DEATH WORE A REDCOAT

Feb 2014

Peter Tyzack

"Death Wore a Redcoat," by Peter Tyzack. ISBN 978-1-60264-701-5.

Published 2010 by Virtualbookworm.com Publishing Inc., P.O. Box 9949, College Station, TX 77842, US. ©2010, Peter Tyzack. All rights reserved. No part of this publication may be reproduced, stored in a retrieval system, or transmitted in any form or by any means, electronic, mechanical, recording or otherwise, without the prior written permission of Peter Tyzack.

Manufactured in the United States of America.

Other Inspector Parsons mysteries

Rooted in Dishonor

Wider Than Blood

To my grandchildren:

Luke, Isabella, Tegan, Zack, Pippa and Troy;

wishing you long and healthy lives that are happy
and fulfilling

1

London, Wednesday, 22nd October, 1881

LORD FREDERICK SAYERS had not felt such elation since the day he was offered a Cabinet post as Colonial Secretary; and although he would never have dreamt of admitting the full extent of his delight to his fellow peers, as he strode purposefully across the Old Palace Yard of the Houses of Parliament he felt as though he was walking on air. As a seasoned politician he could sense that the sentiments he had just expressed in his speech had struck a chord. Such thunderous applause and exuberant waving of Order Papers were rare events in the phlegmatic benches of the Upper Chamber.

On similar occasions in the past he would have been tempted to remain behind and bask in the warm words of praise being offered by his parliamentary colleagues. But tonight he had no wish to engage in a round of inconsequential hand shaking and back slapping from men he knew could do little to help resurrect his career. In due course he would seek a reward from those people that mattered.

The gas lamps on the railings around the Houses of Parliament were barely visible in the dense, swirling, river mist enveloping Sir Charles Barry's majestic Gothic palace. It was a mist that stifled both the shrill chorus of foghorns on the small boats working this stretch of the Thames and the deeper notes of their larger cousins in the great docks to the east.

Sayers acknowledged the halfhearted salute of the bored policeman on duty at the tall wrought-iron gates with an equally casual brush of the silver tip of his black ebony cane against the rim of his silk top hat. He turned south towards Millbank Street, pulling up the collar of his long, black cashmere overcoat as he felt the full force of the bitter north wind falling full-square upon his back from the direction of Whitehall, oblivious to the sound of the bell in the clock tower striking half past ten. His ears were still ringing with the plaudits that had greeted his robust attack on the Government's bill proposing Home Rule for Ireland.

Sayers could well imagine the anger with which Prime Minister Gladstone would receive the news of his former Colonial Secretary's bitter attack on the policy that was so dear to his heart. That was of little concern to Sayers. If Gladstone had expected him to support the ruling Liberal Party's foolish Irish initiative he should not have

schemes of the great civil engineer,
nzalgette. It was thanks to him that raw
'as no longer fed directly into the river.
's innovations had gradually wrought
matic changes that there were even
f salmon once again being seen in the
Sayers had yet to see one of these
fish for himself, but he liked to imagine
en at this very moment, making their
rogress upstream to their traditional
grounds in Berkshire.

ontinued to gaze down at the river for
inutes, the deliberations about his private
ic life for once subordinated to the
effect of the gentle waters. It was but a
ite. There were pressing matters in the
ultuous world of politics to consider,
what the events of the past few hours
an for his future career.

loss of his Cabinet post had come
d. It had been an especially bitter pill for
wallow at a time when he had felt his
be in the ascendant. When it had
he had thought his political life was over,
nthusiastic way in which the evening's
ad been received made him believe that
he age of fifty-two there was time enough
abinet appointment. But whether he
l to support the Liberal Party was another
he Prime Minister would be furious when
d about the speech, and Sayers knew that
likely he would ever find favor again as
Gladstone remained in power. It was

been so hasty to demote him for the Africa business. As far as Sayers was concerned his speech had been no more than Gladstone deserved. If the Prime Minister wanted support for his policies it was well for him to treat a man better. That was part and parcel of the cut and thrust of British politics. And regardless of petty political squabbles Sayers knew that he was right. What he had said reflected the mood in the country at large. Even the most ill-informed of Englishmen knew that the Irish were unfit to govern themselves.

As Sayers lengthened his stride the muffled voices of fellow parliamentarians clamoring for hansom cabs outside Parliament grew fainter. Few of them, he knew, would be heading in his direction. Lambeth was not an area of London in which many of his fellow peers would choose to live. But for the present it suited his own purposes admirably.

As eighteenth-century London had gradually spread its tentacles south of the Thames, the village of Lambeth had acquired a reputation for sordid taverns, disreputable pleasure gardens, prostitutes and political reactionaries. Even with London's rapid growth in more recent years Lambeth had yet to find favor with the respectable middle classes, let alone members of the august House of Lords. But regardless of its unsavory reputation, Sayers was convinced that the area had great potential. Even now it had at least one thing to recommend it. It was within easy walking distance of Parliament.

Sayers shared the opinion of the more speculative of property developers. Like them, he believed that the character of Lambeth could only improve. It was, after all, where the archbishops of Canterbury had chosen to live for centuries; and Sayers could visualize that as London continued its relentless growth that his own small house fronting the river would become worth several times what he had paid for it. In the meantime he would simply have to suffer the tasteless remarks of fellow peers with far grander houses in the fashionable parts of London on the other, more respectable, side of the river.

Sayers' decision to move to Lambeth had been a source of much amusement in the House of Lords and had led to many wry comments amongst those who had little else than petty social matters to occupy their time. After all, they said, why should any man choose to move to Lambeth when his wife owned a house in Regent's Park. Regents Park, the gossips were quick to point out, was not exactly Mayfair, but it was still a perfectly acceptable address. But after the death of her father in 1878, an event that had made his wife the sole beneficiary of a substantial fortune, Lady Vespasia Sayers had made it abundantly clear to her husband that she had no further wish to remain in London. Instead, shortly after Sayers had been deprived of his Cabinet post, his headstrong wife had abandoned her London house and moved back to her father's country mansion in Lancashire. Her North Country accent and manners had never found favor in London society, and she in turn had

seen little to admire
which an ambitious
husband was obliged
to pay Lord Frederic
had been agreed at th
that in itself was not
the house in Regents
befitting a peer of the
allowance Sayers ha
received no remuner
his parliamentary dut
for his move to Lamb

—

IN LESS THAN ten n
cross Lambeth Bridg
when, in an attempt
feelings he still harbo
examine the dark wat
happened when the w
had cleared from t
between Westminster
there was light enoug
quarter to prompt S
much the river had c
career. As a young m
he had been amazed
During the Great Stir
had taken his seat in
had been forced to clc
elsewhere rather than
malodorous fumes.

grandio
Joseph
sewage
Bazalge
such d
rumors
Thames
handsor
them,
stately
breedin

He
several
and pu
calming
brief re
more t
especia
could n

The
unheral
him to
career
occurre
but the
speech
even at
for a
continu
matter.
he lear
it was
long a

perhaps an opportune time to rejoin the Conservative ranks, even though they were the party in opposition. He had formerly been a staunch Conservative, but for reasons that everyone in politics knew were entirely opportunistic had joined the Liberals when he had seen that their star was in the ascendant. It was, Sayers mused, perhaps time for him to cross the floor of the House yet again. But that was not a decision he need take tonight. There were influential people in both parties to approach before he decided which way he would jump.

One of those was Lord Goddard, the new chairman of the Conservative Party, and as fortune would have it Goddard had only that evening invited him to join a weekend shooting party at his Hampshire estate. If he was thinking of abandoning the Liberals there was no better person to discuss this with than Goddard. Of course, the terms would have to be right. There would naturally have to be a gentleman's agreement about a Cabinet post in any future Conservative Government, especially if Goddard were to ask him to continue making virulent attacks against the Liberal party and its leader.

Sayers relished the idea of a weekend in the country. For one thing it would provide him with an opportunity to display his prowess with a shot gun and fishing rod. And for another there was the opportunity of an amorous adventure; especially as it was now common knowledge that, with a wife in Lancashire, he was, to all intents, an available bachelor.

So absorbed was he with his thoughts of shooting several brace of pheasants, landing a fat salmon, and the enchanting prospect of renewing his acquaintance with an attractive young widow who was sure to be among Goddard's guests, that Sayers was unaware of the stealthy footsteps approaching from behind and the revolver being leveled at the back of his head.

A single bullet sufficed. Lord Frederick Sayers, former Colonial Secretary in William Gladstone's Liberal Government, died in an instant, his last thoughts on this earth imbued with his past and present triumphs and the even more glorious personal and political conquests that he imagined lay ahead.

The assassin swiftly dragged Sayers' lifeless body into a sitting position, leant his back against the railings of the bridge, replaced the silk top hat on the peer's shattered skull, and laid his cane by his side. Then he thrust a folded piece of paper into the dead man's mouth. Pausing briefly to admire his handiwork the killer tossed the revolver into the Thames and then walked calmly away in the direction of Lambeth.

2

Keswick, Thursday, 23rd October

THE FAIR-WEATHER CUMULUS clouds drifting lazily across the ice-blue sky were faultlessly reflected in the placid surface of Derwent Water. The barometer in the hall promised yet another fine day for sight-seeing, and to fortify himself for its rigors Inspector Everett Parsons was partaking of a substantial breakfast. Not often in London had he the time, the opportunity or the resources to indulge himself in a breakfast comprised of two fried eggs, three rashers of bacon, a generous helping of kidneys and mushrooms, and several rounds of toast and marmalade. On most days he had to settle for a cold ham roll purchased from a street vendor near his Chelsea lodgings whilst *en route* to his office in Scotland Yard.

Parsons had been invited to the Lake District by the Chapman family: Jasper, the patriarch, Mildred, his wife, and their two adult children,

Captain Reginald Chapman and Louise. Louise had been the real instigator of the invitation, the other members of her family having far less interest in his presence than she.

Much to Parson's delight his relationship with Louise had blossomed since their meeting some seven months prior, although were he to be honest he would admit that this was a state of affairs not entirely to the liking of other members of her family. It had, in consequence, come as an unexpected yet welcome surprise to find himself invited to join the family holiday in Keswick, a charming Cumbrian town at the north end of Derwent Water. And to his delight, his mother had also been included in the party.

He had shyly broached the subject of Louise with his mother on several occasions during the past few months, but prior to this holiday there had been no opportunity for Amelia Parsons to meet her. It was not a situation entirely to Parsons' liking, as he was most anxious that his mother should meet the young woman who had become such an important part of his life. It was simply that circumstances had never before made it possible.

From the start, in spite of Louise's entreaties, the Chapmans had been strongly opposed to their daughter having any sort of relationship with a policeman. Louise had never said that in as many words, but it was clear from the way her parents and brother behaved towards him that they considered that the daughter of a wealthy banker ought not to be contemplating a relationship of any sort with an impecunious police inspector. As a consequence, apart from them seeing one another at church or at a rare dinner party at the home of a family the Chapmans felt they could trust, any other meetings between the two were carefully chaperoned either by Louise's mother or her brother whenever his military duties allowed.

Parsons had found such arrangements to be thoroughly disagreeable. And if it was bad enough to have Louise's fastidious mother for company, he found her brother to be even more tiresome; as once Reginald Chapman had learned that Parsons' father had once been a colonel in the Indian Army he was especially scathing about Parsons' own choice of career.

For Louise's sake Parsons had suffered these taunts with forbearance. As it happened his late father had always fondly hoped that his only son would follow in his footsteps and pursue a military career. But at no time had Parsons ever contemplated that. Although born in a military cantonment in India, from the tender age of eight he had been educated at private boarding schools in England and had spent most of his school holidays in a Dorsetshire parsonage with his maternal grandparents. As a consequence, he had little experience of military life, but from what he had read of the exploits of the army in the far flung corners of the British Empire he had formed a poor opinion of its officer corps; although he had never ventured to express such thoughts to his father. His experiences in solving the murders at Beaumont Castle some twelve months previously had only served to strengthen those opinions. And they had been more recently reaffirmed by his association with Louise's brother.

Reginald had been blessed with many of his father's physical characteristics. Like his father he was tall and broad-shouldered, and possessed an equally loud and intrusive voice. Yet he had inherited none of the banker's shrewd intelligence. In Parsons' opinion he had much of Mildred Chapman's dull nature. It was an unfortunate circumstance that Reginald had chosen to exaggerate partly by his own indolence, and partly by the effeminate lisping speech espoused by young cavalry officers such as himself, and their deliberate practice of mispronouncing each letter 'r' as a 'w'.

"How could you choose such a vulgar twade as a policeman?" Reginald had drawled on more than one occasion. "When you had evewy oppowtunity of joining a faw mowe wo'fwhile pwofession like that of yo' father."

Reginald was always sure to be out of earshot of Louise whenever he made such comments, and would also make a point of standing close enough to Parsons to bring the full advantage of his superior height to bear. On these occasions Parsons was tempted to mention his science degree from London University and to suggest that the intelligence demanded of a detective inspector was somewhat more than that required of an army officer, especially one, such as Reginald, who served in the cavalry. Even he, a mere civilian, knew that it was common knowledge that officers in the cavalry were considered to have less brains than others. But Parsons had refrained from such comments, fearing that they would only elicit further derision. Apart from that he had no wish to upset Louise by arguing with her only sibling, and one she held, for reasons that Parsons could never fully understand, in such high regard. Instead he comforted himself with the knowledge that in due course an opportunity would arise for him to demonstrate his superior intellect not only to Reginald but also to the elder Chapmans.

Reginald Chapman had once disdainfully informed Parsons that Louise's parents had planned that she would marry an Army officer from a good regiment such as his. In view of Louise's physical disability it was unlikely that such a match would ever have occurred, as army officers as a whole expected their wives, like their horses, to be thoroughbreds. It seemed that Louise's parents had finally accepted such an unhappy state of affairs, and had reluctantly accepted Parsons as a possible suitor. For what other reason had he and his mother been asked to join them in the Lake District.

Although Parsons had explained the nature of Louise's disability to his mother, he was anxious, nevertheless, that at their first meeting she betray signs of the initial dismay she had shown when he had first told her about Louise's club foot. He knew only too well that as a doting mother, Amelia Parsons had hoped for nothing short of perfection in any woman her only son considered as a future wife. But he need not have been concerned. Amelia's face had been a picture of happiness when they were introduced.

"My dear Louise," Amelia had exclaimed, "you are so much like that divine child in *'Pot Pourri'*.

The awkward silence that had greeted this remark had prompted Parsons to explain that his mother had merely been referring to John Everett Millais' painting of a young girl holding a basket of flower petals, as it was clear that neither Louise's parents nor her brother were remotely aware of the nature of the compliment. Nor, from the subsequent conversation, did it appear that they were greatly interested in any form of fine art, even Amelia Parsons' comment that she had actually named her son after the painter of *'Pot Pourri'* falling upon deaf ears. In matters of culture, at least, Parsons had reflected, he and his mother had a clear edge over the Chapmans.

For his part, Parsons had considered his mother's comparison of Louise to the young girl in Millais' painting to be most befitting. There was a striking similarity between the two. Both had short, dark, curly hair and large, brown eyes; and, as much as one could tell from the image in a painting, they seemed to share the same sense of childish innocence that had first attracted him to Louise and that he continued to find so endearing.

THE HOLIDAY HAD proved to be an enormous success for Louise, his mother and Parsons. The weather in this notoriously wet part of northern England had been uncharacteristically benign. The towering mountains of Skiddaw Forest, Castlerigg and Derwent Fells, the shimmering surface of Derwent Water, the trees flecked with their palette of rich autumnal shades, and the lush green fields brimming with cattle and sheep, had all served to display the Lake District at its best. It was easy to see why it had become such a haven for artists and poets.

Amelia Parsons' presence had proved to be a godsend to the young couple. No longer was it necessary for one of the Chapmans to act as a chaperone, leaving Parsons, his mother and Louise to explore the countryside together, to cruise the lake, and to dine in the quaint inns in the many picturesque villages. Parsons had been delighted to see how quickly the two women had become firm friends. They were alike in so many ways, being of a similar size with the same trim figures and sweet natures. And whenever Parsons looked at Louise he found himself imagining how much like her his mother must have been as a young girl. Her marriage to a military man many years her senior had no doubt stifled much of her youthful zest for life, but he was delighted to see how much it had been rekindled by her friendship with Louise.

Amelia had also taken the opportunity of the holiday to finally abandon her mourning clothes. It was almost four years since her husband had died, but until recently she had continued to wear the gray, lavender and mauve colors of half-mourning. But in keeping with the season she had chosen bright autumn colors for her visit to the Lake District, the only token of her bereavement being the gold locket round her neck that contained a lock of her late husband's hair. She seemed to Parsons to be once again the mother he remembered from his childhood. The woman who had visited him during the long summer holidays in the Dorsetshire parsonage, and whom he had missed so dearly whenever she returned to India. Those summers had been amongst his happiest memories. But nothing could compare with the past few days spent in such idyllic surroundings with the two most important people in his life.

———————

THE THREE OF them were discussing their plans for the day when Jasper Chapman, seated in his customary place at the head of the table, lowered his copy of the *Times* and solemnly announced that yet another Fenian atrocity had occurred. One of his first actions upon arriving in Keswick had been to ensure that an early edition of the newspaper was brought straight to the house from the first train to arrive from London. As an important figure in the world of finance, he had said pompously, it was his duty to ensure that he kept abreast of events in the wider world.

"Lord Frederick Sayers was assassinated last night," he announced, his bulbous eyes, bushy eyebrows and heavy jowls registering an appropriate degree of gravitas.

"He was shot on Lambeth Bridge," he explained impatiently, in answer to Parsons question, "and there seems little doubt that it was the work of those damned Irish Fenians. It seems that only that night Lord Frederick had made a speech in Parliament about the present state of near anarchy in Ireland and had denounced the Liberal Party's proposals for Irish Home Rule. And quite right of him. Any fool can see that the Irish will need Westminster's steady hand for many years yet."

"Whatever is the world coming to," exclaimed Mildred Chapman in alarm. "Already this year there has been an attempt on the life of our own dear Queen. Apart from that the Russian czar has been murdered, Lord Russell Parker assassinated in Dublin, and only a few months ago President Garfield of the United States was shot. I wonder how any of us can sleep easily in our beds when there are such violent men walking our streets."

Parsons refrained from commenting that whatever anarchists or political activists there might be at large were unlikely ever to be a threat to Mildred Chapman. But Lord Sayers assassination left him in something of a quandary. After such a high profile murder he could well imagine the pressures being placed on his colleagues in Scotland Yard while he was breakfasting in style in the Lake District. Doubtless the Home Secretary would be breathing down the neck of the Police Commissioner, who would in turn be putting pressure on Parsons' own superior, Superintendent Jeffries. Regardless of how much he was enjoying himself, Parsons knew where his duty lay. But how, and when, should he broach the subject of his premature return to London?

That decision was fortuitously taken out of his hands by the arrival of a housemaid bearing a silver salver on which there was an envelope and a paperknife. She was one of three servants brought by the Chapmans from their London home, the others being a cook and a lady's maid.

"A telegram for Inspector Parsons," she announced dramatically.

The curiosity around the table was palpable, even Jasper Chapman deigning to lower his newspaper to watch as Parsons sliced open the envelope.

The telegram was from Superintendent Jeffries, and the message as short and succinct as in the circumstances Parsons might have expected.

"Your leave canceled forthwith," he read. *"Return to London immediately. Jeffries."*

"My superior officer has instructed me to return to London," Parsons explained to the inquisitive faces around the table, "and I'm afraid that I have no option but to leave at once."

Out of politeness Parsons had addressed his remarks to his host, before turning to Louise with what he hoped was a suitably disappointed expression on his face. She and his mother, he could see, were clearly dismayed by the news. It was not simply that he was leaving so unexpectedly. There was also the matter of the engagement between Parsons and Louise that had been the subject of many whispered conversations and girlish giggles between the two women during the past few days; and despite his embarrassed protests it had been decided that Parsons should broach the subject with Louise's father before the end of his holiday. It had not been an interview that Parsons had been anticipating with any degree of pleasure, and if he was completely honest, he did not feel that his relationship with Louise had reached a stage at which an engagement was appropriate. He had been wondering how to resolve this problem without upsetting either Louise or his mother, and this unexpected recall to London had, for the moment, spared him that ordeal.

Apart from matters of a more personal nature, Parsons also relished the prospect of returning to London and becoming involved in such an important investigation. Much as he had enjoyed the holiday and the opportunity of spending time with Louise, he had desperately missed his work and its challenges. Jeffries' telegram seemed also to have served an additional purpose. From the expressions on the faces of Louise's parents Parsons noted with some pleasure that they appeared to be impressed by his unexpected recall to London, and by his involvement in the hunt for the assassin of an important political figure. Only Reginald Chapman seemed less awed by the news, and did not allow the opportunity to pass without making a final disparaging remark.

"So the mighty Scotland Yard detective swings into action," he drawled sarcastically as he nonchalantly buttered a piece of toast. "You need not concern yo'self now, mothah deah. Inspector Pahsons will have the case solved within a few days, and those assassins you are so wowwied about will soon find themselves in pwison."

It was all Parsons could do to refrain from making a suitably cutting response. But hopefully his actions over the next few days and weeks would prove far more effective than any words. He could not have wished for a better opportunity of proving to Reginald and his parents that his work was not only important in itself but, in this instance, was actually a matter of national security.

The telegram had fortunately arrived in sufficient time for Parsons to pack, thank the Chapmans for their generosity, say a few awkward words of farewell to Louise and his mother, and still reach Windermere Station in time to catch the late morning train to London. He even managed to send a telegram to Superintendent Jeffries informing him that he would be in the office first thing on Friday morning.

Parsons purchased as many London newspapers as were available at the station shop, supplementing them with later editions when he changed trains at Crewe. Although the information in these early editions was far from comprehensive, enough had been written and speculated about the assassination and about Lord Sayers himself for Parsons to compile a useful dossier before the train reached Euston Station.

As Jasper Chapman had said, there had been a late night debate in the House of Lords on Wednesday at which Lord Frederick had made a powerful speech attacking the proposed Liberal Party policy in support of Irish Home Rule. The debate had finished shortly after ten-fifteen and the constable on duty outside the Houses of Parliament had confirmed that Lord Frederick was amongst a group of parliamentarians leaving the building at around half-past ten. The constable said that Lord Frederick had seemed somewhat preoccupied, but clearly remembered him walking in the direction of Lambeth Bridge.

It was there that his body was discovered some twenty minutes later by Horace Butcher, a twenty-six year old shipping clerk who was walking from the City to his home in Camberwell. Parsons wondered what had prompted Butcher to take such a circuitous route home, when it would have been quicker for him to have crossed the Thames by way of London Bridge. No doubt that thought had also occurred to others at Scotland Yard. But if Butcher had anything to do with Sayers' murder, thought Parsons, he must have been a cool customer, as he had remained with the body until his cries for help were answered. That help had come in the form of Constable Dewhurst, a policeman from Whitehall Division who, at the time, was patrolling the west side of the river between Lambeth and Vauxhall Bridges.

Dewhurst described how he had found Lord Frederick slumped against the side of the bridge with his top hat and cane lying on the ground beside him. Butcher had later explained that when he discovered Sayers' body he was still wearing his hat, but at that time Butcher had thought he had merely stumbled upon someone who was either ill or the worse for drink. It was only when he had tried to rouse the man by shaking him that the hat had fallen off his head, revealing the nature of his terrible wound.

The later newspapers reported that not long after Constable Dewhurst had arrived on the scene another policeman had come from the Lambeth end of the bridge. Dewhurst did not recognize the man, but accepted his offer to go to the nearby St. Thomas' Hospital for assistance. By eleven-fifteen that help had failed to arrive, and as no other pedestrians had crossed the bridge in the meantime Dewhurst had sent Butcher to the hospital, where it had subsequently transpired that no policeman had ever come seeking assistance. Subsequent enquiries at Lambeth Division had found that at the time of the murder no policeman of theirs had been in the vicinity of Lambeth Bridge.

In the opinion of most newspapers the murder was another political assassination by the Fenians, and the mysterious policeman who had disappeared into thin air had been responsible. It was further speculated that the assassin had felt sufficiently confident at concealing his identity that he had been brazen enough to return to the scene to confirm that his victim was indeed dead and to gloat over the dreadful deed.

All the papers reported that Lord Frederick had been an outspoken opponent of Irish Home Rule, especially after losing his Cabinet post. His recent speech in Parliament had been only the latest of many critical of the Liberal Party's proposed policy. And any doubt about the political nature of the crime was confirmed by the paper found in the dead man's mouth. It was a page torn from *Hansard*, the daily report of Parliament proceedings.

Other events occurring earlier that evening in Kensington seemed to support the general feeling that Sayers' death had been the work of the Fenians. Bombs had been thrown into an army barracks and into the home of a member of parliament, actions that most newspapers were swift to point out were as much a hallmark of the Fenians as Sayers' assassination.

Lord Frederick Sayers, Parsons learned, was fifty-two years old, and had been involved in politics for much of his adult life, having assumed his hereditary title after the premature death of his father. For a short time he had been a member of the Conservative Party but had switched his allegiance to the Liberals after Gladstone had led them to a resounding victory in 1868. Sayers had subsequently been rewarded for this betrayal by being given the Cabinet post of Colonial Secretary when the Liberal Party returned to power in 1880. It was, however, an appointment that had been short-lived, for within a matter of months Sayers had resigned from the Cabinet. The reason for this highly unusual step had never been satisfactorily explained, as the wording of his written resignation was couched in the usual politically ambiguous words. But it was rumored that Sayers had overstepped the bounds of his office by becoming too closely involved in the military campaign that was then being waged against the Boers in South Africa.

Parsons read that Sayers had married Vespasia Broadstone, the only surviving child of a wealthy Lancastrian who had made his money from cotton mills in Manchester. Several newspapers suggested that this had been a fortuitous marriage for Lord Frederick, as his own father had managed to gamble away what remained of the family fortune both at the card table and on the race track before eventually concluding matters by putting a pistol to his head. There were no children of this marriage, and some of the more popular newspapers had made play of the fact that Lord Frederick and his wife were virtually estranged, Lady Vespasia having returned to live in Lancashire soon after her own father had died two years previously.

PARSONS JOINED A disconsolate group of fellow passengers outside Euston Station Parsons waiting patiently in line for the first available hansom cab. There was little attempt at convivial conversation, the principal sound that of rain beating remorselessly upon the phalanx of umbrellas. London, on such a wet night, Parsons reflected, had little to recommend it, especially if one was a weary traveler wishing to get home as quickly as possible.

Even the small confectionery booth at the entrance to the station was closed, depriving those like Parsons who had eaten little since morning, of the chance of a welcome snack. The only sign that the booth had ever been open for business were the boards leaning against it displaying headlines from the evening newspapers. There was, as ever, some difference of opinion among the various banners as to which was the most likely to attract readers, but the majority had favored the same blunt statement:

"Bayswater atrocity. Army officer stabbed."

3

London, Friday, 24th October 1881

PARSONS' SMALL LARDER had been empty when he had eventually returned to his lodgings the previous night. At first he had contemplated going out in search of food but had then decided against it. It was a foul night, and although he was hungry, after such a tiring journey, more than anything he had felt in need of sleep, especially as he intended to make an early start the next day. Mindful of his absence during the early stages of the investigation he had set his alarm for six, intending to make a favorable impression on his colleagues by being amongst the first to arrive at the offices of the Criminal Investigation Department in Scotland Yard.

When he rose he was even more ravenous, but had time only for two thin slices of bread and butter and a mug of watery coffee purchased from a street vendor in Kings Road as he hurried to catch an omnibus. His large, leisurely Lake District breakfasts were already a distant memory.

Arriving at Scotland Yard shortly after seven he was surprised to find many of his fellow detectives already at their desks; and judging by their unshaven faces and disheveled appearance they had been there all night. Superintendent Jeffries, he learned, was also in his office, as the Police Commissioner had insisted that his head of CID should be on call at any hour of the day or night during the nationwide hue and cry that had followed hard upon the heels of Lord Frederick Sayers' murder. There was nothing, Parsons mused as he made his way along the corridor towards Jeffries' office, more likely to engage the attention of a Home Secretary or a Police Commissioner than a political assassination and the prospect of Fenian anarchists stalking the streets in search of other victims from amongst the ranks of the Establishment.

Although the focus of the investigation had primarily been in London, Parsons learned from his colleagues that police forces throughout England, Scotland and Wales had also been put on full alert. Any Irishman or Irishwoman with a record of hostility towards the Crown had been rounded up, and major ports around the country put under close watch lest any of those on Scotland Yard's list of Fenian sympathizers attempted to leave the country. And all of this activity was being coordinated by Superintendent Jeffries.

As yet the military had not been involved, but Colonel Wilson, the Police Commissioner, himself a retired army officer, had prevailed upon the Home Secretary to ask the War Office to put troops on standby. The use of the Army would only be considered as a last resort, as the British people had no particular wish to see redcoated soldiers bearing arms on the streets of London and other major cities. But it was an indication of how serious the Government was in its intentions. Under no circumstances were the authorities going to allow the Fenians to get away with a political assassination on the very doorstep of Parliament.

Parsons had witnessed a similar witch-hunt before. Only two years previously, following a spate of bombings in London, including one at Scotland Yard itself, the CID had been successful in rounding up and imprisoning many of the more militant Fenian members. At the time it was considered that the Fenian threat had finally been eradicated, and like many of his colleagues, he was surprised to see that the group was still active.

Founded in 1858 with the objective of overthrowing British rule in Ireland, the Fenians, also known as the Irish Republican Brotherhood, had been a thorn in the side of the British ever since. Membership of the Brotherhood had fallen dramatically following the punitive measures taken by the British after the abortive Irish rebellion of 1867, and many Fenians had fled to France or America. Those diehards that had remained in Ireland had gradually drifted towards more constitutional means of achieving political independence, and the Irish Home Rule movement led by Charles Stewart Parnell had even gained a degree of support from Gladstone's ruling Liberal Party. However, an industrial slump in England in the late eighteen-seventies had caused severe economic problems in Ireland. The potato harvest had failed again, and although the situation was not as serious as that in the eighteen-forties, famine had again stalked the land, and those Irish tenants unable to grow sufficient crops to pay their rent lived in constant fear of being evicted.

By 1880 more than two thousand Irish families were losing their homes each year, a situation that had precipitated bitter retaliation against both English landlords and their agents. Haystacks had been burned, animals maimed and attempts made upon the lives of the ruling class. Most notably, Lord Russell Parker, the Chief Secretary for Ireland, had been assassinated as he strolled through Dublin's Phoenix Park.

More often than not these atrocities had been led by those Fenians who had remained in Ireland, and who formed the more radical elements of Parnell's Land League. Only eleven days before Lord Sayers' murder Parnell himself had been arrested in Dublin for his continuing links with the Fenian movement and for his outspoken support for Irish tenants against their English landlords. It was an action that many considered to be long overdue, and it was one that was greeted with much popular support in England; although in retrospect it may well have led to the death of such a forthright opponent of Irish Home Rule as Lord Sayers.

SUPERINTENDENT JEFFRIES WAS completing his ablutions when Parsons entered his office. Stripped to the waist with his braces hanging loosely over his trousers, he was wiping the last of the shaving soap from his face. The atmosphere in the room was stale: an unsavory blend of tobacco smoke and body odour. An inveterate pipe smoker, the superintendent rarely opened his windows even in the height of summer, and after a continuous occupation that was now into its second day the visibility in the room was fast approaching that of the thickest London fog.

"Good to see you at last, Parsons," Jeffries said wearily, as he fastened a fresh collar to a clean shirt. "I'm glad to see my telegram had the desired effect."

Jeffries ran a comb through his thinning hair, put on his tweed waistcoat and jacket and slumped into the chair behind his desk.

"I've got a special job for you, young man," he said.

The investigation had been in progress for less than thirty-six hours, but already the signs of the strain and lack of sleep were evident on Jeffries' craggy face. Parsons had seen the superintendent cope with other crises before. But this was no ordinary investigation. A senior British politician had been assassinated within sight of Parliament. The stakes were as high as they had ever been for a CID commander, as the direct responsibility for finding those responsible for the murder now rested firmly on Jeffries' shoulders. Not only the Home Secretary, but no doubt Prime Minister Gladstone himself, would want to be assured that progress was being made.

"Has Harris briefed you?" Jeffries asked, as he began filling his pipe.

"He's not in yet, sir," said Parsons, surprised and pleased that he would be working with Harris again. Harris was probably the most reliable detective sergeant in the department. "But, if you've got the time, perhaps you can tell me what it is you have in mind for me. I spent much of my time on the train yesterday reading every newspaper I could lay my hands on, so I think I'm well up with the background to Sayers' murder."

"It's not Sayers I want you for, Parsons," grunted Jeffries, "though I'm not denying I could do with an extra pair of hands. As you can imagine we're already stretched pretty thin. No, it's the other matter. General Sir Maxwell Latham. With your father being a military man I thought you'd be the ideal person to investigate the murder of an army officer."

"I know nothing about General Latham's murder, sir," said Parsons, disappointed to be unexpectedly sidelined from an important investigation, and already hearing Louise's brother's mocking laugh when he heard the news. "Unless it was the murder I saw referred to on the newspaper boards at Euston Station last night."

"That would've been it, Parsons," Jeffries said as he pressed tobacco into the bowl of his pipe with his thumb. "The poor devil was stabbed to death with a spear only an hour or so after the Sayers' business. And in the chaos that followed his lordship's death I'm afraid to say that the general got rather overlooked. So I can't tell you much about it myself. I put Harris on the case yesterday morning. He'll fill you in, and in due course you can tell me what it's all about. But not for the moment. As you can see I'm rather preoccupied with these wretched Fenians."

Jeffries put a match to his pipe, a sure sign that as far as he was concerned the interview was over.

"I'll get onto it right away, sir," said Parsons, as a fresh plume of smoke melted into the already dense gray cloud overhead.

4

SERGEANT LEONARD HARRIS had arrived at his desk by the time Parsons returned to the general office. He grinned widely when he saw Parsons.

"Good morning, sir," he said cheerfully. "Quite a change from the Lake District I imagine."

"You never said a truer word, Harris," Parsons said with a wry smile. "But if there was one thing I missed it was the sight of your jovial face, not to mention that fine mustache. I can assure you that not one gentleman I saw in Cumberland had anything to compare with it."

Harris affectionately stroked the object in question. Like his heavily macassared hair, Harris' waxed mustache and distinctive brown check suit set him apart from the other detectives, and in the past had made him the butt of many an office joke. Parsons' own stout and diminutive figure had attracted similar attention when he had first joined the department. But the jokes were less cruel and the humor more good-natured now than in the past, for in spite of appearances that were bordering on being eccentric, Parsons and Harris had managed to win the approbation of their peers by dint of their professional competence.

"I understand that the superintendent doesn't want our help rounding up the Irish, Harris. He's just told me we've been given a stabbing. Well, you had all day yesterday. You must be close to arresting someone by now."

Parsons poured himself tea from the large enamel pot that was permanently stewing on the stove in the general office.

"Replenish that mug of yours and follow me, Harris," he said. "Let's discuss General Latham's murder in my office."

———————

PARSONS WAS DELIGHTED to be back in familiar surroundings. He would have had some difficulty in explaining to Louise exactly why that was, but even during the blissful time they had spent together in the Lake District there were times when he found himself missing his sturdy wooden desk and his well-worn leather chair.

"Sit yourself down, Harris," he said, gesturing towards the ancient armchair opposite his desk, "and tell me what you've been up to."

Harris took a sip of tea, placed his mug on the floor, and took a small black notebook from the inside pocket of his jacket.

"Well, sir," he began, "it would appear that just after midnight on Wednesday a woman arrived by cab at General Latham's house in Chester Place. Chester Place is in Bayswater, just off Hyde Park Square. Constable Matthews from Paddington Division was patrolling the area at the time and later reported he had seen her. I've spoken to Matthews, and he confirmed that it was about fifteen minutes past twelve. He said he remembered hearing a clock strike the quarter hour."

"Can he describe this woman?" asked Parsons eagerly.

"Just be patient, sir," said Harris with a weary smile. "I'll come to that. Just let me tell you what I've managed to piece together so far."

Parsons cradled his mug in his hands and leaned back in his chair.

"Go on, Harris," he said with an impatient sigh. "I promise not to interrupt again."

Harris took another sip of tea and returned to his notes.

"The woman was admitted to the house by Bradley, the general's servant," he explained. "Bradley says she was wearing a thick veil, but he says he's sure he knows her identity. He said she'd been to the house before."

Parsons again considered asking Harris the obvious question, but thought better of it. It was better to let the sergeant tell the story in the way he wanted. Over the years he had learned to be patient with the rather pedantic sergeant. Instead he drank the remainder of his tea and placed the mug on his desk.

"According to Bradley," Harris continued, "the woman said that the general was expecting her. Bradley told me he wasn't unduly surprised by that, as it appears unescorted women often arrived at the general's house, even at such a late hour. And, as he had already said, this particular woman had been a regular visitor."

Harris looked up from his notes and raised an eyebrow, an expression that Parsons had learned to interpret as one of disapproval. As a member of what society chose to describe as the deserving lower classes, Harris had strong feelings about the way in which many members of the upper classes conducted themselves.

"Go on, Harris," Parsons said wearily. "You aren't paid to make judgments about those who consider themselves to be your betters."

"No, sir," said Harris glumly. "But you have to admit that the way some of them behave is nothing short of a disgrace."

Parsons resisted the bait being offered by Harris. It was no time to engage in a discussion on morality, or the lack of it. He merely fixed Harris with a polite smile and leaned back in his chair, steepled his fingers and waited for Harris to resume.

"Well, sir," said Harris petulantly, after a further sip of tea, "it appears the general was in his study at the time. According to Bradley that was his favorite room in the house, and it was where he spent most of his time when he was at home. Bradley said he offered to escort the woman to the study but she dismissed him. She told him she knew perfectly well where the general's study was. So Bradley went back to the kitchen where he'd been before the woman arrived. But no sooner had he got there when he heard her screaming. Naturally he rushed back into the hall, and according to Bradley the woman was standing just outside the study. Bradley said that she was still wearing her veil, but he claims that he could see blood on her hands and on her cloak."

"Did she say anything?" said Parsons, for the moment forgetting his previous promise to remain silent.

"No, sir," Harris replied. "Bradley said that as soon as the woman saw him she stopped screaming, but she ran out of the house before he could ask her what had so alarmed her. Bradley said that at first he thought of following her, but then he decided to go into the study. That's when he saw the body. He said General Latham was lying on the floor with his chest covered in blood and a spear of some sort lying on the floor beside him. He could tell at once that the general was dead, and so he decided to leave the house himself to seek help. But the streets were deserted at the time, and it wasn't until he reached Edgeware Road that he found a policeman."

"The same policeman who saw the woman arrive?" asked Parsons. "Constable Matthews?"

"No, sir. It wasn't Matthews," Harris replied, frowning at what he considered to be Parsons' unwarranted interruption. He examined his notes. "I'm afraid I don't know the constable's name," he said lamely.

"Carry on, Harris," said Parsons. "It's probably not that important. What happened next?"

"Well, sir, the constable and Bradley returned to the house and after the constable had verified that the general was dead he sent Bradley to the police station in Paddington Green with a note explaining what had happened and requesting that a more senior officer be sent to the house. All that took some time as you can imagine. It also appears that not a great deal was done when Bradley reached Paddington Green because at much the same time every police station in London received a telegram from Scotland Yard informing them of Lord Frederick Sayers' assassination and the bombs in Kensington, and requesting that the houses of all politicians within their jurisdiction be given police protection. Well, as you probably know, sir, there are several politicians living in the area covered by Paddington Division, and you can well imagine the chaos there was at that time of night getting the information out to the policemen already on patrol and summoning reinforcements from those policemen who were off duty. So in the midst of all that it appears General Latham's murder got overlooked. Even when the superintendent at Paddington arrived at the station he didn't take any action other than deciding that his resources were already spread too thinly to do anything about it. So he passed the buck to Scotland Yard. And that's where it stuck for a few hours more, as we were in a bit of a pickle ourselves. As a result it was not until after nine yesterday morning that Superintendent Jeffries asked me to investigate."

Parsons had listened with growing incredulity to what appeared to him to be a litany of incompetence. No doubt someone would be reprimanded at some stage, although it was difficult to see who that might be. But that was hardly his problem. For the moment it was best to keep his opinions to himself and let Harris finish his report.

"I went straight to General Latham's house and arrived there around about half past ten, sir," Harris said, "and I found everything much as I've described. The general was still lying on his back covered with blood with the murder weapon on the floor beside him. From what I could see he'd been sitting by the fire reading at the time the woman entered the room, and judging by the position of his body it looked as though he had taken a few steps towards her before she stabbed him."

"Are you eventually going to tell me who you, or should I say, who Bradley thinks this woman is?" said Parsons, his patience finally beginning to wear.

"I will, sir," said Harris. "But before I do that I should warn you that Bradley's evidence may be a little suspect."

"And why, pray is that?" Parsons snapped. "If he said he recognized the woman he must've had a very good reason."

"That's true, sir. But don't forget that the woman was veiled."

"I haven't forgotten that, Harris," said Parsons irritably. "I've just been waiting for a suitable opportunity to speak. And now you're telling me that Bradley could have been mistaken after all. Why, for Heaven's sake?"

"Because he appears to have been drunk, sir. Or at least that's what the constable who went with him to the general's house thought."

"I see," said Parsons. "So, if the woman was veiled and Bradley was drunk when he admitted her to the house, what was it that makes you believe he could possibly identify her?"

"It was her accent, sir. Bradley said he recognized her French accent. And Constable Matthews also said that the woman he saw said a few words in a foreign accent to the cab driver."

"So you're finally going to reveal the identity of this mystery woman, Harris," said Parsons, smiling in spite of his impatience.

"I am, sir. And in view of who Bradley says the woman is I don't mind admitting that I'm glad to see you back from your holiday. I didn't feel I had the authority to take matters any further, and what with the superintendent being so occupied with the Sayers' business, I was beginning to feel a little out of my depth. You see Bradley claims that the woman who murdered General Latham was Mrs. Venetta Cordell. And she's the wife of Colonel Cordell, the commanding officer of the Middlesex Light Infantry."

5

"YOU DON'T IMAGINE I'm going to rush out and arrest the wife of a senior army officer merely on the word of a drunken servant, do you, Harris," said Parsons impatiently. "I need more conclusive evidence than I've heard so far. What about the cab driver who dropped her in Chester Place and the one who must have picked her up after she left? Have you tried tracing them?"

Harris' smug smile was enough to tell Parsons that the sergeant had already anticipated the question.

"I did exactly that, sir. After seeing Bradley I visited the companies which generally provide the cabs operating in the Kensington and Bayswater areas, and I asked if enquiries could be made about any of their cabbies picking up a woman wearing a heavy veil and speaking with a foreign accent between eleven and twelve on Wednesday night or in the early hours of Thursday morning. I told them she was probably French, although I'm sure most cabbies wouldn't know the difference between one foreign accent and another. To them anyone who isn't English is just another foreigner speaking a language they don't understand. That's true for most policemen as well. And that includes myself."

He gave Parsons a quick glance that was both critical and envious.

"Not all of us have the benefit of a private education, sir. At my school the master had trouble spelling some of the words in the English language. We had no French, Latin or Greek. So I don't imagine any jury is going to be convinced by a cabbie saying that he remembered a woman speaking in French when it could equally have been Spanish or Italian. As it was the cab owners weren't very optimistic about what any of their men might remember at that time of night. They said that after midnight most of them are drunk."

"Well you never know," Parsons said with a sigh. "We may just be lucky. And bearing in mind Bradley's condition that night, the evidence of these cabbies could be vital. But if General Latham lived in Bayswater why did you include the cabs operating in the Kensington area?"

"Because Colonel Cordell lives in Kensington Barracks, sir. That's where the Middlesex Light Infantry is garrisoned. So I'm assuming that if it was Mrs. Cordell who Bradley saw at Chester Place she would've probably come from the barracks and would have wanted to return there."

"That's good thinking, Harris. You've done well. And what do you suggest is our next step?"

Harris was momentarily nonplussed by the question. He had been anticipating that when Parsons took over the reins he would immediately start making the decisions.

"Well, I'd assumed you'd want to speak with the general's servant, sir. So I warned Bradley we would probably call on him sometime this morning. Then I thought you'd want to see the body. I couldn't leave the poor devil in his study any longer, so I had the body moved to the dead house in Chilworth Street. That's close to Paddington Station. So if you want to have a word with the police surgeon you could send a telegram to the station and arrange to see him later today."

"Full marks, Harris," said Parsons with a smile. "I couldn't have done better myself. We'll do just as you say. And while I'm sending the telegram you can go and find us a cab."

CHESTER PLACE WAS a street of modest three-storied terraced houses, far humbler in design and stature than the mansions in nearby Hyde Park Square. Parsons was surprised to find that General Sir Maxwell Latham had chosen to live there, as he had imagined that such a senior officer would occupy a far grander residence. But possibly Latham did not possess a substantial private income. Army officers, like other members of the Establishment, were not expected to live on the relatively meager salaries they received; and it was unusual to find anyone rising to a position of influence without private money. The house was nonetheless one that Parsons himself would be proud to dwell in with Louise, although he doubted whether his policeman's salary would ever allow him to afford it.

Other then the curtains on the ground floor being drawn there was no obvious sign that there had been a death in the house. There had been time enough for someone in the general's household to have purchased a wreath for the front door. But that clearly had not been done.

Bradley's disheveled appearance when he answered the front door suggested that if he had slept at all it had been in his clothes. His morning shave had left him with slicks of blood on his cheeks, he had not bothered to brush the stray gray hairs from the shoulders of his black jacket, and his shoes were unpolished. At first sight the dark rings in the hollows of the servant's eyes were perhaps a sign of the strain and fatigue he had experienced since finding the general's body, but Parsons was inclined to think that Bradley's bloodshot eyes were the result of him making free with the contents of the wine cellar.

"I believe that you claim to know the identity of the lady who arrived here shortly after midnight on Wednesday night," said Parsons, after Bradley had shown them into the house and the three men were standing in the center of the small hall.

Bradley nodded.

"Yes, sir," he said. "I've no doubt about it. She were Mrs. Cordell, the colonel's wife."

"And why are you so certain of that, Bradley?" Parsons asked. "Sergeant Harris tells me that you said the lady was wearing a thick veil at the time."

"That's true, sir," said Bradley irritably. "But I know Mrs. Cordell well enough. She dined 'ere with the colonel before, and she also come 'ere several times by 'erself."

Bradley looked down at his feet, as though discomfited by having to discuss such unbecoming behavior by a senior army officer's wife with a policeman.

"But that still doesn't explain how you managed to recognize her when she was wearing a veil," said Parsons. "How can you be sure it was Mrs. Cordell when you couldn't see her face?"

"'Cause I recognized 'er voice, sir," Bradley said irritably, a trace of hostility unexpectedly appearing in his bloodshot eyes. "She's a Frenchie, ain't she, an' as I've already said she been 'ere more than a few times."

Parsons could not dispute Bradley's reasoning. Were he in Bradley's position he would have been inclined to do the same. Voices were often every bit as distinctive as a person's physical appearance. In similar circumstances he was confident he would have been able to recognize those of either his mother or Louise even if their faces had been hidden. But a jury would want to hear more persuasive evidence. Identification of a murderer by her voice alone would scarcely be good enough, especially as, in this case, the woman was merely described as having a French accent. Any defending counsel worth his salt would call into question the ability of an uneducated man like Bradley to tell one French accent from another, or indeed, as Harris had already said, one language from another.

"What about her clothes?" Parsons asked. "Apart from the veil, what other clothes was this lady wearing?"

"I couldn't see 'er dress, sir, 'cause she were wearin' a long cloak. Black it were. I'd swear it were the same cloak she always wore when she come 'ere." Bradley coughed nervously again. "Either when she come with the colonel or when she come by 'erself."

"Very good, Bradley," said Parsons. "You're doing well. Now am I right in assuming from what you've said about this lady coming here alone that there is no Mrs. Latham?"

"That's quite correct, sir. The general's wife died many years ago. Long before I knew 'im."

"I see," said Parsons solemnly. "How unfortunate."

He glanced around the hall, noticing the unattractive dark wallpaper that was peeling in several places, and the lack of flowers, paintings, or any bright ornamentation that might indicate a woman's influence.

"Tell me what happened after the lady arrived?"

Bradley pointed to a door on the far side of the hall.

"She went into the study," he said. "She told me the general was expectin' 'er."

"Did you actually see her enter the room?"

Bradley reflected on the question for a short while.

"To be 'onest I can't say I did, sir. When I realized who she was and that the general was expectin' 'er I jus' went back to the kitchen."

Bradley pointed to a dark corridor leading towards the back of the house.

"Where you no doubt continued drinking," Parsons said calmly. "But we'll come to that later."

Bradley was embarrassed enough to blush, before once again taking an unwarranted interest in his unbrushed shoes.

"Were there any other servants in the house that night?" Parsons asked.

"No, sir. There's only me. I been with the general ever since 'e were a major in South Africa. That were before 'e were made colonel and got command of the Middlesex. A man of simple tastes was the general. For the mos' part I could do fer 'im pretty well. It were only when there were a dinner party or somethin' like that, that there were ever need for extra 'elp. An' that were rare enuff."

"So you were an army man yourself," said Harris.

"Yes, sir, but I left after the Middlesex come back from Africa and the general got 'is promotion. 'E said 'e wanted someone to run this 'ouse more or less full time."

"And is there a Mrs. Bradley?"

"No, sir. I never married. Soldiers is never encouraged to marry, an' in any case I liked lookin' after the general too much to want to get involved with no bloody woman."

Parsons could not help thinking that in the absence of a wife for General Latham the presence of a Mrs. Bradley might have brightened the household. But it seemed that the general was content with matters as they were.

"Now Bradley," he said, "just let me be sure of the actual sequence of events that occurred after you went back to the kitchen. You say that you were there when the general was murdered. What actually happened?"

"As I told the sergeant, sir, I 'eard a woman screamin'. An' when I run into the 'all I saw Mrs. Cordell, or should I say the lady in the veil, runnin' out o' the study. She were 'oldin' 'er 'ands up towards her 'ead, as though if she 'adn't been wearin' a veil she would be touchin' 'er face like women do when they've 'ad a shock. And there was blood on 'em. I could see it, right enough, even though she were wearing gloves. She also 'ad blood on 'er cloak."

"You're quite sure she was still wearing her veil," said Parsons.

"Yes, sir, quite sure. If she weren't I would've seen 'er face, wouldn't I!"

"Did either of you speak?" Parson asked, ignoring Bradley's petulance.

"I don't think so, sir. But I can't be sure 'cause everythin' 'appened so fast. One moment she were standin' in the doorway and the next thing I knew she'd run out of the house through the front door."

"Why didn't you follow her?" Parsons asked.

"I thought of that, sir. But then I decided to see what it was she were screamin' about. So I went into the study." Bradley dropped his head. "An' that's when I seen the general's body. That bloody Frenchie done for 'im," he said bitterly.

"It must have been a great shock for you to find General Latham like that, Bradley," said Parsons sympathetically, "A man you'd served faithfully for so many years. So I appreciate how difficult all this must be for you. But I'm afraid there's no other way but for me to ask you these questions. Unless I know exactly what happened on the night your employer died I'll have no chance of bringing his murderer to trial. And now I'd like to go into the general's study and for you to tell me exactly what you saw on Wednesday night."

Bradley led the way across the hall. He opened the door of the study and stood to one side to allow the two detectives to enter. After a few seconds hesitation he followed them, crossing to the window to open the curtains.

To his surprise Parsons found the rather austere study much to his liking. Bradley had claimed that the general was a man of simple tastes, a fact that was amply reflected by the uncluttered way in which the room was furnished. It was a room in which Parsons could imagine himself spending many contented hours. There were two Wolsey easy chairs, one on either side of a large fireplace, in which, he noted, the embers of Wednesday's fire still lay uncleared. Beside one of the chairs stood a small table. An open book lay face-down on it, next to a partially filled decanter, and a cut-glass tumbler containing the remains of the general's last drink. A large, well-upholstered, black leather settee faced towards the fireplace, separated from it by a thick brown rug.

There was a chair and desk in front of the solitary bay window, the surface of the desk bare except for a gas-lamp placed at one corner. Partially filled bookcases occupied the alcoves on each side of the fireplace, on the mantel of which stood a coach clock and four photographs.

Parsons crossed the room to examine the photographs. Two, it appeared had been taken in India. One showed an exuberant group of young men with rifles gathered around the prostrate body of an enormous tiger; the second a similar group on polo ponies wearing pith helmets and brandishing wooden mallets. Judging by the better quality of the other two photographs they had been taken later, and in another part of the world. Perhaps Africa. The first showed a group of army officers in full dress uniform, their neatly trimmed hair and large mustaches making them appear remarkably like one another; the second was of a large body of men formed up in ranks with a solitary figure on horseback at their head. The faces in these photographs were grimmer, the business of war less amusing than that of recreation.

"I assume that General Latham is in each of these photographs," said Parsons.

Bradley crossed to the fireplace and pointed to a young man near the dead tiger in one photograph and the same man dressed for polo in another; then to an older man seated in the midst of the group of officers and mounted on a horse in front of the ranks of soldiers.

"Them two were when the general were a young officer in India," he said. "I never knew 'im then. An' the other two were taken years later when 'e were colonel of the Middlesex in Africa.

"And what of Colonel Cordell?" Parsons asked. "Is he in any of these photographs?"

Bradley pointed to a figure in the two photographs taken in Africa.

" 'e were a major then," he explained.

Parsons looked closely at the photographs before deciding that the quality of the print, the similarity of the uniforms, and the conformity of men's' grooming made it almost impossible to identify one officer from another. Then he strolled slowly around the room, pausing as he did to examine the three oil paintings on the wall opposite the window. As he might have expected, they were all of a military nature: two scenes of red-coated British infantry in defensive squares and one of a dramatic charge of British cavalry against what he imagined was Napoleon's Old Guard at Waterloo. Taken as a whole, the room was clearly that of a bachelor soldier. There was nothing whatsoever to suggest the influence of a woman.

Parsons ran his fingers across the surface of the desk, leaving a faint trail in the light layer of dust.

"I can see what you mean by General Latham not being a demanding man," he said to Bradley.

"No, sir," the servant replied. "The general was never one to make a fuss about 'ouse-keeping.'"

Parsons' initial reaction was that of surprise in finding that a man such as General Latham should have allowed such a state of affairs. The British army, it had always appeared to him, always laid great emphasis on outward appearance, especially its officers. Their uniforms were some of the most glamorous in the world. And here was one of its generals, a man who until recently had commanded an infantry regiment, living in a state that would make most respectable women weep. But perhaps that was the reason. With no woman to organize household affairs it was no wonder that there was dust everywhere. It seemed that Bradley did little in the way of housekeeping, and if that did not concern the general, his servant was no doubt all the more happy for that. Perhaps that was how it was in the army. Behind the facade of spotless uniforms, polished brass and gleaming bayonets, an inspection of the officers' rooms, the soldiers' dormitories, and the regimental kitchens might tell quite a different story.

"Did you move anything in the room after you found the body?" Parsons asked, his eyes straying towards the decanter.

"No, sir. I never touched nothin'."

As though anticipating Parsons next question Bradley pointed towards the rug.

"The General was lyin' there," he said. "If you ask me, 'e'd been sitting by the fire readin' when the woman come in. It looked to me as though 'e put 'is book down on the table before 'e stood up. An' that's when she done for 'im."

Parsons briefly examined the rug and the dark stains that were still visible in the thick strands of wool.

"Can you show me exactly how the General was lying when you found him?' he asked Bradley.

"Yes, sir," said the servant.

Bradley lowered himself gingerly onto the rug, with his head towards the fire and his feet facing the settee.

"And the spear? Where was that?" asked Parsons.

"By 'is side, sir." Bradley patted the rug on his left side. "An' it weren't no spear, sir. It was what they natives call an *iklwa*. We come across 'em of'en enough in Africa. All they bloody natives use 'em, 'specially the bloody Zulus. Some they use mostly for throwin' at yer, like spears. Others they use for stabbin'. They call 'em all *assegai*. But the one used on the general was an *iklwa*. It was shorter an' 'ad a bigger and fatter blade than the one's they throw. They use *iklwas* at close quarters, an' they get their name 'cause of the sound it makes when they stick 'em in your guts and the sucking noise it makes when they pull 'em out. "

"An *iklwa*," said Parsons with a weak smile, flinching a little at the thought of what Bradley had just described. "I'm obliged to you for that information, Bradley. You can get up now."

Bradley rose slowly to his feet.

"Had you seen this particular *iklwa* before?" Parsons asked. "Was it one of the general's mementoes from his African campaigns?"

"No, sir," Bradley answered. "It weren't the general's. You can see that 'e didn't go in for that sort o' thing."

Parsons looked around the room. Other than the photographs and the paintings there were no other items of military memorabilia.

"I see what you mean, Bradley," he said.

Parsons walked over to the small table and picked up the book.

"*A History of Ireland*," he read aloud. "Did you know the general was interested in Ireland, Bradley?"

"No, sir. The General never said nothin' 'bout Ireland to me other than to curse the bloody Paddies. 'E said they was an 'eathen race. No better than the savages 'e come across in India an' Africa."

Parsons replaced the book, then picked up the glass and sniffed the contents.

"Whisky," he said. "Is that your tipple, Bradley?"

"No, sir. I'm a brandy an' water man m'self."

"Is that what you were drinking on Wednesday, before this unfortunate incident?" Parsons asked.

"Yes, sir. An ol' friend from the regiment brought me a bottle."

"Oh, indeed. And who, pray, was that?"

"It were Regimental Sergeant Major Whitehead, sir. 'E come 'bout 'arf six. We served in Africa together. Mr. Whitehead said it was the anniversary of the Battle of Nyumaga an' we should 'ave a drink to celebrate our victory."

An expression of pride appeared unexpectedly on Bradley's face.

"I was there that day, sir. We give 'em natives a good whippin'," he said enthusiastically. "But blest if I could remember the date m'self. But there again I'm not an RSM."

"And did this gentleman, Mr. Whitehead, remain here long?"

"Oh, no sir. 'E 'ad one drink with me an' then he went."

"How nice for you," said Parsons drily. "to have the remainder of the bottle for yourself."

Bradley colored and shuffled his feet. He had no wish to be reminded of what had happened to the rest of the brandy.

"And where was the general while you were drinking with Mr. Whitehead?" Parsons asked.

"In 'is study, sir. 'E just come from the War Office. 'E been there all day. 'E said a few words to Mr. Whitehead like, 'cause they served together in Africa."

"So the RSM went into the general's study," said Parsons.

"Yes, sir. They 'ad a few words, like I said. But if you think Mr. Whitehead killed the general you couldn't be more wrong. They served together for years. Mr. Whitehead was a company sergeant major when the general was colonel of the Middlesex, and they was at Gwadana 'ill together fighting them bloody natives. And, in any case, the general was alive when I took 'im is supper after the RSM 'ad gone."

"One final question, Bradley," said Parsons, as he made his way to the door of the study. "What happened to the *iklwa*?"

It was Harris who answered.

"I had it taken to the dead house, sir," he said. "I thought that after examining the body the police surgeon would be able to confirm that it was the murder weapon."

"Then let us pursue that line of enquiry, Harris," said Parsons with a smile, "and leave Bradley to attend to his household responsibilities."

6

DOCTOR GRAINGER, THE police surgeon, was a tall, slim man with a sallow complexion, and a face that in profile appeared to be thin, but was unexpectedly wide when viewed from the front. He had large, watery gray eyes, the long dark beard and bushy eyebrows of an Old Testament prophet, and an expansive forehead that a receding hairline contrived to make even more prominent. The black frock coat he wore was badly creased and his right pocket needed stitching. Such an unkempt appearance, together with the stray hairs left unbrushed from the shoulders of his coat, suggested at first to Parsons that the doctor was a fellow bachelor, but the wedding band on his left hand indicated otherwise. The good doctor was either a sadly neglected married man; or, what was more likely in view of his advanced years, a widower.

In a suitably solemn tone Grainger confirmed beyond doubt that the naked man lying on the cold tiled slab had been stabbed with the weapon that had accompanied the body to the dead house.

"You say it is called an *iklwa*, inspector," he said. "Well, we learn something every day. But whatever it's name, there's no doubt it was the cause of death of this unfortunate gentleman. I'm told he was a senior army officer. Quite a fitting end for a soldier, wouldn't you agree?"

"I'm not certain General Latham would think that, sir," said Parsons politely. "Had the general chosen to end his life by being stabbed with an *iklwa*, he would doubtless have preferred his death to have been on a battlefield and not in the study of his London home. But that is just my opinion. What I'm hoping you can tell me from his wounds is something of the manner in which the blow or blows were delivered."

As the doctor bent over the body to examine the deep lacerations in Latham's torso Parsons studied the corpse. Even in death there was evidence of the vitality that the general must have displayed in life. Although of no more than average height he possessed broad shoulders, a deep chest matted with tight swirls of black hair, and muscular arms and legs. Parsons also noted the large hooked nose, the luxuriant mustache over his wide sensuous mouth, and the powerful thrust of his jaw. General Sir Maxwell Latham would not, by any means, have been called handsome, but his obvious physical strength and presence would doubtless have been attractive to many women.

"As you can see, inspector," the doctor said, pointing to a deep wound on the left side of the torso, "the *iklwa,* as you call it, entered the chest just below the ribs with considerable force. There was but a single blow, probably by a person using both hands, but it was applied with sufficient skill or good fortune for the blade to rupture the intestine before piercing the heart. The way in which the flesh has been torn also suggests that the assailant withdrew the weapon from the body after the assault."

"That would explain why the *iklwa* was found lying next to the body," said Harris. "The murderer must've pulled it out and placed it on the floor."

"That makes perfect sense, sergeant," Grainger said. "I would have been surprised if you'd told me that the spear was still sticking in the general's chest when you found him."

It also showed that the murderer acted calmly, thought Parsons. Not everyone would remain as composed in similar circumstances.

Grainger pointed to other scars on the general's left arm.

"These were not made at the time of his death," he said. "Doubtless the general received them on some distant battlefield."

"Would there have been much blood?" Parsons asked.

"Oh yes, a considerable amount," the doctor answered as he stroked his beard thoughtfully. "I would expect the person who stabbed this gallant soldier to have had blood on their hands and possibly on their clothes."

"Could a woman have done this, doctor?" asked Parsons.

"Without doubt, inspector."

Grainger lifted the *iklwa* and touched the sides of the blade with his fingers.

"The murder weapon was sharp enough for even a strong child to have made a wound like the one inflicted on the general."

Parsons took the *iklwa* from Grainger and examined it.

"Judging by the burnished edges it looks very much as though the weapon was sharpened before it was used," he said. "Whoever killed the general wanted to be certain of making a good job of it."

———

IT WAS RAINING steadily when Parsons and Harris left the dead house. Hansom cabs were at a premium, and as there was no chance of finding one passing that was empty, the two men were obliged to walk to the cab stand in Praed Street and wait in line for fifteen minutes before one became available.

"Horse Guards Parade," Parsons shouted to the cabbie as he scrambled aboard, sank into the leather seat beside Harris, and left his umbrella to drip on the floor of the cab. Then, oblivious to the gentle rocking motion of the cab as it made its way slowly along Edgeware Road towards Hyde Park, the sound of the rain beating on the roof, or the din of the other traffic, he lapsed into deep thought. It was not until they had reached the end of Park Lane that he spoke.

"As you said at the start, Harris," he said, "it all seems simple enough. This Frenchwoman, who if Bradley is to be believed is Mrs. Cordell, appears to have been involved in some sort of relationship with General Latham. No doubt in time we will learn more about that. It also seems clear that she was in the general's house at the time of his death and from the evidence we have so far it appears likely that she killed him, although it seems strange that she should have drawn attention to that fact by screaming in the way she did. If she had simply left the house quietly Bradley might not have found the body for hours. As it was, her screams ensured that the hue and cry began immediately. There's also the matter of the weapon. Mrs. Cordell, if indeed it was she, would have needed access to an *iklwa* and the opportunity to sharpen it. But that should not have proved a difficult problem for an officer's wife. From what I remember of the Officers' Mess in my father's regiment it was filled with all kinds of weapons."

"And what about the veil, sir," Harris said. "I can't say I've ever worn one myself, nor would I wish to, but if I was a woman intent on stabbing someone I think I might dispense with my veil."

"An excellent point, Harris" said Parsons, smiling at the thought of Harris' waxed mustache concealed beneath a veil. "But we'll return to this French woman later. For the moment I'm more intent upon learning something more about General Latham. Other than what Bradley has already told us we know little about him other than that he served in India and Africa, and that he was a widower with an eye for the ladies. I'm hoping the War Office will have records about his career which may suggest other avenues of investigation."

The rain was easing as the cab reached the end of Constitution Hill and passed Buckingham Palace on its way into the Mall.

"The trees in St. James' Park look particularly well at this time of the year, don't you think, Harris?" said Parsons, looking through the window on the right side of the cab.

Harris did not reply. Having been brought up in a treeless back street in East London he had little appreciation for the cycle of Nature that led each year to such vivid autumn colors.

Once part of the grounds of St. James's Palace, the park had been arranged into its rhomboidal shape during the reign of Henry VIII. Over the centuries other monarchs had endeavored, to one extent or another, to leave their imprint upon it. Perhaps the one most devoted to the park had been Charles II, whose unfortunate father of the same name had walked through its grounds from St. James' Palace on a cold morning in 1649 on the way to his execution in Whitehall.

As the cab approached the end of the Mall, Parsons instructed the driver to turn right at the Admiralty building, and stop at the edge of the graveled parade ground behind Horse Guards. It was a simple manoeuvre that avoided the invariable delay caused by the heavy traffic in Trafalgar Square. From the parade ground it was but a short walk through the arch of the Horse Guards building to the War Office, where they were directed by a clerk to the second floor office of Lieutenant Morrisey, the late General Latham's *aide-de-camp*.

"I confess I've been expecting a visit from the police," the young, fresh-faced officer said jovially, "and as I imagined you would be wanting to know more about the general I took the liberty of preparing a summary of his career for you. I can't tell you what a shock it was to hear of the general's death. He was here only two days ago as large as life and keen to take up his new post."

He handed Parsons three sheets of paper.

"That's most thoughtful of you, lieutenant," said Parsons, noting from the large, ill-formed handwriting that Lieutenant Morrisey, although a far more friendly and polite young officer than Louise's brother, appeared to have benefitted little more than Reginald Chapman from an expensive private education.

"Well, to be honest, inspector," Morrisey explained. "I'd only recently been appointed as the general's ADC, and just before this unfortunate event I'd been doing some research on his career for my own benefit."

"So you know the general's next appointment," said Parsons.

"Oh, yes," said Morrisey. "Although when I learned it myself I confess that I wasn't at all happy to be leaving London. And to be perfectly frank I'm not altogether sure that the general himself was too thrilled when he heard where he was going. But he told me a good soldier should just do as he's told. He also convinced me that the move would be good for my career, and assured me that if I did a good job as his ADC he'd see that I was promoted."

"You can tell me more about that when I've finished reading this," said Parsons, turning his attention to the papers the lieutenant had provided. He read each sheet carefully and without comment before passing it to Harris.

General Maxwell Latham, he learned, was forty-eight years of age at the time of his death. He had first purchased a commission in the Middlesex Light Infantry in 1853, at the age of twenty, had served in the Crimean campaign and fought against the Russians at the Battle of Inkerman and at the Siege of Sevastopol. Parsons read that a spell in England recovering from wounds had followed, remembering as he did the scars he had seen on the general's left arm. Latham had rejoined his regiment in India, and had won the Victoria Cross during the mutiny of the native sepoys by leading a frontal assault against the heavily fortified fort at Burnai. Whilst still in India, he had purchased the rank of captain.

Latham had returned to England with his regiment in 1865, and after purchasing his majority in 1870 been given command of a company before the regiment was posted to southern Africa in 1875. In Africa he had fought on the eastern frontier of Cape Colony in the wars against the Xhosa tribes, and when the commanding officer of the Middlesex Light Regiment was killed Latham had been given command. Colonel Latham and the Middlesex, Parsons read, continued to distinguish themselves in further wars against the Xhosa and Zulu nations, and in his final African campaign Latham himself had received a commendation for his leadership during the war against the Boers in Transvaal. This had led to further promotion and to a knighthood on his return to England. That had been six months ago. Since then he had been on home leave awaiting his next appointment.

Parsons passed the last of the papers to Harris.

"General Latham was indeed a remarkable man," he said. "And at his relatively young age I've no doubt he was destined for further promotion. But from what you said earlier you were both soon to be leaving London."

"That's perfectly true, inspector," said Morrisey. "The London Gazette published his appointment as Commander-in-Chief of British troops in Ireland only last week. It was an excellent choice. The General would've stood no nonsense from the Irish, although if the truth be told he would have far preferred to return to Africa."

"So that explains the book he was reading at the time he was murdered," Parsons murmured.

"But what of his family?" he asked Morrisey. "I see nothing in your excellent notes about General Latham's family."

"As far as I could tell from army records he had no direct family, inspector. I believe he was married once, but his wife died many years ago, and there is no record of him ever having any children."

"What about his next-of-kin?" Parsons asked. "There must be some record in his papers of somebody to contact in the event of his death."

"The only person listed in his records is his half-brother, Colonel Cordell, the gentleman who succeeded him as commanding officer of the Middlesex. The two men served together in South Africa. Cordell commanded one of the companies."

Parson and Harris exchanged a glance at this new and unexpected information about the relationship between General Latham and Colonel Cordell, but neither of them made any comment.

"Thank you, lieutenant," said Parsons as they shook hands. "Your notes have been most helpful. But now you must excuse us. I think it's time we paid our respects to General Latham's half-brother."

7

"I'M GLAD I waited for you to return from the Lake District before deciding to make an arrest, sir," said Harris, as the two men walked briskly along Whitehall towards Trafalgar Square. "What seemed to be relatively straightforward has suddenly taken an unexpected twist."

"Murders are rarely simple matters, Harris," Parsons said. "Human beings are complex creatures, and at times of stress can be relied upon to behave irrationally. Even in a highly structured organization like the army."

Harris was right. The fact that the chief suspect was the wife of victim's half-brother was altogether unexpected. Not to mention both men being senior officers who had served together in the same regiment.

While Harris was finding a cab Parsons purchased two meat pies for their lunch from a street vendor in Trafalgar Square. For the moment Parsons had decided not to confront Colonel

Cordell with his suspicions about his wife's involvement in General Latham's death, but to interview the colonel as though he were no more than the general's next of kin. Depending upon the outcome of that interview he would then decide how to proceed. It was just possible that the colonel might be aware of her motive. And Parsons had no wish to arrest Mrs. Cordell until he had a better idea of what that might be.

———

THE TRAFFIC IN Piccadilly was almost at a standstill. As the major access road between central London and the wealthy residential areas to the west and south west of the city, it was a route much traveled by cabs. For that very reason it was one thoroughly disliked by cab drivers, as the fares they could charge were regulated by the distance their cabs traveled, and not by the times the journeys took.

As Parsons' cab had made its dilatory progress towards Hyde Park Corner past the expensive shops and imposing residences their driver's language had worsened. He had not been in the most civil of moods when they had first boarded, but the curses and obscenities he directed towards other vehicles had become so loud and offensive that Harris, who had as great an aversion to foul language as he had for strong drink, had rapped repeatedly on the roof of the cab. But his protests had gone unheeded, and the torrent of abuse continued unabated. Parsons had to admit some sympathy for the driver. What other way was there for a man in his situation to vent his frustration? Had the fortunes of life conspired to make him a cab driver, Parsons had no doubt that he would have acted in a similar fashion.

Apart from these occasional attempts at stemming the flow of invective Harris had been unusually quiet, and Parsons sensed that something he had heard at the War Office was troubling him.

"I don't understand this business about purchasing commissions, sir," he said eventually as the cab finally emerged from Knightsbridge and the horse raised a steady trot along Kensington Road. "Does that mean that army officers are able to buy promotion?"

"That was certainly the case until 1871, Harris," explained Parsons, as he absent-mindedly watched the stately progress of two elegant ladies riding sidesaddle along Rotten Row. Dressed in black top hats, long black riding skirts, and tight black jackets over their white silk blouses they made a fine sight, and he could not help admiring the grace and skill with which they controlled their mounts. "It was only then that Edward Cardwell, the Secretary of State for War, abolished the purchase and sale of commissions. The system had been considered far from perfect for years, but it took the newspaper reports of the disastrous Crimean campaign to bring matters to a head. After such public exposure of the incompetence of our military leaders it was clear that something had to be done. I'm sure you'll have heard of the gallant but foolish cavalry charge of the 11th Hussars at Balaclava. If you recall they attacked the wrong Russian guns. Tennyson even wrote a poem about it. But what you might not know is that the Earl of Cardigan, the officer leading that charge, was reputed to have paid forty thousand pounds shortly before the Hussars left for the Crimea for the honor of commanding the regiment."

"Forty thousand pounds, sir!" Harris exclaimed in amazement. "Just to wear a smart uniform and ride at the head of a few hundred soldiers."

Harris sat deep in thought for several minutes.

"That's more than I'll earn in my lifetime, sir!" he said indignantly. "In fact I wouldn't earn that much in several lifetimes! Why are men like that be given so much responsibility? How could the Government have allowed it? It's not like that in the navy! At least in the navy the officers have to know how to navigate their ships in all weathers and in every part of the world. But it doesn't sound as though army officers are capable of reading a map!"

Parsons could not argue with what Harris had said. In the past the British army had often been led by men of little intellect, and if Reginald Chapman was an example of a modern officer little had changed in spite of Cardwell's reforms. But as Harris knew nothing of Reginald or of Parsons' relationship with Louise, he had no wish to prejudice Harris against her at this stage by admitting that the object of his affection had a brother who was an army officer. It would be far better to let Harris meet Louise at an appropriate time and allow him to form his own opinion.

"Don't think for one moment I'm making an excuse for the system as it was, Harris," Parsons said, "all I can tell you is that by allowing officers to purchase their commissions it was intended to attract men of fortune and good character into the army. Men who, it was considered, would know how to best protect the nation's interests. To some extent it worked. It produced outstanding leaders like Marlborough and Wellington. But for every great man like that there were hundreds of dilettantes masquerading as officers. The system also assumed that a fixed price would be paid for a given rank. But that was never the case. There was always a ready market for those commissions that were considered to be of greater prestige than others. For instance, the price for the rank of colonel in a Hussars or Guards regiment far exceeded that of one in a more junior infantry regiment. It was also considered inappropriate for one officer to approach another with a view to buying his commission. Someone had to act as an intermediary. And that gave rise to agents who bought and sold commissions like company shares. You may find it difficult to believe, but many officers regarded the purchase of a commission as a form of investment. You see, after purchasing a commission an officer considered that he effectively owned it, and could sell it to the highest bidder whenever he chose. In other words he was anticipating a sizable return on his investment when he eventually left the army. So it was no wonder that many officers opposed Caldwell's changes, because although every officer was compensated by the Government when the purchase system was abolished, the money many received was actually less then the inflated price they had previously paid for their rank and considerably less than what they ultimately hoped to sell it for. As you can imagine, some officers actually lost large sums of money."

"What about General Latham, sir?" asked Harris. "Do you think he was one?"

"I don't think it likely, Harris. From what I read about him at the War Office he only purchased his commissions up to the rank of major. His subsequent promotions to colonel and general would doubtless have been made on merit."

THE MIDDLESEX LIGHT Infantry was stationed in the leafy suburbs of Kensington. Their barracks was in Church Street, a quiet tree-lined road off Kensington High Street, less than a quarter of a mile from Kensington Gardens and Hyde Park. Although regarded primarily as a residential area with middle and upper class pretensions, Kensington also contained areas that were distinctly artisan, and the presence of the army had ensured that there was a sprinkling of cheap shops, bawdy public houses, and houses of ill repute.

"This will do nicely, driver," Parsons shouted, at the same time rapping on the roof of the cab as it drew level with a pair of tall, black wrought-iron gates with the Union flag of England, Ireland and Scotland on one side, and the red, yellow and blue stripes of the Middlesex Light Infantry on the other. Both flags had been lowered to half-mast as a sign of respect for the late commanding officer.

"I'd like to see Colonel Cordell," Parsons explained to a sentry dressed in a red five-buttoned serge frock coat, navy serge trousers and wearing a blue cloth-covered helmet with the Middlesex regimental crest on a thin brass plate.

"You can't do tha' without permission, sir," the sentry replied sourly. "I'll need to call the guard commander."

The guard commander in turn had to seek further permission from the Regimental Sergeant Major, and it was fully ten minutes before a clean-shaven, slim man of medium height with a ramrod-straight back appeared at the gate with a silver-topped cane tucked tightly under his left arm.

"I'm Regimental Sergeant Major Whitehead, gentlemen. And what exactly is your business with Colonel Cordell."

Whitehead's enquiry was polite but firm, the coolness in his clear gray eyes suggesting that his was an authority that was rarely, if ever, challenged. Parsons first impression was that they were the eyes of a man who had faced obstacles in his life and overcome them.

"My business concerns the murder of General Latham, sergeant major," said Parsons. "I've no doubt you will have heard about it."

"I have indeed, sir," Whitehead replied in a less severe tone. "A terrible business. The general was a fine gentleman. I had the honor of serving with him in Africa. I only hope you catch the devil who murdered him. Hangings too good for someone like that. We should hand him over to the bloody natives. I've seen what they do with their prisoners."

Whitehead turned sharply on his heel without waiting for a response.

"Follow me, gentlemen," he said over his shoulder. "I'll escort you to the colonel's house. I happen to know that he left his office not long before you arrived."

Much of the space in the center of the barracks was occupied by an expansive parade ground, which appeared to Parsons to be the main focus of activity. Whitehead set off at a sharp pace along that side of the parade ground that ran parallel to Church Street, bellowing as he did at the squads of soldiers drilling on the square. Both Parsons and Harris had been initially startled by this, as they had imagined that these loud words of command had been directed at them.

"Why is it necessary for soldiers to spend so long on the parade ground?" asked Parsons innocently, thinking as he did that there could be no greater waste of time than that spent repeating endlessly what he regarded as being pointless drills.

Whitehead gave Parsons a look that might well have been reserved for ill-behaved children and imbeciles.

"Because the British Army is nothing without the discipline learned on the parade ground," he said coldly. "Without discipline a soldier loses his bearings. Discipline is the mortar that holds a regiment together. It's discipline that wins wars, sir. Discipline."

Parsons did not respond, but took some comfort from the fact that the RSM had at least stopped shouting and instead had turned his attention to the buildings around the parade ground.

"That's the Guard Room, gentlemen," he said, turning and pointing his cane at the solitary building near the gate. "The building on your left contains the Regimental Headquarters and the Orderly Room. That's where the colonel and I have our offices. Beyond that is the Armoury, and in the far corner the Sergeants' and Warrant Officers' Mess."

Whitehead waved his cane towards the buildings on the opposite side of the drill square, on the south and east sides of the barracks.

"Those are the soldiers' accommodation blocks. There is one for each of the three companies, with a mess hall on the ground floor and sleeping quarters on the two floors above. And in the far corner," the RSM pointed to an area between two of the accommodation blocks, "are the stables where the officers keep their horses."

Whitehead indicated two buildings at the northern end of the barracks, each of them partly hidden by a high privet hedge.

"The colonel's house and the Officers' Mess are over there," he said.

"If, as I imagine, the smaller of the two buildings is the colonel's house," said Parsons, who was beginning to wilt at the fast pace the RSM was setting, "why is it that we are walking around the edge of the parade ground when it would be far quicker to take a direct line across it?"

Whitehead came abruptly and unexpectedly to a halt and regarded Parsons with an expression of abject horror.

"Because no one, sir," he said with an outraged expression on his face, "and I mean no one, unless he is the commanding officer or one of the company commanders, dare set foot on that hallowed ground unless it is for the purpose of drilling. Not even me."

Whitehead fixed Parsons with an icy gaze.

"No one, sir," he repeated.

Parsons did his best to meet the RSM's fierce glare, but he failed. After years of staring down recalcitrant soldiers RSM Whitehead had become adept at dominating others with the intensity of his gaze, and Parsons realized immediately that at least in this respect he had met his match.

"I believe you were at the General's house yourself on the night he was murdered," Parsons said, anxious to move onto a less contentious subject than parade grounds and their purpose.

"Quite right, sir," said Whitehead as they resumed their brisk march. "I took his man, Bradley, a bottle of brandy to commemorate an action we saw together in Africa. And while I was there I took the opportunity to pay my respects to the general. As I said before, sir, he was a fine man. One of the old school. A disciplinarian if ever there was, but an officer the men were proud to follow. I only wish there were more like him."

"What time was it when you saw the general?" Parsons asked.

"I'd say somewhere between six-thirty and seven, sir. I'd agreed to meet one of the sergeants for a drink at seven-thirty, and I'm always punctual. It wouldn't do for me to be late."

He gave Parsons another sharp glance.

"Where would the army be if senior noncommissioned officers like me couldn't be relied upon to keep time?" he asked. "I can tell you, sir. It would be in a far greater mess than it already is."

In spite of his feelings about the questionable value of monotonous parade ground drills Parsons' knew that there was some truth in what the RSM had said. Much of the success the British army had attained on the battlefield had been due in no small measure to the strict discipline instilled into soldiers by men like Whitehead. Commissioned officers, of whom the Earl of Cardigan was a prime example, were often no more than expensive window dressing.

THE COMMANDING OFFICER'S house was a square granite building surrounded by a black wrought iron fence against which grew the thick, neatly trimmed privet hedge they had seen from a distance. The hedge was surprisingly effective at filtering noise, as once inside the gate Parsons was surprised to discover how effectively the sounds of the parade ground were absorbed by the foliage. So quiet was it that it was difficult to believe the well-tended garden of shrubs and standard roses and the neatly trimmed lawns fronting the house were only a short distance from the parade ground and the barrack blocks in which hundreds of soldiers lived.

The signs of mourning were mixed. There was a wreath on the front door, but the curtains had not been drawn as was the custom when a household was in mourning.

"I'll leave you gentlemen here," said Whitehead, once he had been assured by the servant answering the door that the colonel was at home. Then he saluted, executed a smart about turn, and marched swiftly away.

——— ——— ———

PARSONS' FIRST IMPRESSION upon seeing Colonel Cordell in the flesh, rather than as one of many indistinct faces in a photograph, was that he was not at all as he had imagined the commanding officer of an infantry regiment to be. It was foolish, he knew, to ever allow himself to have set preconceptions about how individuals should look, but after having only recently seen General Latham's corpse, Parsons was surprised to find that his half-brother bore no physical resemblance to him whatsoever. Cordell was barely taller than himself, and in contrast to the general's robust physique, he had a slim, willowy frame, and the narrow, pinched face of an aesthete. His dark hair was cut short, parted severely down the center and liberally dressed with macassar oil; and his slim mustache gave the impression of having been drawn with two quick strokes of a fine-nibbed pen. The overall effect was less than impressive. In fact Parsons could not have imagined anyone looking less like a senior army officer. Were it not for a pair of piercing blue eyes the sense of pusillanimity would have been overwhelming. But even in those eyes Parsons sensed a weakness and a lack of confidence quite out of keeping with his rank, and a marked contrast to the eyes of the man who had just escorted them to the house.

Cordell was wearing a red jacket and navy trousers similar in color to those worn by the sentry. But the material was of a far superior quality, and had been better tailored. The jacket, in particular, had been amply furnished with gold braid: on the epaulettes to delineate the star and crown of the colonel's rank, together with an elaborate scroll on each sleeve.

"Well, inspector," he said brusquely, with the slightest trace of a lisp. "How can I be of assistance?"

They had moved from the large entrance hall into a small study with paneled walls, an easy chair on each side of a fireplace, and a desk with a sea captain's chair facing out towards the front lawn. Papers scattered across the desk suggested that prior to their arrival the colonel had been working there.

There was a striking similarity in the way the furniture was arranged in this room and the one in which General Latham was murdered, but it was only superficial. The difference was in the detail. In contrast to the study in Chester Place, this room was replete with military memorabilia: rifles, pistols, sabres, lances, and, Parsons could not fail to notice, a collection of *assegais* assembled in a tall brass pot on one side of the fireplace. It was as though, unlike his half-brother, Colonel Cordell had to prove his military pedigree with a lavish display of weaponry.

"I believe you are General Sir Maxwell Latham's half-brother, sir," Parsons said. "Please allow me to offer my condolences. From what I have heard he was an outstanding officer and a fine gentleman."

"You have been correctly informed about our relationship, inspector," Cordell replied, who had remained standing with his hands clasped behind his back. "The general and I had the same mother, but different fathers."

"But you nevertheless followed the same military career, sir," said Parsons. "And with evident success."

Cordell accepted the compliment with a weak smile.

"And other than confirming that the general and I were half-brothers, inspector," he said impatiently, "how can I be of assistance to you?"

"Would you be so kind as to tell me where you and Mrs. Cordell were on Wednesday night, sir," said Parsons. "It is just for the record, you understand."

Cordell unclasped his hands and stroked each side of his mustache with the index finger of his right hand in a manner that struck Parsons as surprisingly feminine.

"Mrs. Cordell and I were entertaining on Wednesday," he said. "We had a dinner party for some of the regimental officers. Two of the company commanders were present, one of whom brought his wife. And there was Captain Simpson. The dinner was in the way of being a small celebration for Captain Simpson. He is shortly to be awarded the Victoria Cross for his bravery in Africa. Although the patrol that he so gallantly led took place several months ago, the announcement of his award was made only recently."

Cordell's mouth twisted in a wry smile.

"The wheels of military bureaucracy turn slowly," he said.

"That must be a great honor for the regiment, sir," said Parsons, "and especially for you as his commanding officer."

"Well, as it happens I was not the commanding officer at the time," Cordell explained frostily. "That honor fell to my half-brother. But I am, nevertheless, proud to say that I was Captain Simpson's company commander."

"Then no doubt congratulations are even more in order, sir," said Parsons, "as no doubt you were that much closer to the action."

Cordell acknowledged the approbation with another feeble smile and continued stroking his mustache.

"And this dinner party concluded at what time, sir?" Parsons asked.

"Around eleven, inspector. Mrs. Cordell said that she was feeling unwell and wanted to go to bed, and naturally when our guests realized that they left immediately afterwards."

"And can you remind me again who those guests were, sir," said Parsons. "Just for the record."

"I really don't see what my guests have to do with your investigation, inspector," said Cordell, his blue eyes suddenly turning to ice.

"That is for me to decide, sir," replied Parsons calmly. "Now, sir. Please. Their names."

Cordell glared at Parsons for a few seconds, in an unsuccessful attempt to impress the young inspector with his superior rank and authority.

"Very well," he said icily. "If you insist. My guests were Major Mark Holland of A Company, Major Charles Arbuthnot of B Company and his wife, Lady Cordelia. And, as I said before, Captain Audley Simpson."

"I might have expected to find General Latham among the guests. Did you not say that he was Captain Simpson's commanding officer, and was not his own promotion and knighthood a direct result of the regiment's actions in Africa?"

Cordell's jaundiced expression suggested to Parsons that what the colonel might first have considered saying about his dead half-brother might have been less than flattering. Instead he said bitterly:

"I had invited the general, but he declined because of a previous engagement."

"That is to be understood, colonel," said Parsons. "The general must have been a very busy man, especially after learning of his new appointment. Would you have said he had any enemies?"

"Not that I know of, inspector," said Cordell. "Unless, of course, you count a few thousand natives in India and Africa. But I imagine that most of those are already dead. But what of these Fenians and the atrocities in Ireland I am constantly reading about? Bearing in mind that the general was about to take command there I would think that his murder could well be their work. Especially as it happened not long after Lord Sayers was shot."

"An excellent point, sir. And one the police have not overlooked, I can assure you."

Parsons knew that this was far from the truth. Neither Superintendent Jeffries nor any of the other detectives had at any time suggested there might be any connection between the two deaths.

Parsons gazed over the Colonel's shoulder towards the fireplace. "But in my experience," he said, "the Fenians have never before resorted to the use of *iklwas* like the ones I can see in this room, and like the one that was used to murder your half-brother."

Parsons was unsuccessful in engaging Cordell's eyes. The Colonel seemed intent only in leading the way towards the front door.

"That is a most interesting point that you make, inspector," he said. "But now you really must excuse me. I have other more important matters to attend to."

8

"**H**AVE YOU CHANGED your opinion of the British Army now that you've had the opportunity of seeing it at close quarters, Harris?" Parsons asked. "I notice you didn't have much to say whilst we were in the barracks."

Their cab was passing the Natural History Museum in Cromwell Road. The museum had only recently been completed in a Romanesque style that Parsons found much to his liking. In his opinion it provided a welcome contrast to the more elaborate Gothic Revival buildings that had become so popular. The museum had been built with profits made from the Great Exhibition in Hyde Park in 1851, and was part of what the late Prince Albert had envisaged as being a national center of arts and science. Had he lived to see his dreams come to fruition Albert would doubtless have been a proud man.

Parsons had decided to return to Scotland Yard before interviewing Venetta Cordell. As things stood the only person claiming to see her at Chester Place at the time of General Latham's death was the general's servant. And a reliable witness had suggested that Bradley was drunk at the time. On the other hand, if any of the cabbies operating in Bayswater and Kensington had also seen a veiled woman with a foreign accent traveling between Kensington Barracks and Chester Place around and about midnight the case against Mrs. Cordell would be that much stronger. And with luck that information would be awaiting them at Scotland Yard.

"I've never had a good opinion of the army, sir," Harris replied morosely. "And nothing I've seen or heard in the last few days has made me change my mind. In my experience any family who ever had a son wear a red jacket was generally ashamed of him. It's all very well people boasting about the famous thin red line and how our glorious victory at Waterloo saved Europe from Napoleon, but when I was a young constable pounding a beat in the East End I saw those fine young men in their red jackets for what they really were. And I can tell you, sir, they were the scum of the earth. And as for their officers, as you said yourself, you don't have to look any further than the Crimean War to see how incapable they are. I don't know too much about what's going on in Africa, but it wouldn't surprise me to hear that it was nothing that we should be proud of."

Parsons was not unduly surprised by Harris' outburst. In spite of his own late father being a senior officer he shared many of those opinions, although he was inclined to be less critical than the sergeant. It was true that the army recruited from the lowest classes, and it was an unfortunate fact that soldiers were not only known for their drunkenness, but as many as twenty per cent of them at any one time were suffering from venereal disease. Yet, in spite of all that, Parsons felt that the army played a useful role in society beyond that of defending the country. Soldiers were generally recruited from men with little prospect of work, and in his opinion it was better for such men to be trained and given a sense of discipline within a military organization than for them to remain as disillusioned and rebellious civilians who might at some point become a threat to society. And after all, these were the men who more often than not performed valiantly in battle, in spite of the poor quality of their leaders; leaders, who for the most part came from the privileged upper classes, and for whom army life was intended as no more than a short and pleasant interlude in a life of comparative idleness.

In spite of the pre-eminent position Britain held in the world compared to other major European powers, she was ill prepared for war. The first signs of the army's deficiencies had become apparent during the Crimean War, but the real gravity of the situation had not become clear until 1870 when the newly unified Germany's modernized army had overwhelmed that of France. It was clear then that drastic changes would be necessary if the British Army was ever to be capable of fighting a modern war.

Cardwell's reforms were intended to begin the process of modernization. As well as abolishing the sale of commissions, it was also proposed, that like Germany, the British Army should have a professional general staff, an intelligence section to advise the commander-in-chief, and a Reserve force that could be used to bring peacetime battalions up to a war footing to meet any threat to the country.

As was often the case, these reforms had been implemented slowly, and had little influenced the conduct of the smaller campaigns that Britain continued to wage around the world. Campaigns such as those that had been fought in India, China, New Zealand, Canada, Abyssinia, and now in Africa. The scale of these campaigns was generally so small that, unless the results proved disastrous, there was scant coverage in the newspapers and little public reaction. But then, only two years previously, there had been Isandlwana. At Isandlwana a force of two thousand British soldiers had been annihilated by African Zulus armed mainly with primitive weapons. And it was in similar campaigns in Africa, Parsons deliberated, that the late General Latham had won two promotions and gained a knighthood.

———

AFTER REACHING SCOTLAND Yard the two men separated. Parsons went straight to his office, and had barely time to glance through the papers on his desk before a beaming Harris entered.

"Listen to this, sir," he said excitedly. "I've a report from the cab company in Kensington about one of their cabs collecting a woman from a street near Kensington Barracks not long before midnight and delivering her to Chester Place; and another from Bayswater stating that a distraught woman was collected from Stanhope Street - that's a street close to Chester Place, sir - at around half past twelve and taken to Kensington Barracks. Both reports say that the woman was dressed in a dark cloak, wore a heavy veil, and spoke with a foreign accent. One of the drivers even went as far as to say that he thought she was French."

9

Saturday, 25th October 1881

REGIMENTAL SERGEANT MAJOR Patrick Whitehead had been up since five o'clock. He was always one of the first in the regiment to rise. Only the cooks in the soldiers' mess halls and the servant who brought him his morning tea and hot shaving water rose earlier. He shaved, dressed quickly and efficiently, and scrutinized himself in the full-length mirror on the back of his door to ensure that there was not the slightest blemish in his appearance.

Like the majority of men joining the army as common soldiers Whitehead's background had been harsh. The only son of poor Irish immigrants to the north of England, he had been orphaned before the age of ten. His father had died in an accident whilst working on the railways and his mother had followed soon after, the victim of a fire that had swept through a row of small sweatshops in the back streets of Manchester.

Whitehead had avoided the repressive clutches of the orphanage, choosing instead to live from hand to mouth in the slums, taking whatever jobs were available, and occasionally resorting to begging and petty crime.

But even amongst the squalor in which he was forced to live he never lost sight of his goal. He had always remembered the shame his parents felt at their inability to read, and in an age when schooling was available only to a privileged few Whitehead had never abandoned the dream of receiving an education.

Fortunately for him a Ragged School had recently opened in Manchester, one of dozens that had gradually spread from London to the industrial cities. These unofficial schools were organized, funded and taught by philanthropic Christians, who took verminous, ragged children from the slums, clothed and fed them, and taught them basic literacy, numeracy and rudimentary social skills.

The Ragged School that Whitehead had attended had been established by a clergyman who had previously been a missionary in Africa. This most excellent man scrubbed his pupils from head to foot, deloused them, and mercilessly flogged girls and boys alike when they were inattentive in class or had forgotten what it was they had been taught in a previous lesson.

The experience was pivotal in Whitehead's development. He had acquired a strong sense of self-improvement, had learned the importance of self-discipline, and after listening enthralled to tales of missionary life in Africa had determined upon seeing the world.

After reluctantly accepting that Whitehead had no calling for missionary work his mentor had encouraged his star pupil to join the army, and in 1861 the young man had traveled to London, had cheerfully accepted the Queen's shilling from a recruiting sergeant, and joined the Middlesex Light Infantry. It was a decision he had never regretted. The regiment had become his family, and his love for it had been reciprocated. By the age of thirty-eight he had reached the rank of regimental sergeant-major, an achievement that was as much as any common soldier could expect.

But Whitehead was not content to let matters rest. His ambitions knew no bounds. He dreamed that a day would come when he would command his regiment. It was a step far greater than most common soldiers would ever consider possible, one step beyond that achieved by Major Plumb, an experienced soldier with a similar humble background to Whitehead. But Whitehead felt he was capable of taking that step. He knew he was better qualified to be commanding officer than any other man in the regiment, and especially more so than the present incumbent.

THE BUGLER WAS playing the strident notes of Reveille as Whitehead left the Sergeants' Mess and marched swiftly alongside the parade ground to the Guard Room. The response by the guard to the recent attack by the Fenians had, in his opinion, been far from satisfactory, and the sergeant commanding the guard that night had, at Whitehead's insistence, been reduced to the rank of corporal.

Whitehead scrutinized the guard report for any irregularities before turning his attention to the prisoners undergoing punishment, satisfying himself that they had been roused and set to work scrubbing the Guard Room floor. Then he made his way to A Company mess hall to see how the preparations for breakfast were progressing.

In Whitehead's opinion nothing was more important for the morale of a regiment than the quality of its food. Most soldiers, he knew, came from similar backgrounds to himself and were prepared to put up with considerable hardship and discipline provided they were well fed. But the men serving as cooks in the army were generally inadequately trained and poorly supervised, the victuals were of poor quality, with the result that the meals were tasteless and unnourishing. That might happen in other regiments, but Whitehead was determined it would never happen in the Middlesex. Not as long as he was RSM.

He declined the mug of strong tea offered him by one of the cooks, choosing instead to inspect the kitchen, his keen eye checking both the quality of the food being prepared and the cleanliness of the cooks. As a young soldier he had often been forced to eat food that was only fit for pigs, and on active service had witnessed more soldiers laid low by disease and unsanitary food than by enemy action.

At half past six the bugler played the call to the Cookhouse and shortly after that the first of the soldiers began to arrive. Whitehead stood at the end of the serving line as each man ladled porridge, scrambled eggs and sausage into his mess tin, and filled a tin mug with hot tea. He had said on countless occasions that a soldier's morale could be judged by the look in his eyes, and at each breakfast Whitehead made a point of checking that for himself by engaging each man directly and greeting him by name. By rotating through each of the three companies on a daily basis Whitehead was sure of seeing every soldier in the regiment at least twice each week. In that way he had learned the names of each of the nine hundred and sixty men in the regiment. No one else in the regiment could boast of that.

By seven o'clock Whitehead had seen enough to know that the men in A Company were in good heart and well satisfied with their breakfast. Only then did he make his way towards the Sergeants' Mess for his own meal.

MAJOR MARK HOLLAND had breakfasted before seven. Since rejoining the regiment in London he had made it his custom to ride each morning in Hyde Park. There was no better place in the London than Rotten Row to meet fashionable young ladies from wealthy families; and after his recent promotion he considered it high time to embark upon the serious business of finding himself a wife with a private income in keeping with his ambitions.

By most people's standards Holland would be considered wealthy. He had been born into an affluent farming family, but as the second-born son he had known from an early age that it was his elder brother, Matthew, who would one day inherit the house and the thousand acres of Devonshire farmland. Mark would have to make his own way in life with the only help the few hundred pounds his father allowed him each year.

Like his brother he had been schooled at Wellington College, the national monument to the great Duke of Wellington, and it was there, in the classically inspired buildings set in four hundred acres of verdant Berkshire countryside that he had decided upon a military career.

The Caldwell reforms had made it unnecessary for Mark to purchase his first commission. It was, nevertheless, incumbent upon him to have a private income of sorts, not only to compensate for the inadequacy of his army pay, but also for him to live in a style befitting that of an officer in Her Britannic Majesty's land forces.

It was at Wellington, and later at the elite military college at Sandhurst, that Mark had first learned of the great disparities in private income that existed even amongst the wealthy upper classes. At Sandhurst he had fondly imagined himself becoming a Guards officer until politely being advised that his pedigree was not of sufficient quality for him to join such exalted ranks and his private income fell below that required to afford the lavish lifestyle of such exclusive regiments. So he had been obliged to settle for a less glamorous regiment like the Middlesex Light Infantry.

His time on the general staff in Africa had only served to reinforce his opinion about the importance of money. As a conscientious staff officer his energy and willingness to ingratiate himself with officers more senior than himself had earned him promotion to major at the age of thirty, several years ahead of what was considered to be usual. But it was clear to him that if he wished to rise higher he had to seriously consider finding himself a wealthy wife, as most officers he had met in the rank of colonel or above, either had large private incomes of their own, or had married judiciously. In that respect Colonel Cordell appeared an exception. As far as Holland could see neither he nor his new wife had any money of their own that was worth mentioning. But, on the other hand, Cordell's half-brother had been a general.

But money in itself was not sufficient. A man also had to have ambition. There were officers who had the one and not the other. Charles Arbuthnot was one. Charles had a wife with enough money for him to achieve the highest rank. But he had no ambition. He regarded the army merely as a socially acceptable profession with which to occupy himself for a few hours each day. His real interests lay elsewhere.

While his servant carefully brushed the shoulders of his uniform jacket Holland examined himself in the mirror. He was pleased with what he saw. If ever, he imagined, there was a sight to gladden the heart of every rich woman of tender years it was the handsome bachelor major he saw reflected in the glass. Satisfied that every hair on his head was in place he ran a small comb through his mustache until he had achieved the desired symmetry. Then he picked up his hat, his gloves and his riding crop and set off for his morning ride.

WHITEHEAD PASSED HOLLAND on his way to the stables. He greeted the young major with a crisp salute, only to find it reciprocated by a perfunctory nod and a halfhearted wave of Holland's riding crop. It was a gesture that never failed to irritate Whitehead. To his way of thinking Holland's perfunctory response epitomized the indolent life-style enjoyed by commissioned officers. Even when they were in barracks it was rare to see them for more than a few hours each day, and with their generous leave allowances they were often absent from the regiment for several months at a time, much of it spent visiting the large country estates of their family or of other wealthy members of their fraternity.

Major Plumb was the only officer in the regiment who was excluded from this privileged lifestyle. Plumb and his wife were not of the same class as the other officers. They were never going to receive invitations to country estates or house parties, and during periods of extended leave had insufficient funds to travel any further than their small house in Battersea.

It was another reason why Whitehead was pleased that he had remained single. The army did not encourage marriage among enlisted men, and Whitehead was grateful for that. As he had steadily risen through the ranks he had decided that if he ever married it would only be to a woman suited to being the commanding officer's wife. Someone like Gertrude Plumb would only be a handicap.

———

THE MONTHLY COMPANY commanders' inspection of the soldiers accommodation and equipment began at nine. Similar inspections were carried out more frequently by the noncommissioned officers in each company, but once each month each of the three companies was inspected by their commanders: Major Holland of A Company, Major Arbuthnot of B Company, and in the absence of Major Plumb on annual leave, Captain Simpson of C Company.

In Whitehead's opinion Holland, Arbuthnot and Simpson were unfit to command soldiers. Holland had spent much of his career on the staff ingratiating himself with senior officers, and had little experience of leading men in action. If he ever made general, which, in Whitehead's opinion was quite likely, it would be a result of his social contacts and not his qualities as a leader. Arbuthnot, on the other hand, made little attempt to cultivate the good opinion of senior officers. It was common knowledge that the rich woman he had married considered that rightfully he should be commanding the regiment. But Whitehead knew that would never happen. Arbuthnot had little interest in the regiment. He was more often than not hunting and shooting with men equally as unambitious as himself. And there were rumors that he was a reckless gambler.

With Major Plumb absent on leave his company was in the hands of Captain Simpson, a young man especially favored by Colonel Cordell. He had been in Cordell's company in Africa, and was serving under Cordell when he had won his Victoria Cross. But since returning from Africa Simpson had begun to drink heavily. In Africa Whitehead had considered that Cordell and Simpson had behaved in a manner that had no place in the army. Fortunately Cordell had chosen to marry when he was promoted, but the army could do well to dispense with the likes of Simpson. But Whitehead knew that would never happen. Not every regiment could boast an officer who had won the Victoria Cross. It was good for the image of the regiment and it helped recruitment.

MAJOR CHARLES ARBUTHNOT was breakfasting alone. It was rare for Lady Cordelia to join him at that hour. She far preferred to breakfast later in her own bedroom, and as the Arbuthnots slept in separate wings of the house there were many days when they managed to avoid one another completely. It was a situation that they both found congenial.

From the start their relationship had been no more than a business arrangement. For his part Charles had provided the veneer of a respectable marriage for the only child of a titled West Country family with several thousand acres of prime dairy farmland. It was her role to ensure that her substantial private income and title was available for Charles to further what she and her parents had fondly imagined would be a successful career in the army. They were only too relieved that their difficult daughter had finally found a husband. Not only had her plain looks failed to attract the attention of the eligible young men from the neighboring counties, there had also been unfortunate rumors of behavior that was far from ladylike. There had been reports of her foul temper, her mistreatment of horses, and even of a whipping she had given to one of the grooms.

In those halcyon days after their engagement had first been announced Cordelia had spent many happy hours imagining how grand it would at some future time to be known as the wife of Colonel or even General Arbuthnot. She had finally decided that she would be happier if Charles were to become a general, and had spent so many idle moments at her escritoire writing 'General Charles and Lady Cordelia Arbuthnot' that she had actually begun to believe that it was only a matter of time before two such people would actually exist.

Charles had singularly failed to fulfill those dreams. He was invariably charming and dutiful to her in public, but in their private life he virtually ignored her. She had made it clear to him from the start of their marriage that her substantial fortune was available to ensure his smooth and effortless rise into the senior ranks, but it had become all to clear to her that the only use Charles intended for her money was to pay his considerable gambling debts.

The previous evening had been the latest in a long line of disastrous evenings spent playing faro at the West End gambling club Charles frequented. Unlike many such gentlemen's clubs *Lasiters* allowed a degree of latitude over the matter of settling debts, especially for a man like Charles whose wife had a seemingly bottomless purse. As a regular and heavy gambler Charles was allowed to settle his account on a monthly basis. That date was fast approaching, and unless his luck changed within the next few days Charles knew he would be in debt to a sum approaching one thousand pounds. That would mean going cap in hand to Cordelia yet again, which would in turn inevitably lead to another angry scene; and with a tiresome barrack inspection imminent it was one that was best delayed until later.

Charles looked at his watch. It was already half past eight.

"Tell Cooper to have my horse ready," he informed the servant who had been serving his breakfast. "I'll be out in five minutes."

CAPTAIN AUDLEY SIMPSON had been having a nightmare. It was one with which he was all too familiar. He was alone on the veldt surrounded by the bodies of his soldiers. Night was falling and the Zulus were closing in. He could see their *iklwas* gleaming in the light of the full moon. There were hundreds of them, and he had only a few rounds of ammunition left. Already he could see the whites of their eyes and smell the sweat on their bodies.

He was quite alone. The rest of the regiment was miles away.

"Hector," he screamed. "How could you have done this to me!"

Then he awoke, his nightshirt wet with his own sweat, and his head throbbing from the effects of the whiskey he had drunk the night before.

Simpson glanced at the clock on his bedside locker. It was half past eight, and the bloody barrack inspection was at nine. He could imagine the furious expression on RSM Whitehead's face when he was late yet again.

"Damn and blast that man," he said angrily as he struggled out of his night shirt and threw it onto the floor.

He opened the door of his room and yelled down the corridor.

"Henderson! I need hot water. Now!"

Simpson pulled on his uniform trousers and began shaving as soon as his servant arrived with his water. It was unusually quiet outside. For once there were no soldiers stamping their wretched feet on the parade ground. They were all in their rooms waiting to be inspected. Damn them!

"What a complete waste of time," he mumbled angrily as he fumbled with the buttons on his uniform jacket. Then his eyes fell on one of the two photographs on his desk. "And damn and blast you, Hector," he shouted, seizing the photograph and hurling it against the wall.

10

ARMED WITH THE fresh evidence against Venetta Cordell, Parsons and Harris returned to Kensington Barracks, on their way stopping at the dead house to collect the *iklwa* that had been used to stab General Latham.

"I'll put it out of sight in my coat pocket," Parsons said. "I don't want any problems with the sentry or the RSM. If I was found carrying a weapon like this I don't imagine they'd let me enter the barracks.

"Don't you think Colonel Cordell may be right?" asked Harris in the cab. "To my way of thinking it seems too much of a coincidence that the general's death took place so soon after Lord Sayers' murder and the two bombings. It would be a real propaganda coup for the Fenians to murder two prominent figures within a few hours right in the center of London, one of whom was an outspoken opponent of Irish Home Rule, and the other a military hero with a ruthless reputation who had just been appointed military commander in Ireland."

"I'm not entirely ruling out the possibility of the Fenians being involved in Latham's death, Harris," Parson replied. "I'm just dealing with the facts as I see them. But now that you mention the Fenians, there's just a possibility that Mrs. Cordell could be an Irish sympathizer. Who's to say that her motive for murdering Latham wasn't political. A few Fenians fled to France after the 1867 rebellion, and there are plenty of French men and women who still feel an animosity towards we British. Napoleon is still revered by a majority of the French, and they continue to hold us responsible for his defeat at Waterloo. Some of them even think we murdered him while he was our prisoner on Saint Helena. But I confess I'm having difficulty imagining a Fenian sympathizer with a spear in her hand. For the moment, I'm inclined to agree with Superintendent Jeffries and consider the two incidents as being quite separate."

COLONEL CORDELL WAS sitting by the fire in his study reading when the two policemen were announced. He made no attempt to stand and acknowledge their presence.

"Well, what is it this time, inspector?" he asked irritably as he set his book to one side.

"I'd like to speak with Mrs. Cordell, sir," Parsons said politely. "Your servant has confirmed that she is in."

"And what, pray, is your reason for speaking to my wife?" Cordell demanded.

"I'd rather not discuss that with you, sir," Parsons replied. "I wish to speak with her in private."

Cordell rose from his chair and took a few steps towards Parsons.

"If you don't allow me to be present at any interview you have with my wife, inspector," he said icily, "I'll have you both thrown in the Guard Room."

"And I can imagine how the newspapers would report that, colonel," Parsons said calmly. *"Scotland Yard detectives investigating murder of General Latham placed under close arrest by his half-brother!"*

"Don't try to be clever with me, Inspector Parsons," Cordell said in a shrill voice. "This is my barracks, and I'll do what I damn well please here."

After their earlier visit Parsons was not entirely surprised by Cordell's outburst. The colonel seemed to be suffering from nervous exhaustion, a condition that might well have been caused by his experiences in Africa. On the other hand, it could have been a result of more recent events. But whatever the reason, if his reaction was any indication of his emotional state it might well prove informative to allow him to remain in the room whilst his wife was being interviewed.

Especially to see how he responded when she was accused of murdering his half-brother.

"Of course you may stay, sir, if you insist," said Parsons tactfully. "But I would ask that you be silent whilst I'm questioning your wife. If I think your presence is in any way influencing her answers I will have Sergeant Harris escort you from the room."

———————

VENETTA CORDELL WAS several years younger than her husband. The colonel, Parsons had calculated, was a man in his early forties, whereas his wife did not appear to have yet reached thirty. She was as tall as the colonel and of a similar build, but there the similarity ended. Whereas Parsons saw only weakness and indecision in Cordell's gray eyes, there was fire and intensity in the dark Latin eyes of his wife. Her ebony hair complemented those eyes, and she wore it gathered in a bow on top of her head with a light fringe over her forehead. In contrast the crimson beige dress with satin kilting accentuated her trim waist. Parsons could never imagine Louise wearing such a vibrant color, but it was one that seemed to suit Venetta's temperament. If eyes are the windows of the soul, he mused, then this was a woman with a mercurial and impulsive nature.

Mrs. Cordell cradled a small black poodle in her arms. It bared its teeth and growled when it saw Cordell, and to Parsons' surprise she had made no attempt to silence the dog.

"Please sit by the fire, Mrs. Cordell," Parsons said, indicating the chair in which her husband had previously been sitting. "Perhaps you, sir, will be kind enough to sit at your desk."

"I'd like you to sit opposite Mrs. Cordell, Sergeant Harris," said Parsons, indicating the other fireside chair. "And if you have no objection, I will remain standing."

Parsons felt he had little choice. In his long winter coat it would have been unbearably hot close to the fire, and to remove it might have meant revealing the *iklwa* concealed in his inside pocket.

"Would you be kind enough to start by telling me something of yourself, Mrs. Cordell?" Parsons asked, after she had settled the dog in her lap and arranged the folds of her dress to her satisfaction. "I believe you are French. Perhaps you can begin by telling me how you came to meet your husband."

Mrs. Cordell acknowledged her husband's presence with a swift hostile glance.

"I met 'im in Rochefort earlier this year, inspector," she said in perfect English. "'E was taking the waters at the spa with Captain Simpson, another officer from the regiment."

"And you, madame. Were you also taking the waters?"

"*Mais oui*, inspector. It was by way of being, 'ow you say, a treat for myself. You see I was still mourning the unexpected death of my 'usband. 'E 'ad died only one year before. Like 'ector 'e was also a soldier."

Until that point Parsons had been unaware that the colonel's first name was Hector. It was unusual, but admirably fitting for a man who was a soldier. When the Greeks had laid siege to Troy, Hector had been considered the bravest and greatest soldier in the Trojan army. But his military skill was no match for the Greek hero, Achilles. Achilles had killed Hector and triumphantly dragged his body around the walls of Troy behind a chariot, much to the joy of the Greeks and the despair of the Trojans. From what he had seen of her, Parsons considered that if Venetta had been born a man she could well have been named Achilles. She appeared in every way to be a match for her husband.

"And the name of your late husband, madame?" Parsons asked.

There was an almost imperceptible pause before Venetta answered during which she bent to kiss the top of the poodle's head.

"'E was called Claude de Verney, inspector," she said quietly. "Major Claude de Verney."

"Thank you, madame," said Parsons. "And now, if I may, I would like to ask you a few questions about Wednesday night. I believe a small dinner party was held here in honor of Captain Simpson. This I imagine was the same Captain Simpson who accompanied Colonel Cordell to Rochefort."

"That is correct, inspector," Venetta replied. "The very same man."

"Your husband tells me that you were not feeling well that evening, and that you went to bed early. Could you tell me what time that would be?"

Venetta looked towards her husband as though expecting him to reply. But the colonel remained silent.

"I can't be certain,' she said. "But I think it was around eleven."

"I see," said Parsons. "And may I ask if your husband and you share the same bedroom?"

Venetta's dark eyes flashed briefly. Then she blushed.

"*Non,*" she snapped. "We sleep in separate rooms, inspector. It is, I believe, the way of you English. In France we do not understand such things."

"So, if you were to have left this house later that night," Parsons said, "your husband would probably not have known."

Parsons detected a slight movement from the corner of his eye. At first he thought that Cordell was going to stand up or say something. But the colonel remained silent and did not leave his seat.

"I am waiting for your answer, madame," said Parsons.

"*Oui*, it would be possible, inspector," she said coldly. "But I did not go out. Why should I? Where would I go at that hour?"

Parsons waited for some time before answering, allowing the tension that he could feel between the husband and wife to grow.

"There are reports that you were seen in Chester Place at the home of General Maxwell Latham shortly after midnight that night, madame.

His servant, Bradley, says he saw you there. There are also other witnesses. A policeman reported seeing a veiled woman dressed in black enter General Latham's house at that time. And we have the testimony of two cab drivers. The first collected a woman of that description in a street not far from here shortly after eleven-thirty, and the second picked up a similarly dressed woman from a street near Chester Place between twelve-fifteen and twelve-thirty and returned her to the barracks."

Colonel Cordell leapt to his feet.

"You say a veiled woman, inspector," he shouted. "Then how in God's name can anyone say it was my wife?"

"Because General Latham's servant claims to have recognized your wife by her French accent," Parsons said quietly. "I believe that you had both previously dined with the general, and Bradley claims that Mrs. Cordell visited the general alone on several other occasions."

"Is this true, Venetta?" demanded Cordell, advancing towards his wife, who in turn had risen from her chair to meet his challenge. "Did that swine seduce you as well?"

He took her by the shoulders and shook her.

"Yes," she shouted, her eyes flashing. "'E did, and I went gladly. 'E was a real man. Not like the one I married."

Cordell's response was immediate. He slapped his wife hard across the face, an action for which he was rewarded by being nipped by the poodle.

"You bloody little whore," he said, as he retreated from the little dog's sharp teeth.

"So that explains why my dear brother Maxwell felt unable to accept my dinner invitation," he said bitterly. "Go on, inspector. Let's get to the bottom of this."

11

PARSONS HAD WATCHED in amazement as the angry scene between the Cordells unfolded. He had almost intervened when Cordell had slapped his wife, and he noticed that Harris had risen from his seat probably with the same idea. But then he decided against it. Even from what little he had seen of her, it seemed that Mrs. Cordell and her small dog were more than a match for her husband.

And what had been said had been most revealing. Venetta Cordell had brazenly boasted of cuckolding her husband with a man who was not only his former commanding officer, but also his half-brother. And not only that. She had also thoroughly shamed him by announcing that she had begun the affair because Cordell had been less than a husband to her. She could scarcely have revealed her passionate nature in a more dramatic manner. But was she capable of murder? And if she had murdered her lover, what had been her motive?

"Would you both please sit down," Parsons said politely but firmly to the Cordells. "And as the colonel has said, let us try to understand what happened on Wednesday night."

He waited for them both to resume their seats, Cordell glaring angrily at his wife from his seat in front of the desk and she, with a red mark already appearing on her cheek, regarding her husband with undisguised hatred.

"Well, what is it you want to know, inspector?" she snapped, after she had finally turned her attention from her husband to Parsons.

"I would think that was only too obvious, madame," said Parsons quietly. "I want to know more about your relationship with General Latham. When, for instance, did it start?"

"I slept with 'im, if that's what you mean," she said defiantly. "Almost from the first day we met. That was, *peut etre*, about four months ago."

A half-smile briefly lit up her face.

"Maxwell was extremely persuasive," she said. "''E was also a man of great passion."

She turned towards her husband with a look of contempt.

"And in that respect I 'ad been very disappointed with my own marriage."

Parsons expected Cordell to respond to this taunt, but he remained silent. Instead, he lowered his head slightly, as though acknowledging the dereliction of matrimonial duty of which he stood accused.

"How often did you visit General Latham?" Parsons asked.

"Normally once each week," Venetta said. "Sometimes twice. Maxwell would send me notes telling me when I should go to 'is house."

"Your assignations were always at his house?"

"*Oui*," she said. "Normally at night, but sometimes during the day."

"And how did you come and go without drawing attention to yourself, madame. Especially at night. I would imagine the sentry at the gate would have been surprised to see the colonel's lady leaving the barracks after dark."

"Because I wore a veil, inspector," she explained. "And because I always used the side gate."

"There is another gate to the barracks other than the main gate, inspector," Cordell said in a subdued tone. "It is behind this house and between it and the Officers' Mess. Only a few people have a key. All the commissioned officers have one and a few of the more senior noncommissioned officers living in the barracks like the RSM and the Chief Clerk."

"Thank you, colonel," said Parsons. "Perhaps I could ask you to provide me with a list of these key holders in due course."

Cordell moved his head almost imperceptibly in acknowledgment.

"I'll see the RSM provides you with the names," he said.

"Tell me more about these notes, madame," said Parsons, turning his attention again to Venetta. "Were they always sent to this house?"

"*Non*, inspector. Maxwell did not think that was wise. 'E knew that all the mail for the barracks is first taken to the Orderly Room for the clerks to sort. So Maxwell devised a plan. 'E 'ad 'is servant deliver the notes to a newsagent in Silver Street. It is a small street not far from the barracks. I believe it is not uncommon in this country to pay newsagents a small sum to use their premises for letters and notes of a personal nature."

"And you collected these notes yourself, madame?" asked Parsons.

"*Non*, inspector. I 'ad them collected by Edith, my lady's maid. Like me she is French. So I knew I could trust her."

The last sentence was accompanied by a haughty toss of her head and a disdainful look that defied any of the men in the room to challenge her view of the French as being a more trustworthy race than the English.

"How did you know when to send your maid to the newsagent, madame?" asked Parsons.

"I did not know for sure," she said, "so I sent 'er several times each week. In that way a note would never be left at the newsagent for more than a day or two before it was collected."

Parsons asked "Have you kept any of these notes, madame?"

"*Oui. Naturelment.* What woman would not keep such notes? If you wish I will send for them."

Venetta rose from her chair and tugged at the bell cord at the side of the fireplace, and almost immediately one of the servants appeared at the door.

"Tell Edith to fetch my jewelry box," she instructed. "She will know where to find it."

Venetta's pretty maid arrived with the box within the space of a few minutes. She curtsied and presented it to her mistress.

"*Merci, Edith.*" said Venetta, *"Vous pouvez aller. Et vous pouvez prendre Phooby."*

Edith took the poodle from her mistress. She curtsied again and left the room. As soon as she had gone Venetta opened one of the drawers in the jewelry box and removed a bundle of papers.

"'Ere you are, inspector," she said. "Make what you will of them."

Parsons took the papers and examined them. If he had hoped to find them written in the general's hand he was disappointed. As Venetta had said Latham was no fool. There was little about them that could be regarded as incriminating. Each of the notes had been constructed by cutting words from newspapers and pasting them onto a sheet of note paper.

"You see 'ow clever was Maxwell," Venetta said with a smile. "'E 'ad no wish for anyone to ever know that it was 'e who sent the notes."

"Very clever indeed, madame," said Parsons. "But perhaps you can select from these notes the one that prompted you to go to Chester Place on Wednesday night."

Venetta's shoulders raised and lowered in a Gallic shrug. After admitting her affair with Maxwell Latham and having heard the evidence placing her at the scene of the crime, she appeared to have decided that it was foolish to continue denying that she had been at the general's house on the night he was murdered. She selected one of the notes and handed it to Parsons.

"Edith collected this one on Monday afternoon," she explained.

The message contained three words: *'Wednesday after midnight'*. Two of these words had been cut from a newspaper, but the word 'midnight' had been printed in large ill-formed letters, as though written by a child, or by a person deliberately trying to disguise their hand.

Parsons briefly examined the other notes. Each contained a similar brief message, but he noticed that the words used on the earlier notes were of a distinctively different typeface than that used on the last.

"I notice, madame," he said, "that this is the only message asking you to visit General Latham at such a late hour, and the only one in which the time has been spelt. In the other notes numerals have been used. Why do you think that was?"

"*Je ne sais pas,* inspector," she said, with another Gallic shrug of her shoulders.

For the first time since their arrival Harris spoke.

"Perhaps it was the fact that it was after midnight, sir," he said. "If Mrs. Cordell usually visited the general during the day or in the evening it would probably have been easy enough to find the appropriate numerals in a newspaper. But if General Latham had written '12', Mrs. Cordell could not have been sure whether that meant 'midday' or 'midnight'. Perhaps the general was unable to find the word 'midnight' in the newspapers, and decided to print it."

Parsons was impressed. Every so often Harris provided an insightful gem of this kind.

"Excellent, Harris," he said enthusiastically. Then he turned again to Venetta.

"So you don't deny that you were at General Latham's house shortly after midnight on Wednesday, madame," Parsons said quietly. "And that you went in response to this note."

"I was there, inspector," she said. "But I did not kill 'im. 'E was already dead when I arrived."

"But his servant, Bradley says he saw you with blood on your gloves and on your cloak. How can you explain that?"

"Because when I saw poor Maxwell lying on the floor with blood over 'is chest, I could not 'elp myself from touching 'im. What woman who 'as loved a man would not do the same?"

"And where was the murder weapon at that time, madame?"

"*Je ne sais pas*. I was too much in shock to notice something like that.

"Then how do you explain this, madame?"

Parsons opened his overcoat, reached inside and removed the *iklwa*.

"This was the weapon that was used to stab General Latham to death. When his servant, Bradley, discovered his body it was lying by his side"

Venetta looked at it in horror.

"I 'ave never seen this filthy thing before," she said.

"Oh, but I think you have, madame," Parsons said "If I am not mistaken, this rightfully belongs with the other spears in that brass pot by the fireplace."

Cordell sprang from his chair, took the spear from Parsons, and examined the shaft. As he did the color drained from his face.

"My God," he said in a hoarse whisper. "You're right, inspector. This is one of my Zulu *iklwas*. I can tell that from the date I carved on the shaft. If you care to look you will find that I have carved similar dates on each of my spears."

Parsons looked to where the colonel was pointing, furious with himself for overlooking what had proved to be an important piece of information. With some difficulty he read the crudely carved Roman numerals 'MDCCCLXXIX' near the bottom of the shaft. Then he examined a few of the other *iklwas* by the side of the fireplace. Each had a similar mark carved on the shaft.

"1879," Cordell explained when Parsons asked the meaning of the inscription. "In July that year we gave the Zulus a whipping at Ulundi. That was the final battle of the Zulu War."

12

PARSONS' FIRST INSTINCT had been to arrest Venetta Cordell. But then he changed his mind. The evidence against her was persuasive, if not overwhelming, and she made little attempt to hide her passionate nature. But he still had some difficulty in imagining her taking an *iklwa* from her husband's study, sharpening the blade, traveling to Chester Place with it hidden under her cloak, and stabbing her lover in such a cold-hearted fashion. And apart from all that, her motive was not at all clear. If she was having an affair with the general, and there seemed little doubt about that, why would she suddenly decide to kill him? And why would she draw attention to what she had done by screaming, when most people would have chosen to leave the scene as quickly and quietly as possible?

As yet he had only heard from the general's servant and the Cordells. There might well be others who knew about this unusual *menage a trois*. An army regiment was, after all, a closely-knit community. For a start there were those who had dined with the Cordells on the night of the murder. Not only had the officers served together in Africa, there was also a good chance that a woman like Lady Cordelia Arbuthnot would have have an opinion about the commanding officer's recently acquired young French wife that was worth hearing.

So, for the moment, Parsons decided to do no more than ask Colonel Cordell to guarantee his wife's safekeeping. It was a task that he did not imagine would be difficult. With sentries and high iron railings an army barracks was every bit as difficult to escape from as most police stations.

"That will not present a problem, inspector," Cordell said with obvious relief after Parsons had explained his decision. "It will simply be a matter of telling the RSM to issue instructions that my wife is not to be allowed to leave the barracks without my permission. That will ensure that she will not be able to use the main gate. I will also see that she surrenders her key to the other gate."

"And what possible reason will you give the RSM for that unusual step, sir?" Parsons asked.

"I will tell him that after hearing of General Latham's death my wife is suffering from melancholia, and as a result I do not wish her to leave the house until she has had time to recover."

"Can you rely upon the RSM's discretion?"

"I have known Mr. Whitehead for many years, inspector. He was my sergeant-major when I commanded A company in South Africa. I assure you that there is no more honorable man in this regiment. I know I can rely upon his discretion."

Cordell squared his shoulders and looked Parsons straight in the eye.

"And you need not be concerned that my wife will come to harm by my hand," he said. "Even after learning about her infidelity you may rest assured that she will be perfectly safe here."

"Thank you, colonel," Parsons said. "I'm sure I can rely upon your word. In the meantime I'd like to interview each of your dinner party guests. Do you have any idea where I might find them?"

Cordell consulted his watch.

"I'm sure you'll find Major Holland and Captain Simpson in the Officers' Mess," he said. "By now they'll have finished inspecting the men's billets. They're both bachelors, and I imagine they'll be having a drink before lunch. Major Arbuthnot, on the other hand, will probably have gone home. The Arbuthnots live in Belgravia. Number 5 Eaton Square. If you call you may find them both at home."

IT WAS CLEAR from the disapproving expression on the ruddy face of the Officers' Mess Sergeant that in normal circumstances two such inappropriately dressed civilians would not have been allowed to cross the threshold of the Officers' Mess. Harris' brown suit, in particular, met with the portly sergeant's singular disapproval. Parsons was prepared to concede that the sergeant had a point. He would have been the first to admit that Harris and he did look out of place in the entrance hall of the Mess amongst the regimental flags and guidons, sabres and muskets, and large oil paintings depicting epic battle scenes from the regiment's illustrious history.

"If Major Holland and Captain Simpson are in the Mess I'd like to speak with them in private," Parsons said to the still sceptical sergeant. "And I'd like to see them one at a time. Major Holland first, if that's possible. Is there a room where we can be sure of being undisturbed?"

Convinced eventually of their *bona fides*, the sergeant escorted the two policemen along a corridor, the walls of which were adorned with stuffed and mounted heads of animals from many exotic parts of the world, each of them bearing testimony to the marksmanship of the officers of the regiment. One tiger's head in particular Parsons considered to have a passing resemblance to the one he had seen in the photograph in General Latham's study.

"Please wait here, gentlemen," the sergeant said with a barely concealed sneer. "This is the Ladies' Anteroom. You'll be sure to have some privacy here. I'll see if Major Holland is available."

Parsons surveyed the room and its contents. In contrast to the overt masculinity encountered elsewhere in the Mess, a halfhearted attempt had been made, doubtless by a bachelor officer, at establishing a style more in keeping with a room intended for the use of ladies. The furniture was still sturdy and utilitarian, but it had been softened and made to appear more feminine by the use of a few cushions and some colorful drapes. A few bright prints of idealized country and domestic scenes adorned the walls, and a handful of old magazines had been arranged in a fan on one of the occasional tables, together with a vase of wilting flowers.

Parsons draped his overcoat over the back of an upright chair and took a seat beside Harris on one of the leather arm chairs. They did not have long to wait.

Major Holland was a tall dark-haired young man with a narrow waist and broad shoulders. Parsons imagined him to be in his early thirties, no more than a few years older than himself. But sadly, he reflected, that was as far as the resemblance went. In his dashing red tunic Holland presented a fine figure of a man, and as though happily aware of that fact, had allowed his ample mustache to curl down over the edges of his mouth in a manner that accentuated the obvious sense of superiority that he exhibited in his haughty dark eyes.

Without waiting to be invited he lowered himself into a brown leather armchair opposite the two policemen and draped his left leg over one of its arms.

"I hope this won't take long, inspector," he said, in the crisp, nasal tone that sounded remarkably like that of Reginald Chapman. "I've yet to lunch, and I'm riding with Simpson this afternoon in Hyde Park."

"Be assured that I won't keep you any longer than is necessary, major," said Parsons. "I merely want to ask you a few questions about the dinner party that I believe you attended at the Cordell's house on Wednesday night."

"Whatever for?" Holland demanded.

"Because as you are doubtless aware, major, General Sir Maxwell Latham was murdered on Wednesday night. To be precise he was stabbed with a weapon that, I'm led to believe, members of this regiment are all too familiar with."

Parsons rose, removed the *iklwa* from his overcoat pocket, and held it up for Holland to see.

"In fact the murder was committed with this very weapon," he said.

Parsons returned to his seat, allowing Holland time to digest the full significance of his last statement.

"Now you may think that this might suggest that the assailant was a native," he said. "But I do not believe that to be true. I think it far more likely that the murderer was a person much closer to home. You see, this particular *iklwa* was taken from Colonel Cordell's study."

"My God!" exclaimed Holland, his arrogant tone for the moment forgotten. "Are you suggesting that someone in this regiment murdered the general?"

"I'm really not prepared to say any more than I've already told you, major," said Parsons calmly. "All I want from you is information about what occurred at the dinner party. For a start you can tell me who was present, something of the mood of evening, and the time at which the guests left."

Holland removed his leg from the arm of the chair and sat up straight in the manner of a schoolboy who has just received a reprimand from a master, his nonchalant swagger for the moment forgotten.

"That's not difficult," he said. "There were only six of us. Colonel and Mrs. Cordell, Major Arbuthnot and his wife, Lady Cordelia, and Audley Simpson and myself."

"You will forgive my ignorance of military organization, major," Parsons said. "But I wonder if you will be so kind as to tell me the responsibilities you and the other officers have in the regiment. You need not mention Colonel Cordell as I am well aware that he is your commanding officer."

"Major Arbuthnot is the officer commanding B Company, Captain Simpson is the second in command of C Company, and I command A Company."

"Thank you, major. That is most enlightening. But who is it, pray, who actually commands C Company?"

"Major Plumb," explained Holland.

"And where was Major Plumb on Wednesday night?" Parsons asked. "Surely he would have been invited to dine with the other company commanders."

"I don't believe he was, inspector," Holland said, a trace of the former superiority creeping back into his voice. "Major Plumb is on leave just now. But even were he not, I do not believe that Colonel Cordell would've chosen to invite him. That would have meant inviting Mrs. Plumb, which would have been rather awkward."

"Perhaps you will be kind enough to explain exactly what you mean by that, sir," Parsons said. "I would think that as one of the company commanders Major Plumb would naturally have been included in a dinner party of this nature, especially as Captain Simpson is one of his officers."

"Plumb is a bit of a rough diamond," Holland explained. "Unlike other officers in the regiment, he rose from the ranks. Major Plumb and his wife are rarely included in regimental social events. He and his wife don't quite fit, you see. Especially his wife."

"And yet, as I understand it, the purpose of the dinner party was to celebrate Captain Simpson's forthcoming award for bravery," Parsons said in surprise. "Surely that was one occasion when all the company commanders and their wives would be present."

"Well, I wouldn't know about that, inspector," said Holland with a sneer. "I didn't send out the invitations."

Parsons knew how all this must sound to Harris. If there was one thing that infuriated the sergeant more than any other it was the sort of disdainful comments they had just heard. But the last thing that Parsons wanted was for Harris to say anything at this stage.

"And the mood during the evening, major," Parsons said hurriedly to pre-empt any comment from Harris. "How would you describe that? Would you say it was celebratory?"

Holland thought for a moment before answering.

"I wouldn't call it exactly that," he said reflectively. "I'm afraid dear Audley was a trifle drunk, which naturally offended dear Cordelia. It also seemed to upset Venetta Cordell, as she was not as vivacious as I've known her to be. She generally attempts to irritate the colonel by flashing those dark eyes of hers at any other men in the room. But on Wednesday she was rather subdued. Charles Arbuthnot and I did our best to jolly things along, but on the whole I wouldn't describe the evening as being a great success."

"Now am I correct in thinking that all of the gentlemen present were in the South African campaign together at the time that General Latham was commanding the regiment?"

"That is correct, inspector. Colonel Cordell was then commanding A Company, which is my company now; Arbuthnot was in charge of B Company, and Plumb had C. Simpson was a platoon commander in A Company. That's to say he was a lieutenant."

"And what were you doing, sir," Parsons asked innocently.

Holland appeared momentarily discomfited and embarrassed by the question.

"I was a captain on the General Staff," he said pompously, but without a great deal of conviction.

"So you weren't actually involved in the campaign in which Captain Simpson performed so heroically."

Holland shook his head.

"No," he said quietly. "I was at Headquarters."

Harris was beginning to wonder where all these questions about Africa were leading, but he knew Inspector Parsons better than to interrupt. In previous cases he had seen the inspector approach an investigation in an altogether different way from that which he would have chosen himself.

"I won't keep you much longer, sir," said Parsons with a smile, "especially as I've no wish to delay your ride or to interrupt Captain Simpson in the middle of his lunch; but before you go can you tell me what time it was when the dinner party ended?"

"I would say it was somewhere between half past ten and eleven, inspector," Holland said. "I'm afraid I can't be more precise. I wasn't paying much attention to the time. All I can tell you is that it was earlier than I had anticipated. You see it wasn't long after the ladies had left us to our brandy and cigars that Cordelia came back into the dining room to inform us that Venetta was not feeling well and had gone to bed, and that she, that's to say Lady Cordelia, had no intention of sitting alone in the withdrawing room. She told Charles she wanted to go home, and as she wasn't in the most charming of moods, Charles didn't argue. And soon after they'd gone Audley and I also decided it was time to leave."

"Thank you, major. That has been most useful," said Parsons. "Do I detect from what you've told us that you are not married yourself?"

"Not on your life, inspector," Holland said. "Although now that I've been promoted perhaps I should consider it. You know what they say in the army about marriage.

"No, sir, I don't," said Parsons. "Perhaps you will be so kind as to enlighten me."

Holland laughed heartily in anticipation of what he was going to say.

"They say that lieutenants must not, that captains should not, that majors may, and that colonels must."

And what does that say about the prospects of a penniless detective-inspector, Parsons thought, as his thoughts turned briefly to the possibility of his own engagement to Louise.

"Thank you, major," he said. "That has been most enlightening. Now perhaps, you will ask Captain Simpson if he will be kind enough to join Sergeant Harris and me."

CAPTAIN AUDLEY SIMPSON was a tall, graceful man in his mid-twenties. His long straw-colored hair of loose curls, his fair skin and his pale blue eyes had almost an angelic quality, and were it not for a light wispy mustache he might, at first sight and at a distance, have been mistaken for a woman. But at closer range his complexion was less flawless than it initially appeared, and the likelihood of confusing his gender less likely. His breath also smelt strongly of whisky, and as he took his place in the chair previously occupied by Major Holland, Parsons sensed a tension and uncertainty that had been absent in his brother officer. Unlike Holland, Simpson did not choose to drape an elegant leg nonchalantly over the arm of the chair. Instead he sat tensely with his legs crossed, looking apprehensively at the *iklwa* by the side of Parsons' chair, and nervously flicking ash from his cheroot into a glass ashtray on an adjacent table. It was an action that drew Parsons' attention to his badly bitten nails. The first impression of Captain Audley Simpson was that he appeared an unlikely hero.

Simpson's recollection of events on the night of the dinner party was vague, lending support to Holland's comment that he had been drinking. When asked his opinion about the other people at the dinner he was lavish in his praise for Colonel Cordell, but less complimentary about his wife. About the Arbuthnots he had little to say, but in contrast to Holland, when Parsons commented on the absence of the Plumbs, Simpson was unexpectedly warm in their praise.

"Albert Plumb is probably the finest officer in the regiment," he said. "And his wife cooks a fine game pie."

"So you have been to the Plumbs house, sir," Parsons said, somewhat surprised after hearing Holland's comments about the social standing of the Plumbs.

"I've been there often enough for Sunday lunch, inspector," explained Simpson. "I've no time for the dull Sunday routine here in the Mess: a thoroughly boring church service followed by drinks with my sanctimonious brother officers. I far prefer a few pints of ale with Albert, and Gertrude's Sunday roast. As you probably know Major Plumb is my company commander, and if I ever had to go to war again I wouldn't choose to be with anyone other than Albert. He's got more experience than the rest of us put together."

"And would that include Colonel Cordell?" asked Parsons. "Wasn't he your company commander in South Africa, and isn't he now your commanding officer?"

Simpson drew nervously on his cheroot.

"Between you and me, inspector," he said, "were it not for the fact that his half-brother is, or should I say was, General Latham, someone else would be commanding the Middlesex today. Latham may have been an unpleasant bastard, but he was a fine leader of men, and much as I admire many of Hector Cordell's qualities, even a junior officer like myself can see that he's out of his depth as commanding officer."

"Who do *you* think should be commanding the regiment?" Parsons asked.

"Oh, I don't know," Simpson slurred. "Rightfully it should be Albert Plumb. But we all know that will never happen. Arbuthnot would probably do a better job. He's got a certain style that appeals to the soldiers, and his wife's got money. That's a pretty good combination in the army. There's only one drawback. And that's Charles' dreadful wife."

Simpson rolled his eyes.

"What a woman!" he said. "What do they say about mutton being dressed up as lamb? And Cordelia doesn't try to hide how much she resents Venetta being the colonel's lady. As far as Cordelia's concerned that's a role she should be playing. And God help us all if she ever did. I, for one, would leave the regiment. And I'm sure others would follow me."

Simpson's bitterness towards his brother officers came as a surprise to Parsons, especially as from what he had heard the young captain appeared to be held in such high esteem. His comments about Lady Cordelia Arbuthnot were also revealing, but in view of the nature of English society they were hardly surprising. An older titled lady would invariably have a poor opinion of a younger woman holding a socially more advantageous position than herself. Especially if that woman happened to be a foreigner.

"I hear you are shortly to receive the Victoria Cross for your bravery," Parsons said. "Allow me to congratulate you. I've never before had the privilege of meeting anyone who has earned the highest award for valor the country has to offer, and I probably will never have that chance again. I'm sure you must by now be tired of people asking you, but if I could crave your indulgence again I would greatly like to hear what actually happened."

Simpson ground out his cheroot in the ashtray and immediately lit another.

"Very well, inspector. If you insist," he said, drawing heavily on the cheroot. "Although it's probably nothing like you imagine. I didn't lead a gallant charge against an impregnable enemy position. Quite the contrary. My men and I were actually running away and fighting for our lives at the time."

The hand holding the cheroot shook noticeably and ash fell unnoticed upon Simpson's red jacket.

"If you've read anything about South Africa, inspector," he said, "you'll know that late last year the wretched Boers in Transvaal declared themselves independent of British rule, and had the temerity to attack our forts. As you can imagine, we weren't going to put up with that for long, and the powers that be dispatched a relief column to the Transvaal to sort them out. The Middlesex was part of that column. We thought it would be plain sailing as the Boers were far fewer in number than we. But almost as soon as we reached the frontier between Natal and Transvaal we came under heavy Boer fire. They had all the advantages. They knew the land, they held the high ground, and to be honest, they were better marksmen. I was a platoon commander in Cordell's company then, and when he was given orders to send a patrol through Zululand to attack the Boers from the rear he chose me to lead it. In theory it seemed a good plan. At least it was to the senior officers who weren't going to take part in it.

But like so many other things that happen in war, when it came to executing the plan it didn't quite work as anticipated."

Simpson attempted a wry smile, but instead a look of abject misery crossed his face.

"You may well have heard of the Zulus, gentlemen," he said. "A more warlike bunch of natives you can't imagine. They gave us a good run for our money until we eventually licked 'em in '79. After that the politicians agreed to some sort of peace treaty. Of course, we poor bloody foot soldiers are generally the last to know the details of such things, and frankly when it's in their best interests our commanders often ignore such niceties as treaties with natives. The infantry are only the pawns on the chess board, and we soldiers just go where we're told, treaties or no treaties. As far as politicians and generals are concerned we're expendable."

Simpson nervously drew on his cheroot.

"Well, as it happens, this particular treaty prohibited any British force from using Zululand as a route into the Boer territories. And if the bloody Army High Command knew that, they certainly didn't bother to tell us."

Simpson suddenly glanced down in disgust at the ash that had collected on his red jacket and irritably brushed it off.

"My men and I walked right into it, inspector," he said bitterly. "We were only a few days march into Zululand when we were attacked by hundreds of the bastards. I'd faced them before, and I can tell you there's no more terrifying sight in this world than seeing a Zulu *impi* advancing towards you beating their shields and waving their *iklwas*. And the chanting. It makes your skin crawl I can tell you. Even now I get the shakes whenever I think about it."

Beads of sweat had broken out on Simpson's brow, the little color he had in his face had drained away, and his hands had begun to shake.

"You'll have to forgive me, inspector," he said, "but speaking about this again brings it all back. I need a drink."

Simpson stood up and began walking towards the door.

"I'm sorry, sir," said Parsons. "I had no right to stir up these memories. You've no need to continue. I think I can guess what happened. But may I crave your indulgence to answer one last question and then you can go. General Latham was stabbed with one of the *iklwas* you have just described. Do you have any idea who might have done it?"

Simpson turned when he reached the door.

"I've absolutely no idea, inspector," he said. "I'm sure a bastard like Latham must have made many enemies. But most of them are long dead and buried in some Godforsaken part of the world. Just like my men."

13

PARSONS AND HARRIS left Kensington Barracks for the Arbuthnot's house shortly after one-fifteen, much to Parsons' surprise and Harris' embarrassment receiving a halfhearted salute from the sentry at the main gate. It was a fine autumn afternoon, and encouraged by the unseasonal sunshine Parsons suggested that, rather than take a cab, they walk the two miles to Eaton Square, and make a detour through Kensington Gardens and Hyde Park.

"A good decision, you must agree, Harris," said Parsons enthusiastically, as the sound of a military band greeted them as they entered Kensington Gardens. "It's probably the Household Cavalry band from Knightsbridge Barracks. I often come here on Sunday afternoons after church to listen to them. Say what you will about the army, you can't beat the sound of a good military brass band on a fine afternoon."

They followed a leaf-strewn path through the trees towards the bandstand.

"It sounds as though they're giving us a little Gilbert and Sullivan," Parsons said. "*The Pirates of Penzance* if I'm not mistaken. An excellent choice, don't you agree. I can't say I've ever been to Penzance or anywhere in Cornwall, but from all accounts it's a beautiful county. An ideal spot for a honeymoon, wouldn't you say?"

"I'm sure I wouldn't know about that, sir," said Harris morosely. "When I got married we moved straight in with my in-laws, and that wasn't what I would call a honeymoon. But I didn't know you were contemplating marriage, sir."

A sizable crowd seated on deck chairs had gathered around the bandstand. Judging by the gentlemen's top hats, the elegant dresses and gay parasols of the ladies, and the smartly dressed children - sailor suits for the boys and frilled three-quarter-length dresses for the girls - they were mainly wealthy families from Bayswater and Kensington. Less fashionably dressed people stood at the edge of the crowd, among them a few soldiers in red jackets casting covetous eyes at pretty nursemaids, men selling balloons, and, much to Parsons' delight, an ice-cream vendor. His comment about a honeymoon in Cornwall had been made without thinking how it might sound to Harris. The possibility of his marriage had never been mentioned before, and Parsons was fairly certain that as far as Harris was concerned he was perfectly content with his life as a bachelor.

"I think we should add to the pleasure of the afternoon by having an ice-cream, Harris," said

Parsons by way of a reply, hurrying away before Harris had time to pursue the subject of marriage.

"You're right, sir," said Harris, as he licked his ice cream. "I'm quite enjoying the band. Maybe the army isn't as bad as I thought. But if I ever considered becoming a soldier I wouldn't care to be led by any of the officers we've met so far. And if that Captain Simpson is the army's idea of a hero he certainly isn't mine. It was barely midday when we spoke to him and he was already drunk. And what's this Victoria Cross I keep hearing about? I thought it was only awarded for doing something really brave. But from what Simpson told us he got himself in the wrong place at the wrong time and then decided to run away."

"Don't be so cynical, Harris," said Parsons as he took a clean white linen handkerchief from his pocket and began wiping ice-cream from his fingers. "It wasn't his fault that he ended up somewhere he shouldn't have. That seems to have been the result of a poor decision taken by his superiors. We've all suffered from those at one time or another. As Simpson said, the wretched foot soldiers merely do as they're told. Tennyson was right: *'theirs not to reason why, theirs but to do or die'* And what if Simpson did decide to retreat in the face of the enemy. That's a perfectly acceptable military tactic. Wellington adopted just such a strategy earlier this century in Portugal during the war against Napoleon. And what else could Simpson do? I can't say I'd much relish being set upon by a crowd of angry Zulus. And if it was anything like as bad as Simpson said I'm not surprised he's in the state he is now."

The continuing look of skepticism on Harris' face prompted Parsons to continue.

"I don't know much about the Victoria Cross," he said, "other than that it was first awarded during the Crimean War and that the medals are cast from metal from the Russian cannons captured at Sevastopol. My father told me once that an officer from his regiment won a Victoria Cross during the Indian Mutiny. My father was very proud of that. If you remember it was during the mutiny that General Latham won his. From what my father said the medal is only awarded for acts of conspicuous bravery or for extreme devotion to duty in the face of the enemy. So without knowing the exact details I'd say that there was no reason to think that Captain Simpson wasn't as well qualified as anyone to receive the award."

"At least he isn't a snob like the others," said Harris. "I'll say that for him. Unlike Colonel Cordell and Major Holland, Simpson doesn't appear to be too grand to eat with the Plumbs. I thought the police force was bad enough when it came to that sort of snobbery, but it strikes me that the army is a damned sight worse."

"To some extent that was the whole point of the Victoria Cross," explained Parsons. "In the past most awards and decorations were only given to senior officers. The Victoria Cross, on the other hand, is intended as an award for men of all ranks."

"It sounds as though the senior officers who received awards in the past were the very same ones who'd purchased their rank in the first place," Harris said bitterly. "Now that really does sound like justice!"

"I can see that the band has done nothing to improve your spirits after all, Harris. And as you appear to have finished your ice-cream at last I think it's high time to see what of sort welcome we get from the Arbuthnots."

―――――

THE PATH LEADING from Kensington Gardens into Hyde Park skirted the southern edge of the park and offered a fine view of the fashionably dressed men and women riding along Rotten Row. Much to his father's dismay, Parsons had never been comfortable on the back of a horse, and had ridden only with the greatest reluctance. Regardless of that, he never failed to be impressed by the skillful way in which other people handled them. Especially the women. There was something about a stylish woman riding sidesaddle that never failed to set his pulses racing. But that was not a subject he would ever want to discuss with Louise.

They left the park through the Albert Gate, crossed Knightsbridge into Belgravia and in less than ten minutes had reached Eaton Square, one of three residential garden squares built by the Grosvenor family in the early years of the century. Each of the squares followed a similar pattern with handsome terraces of gracious four and five storied mansions built in a simple classical style and faced with white stucco. There was a mews behind each terrace with stabling for horses and carriages, and in the center of each square an expansive stretch of lawns and flower beds sheltered by large trees for the private use of residents. Each square also had its own classically inspired Anglican church. In Eaton Square it was St. Peter's, its six-columned portico and clock tower at the east end of the square offering a comforting presence and constant reminder to residents that it was indeed possible for a rich man to enter Heaven through the eye of a needle.

It was clear that the Arbuthnots lived in a far grander style than either General Latham or Colonel Cordell, a fact that Parsons could well imagine causing resentment in a strictly hierarchical organization like the army in which wealth played such an important role. It was an opinion that was further reinforced by the expression of unconcealed distaste on the face of the liveried servant answering the door. It was clear that he thought that the two policemen had come, if not to the wrong house, at least to the wrong door.

"Do you have an appointment with Major Arbuthnot?" he asked in an incredulous tone.

"I do not," said Parsons politely. "But if the major is in I would be grateful if you will inform him that we are here in connection with the murder of General Latham. I'm sure that when he hears that he will want to see us."

The servant admitted the two policemen into a large circular hall, took Parsons' card and made his stately progress up a wide central staircase.

"Please be so good as to follow me, gentlemen," he said when he returned. "But first be so kind as to allow me to relieve you of your hat, sir."

The words were addressed to Harris, who had yet to remove his brown bowler hat from his head, and since entering the house had stood gazing in undisguised awe at the large crystal chandelier suspended over the circular hall and at the large oil paintings adorning the walls.

"And you, sir," the servant said, turning to Parsons, "may I take your coat?"

"Thank you, but I prefer to keep it with me," replied Parsons, not wishing the servant to know that he was carrying a spear.

"As you wish, sir," the servant said with a frown, his poor opinion of policemen reinforced by such a blatant breach of etiquette.

"INSPECTOR PARSONS AND Sergeant Harris," the servant announced solemnly, before withdrawing and discretely closing the door behind him.

The two detectives found themselves in a large sitting room with fine views of the central gardens from long sash windows draped in thick red velvet curtains.

A tall, handsome man with dark hair, a neatly-trimmed mustache and long side whiskers lowered his newspaper, rose from his chair and walked across the room with his right hand outstretched.

"Charles Arbuthnot," he said in a well-modulated voice, as he shook the hands with both policemen. "Allow me to introduce my wife, Lady Cordelia."

Lady Cordelia Arbuthnot placed the magazine she had been reading on a table by the side of her chair with an undisguised display of irritation, and surveyed the two policemen with obvious disdain, an especially contemptuous glance being given to the overcoat that Parsons was still wearing.

For his own part Parsons found Lady Cordelia to be extremely unattractive. Admittedly the color of her flaxen hair was unusual and her azure eyes were striking, but these attractive features were marred by a jaw that was overly broad and a down-turned mouth that was excessively wide. And regardless of the large diamonds in her rings, the conspicuous precious stones in her necklace, and the low-cut black cashmere dress that strove to emphasize the attractions of an overlarge bosom, the overall effect was marred by a sour, disapproving expression. Had he been asked to describe her he would have said that she resembled the sort of overweight, fleshy wife of a prosperous Amsterdam burgher that was frequently painted by seventeenth-century Dutch masters.

It was easy to imagine her being irritated by Simpson's boorish behavior, and why in turn both the young captain and Major Holland would have found her so unappealing. But at present the opinions of these two young men were of less importance than what Lady Cordelia thought of Venetta Cordell, a woman who was not only the wife of her husband's commanding officer, but one who was much younger and undoubtedly more attractive.

Arbuthnot gestured towards two vacant chairs, and watched with some bemusement as Parsons carefully removed his coat and placed it on the floor.

"I understand that you gentlemen are investigating General Latham's murder," he said, after resuming his own seat. "I will, of course, be happy to help you in any way I can, but I'm blest if I can see how."

Parsons began by asking a few questions of a general nature about the Cordell's dinner party which Arbuthnot answered. Then he turned his attention to Lady Cordelia.

"I believe that after leaving the gentlemen to their brandy and cigars you spent the latter part of the evening with Mrs. Cordell," he said. "Perhaps you will be kind enough to tell me what you talked about."

Lady Cordelia smiled disparagingly.

"What sort of conversation do you think I would have with that French adventuress," she said haughtily. "She may be some people's idea of a lady, inspector, but she is certainly not mine."

Major Arbuthnot stirred uncomfortably in his chair.

"Cordelia, my dear," he said, "I really do not think that this is the time for such remarks."

"Be quiet, Charles," she said dismissively. "I think it only right that Inspector Parsons hears what I have to say about Venetta Cordell, and also about her despicable little husband."

"Please continue, Lady Cordelia," said Parsons, before her embarrassed husband had time to reply. "You have my undivided attention."

She smoothed the slightest of wrinkles on her dress and for the first time since their arrival the barest trace of a smile appeared on her face.

"You are no doubt aware that Colonel Cordell met this woman at a spa in Rochefort," she said with unconcealed disgust. "He must have been easy pickings for her. A newly promoted colonel with little experience of women who was desperately in need of a wife. It was hardly surprising that he fell for what little charms that vixen has to offer."

Charles Arbuthnot shuffled anxiously in his chair. But although he looked distinctly uneasy it appeared he was not, at least in public, in the habit of interrupting his wife. It could have been no more than good manners on his part, thought Parsons, but on the other hand it might have been a situation he had been obliged to accept. It was, after all, Lady Cordelia who possessed the title, and in all likelihood the fine house in which they lived might also be hers.

"Well, really, Cordelia," was all he managed to say.

His wife ignored the weak entreaty to remain silent.

"In view of General Latham's death it has to be said, Charles," she said firmly.

"Are you suggesting that it was possible there was a relationship between Mrs. Cordell and General Latham, Lady Cordelia?" Parsons asked innocently.

"I would not be in the least surprised," she said. "What else would you expect from a womanizer like Maxwell Latham and a common little courtesan like Venetta. After capturing a colonel she no doubt had her sights set on a general, especially one who has just been knighted. But whatever plans she might have had for a future with General Latham were doomed. I told her as much on Wednesday night."

"What do you mean by that, Lady Cordelia?" Parsons asked.

"I told her that General Latham had just become engaged to a wealthy Irish widow with a fine London house, a palatial mansion in Dublin and large estates in County Wicklow," she said. "You should have seen her face. She was furious. That's why she suddenly claimed to feel ill and went to bed."

Charles Arbuthnot appeared as surprised as Parsons at the news.

"When did you learn that, Cordelia?" he said, "and why didn't you say anything to me?"

"Because you never pay attention when I tell you about such things," she said angrily. "I despair of you, Charles. Haven't I told you a hundred times that if you don't keep your eye on what is happening in society you will never make colonel."

For the first time Parsons noted a flash of anger sour Arbuthnot's handsome features. He opened his mouth to speak but then thought better of it, allowing his wife to continue.

"If you must know, Charles, I only learned it myself less than a week ago," she said. "A friend of mine told me she had read about the engagement in the *Court and Society Review*. It appears to have been all very sudden, and even my contacts at the War Office knew nothing about it. You know as well as I, Charles, that Latham was a sly fox. After all, you were with him in Africa. He must have had some inkling as to where he was going. Not that I can imagine him being pleased to be sent to Ireland. Who in their right mind would want to go to that dreadful place. If you ask me he was being punished for some past indiscretion. And I'm not talking about women when I say that. No, I think influential figures in Government and the War Office decided to promote him and give him a knighthood before shipping him off to a place where he couldn't do any serious harm or further embarrass them."

The ghost of a smile briefly lifted the downcast corners of Lady Cordelia's wide mouth, leaving Parsons to ponder whether this fleeting sign of amusement was due to her being privy to such information or simply because she enjoyed spreading malicious rumors.

"But you can always rely on Maxwell to make the best of things," she said. "From what I've learned in the past few days he'd been courting this Mrs. Fitzgerald for weeks. I can't say I'm altogether surprised. If you've just been promoted general and had as little money as Latham, you'd want to find yourself a rich wife. Especially if you've been appointed to a position in which you're expected to entertain the natives lavishly instead of just slaughtering them."

"And you're saying that the first Mrs. Cordell knew of this was on Wednesday night after dinner?" said Parsons.

"That's right, inspector," she said. "I speak only a little French, but it was enough to know that whatever she said about General Latham in her native tongue after I told her about his engagement would not bear repeating in respectable company."

Lady Cordelia laughed scornfully.

"It wouldn't surprise me if Venetta hadn't murdered that old Casanova," she said. "And right under the nose of that pathetic husband of hers."

"You seem to have a poor opinion of Colonel Cordell, Lady Cordelia," Parsons said.

"And why shouldn't I, inspector?" she said acrimoniously. "If it wasn't for the fact that he was Latham's half-brother he would never have been made commanding officer of the Middlesex. That position rightfully belongs to Charles. Whatever faults my husband may have he's still a finer officer and a more inspiring leader than a pathetic creature whose father was an Italian painter called Giovanni Cordellano."

"Are you talking about Colonel Cordell's father?" Parsons asked.

"Of course I am," she said. "Cordellano was his mother's second husband. Her first was a military man who drowned when his troopship went down on its way to India. And Cordellano wasn't much use to her either. He was a failure as a painter, and drank himself to death when their son was still a young boy. Cordell, as he now calls himself, is seven years younger than his half-brother, and without Maxwell Latham's patronage he would never have been promoted above captain. Not that, as far as I could see, Latham had any real affection for Cordell. But for some reason he seems to have fended for his useless half-brother for most of his life."

"Why do you imagine he did that, Lady Cordelia?" asked Parsons.

"You'd have to ask General Latham that, inspector. And now that he's dead he can't tell you. But it's probably something to do with him taking on the role of a father-figure in the absence of a man in his mother's life. You men, it appears, are always trying to please your mothers. Even old lechers like Latham."

"And is Mrs. Cordellano still alive?" asked Parsons.

"No, she died just after Hector Cordell received his first commission. Naturally he went into the same regiment as his brother, and his brother has been looking out for him ever since."

Parsons turned to Arbuthbot.

"I regret to say that my knowledge of the army and its customs is sadly lacking, major," he said innocently. "But I believe until quite recently it was customary for officers to purchase their commissions."

"That was true until 1871, inspector," Arbuthnot replied. "Then the Secretary of State, in his wisdom, decided to abolish the system."

Lady Cordelia interrupted her husband.

"And a disaster that has proved to be for men of ability like Charles," she said haughtily. "With money behind him Charles would've been at least a colonel by now. I would've seen to that."

If Cardwell's reforms had proved upsetting for many serving officers, thought Parsons, they must also have dismayed their rich, ambitious wives like Lady Cordelia. Wives who might well have married in the secure knowledge that their money alone would ensure for their husbands and themselves ranks and positions to flaunt in society. And once that rank had been purchased there was every likelihood that in due course their husbands would also aspire to a title. And without the ability to purchase her husband a promotion he could imagine how galling it must have been for a woman like Lady Cordelia to find that someone like Venetta, a younger woman with probably little money, nothing in the way of social standing, and a foreigner to boot, had married the colonel of a regiment in which her husband was still a major. It was easy to imagine her delight when she was able to crush Venetta with the news of General Latham's engagement.

"Would you happen to know how General Latham and Colonel Cordell managed to purchase their first commissions?"

Parsons had directed the question to Arbuthnot, but he was not surprised to find that it was his wife who answered.

"As I understand, their mother had money enough of her own to put them through school and Sandhurst and also purchase their commissions in the Middlesex," she said. "I believe that she was also able to purchase Latham his captaincy. But when she died sometime in the late sixties that money dried up, obliging Latham to find a wife with a reasonable income of her own. Without that he would never have become a major."

"What happened to General Latham's first wife?" asked Parsons.

"She died in childbirth in 1874, inspector," Arbuthnot explained. "The child died at the same time. From what I remember Latham was pretty shaken up at the time. Fortunately for him the regiment was shipped to Africa not long afterwards and he was able to immerse himself in the campaigns we fought there."

"And arrange the promotions for his pathetic half-brother that he would never have achieved for himself," said Lady Cordelia. "How else can you explain a man like Cordell being promoted from captain to colonel in the space of eight years. No wonder it was that Latham felt entitled to sleep with Cordell's wife."

14

WHILE PARSONS AND Harris were in Eaton Square, Major Holland and Captain Simpson were riding in Hyde Park. It was not exactly Holland's idea of a ride. Simpson had had several more stiff drinks during lunch, and was even now resorting to frequent slugs from his hip flask. That he was still capable of riding was to Holland, a moderate drinker himself, something of a miracle.

"What do you make of all this business, Simpson?" he asked as they walked their horses slowly along Rotten Row.

In their red jackets and blue jodhpurs the two men made a brave sight, their polished black riding boots and the well-brushed coats of their horses catching the shafts of autumn sunlight through the trees. The heart of more than one young lady strolling through the park fluttered at the sight of two such heroic figures mounted on fine beasts that were seemingly marching in time to the notes of the distant band.

"What business are you talking about?" Simpson slurred, as a gust of wind sent more leaves spinning from the stately elms.

"Oh, for heaven's sake, Audley. I'm talking about Latham's murder. Whatever else?"

"What's that got to do with you or me, Holland?" Simpson said angrily.

"Nothing at all, I sincerely hope, old boy," Holland replied. "I'm more concerned about what it could mean for the good name of the regiment. That bloody little upstart of a police inspector as good as told me that he thought one of us had murdered the general."

"If by *one of us* you mean one of the regimental officers, then I've no idea what you're talking about. It doesn't follow that *one of us* killed the old sod just because he was spiked with one of Cordell's *iklwas*. Anyone could've stolen it from the colonel's study. The colonel's servants or any of the soldiers living in the barracks."

"But why for God's sake?" asked Holland. "Why should anyone in the regiment want to murder the general?"

Simpson reined in his horse, took another slug from his hip flask and glared at Holland.

"Because he was a ruthless bastard prepared to sacrifice others for his own glory. If I thought he'd singled me out for that bloody patrol I might cheerfully have rammed that spear into him myself. But I know it was Cordell I have to thank for that. It was he who picked me for that suicide mission."

"I don't think that's entirely true, Audley," said Holland. "Whatever he may have said later it was not Cordell. You two were pretty close. If Cordell had to send one of his officers on a dangerous mission he would've picked anyone but you. As far as we knew at headquarters it was Latham who selected you. At least that's what he said in his report."

"Then don't you think that gives me an excellent motive?" said Simpson with a bitter laugh.

Holland looked at his friend in horror.

"You're drunk, Audley," he said in disgust. "You don't know what you're saying. Why would you want to kill him? For heaven's sake, if it wasn't for Latham you wouldn't be getting a VC. And the rest of us would give their right arm for one of those."

'Well, give me yours, my dear Mark," Simpson said with a wry laugh, "and you can have my bloody medal."

He took another slug from his flask.

"And who are you to question my drinking, Mark?" he said bitterly. "What would you know about what I went through. You were on the bloody staff ordering poor buggers like me to risk their lives and those of our men. You've no right to criticize me. If you'd been through what I have you'd feel quite capable of murdering anyone you thought was responsible. Don't you know I've not been the same since that bloody patrol. Do you think I've always drunk as much as I do now?"

From what he had heard since rejoining the regiment Holland knew that what Simpson said was true. His heavy drinking had only begun since returning to England.

"I'm sorry for what happened to you and your men, Audley," he said. "But I've told you before that those orders didn't come from the staff. Latham made the decision himself. He said in his report that if his plan had worked in the way he had hoped a lot of lives would've been saved."

"Did he now," said Simpson sourly. "Well, I know a few men whose lives weren't saved. They were with me at the time. And whatever you or anyone else may think about Latham, as far as I'm concerned he was a cold blooded devil. And I'm not sorry he's dead."

Holland had never heard Simpson talk like this before. Whether it was true or not, if any of what he said reached the wrong ears his friend could easily find himself in deep water. And as it happened it would have been relatively easy for Simpson to have taken the *iklwa*. The Officers' Mess was only a short distance from the Cordell's house, and as Cordell's friend no one would have thought twice about seeing him enter. And Simpson was frequently so drunk at night that he scarcely knew what he was doing.

Simpson had seen the expression on Holland's face.

"Don't look so worried, Mark," he said. "I didn't do it. But I think I may know who did. And that fellow Parsons may be right about it being someone in the regiment. Or at least someone with a close connection."

"Are you going to tell me who you think that is?"

"Not on your life, Mark. I know you. You can't keep anything to yourself."

"What about the police? Are you going to tell them of your suspicions?"

"Certainly not. I've no wish to help that fat little inspector."

Holland was confused. He was no longer sure whether Simpson really knew what he was saying or whether the drink was effecting his mind.

"So what do you think about Cordell's little French woman?" he asked, steering the conversation away from Latham's murder. "You were with him in Rochefort when he met her. Didn't it come as a surprise to you that Cordell fell for her charms so quickly."

"Mind your own bloody business, Holland," Simpson said angrily. "Hector only married that woman because it was his duty. As commanding officer he was badly in need of a wife. Someone to help him entertain. At least that's what he told me. It was just unfortunate for him to meet a devious woman like Venetta. She made a play for him as soon as she realized who he was and that he was desperately seeking for a wife."

"I can see why *you* wouldn't like her," said Holland with a laugh. "She certainly changed your relationship with Cordell. You were never as chummy with him as you were before Venetta arrived on the scene."

Holland drew his horse close to Simpson's. He leant over and patted the young man on the shoulder.

"But if you're honest with yourself you couldn't expect that sort of relationship to last, Audley," he said sympathetically. "It's one thing to be friendly with a major when you're in his company, but when that major becomes your commanding officer everything has to change. You'll just have to accept that and find a new interest in your life. Someone who can cheer you up and stop you drinking as much as you do. What you need, Audley, is a woman."

Holland had already decided that he needed a woman himself, and just at that moment spotted two attractive young women riding in their direction."

"Action stations, Audley," he said enthusiastically. "Take a gander at what's on the horizon. I'll take the blonde. You can have the brunette."

"As far as I'm concerned you can have them both, Mark," said Simpson, abruptly tugging at his horse's reins and wheeling it round in the direction of the barracks.

"I'm not in the mood for women," he shouted over his shoulder as he trotted away.

"When are you ever?" muttered Holland, as he spurred his own horse towards the two women. "Perhaps what they say about you, my dear Audley, is true after all."

15

"CORDELIA, THE WAY you speak to me in public is quite outrageous," said Charles Arbuthnot angrily to his wife when they were alone again. "Did you really have to humiliate me in front of those two detectives?"

"I don't have to humiliate you, Charles," Cordelia said, calmly returning her husband's indignant words with a fierce gaze of her own. "Other people only have to see the way you behave to see what a pathetic creature you really are. You should be grateful that I speak up for you at all. Any other woman would have given up on you years ago, whereas I continue trying to salvage something of your career."

"My career, Cordelia! What do you possibly care about my career, other than wanting to be married to a man with a rank that matches your own precious title."

"And what if I do! I have a right to that! Haven't I supported you all these years. Haven't I paid your tailor's bills, purchased the best horses for you, and enabled you to live in a fine house like this. A house which you could have used to entertain the sort of influential people to further your career."

Cordelia's anger was subsiding into despair.

"If you'd only done as I asked, Charles, you could have been commanding the regiment instead of that fool Cordell, or even been a general like Latham. And had you done that I would've been content. I would even have been happy to pay your gambling debts."

Charles had been waiting for a suitable moment to broach that very subject. It was the one reason he had chosen to stay at home after lunch instead of going for a ride in Hyde Park. And then those two wretched detectives had arrived.

"Well, now that you've raised the subject, my dear," he said. "I do happen to need a bit of help this month. I seem to have had another run of bad luck."

"How dare you, Charles," Cordelia hissed. "Have you no shame at all. You take all I have to offer, and in return you give me nothing. Nothing! For the most part you abandon me, and then you have the nerve to ask me for money. No, Charles. There will be no more money until you do something for me in return. And you can start by considering how best to get yourself promoted. Until you do that you can fend for yourself. And perhaps when the news that I've decided to tighten my purse strings reaches your precious club you'll find your chums there less patient about allowing you credit."

"And what possible good will it do for my chances of promotion if I'm unable to pay my debts. Were my credit and good name to become suspect my reputation will be ruined. You know as well as I that there's only one thing worse than being unable to meet one's obligations, and that's to be caught cheating."

"Then you have a choice, Charles. Either you pull yourself together, or you risk losing everything in life that you cherish. Your clothes, your horses and your gambling. I'm no longer willing to support a man whose only interest in life is the faro table. You owe it to me to make something more of your life."

"Damn you, Cordelia. I owe you nothing. Had I not married you, you would have remained a spinster to this day. I knew all about your foul temper before I married you. Your dear father was gentleman enough to tell me about the stable boy you flogged. I was prepared to take you in spite of that. But if you push me too far I'll see that you go back from whence you came. And you'll go without your money, my dear Cordelia. If I divorce you I'll take you for every penny I can get."

Cordelia rose from her chair in a blind fury, seized a porcelain statue of a shepherd girl from the mantel and hurled it at her husband. Seeing what she had in mind, Charles had made a hasty retreat. He ducked out of the path of the statue, and turned to watch it smash against the wall.

"I can already hear my lawyer describing that in the divorce court, Cordelia," he said with a humorless laugh, as he surveyed the shards of porcelain on the floor. He bowed mockingly towards his wife. "And now, my dear, if you'll excuse me, I'm going to my club.

———————

CORDELIA NEEDED LITTLE reason to indulge her appetite for wine at the best of times, but her anger and frustration at her husband's behavior was such that it took her less than half an hour to empty a decanter of Bordeaux. Then she ordered her carriage.

"The landau or the barouche, my lady?" the servant had asked.

"The landau, of course, you fool. And tell Cooper to make sure the roof is up. I've no wish to catch a chill."

———————

COOPER, THE ARBUTHNOT'S broad-shouldered coachman, was lying on his bed in the attic of the mews in his undergarments reading a copy of *Sporting Life* and planning his next investment on the race track when he received the summons.

"So 'er ladyship's been left by 'erself again," he said with a coarse laugh. "'Is lordship's gone off to 'is club, she's in a foul mood and she's 'ad a drink or two. And now she wants me to take 'er for a drive."

Cooper rose from the bed, stretched, swallowed the last dregs from the bottle of stout he had been drinking, belched loudly and reached for the livery that was hanging on a hook on the back of the door. For a moment he considered shaving but decided against it. He doubted whether Lady Cordelia would care whether he had stubble on his chin.

Cooper had once been Charles Arbuthnot's soldier-servant, but when Lady Cordelia had seen his broad shoulders and deep chest during the short visit she had paid to Africa she had prevailed upon her husband to dispense with Cooper's services and make him her coachman. At the time Charles had been in dire need of Cordelia's money to pay a large debt, and he had readily complied. He had never much liked Cooper. Apart from being lazy he was inclined to drunkenness and not long after Cordelia's request Cooper had struck one of Arbuthnot's company officers.

A serious offense such as that, especially on active service, merited an equally severe punishment. It had also provided Charles with an excellent excuse to dismiss Cooper and send him back to England with Cordelia. Replacing Cooper had been no problem. There were always soldiers more than willing to forsake the more arduous life of a rifleman for that of an officer's servant.

THE ARBUTHNOT'S LANDAU was but one of many carriages making their way along Park Lane towards Edgeware Road. The snail-like pace did little to improve Lady Cordelia's humor, and her mood only lifted when the carriage drew up some forty-five minutes later outside *The Marchioness,* one of many small hotels in the back streets of Paddington not far from the station. By then she was wearing a thick black veil.

"That should be enough to ensure that a room is made available, Cooper," she said, handing the coachman two sovereigns, and leaning heavily on his strong right arm as she alighted from the landau.

"Take the carriage round to the stables," she instructed, after the receptionist had confirmed that there was indeed a vacant room. "And be careful you are not seen coming upstairs. Something Captain Simpson said to me at dinner the other night makes me think he knows something."

"Don't worry about Captain Simpson, your ladyship," Cooper said. "I can deal with that milk sop. I still have a friend or two in the regiment who can keep their eye on what he's up to."

Cordelia need not have been overly concerned about any curiosity the receptionist might have shown. He was only too pleased to pocket fifteen shillings of the money he had received for the room to ever pay much attention to the heavily-veiled woman who frequently arrived at the hotel without luggage.

———

THE BEDROOM ON the second floor was smaller and dirtier than the humblest servant's room in

Eaton Square, but the large bed occupying most of the room had clean sheets and was comfortable enough. And as far as Cordelia was concerned that was all that mattered.

She removed her veil, undressed and slipped between the white sheets.

"Come in," she said, in answer to the discrete knock at the door, her excitement growing as Cooper entered the room, locked the door behind him, removed his clothing and tossed it into an untidy pile on the floor. Even from where she lay she could smell the stale odor of his unwashed body. It was a smell that had at first revolted her. But now she welcomed it, in the same way that she lusted for the strong body with its thick mass of black hair. Cooper possessed the body of a warrior. With his fierce dark eyes, his unshaven face, and the broad expanse of his chest and back he was a magnificent specimen of virile manhood. Whenever she saw him naked she congratulated herself on her choice. As soon as she had seen him and heard that he had been flogged she had wanted him. She would have liked to have taken a whip to his broad back herself. But for now that would have to remain the stuff of her dreams. She would have to be content to use her sharp nails. She had also fantasized of Cooper tearing off her clothes and taking her by force. But that could never happen as long as she remained the mistress and he her servant. It was inconceivable to think of her returning to her lady's maid with her clothes in rags.

Cordelia's eyes devoured the strong muscles on Cooper's powerful thighs as he approached the bed. He was hung like a stallion, his manhood dwarfing what she remembered of Charles' poor specimen.

Thoroughly aroused, she kicked off the bedding, stroked the taut nipples on her ample breasts and opened her corpulent thighs.

"What are you waiting for, Cooper?" she urged. "We don't have all day."

16

AFTER RETURNING THE *iklwa* to his office in Scotland Yard Parsons spent much of the evening at the *Crook and Shears.* It was his favorite pub in Chelsea. The beer was excellent, the food varied and plentiful, and, as a regular customer, he was always made to feel especially welcome by the jovial landlord and his wife. He was, nevertheless, unsure of what their reaction might have been had he been discovered carrying a spear. As far as the landlord and his wife and other regulars were concerned he was one of the countless number of civil servants working in London. From the tone of his voice and his physical appearance they could hardly mistake him for anything else. Parsons was not at all offended. He had never admitted to being a detective, as he had felt that the knowledge of his true profession might well have cooled the warmth of his welcome. Even the most law-abiding of citizens tended to choose pubs in which they were not rubbing shoulders with policemen.

Three pints of strong ale and a dinner of mutton chops, carrots and baked potatoes had put Parsons in an excellent frame of mind to write to Louise, and shortly after nine he retired to his lodgings. He had not written since leaving the Lake District, and his conscience was beginning to prick.

There were few people abroad on the foggy streets as he made his way to the modest terraced house in Elm Park Avenue where he had lodgings. Most people were content to be at home, and after the conviviality of the pub Parsons was himself glad to escape from the cold, damp night air to his cozy sitting room on the top floor.

The bedroom and sitting room he rented were not large, but they met his simple requirements more than adequately, and were a vast improvement on his previous cramped accommodation in a Clerkenwell attic. The domestic arrangements were also eminently satisfactory. His landlady was a treasure, and the only other lodgers in the house, a young bookkeeper and his wife, who had rooms on the floor below his, were polite and considerate.

The house was owned by Mrs. Oakley, the widow of an art dealer whose premature death from typhoid fever at the age of forty eight had obliged her to take lodgers out of financial necessity. With no children of her own, Mrs. Oakley had made the best of her misfortune by selecting as tenants people young enough to stir her own unrequited yearnings for motherhood, and although she would never have presumed to mention it, she fondly hoped that it would not be long before the bookkeeper and his wife made her a surrogate grandmother. Parsons had not, as yet, mentioned the seriousness of his relationship with Louise, as he had no wish to encourage further excitement in the good lady. But he was more than content to accept her generous offer of shopping for his bare necessities, and of adding his laundry to that of hers when the laundress came to the house each Monday.

He hung his overcoat on a hook behind the sitting room door and gazed with affection at the aging leather chairs on each side of the fireplace and the growing library of books that were already beginning to fill his handsome oak bookcase. He would be reluctant ever to have to leave such agreeable lodgings. For a start he doubted whether he could afford anything better, although were he to marry Louise he knew he would have little choice. The rooms were of inadequate size for a married couple, especially for someone like Louise used to living in far grander surroundings. There was also the not inconsequential matter of Louise's disability and the problem the narrow stairs would present. It was a situation that greatly concerned Parsons whenever he allowed himself to think about it.

He lit the gas lamps, removed his boots, slipped on his dressing gown and slippers and put a match to the kindling in the fireplace. Then he lit his small paraffin stove. When he had left that morning the milk in his larder had still been fresh, and after a perfunctory sniff he poured what was left into a saucepan and placed it on the stove. Then he measured a spoonful of cocoa into a mug, added sugar and waited for the milk to boil.

He had thought of Louise often since returning to London, although were he to be honest he would have had to admit that now that he was fully engaged in an absorbing investigation she had entered his thoughts less frequently than he had imagined. When they had been together in the Lake District he could think of little else, but now that he was once more immersed in his work she entered his consciousness only at such times as the present, when he was completely alone.

Parsons removed the boiling milk from the stove and poured it into his mug. Then he settled himself at his small desk and began his letter. He told Louise as much about General Latham's murder as he felt able, omitting the names of any officers he had questioned lest she relate that information to her odious brother. He mentioned his visit to the barracks in Kensington, but dwelt more on the band in the park, saying how much he had wished she had been with him to enjoy the music. He closed by asking Louise to give his love to his mother. As he did so he felt a twinge of guilt. Only recently it would have been his mother to whom he would have been writing. He could, of course, have written a second letter, but he chose not to; and torn between this sense of remorse and his sudden tiredness, took the easier of the options and went to bed. Within five minutes he had fallen into a deep sleep, his last thoughts spent in contemplating the mysterious nature of women; and how, at one extreme, there were ladies of such virtue and sweet nature as his mother and Louise, and at the other, unfaithful, cold-blooded killers like Venetta Cordell.

17

Sunday, 26th October 1881

KING'S ROAD, CHELSEA on a crisp sunny Sunday morning in Autumn was as fine a place to be as anywhere in London, thought Parsons, as he perused his copy of the *Sunday Times*. It was the only day in the week when the normally busy road running from Putney Bridge to Sloane Square could be said to be quiet. Shops other than newsagents were closed, it was too early for the public houses to be open, and the few carriages and cabs on the road seemed to be moving at a less frantic pace and with a greater sense of decorum than at other times of the week. Even the pavements were bereft of pedestrians, as there was still an hour before the sound of the church bells would begin to summon the faithful.

Parsons was beginning his Sunday with a substantial and leisurely breakfast at his favorite coffee shop, a regular habit of his that afforded him much pleasure. It also enabled him to catch up on the week's news, especially that pertaining to the Sayers' investigation. At the newsagent he had also confirmed that the notes sent to Venetta Cordell by General Latham had been compiled from only two newspapers: the *Times* and the *Daily Chronicle*, although the words cut from the *Chronicle* had only been used in the last note. It struck him that it was a curious combination of newspapers for Latham to have used. Parsons could well imagine the general reading a highly respected newspaper like the *Times*, but the more radical *Chronicle* was quite another matter, unless he was endeavoring to gain an insight into the opinions held by the more extreme elements of society. It was, of course, possible that the *Chronicle* was Bradley's choice of newspaper, and Parsons made a mental note to ask Bradley about that and what he knew of the general's notes when he next saw him.

It was clear from what he read that the police were making little progress in finding Lord Sayers' killer. There had been arrests in many parts of the country on a variety of pretexts, but no one as yet had been charged with murder. In the meantime, Parsons read, the victim had been buried, the funeral having taken place at a private ceremony at his wife's home in Lancashire.

Some of the reports, especially those in the more sensational popular press, spoke with considerable vitriol about this unsatisfactory rate of progress and of the woeful incompetence of the police. Questions had even been asked in Parliament, and the Prime Minister himself had seen fit to make a statement in an attempt to reassure a nation made increasingly nervous by recent Fenian activities. Doubtless, Parsons mused, this would only add to the pressures on Superintendent Jeffries and his colleagues, and as he spread marmalade liberally upon yet another piece of toast Parsons congratulated himself on his good fortune in having been given a relatively straightforward case to solve.

It being one of the few Sunday mornings since early August that the sun had chosen to shine, after several minutes spent wrestling with his conscience, Parsons abandoned any idea of going to church, and instead decided to take full advantage of the weather by going for a walk. After such a substantial breakfast he felt the need for exercise. At first he considered returning to Kensington Gardens to hear the band or even wandering further afield to Regents Park, but prompted by a curiosity that had been born of reading the morning papers he decided to revisit Kensington with a view to seeing for himself exactly where the bombs had been detonated on the evening of Lord Sayers' murder.

The intended targets for the two bombs had been widely reported as being the home of Sir William Fawkus, the Conservative Member of Parliament for Kensington, and Kensington Barracks itself. In retrospect Parsons regretted not enquiring about the latter during his previous visits to the barracks. Regardless of that, it was indicative of the shallowness of newspaper reporting that nothing he had read since the event had ever given a detailed description of the actual location of the bombs or the extent of the damage they had caused. It was true what they said about newspapers. They reported only what the public wanted to read, which at present was the laggardly progress of the police.

———————

A SOLITARY SENTRY was patrolling outside the main gate of the barracks when Parsons arrived shortly after midday. The young man seemed less concerned about his duties than he was in exchanging banter with the steady stream of young soldiers leaving the barracks. And judging by what Parsons could hear they were heading for the local hostelries to meet the sort of young women who found red-jacketed soldiers irresistible.

"I'll 'ave one fer you, mate," several said jokingly to the sentry. One or two even mentioned the names of women they were planning to meet, and taunting the sentry as they passed with lewd suggestions as to what they had in mind to do. All of this was taken in good humor by the sentry, who was no doubt content in the knowledge that by the following Sunday the roles would be reversed, and that he would be amongst the revelers in the pub and one of their number would be engaged in guard duty.

As far as Parsons could see through the railings there was little activity within the barracks. No squads of soldiers were pounding the parade ground and no drill sergeants were shouting shrill words of command. Sunday, it appeared, was as much a day of rest in the army as elsewhere. Perhaps, even at this late hour there were soldiers still abed, especially those without the wherewithal to buy themselves a beer.

Parsons followed the railings north until he reached the intersection of Church Street with Holland Street. Then he turned right, within two hundred yards reaching the second gate into the barracks, the smaller one that he had been told was used only by a select number of key-holders, and the one Venetta Cordell had used on her last fateful visit to General Latham. As he had expected, the gate was locked.

The privet hedge he had previously seen from within the barracks also grew alongside this stretch of the railings. It effectively blocked his view of the commanding officer's house and the Officers' Mess apart from a spot where the shade of a lime tree had inhibited its growth. The hedge was much thinner there, sparse enough for Parsons to see the back of the Officers' Mess and one of the servants emerging from a back door to smoke a cigarette.

Parsons continued walking for just over a hundred yards more, at which point the barrack railings turned abruptly south along the edge of the long gardens behind the large houses in Kensington Palace Gardens and he could follow them no further.

From what he had seen during what was admittedly a cursory inspection Parsons decided it unlikely that any bombs had been thrown into the barracks from Church Street or Holland Street. Either that or they had caused negligible damage. Nor did he think it likely that any prospective bomber would have chosen to launch an attack from the well-tended lawns of the wealthy owners of the houses in Kensington Palace Gardens.

There was only one other possible access to the barracks, and that was from the south. But on retracing his steps past the main gate he also discovered the difficulty of an approach from that direction. For the most part access to the barracks from that side was blocked by terraces of small working class houses built at right angles to the barrack railings. Like similar dwellings in many parts of London these houses were without front gardens and had only small back yards with barely room for outside privies and washing lines. From what Harris had once told him they must have been similar to the house in which he lived with his wife and two children.

Parsons explored each of the narrow dirt roads leading past the fronts of these houses and the dark passages to their back gates, concluding as he did that although it was indeed possible to reach the barrack railings from any of these routes there seemed little there to interest a bomber. The only building visible was one of the large three storied barrack blocks used as soldiers' accommodation. It was hardly a satisfying target for a Fenian bomber, and even had an attack on the barracks been mounted from this direction there was little evidence of any damage ever having been done. As far as he could see the railings were still intact and if any bomb had detonated against the soldiers' accommodation it had caused little damage.

By now Parsons had become thoroughly frustrated at what he now felt to have been a waste of a perfectly fine afternoon, and he was about to leave the area when he was hailed by an old man dressed in a battered bowler hat and a torn jacket. The man had been sitting outside the front of one of the houses in a battered cane chair watching Parsons with evident curiosity.

"Are you fr'm one o' they papers, mate?" the old man asked, removing his pipe from his mouth in order to wipe a drip from the end of his nose with the back of his hand. "I thought you people would've know all yer want by now."

"And what exactly would that be, sir?" asked Parsons politely. "As it happens I'm not a newspaper reporter. But I've read about the bombs in the papers, and as I was just passing this way I thought I would see for myself what damage had been caused."

The old man laughed, cleared his throat and spat on the ground.

"There weren't no damage, mate," he said, "leastwise not wha' I'd call damage."

"How do you know that, sir?" Parsons asked. "Did you happen to see anything?"

"I seen an' I 'eard, mate," the old man said with a wink. "an' so did 'arf the people in the street. 'Twas just ar'ter nine on Wen'sday night. I woz jus' goin' to bed when I 'eard a loud noise comin' frum inside the barracks. First I thought it were one o' those bloody soldiers messin' 'round, 'cause when I come to the front door I saw smoke, jus' behind the soldiers' quarters."

The old man pointed to the end of the street towards the railings.

"Then I saw someone runnin' down the street towards Kensin'ton 'igh Street."

"Just one man?" Parsons asked.

"Yes, mate. Jus' one. But I didn' see 'im fer long, cause 'e run into the 'igh Street almost as soon as I catch sight ov 'im."

"Have you told the police about this?" Parsons asked.

"Oh, yes, mate. I tol' everyone that wanted ter know."

"And what about the barracks?" Parsons asked. "Could you tell if much damage was done inside the barracks?"

"No, mate. There weren't much o' that'. Jus' a few winders wiv broken glass. An' they fixed 'em the nex' day."

"What did this man look like?" Parsons asked. "How tall was he and what was he wearing?"

"It was dark, mate, and there ain't much light in these streets," the old man said. "They only put they new fangled gas lamps in the streets where the toffs live. But I seen 'im well enuff. I'd say 'e were a big man. 'E were taller than you, an' 'e were fatter. Leastwise 'e appeared tha' way to me as 'e didn' run too well."

"What about his face?" Parsons asked. "Can you describe what he looked like?

" 'E 'ad a beard or a thick mustache. But 'e had a 'at over 'is eyes, so I never got a good look at 'is face. An' 'e were wearing a long dark coat. More than tha' I couldn' tell you."

———

IT WAS A similar story at 6 Pembroke Road, the home of Sir William Fawkus. The Kensington MP's home was no more than ten minutes walk from the barracks, and according to the servant who answered the door to Parsons, it had been just before nine fifteen on Wednesday night that a small bomb had been thrown into the front garden. No damage had been done other than to some of Lady Gladys' favorite standard roses. Lady Gladys had been most upset about that, the servant explained, but as it happened, both she and Sir William were dining out that evening, and in consequence, apart from the damage to the flowers, neither had been greatly inconvenienced by the incident.

———

AS FENIAN BOMBINGS went, Parsons thought, these two must rank as the most ineffective he had ever heard of. Judging by the times and the distances between the barracks and Pembroke Road it appeared almost certain that the same person had thrown both bombs, but it also seemed evident that there had been little intention to kill or to maim, or to cause anything other then the slightest of damage. And that had never before been the case with the Fenians.

If any of his colleagues at Scotland Yard had investigated the scene they must surely have come to the same conclusion. But the fact that the two relatively harmless attacks continued to be labeled as the work of Fenians suggested otherwise. And as far as Parsons was concerned an oversight such as that threw an entirely new light on Lord Sayers' assassination. One that he intended pursuing with Superintendent Jeffries at the earliest opportunity.

18

Monday, 27th October 1881

THE WEATHER HAD reverted to a gloomy pattern of steady rain that was more typical for the time of year and had pedestrians clattering into each other as they scurried along the wet pavements under their umbrellas. It was as if the previous day's sunshine had been merely a dream or a collective figment of London's imagination. As ever Whitehall was jammed with impatient vehicles jostling for position and the hive of government clerks hastening to their desks to begin another week of bureaucratic monotony.

The offices of Scotland Yard were uncommonly quiet. The lack of any real progress after the early flurry of activity had left Parsons' colleagues despondent and unsure of where next to turn. Parsons did not speak to any of them. Their downcast and weary expressions told him all he needed to know. Instead he made straight for Jeffries' office, where he found the superintendent in the process of angrily closing his window. Doubtless one of the clerks would soon feel the superintendent's wrath for daring to think that the room needed airing.

Lack of sleep, the strain of the investigation, a failure to make any genuine headway in finding Sayers' killer, and the pressures from the Commissioner and senior political figures were all deeply etched on Jeffries' craggy continence. Parsons had never before seen his superior looking so tired and careworn.

"I hope you've got something positive to report, Parsons," Jeffries said wearily. "I could do with some good news."

"I gather the Sayers' case isn't going too well, sir," Parsons said, with what he hoped was an appropriate degree of sympathy.

Jeffries merely grunted by way of response, took a tobacco pouch from his jacket pocket and began filling his pipe.

"Enough of my problems, Parsons," he said as he pressed the dark shag into the bowl. "What have you and Harris been doing with yourselves?"

Jeffries listened attentively as Parsons outlined the progress he had made.

"And you're convinced this Mrs. Cordell murdered the general?" Jeffries asked after Parsons had concluded his report.

"The evidence certainly points that way, sir," Parsons replied. "She admits to having a relationship with General Latham, and for his part he appears to have been a gentleman with a reputation for that sort of thing. But it was a relationship that Latham was about to bring to an end after becoming engaged to a wealthy Irish widow. Mrs. Cordell does not deny that she was at the general's house on the night he died, and even had she done so we have other witnesses - a policeman and two cab drivers - who saw and heard a veiled woman with a foreign accent entering the general's house. Bradley, the general's servant, has no doubt it was Mrs. Cordell. She had been to the general's house with her husband several times before, and Bradley recognized her voice and the clothes she wore. And there's the weapon. The *iklwa.* There's no doubt it came from Colonel Cordell's study. He identified it by the date carved on the shaft."

"And you think she's capable of murder," Jeffries said.

"I do, sir," Parsons replied. "She's a woman with an extremely fiery nature, and she made little attempt to conceal it from Harris and me. There's also the information we obtained from Lady Cordelia Arbuthnot, the wife of one of the officers in the Middlesex regiment. She implied that Mrs. Cordell was no better than a courtesan, who seduced the colonel and then decided to set her sights on the general. But perhaps it's only to be expected that Lady Cordelia would say that. Mrs. Cordell is not only younger and prettier than she, she is also the wife of the commanding officer, a role that Lady Cordelia rightfully considers to be hers."

A long plume of smoke drifted up to the ceiling from Jeffries pipe. He sighed wearily.

"I wouldn't be too concerned with what the likes of this Arbuthnot woman has to say, Parsons," he said. "People like her have got nothing better to do with their time than spread malicious rumors about women they don't like, especially if they're younger and prettier. If you were married, young man, you'd understand things like that. It sounds like petty jealousy to me. Just get on and arrest Mrs. Cordell, colonel's lady or not. From what you've said I think she's as guilty as sin, and I could do with some positive news like that reaching the newspapers. It might take some of the heat off me."

"I had that in mind, sir. But I decided to speak with you first, because there's still another angle I'd like to pursue."

"And what is that for Heaven's sake," said Jeffries in exasperation. "It all looks cut and dried to me."

"It's a question of a motive, sir. On the face of it Mrs. Cordell being a jilted lover could indeed be the reason she murdered the general. But before I arrest her I'd like to know more about her background. There's a slim chance she may have some connection with the Fenians. As you probably know a few of them fled to France after the rebellion in Ireland in 1867. It's just possible that she could be one of their French supporters."

Jeffries looked far from convinced.

"That doesn't make any sense to me, Parsons. Nor does it alter the fact that everything points towards her having murdered Latham. Just arrest her. You can sort out the details later."

"As you wish, sir," said Parsons. "But I still think I'll send a telegram to Paris to see if the French police have any information on Mrs. Cordell, or should I say, Madame de Verney. That was her name before she married Cordell. And don't worry about her running away in the meantime. She's as much a prisoner in the barracks as she would be in police custody."

Jeffries began sifting through the pile of reports on his desk. It was clear that, as far as he was concerned, the interview was over. But Parsons had decided otherwise. He had no intention of leaving without discussing the previous day's discoveries.

"Can I ask you about the bombs, sir?"

"By that I assume you mean the two bombs the Fenians planted on the night Sayers was murdered," Jeffries said with a sour expression on his face. "If you've got anything to say about them that's at all relevant to your investigation then get on with it. As you can see I've work to do."

Parsons knew that what he was about to say would not be well received.

"With great respect, sir," he said, "don't you think it's more than a coincidence that these bombs were planted not only on the same night as Lord Sayers was assassinated but also within a few hours of General Latham being murdered? And don't you think that there was something highly unusual about them? I spent yesterday afternoon in Kensington checking the places where the bombs were thrown, and I'm convinced that neither of them had any of the hallmarks of previous Fenian bombs. From what I could see there was no real intention of damaging property or killing anyone. And when has that ever been a Fenian *modus operandi*? In fact, if you were to ask my opinion, I'd say the bombs were intended as no more than a diversion from Lord Sayers murder - and possibly General Latham's."

For a moment Parsons thought that Jeffries was going to have a fit. His faced had turned puce, and his tightly clenched hand shook as he removed his pipe from his mouth.

"What the hell d'you mean by sticking your nose into *my investigation* without my say so, Parsons. You've got work of your own to do. And as far as I can see you're dragging your feet over that. Just get on with what I've told you to do. Arrest that bloody French woman and leave me to worry about the Fenians. And just for your interest, late last week we received positive evidence about the bullet found in Lord Sayers' skull. It was fired from a Webley revolver. A weapon, I need hardly remind you, Parsons, that the Fenians are extremely found of using. Whereas your man, as you keep telling me, was murdered with a bloody native spear!"

Parsons had never before seen Jeffries so angry. There was no saying what he might have done had Parsons pointed out that Webley revolvers were not solely used by Fenians. They were also in common use in the army and the police. But the superintendent was clearly in no mood for further discussion of bombs or pistols. And there was no chance whatsoever of him answering the other question Parsons had intended asking. He would have to use other channels for that.

———————

HARRIS WAS IN the General Office drinking a mug of tea with a few of his colleagues when Parsons beckoned to him from the door.

"A word, Harris," he said. "I've a small task that requires your unique powers of diplomacy. I'd do it myself but I've just upset Jeffries so much by asking him questions about the Sayers' business that if he hears that I've ignored his warning to drop the matter he could well suspend me."

"What do you want me to do, sir?" Harris asked with a smile. He knew how bumptious Parsons could sound at times with his use of long words and Latin phrases. He had often been tempted to mention it to Parsons himself, but as a sergeant he did not feel it was his place. On the other hand, Jeffries was not only Parsons' superior, he was also known to have a short fuse; and in the middle of a high profile investigation that by all accounts was not progressing well, the superintendent was unlikely to have been pleased to receive one of Parsons' helpful suggestions. Especially if Parsons had managed to imply that Jeffries might have overlooked something.

"You remember the paper that was found in Lord Sayers' mouth," said Parsons.

"You mean the report about what was said in Parliament, sir."

"Exactly, Harris. The page from *Hansard*. I want to see it, and I want you to get it for me. Ask one of the other sergeants where it is, and when you have it bring it to my office. But don't for God's sake let anyone know it's for me. Just say something vague like you've never seen a page from *Hansard* before and you're curious to see what one looks like. They'll probably think you're crazy, but what does that matter. They already know that."

———

HARRIS APPEARED IN Parsons office fifteen minutes later with a grin on his face and a buff-colored folder in his hand.

"I don't think you'll learn much from this, sir," he said, handing Parsons the folder. "You'll soon see what I mean."

There was single sheet of heavily stained paper inside the folder. Judging by the number of creases the paper had been folded six times. Enough to make it small enough to fit into Lord Sayers' mouth.

Parsons examined the paper with his magnifying glass.

"You're right, Harris," he said. "I can't read this, what with the dried blood and the creases. But fortunately the most important part is still intact."

"And what's that, sir?" asked Harris.

"The page number and the date," said Parsons. "Although this page may be illegible I'm sure I'll be able to find the relevant copy of *Hansard* in that excellent reference library at the Guildhall. But that will have to wait for a few hours. First I have a telegram to send to Paris, and then you and I are going to Brompton to seek B Division's assistance in arresting Mrs. Cordell."

19

VENETTA CORDELL'S ARREST was not without incident. RSM Whitehead had at first refused to allow Parsons, Harris and the two policeman from the Chelsea station into the barracks. Only when Parsons had demanded to see the commanding officer had Whitehead relented and allowed the quartet to proceed to the Cordell's house.

"I hope you know what you're doing, Inspector Parsons," Cordell had said icily as his wife was led to the awaiting police carriage, "or by God I'll see that Colonel Wilson hears of your incompetence."

Parsons knew that it was no idle threat. It was common knowledge in the Metropolitan Police that Colonel Wilson, the Commissioner, continued to lunch at the Army and Navy club, and thereby maintained an acquaintance with many of the senior army officers in the London district. Doubtless Colonel Cordell, as the commanding officer of a regiment garrisoned in London, was one of them. Whilst not entirely unprecedented, the arrest of a senior army officer's wife on a charge of murder was an unusual enough occurrence for it likely to be a subject for discussion at that venerable institution. And should it later transpire that Parsons, as the arresting officer, had been hasty or erroneous in his actions, doubtless considerable pressure would be exerted upon the Commissioner to see that a blunder of such magnitude did not go unpunished.

For her part, Venetta was anything but cooperative, and continued to protest her innocence as she was taken to the police carriage in a voice that carried far beyond the confines of her house and garden. Such had been the volume and pitch of her shrieks that many of the soldiers on the parade ground had become disorientated, and had taken her loud cries to be their drill instructors' words of command.

Venetta had continued in a similar vein during the journey to Chelsea, whilst she was being booked into the police station, and even when being escorted to her basement cell.

"We'll give her time to cool off before interviewing her," Parsons had told the desk sergeant before taking Harris to a nearby coffee shop and ordering a pot of coffee and two rounds of toast. Harris had settled for tea.

THEY FOUND VENETTA calmer when they returned. The effect of confinement in a dark, damp cell below street level usually had a salutary effect on most prisoners, especially if it was their first experience of custody and they were women from a higher social class like Venetta Cordell.

"I tell you I am innocent, inspector," Venetta said tamely, when the two detectives entered her cell.

"But you don't deny your affair with General Latham or that you were in his house after midnight last Wednesday," said Parsons.

She shook her head wearily.

"*Non,*" she said weakly. "I do not deny that any of that. I visited 'is 'ouse on many occasions. First with my 'usband, and then by myself. But as I 'ave already told you, Maxwell was dead when I arrived. That was why I screamed and ran away."

"When was the last time you saw General Latham alive before last Wednesday?" asked Harris.

Venetta mumbled a few words in French before answering.

"I t'ink it was a Thursday," she said. "*Oui, je suis certain.* It was the Thursday of the week before 'e died."

"And what about the *iklwa* taken from your husband's study? How do you think that found its way to the general's study?"

Venetta shrugged her shoulders.

"*Je ne sais pas,*" she said. "I know nothing of these *iklwas*, as you call them. I know that 'ector 'ad some native weapons in his study. But I never touch them. Never, never, never. Such things disgust me."

"Then if not you, who else do you think may have murdered General Latham?" asked Parsons. "Do you know of anyone else who may have held a grudge against him?"

"I know I was not the first woman to 'ave an affair with Maxwell, inspector," she said. " 'E made no secret of 'is many conquests. There must be many 'usbands who would want to kill 'im if they discovered their wives 'ad been unfaithful."

"Would you care to give me their names?" Parsons asked.

In spite of the circumstances in which she found herself Venetta managed a weak smile.

"Only that of my 'usband," she answered. "Maxwell never told me the names of any of 'is other mistresses. And why should 'e? I never wished to discuss them with 'im."

Then after a short pause she said: "But I do know of one woman who 'ad made advances to Maxwell and been rejected. Per'aps it was she who murdered 'im."

She laughed mockingly.

"And now that I know 'er better I would not be surprised," she said. "Maxwell told me 'ow she 'ad tried to seduce 'im soon after the regiment 'ad returned to England."

Venetta laughed again, this time with greater enjoyment.

"An' Maxwell told 'er she was too ugly. 'E said that 'e did not sleep with ugly women."

"And who was this lady?" asked Parsons.

"Lady Cordelia Arbuthnot, inspector," she said. "If you 'ad met 'er you would know what I mean. Maxwell was right. She is an ugly cow. I remember Maxwell laughing when 'e told me 'ow mad she 'ad looked when 'e said that 'e did not want 'er. She 'ad come to 'is 'ouse and offered 'erself to 'im 'oping that by doing that 'e would make 'er 'usband the colonel."

Venetta laughed until tears appeared in her eyes.

"And did General Latham tell you how she reacted to that?" asked Parsons.

Venetta's dark eyes flashed.

"She said she would kill 'im," Venetta said with an ironic laugh. "And per'aps she did. She 'ad as much opportunity as me. She was at my 'ouse on the night Maxwell was murdered. It was she 'oo told me about Maxwell's engagement to this other woman. Per'aps it was she 'oo killed Maxwell, knowing that it was I 'oo would be blamed."

"WELL, WHAT DO you think of what Mrs. Cordell had to say about Lady Cordelia, Harris?" Parsons asked as he tucked the end of a clean white napkin into his jacket and began his assault on the plate of boiled leg of mutton and caper sauce, mashed turnips and carrots, and boiled potatoes that had just been placed in front of him.

After their interview with Venetta they, or more accurately, Parsons, had decided to lunch at *The Mitre*, a chop house in Sloane Street. When Harris had protested that the cost of the meal was beyond his pocket, Parsons had brushed his protest aside.

"My treat, my dear Harris," he had said enthusiastically. "This case is becoming more interesting by the day. And I think we should celebrate."

Parsons had chosen a pint of Guinness to accompany his meal, Harris a glass of lemonade. How unfortunate it was, thought Parsons as he watched Harris take a sip from his glass, that the sergeant felt unable to enjoy a real drink. It was, he had sadly decided, a case of their very different upbringing. Whereas he had grown up in a household in which his father enjoyed a whisky and water, his mother a glass of sherry, and they had both taken wine with their meals, the less fortunate Harris had been brought up in a neighborhood in the East End of London in which alcohol more often than not brought nothing but misery. Not only the men, but also the women and children became its unfortunate victims. Harris' father-in-law had himself been an alcoholic who had died from excessive drinking. It was no surprise, therefore, to learn that Harris' wife and mother-in-law had become members of the Abstinence Society, and that Harris himself had become a teetotaler.

"I never like to think any woman capable of murder," Harris replied. "Nor will I ever understand why women with the sort of advantages that both Mrs. Cordell and Lady Arbuthnot possessed should ever resort to it. Look at them both. They have the kind of homes that my wife would give her right arm for, husbands with respectable and responsible positions, and as far as we can tell no worries about money. Why should either of them want to forfeit all that by murdering a lecherous old general?"

"Because, Harris, the lecherous old general apparently turned them both down for another woman. And we all know that saying about the fury of Hell and a woman spurned. Just think about it. We have here a classic case of two women hating the same man because, for one reason or another, he had decided he no longer wanted them. In the first instance we have wealthy Cordelia being told by Latham that she is too ugly, and then a beautiful woman like Venetta learning that he no longer wants her because he has found an older woman with money. Are both of these not excellent motives for murder? Perhaps not for the likes of you or me, Harris, but we don't happen to be women."

"You seem to have suddenly made this Lady Cordelia a suspect simply because of what Mrs. Cordell said," interjected Harris. "What proof do we have that she ever attempted to seduce the general or that he turned her down?"

"Because it makes perfect sense, Harris," Parsons said. He took a sip of his stout. "Can't you see how ambitious that woman is. She's desperate for her husband to become a colonel, but because the army has abolished the purchase of commissions she knows that her money can no longer guarantee his promotion. And she knows her husband well enough to realize that if it's left to him she'll remain a major's wife for ever. And that, as far as she's concerned, would be a social disaster. Whereas if she can bring her feminine charms to bear on Latham, a man with a reputation for seducing women who has recently been knighted and promoted to general, she might well persuade him to recommend to the War Office that her husband be made colonel of the Middlesex."

"But that didn't work, sir," said Harris. "Latham not only rejected her, he also ensured that his half-brother became colonel."

"Exactly, Harris. And you can imagine how furious that would make Cordelia. Not only does Latham have the gall to call her ugly to her face, he pours salt on the wound by ensuring that Hector Cordell is made colonel. A man seemingly less qualified than her husband. And now that I've met Lady Cordelia I'm inclined to agree with the general. She is a most unattractive woman."

Parsons wiped his mouth with his napkin.

"But let us move forward in time and try to imagine events as they were a few months after Cordelia's rejection. Not only has Cordell become colonel, he has also married a woman much younger and far more attractive than Cordelia, a woman who effortlessly finds her way into the general's bed almost before the ink on her marriage license is dry."

"How do you think Lady Cordelia knew about that, sir? From what Venetta told us the general and she were very discrete."

"Oh, Harris, how can you be so naive? Women like that know everything that's going on.

You don't mean to tell me that Venetta Cordell went to the general house as often as she did without other people discovering."

Parsons could see that Harris still looked unconvinced.

"Imagine how angry that would make Cordelia feel, Harris, and how much she would want to revenge herself on both Latham and Venetta. And then the perfect opportunity presents itself. Cordelia learns that Latham has become engaged to an older woman with money. At the first opportunity she tells Venetta, knowing that her fiery temperament was likely to goad her into action. And imagine her delight when Venetta immediately takes the bait and goes to the general's house on that very night."

"But Venetta is claiming that Lady Cordelia murdered the general, sir," said Harris, a puzzled expression on his face.

"And I think she may well have done, Harris. Or at least paid someone to do it for her. She has money enough. And if Cordelia was responsible then Venetta has been telling the truth all along. Latham *was* dead when she arrived."

"Don't you think you're making too many assumptions, sir?" said Harris.

"Maybe I am, Harris. And that's where you come in. I want you to recheck the cabbies' stories and that of the policeman who claimed he saw a veiled woman arrive at Latham's house. Especially the timings. Tell them all they'll have to stand up and swear in a court of law that the information they gave us is one hundred per cent accurate. If they know that they may think twice about what they told us. And, if as I now suspect, Lady Cordelia Arbuthnot was involved in the general's murder I want you to find out all you can about her. Where she's been going and who she's been seeing since the general's engagement became public."

"And how do you think I'm going to find that out, sir. She's not likely to tell me."

"Then use your imagination, Harris," Parsons said irritably. "For a start Lady Cordelia has a house full of servants. I'm prepared to bet she's got a coachman. He must know where she goes."

"And what will you be doing in the meantime, sir?" asked Harris despondently.

"This afternoon I'm going to Cheapside to the Guildhall Library," Parsons replied. "And tomorrow I'll be going to General Latham's funeral. There was an announcement about it in this morning's *Times,* and I want to see who attends. Let's meet in the office on Wednesday, the day after tomorrow. That'll give you plenty of time to do what I've asked."

20

THE LONDON GUILDHALL had been the financial powerhouse of the City since the twelfth-century. In those days the Lord Mayor of London had often rivaled the monarch in influence and prestige, and had frequently exceeded him in wealth. Mayor Whittington, whilst entertaining Henry V, had ostentatiously displayed that wealth, much to the great relief of the noble king, by burning the monarch's promissory notes worth sixty thousand pounds on a sandalwood fire and thereby releasing him from the debt.

The Great Fire of 1666 had destroyed much of the medieval city. The fire had consumed thirteen thousand houses, eighty seven parish churches, St. Paul's cathedral, and the Great Hall of the Guildhall; and it had taken many years and the genius of Sir Christopher Wren before the City had risen again. Fifty-one of the majestic churches now dominating the City skyline had been a direct result of the imagination of this great man.

But it was the great white stone entrance of the Guildhall, built by George Dance in 1788, that most impressed itself upon Parsons as he hurried across the wide courtyard. Dance's work had attracted much criticism, his style often being despairingly described as 'Hindoostani Gothic'. It was an expression that much irritated Parsons, and, in his opinion, served only to reflect the ignorance of the building's critics. Anyone with the slightest knowledge of Indian architecture would know that the style reflected in the Guildhall had nothing to do with the Hindus, but was that of the Mughals, the last rulers of India before the British Raj.

In Parson's opinion there was much to admire about the way in which Dance had attempted to merge the medieval style of Europe with that of India. If for no other reason than that it reminded him of his own childhood in Rajasthan.

Inside the Great Hall, Parsons paused to admire the vast timber roof and the monuments of a grateful nation to Pitt, Nelson and Wellington, before paying his own tribute to the large wooden statues of the fierce, bearded giants, Gog and Magog. Their presence in the heart of London had always fascinated him after he had learned that earlier images of these two figures had once been carried in the Lord Mayor's annual procession. Although the reason for that had been lost in the mist of time, if legend was to be believed its origins lay in a link between Britain and ancient Rome.

The daughters of the Roman Emperor Diocletian, led by Alba, the eldest, had murdered their intended spouses, and as punishment had been set adrift on the open sea. Eventually they were washed ashore on a windswept northern island, which they named Albion in honor of their leader. It was a name still associated with Britain. There the women mated with the indigenous demons and gave birth to a race of giants, two of whom were Gog and Magog.

It was somewhat of a stretch of the imagination to link these two mythological giants with the City of London, but, as far as Parsons was concerned, there was every reason to believe that the legend was true. The evidence was plain to see. During and after the Crimean War it had become fashionable for men to wear beards as a gesture of support for the troops, and on any one day the streets of London were filled with smaller, but equally hirsute and wild-looking replicas of Gog and Magog. One of them was even working in the Guildhall library and had answered Parsons' request for a copy of *Hansard* by directing him to the appropriate reference section.

IT HAD ALWAYS been assumed by the police and press alike that the page of *Hansard* thrust into Lord Sayers' mouth at the time of his murder had some bearing on the motive for his death. Parsons had believed that himself. For what other reason would an assassin have made that gesture unless intending to draw attention to the cause he served. And in Sayers' case that cause had been assumed to be the Fenian response to his outspoken and frequent attacks in Parliament upon Government policies supporting Irish Home Rule.

But the actual information contained on the page found in Sayers' mouth did not support that assumption. Admittedly the report contained the details of a speech made by Lord Sayers. But it was not a speech on Ireland. The subject of the speech reported in *Hansard* had been Africa, a continent Lord Sayers had eloquently described as having great commercial opportunities for Britain if she was but willing to take firm and positive action against anyone standing in her path. And by that, Parsons assumed, Sayers was referring to the native tribes and the Boer farmers.

Parsons was intrigued by what he read, as it suggested that he could well have been correct in thinking that, after all, there was a connection between Sayers and Latham. But that connection was not Ireland as he had first imagined. It was Africa. And it was a connection that made the use of an *iklwa* as a murder weapon that much easier to understand.

Regardless of what he had discovered, Parsons knew that the link between Africa and the deaths of Sayers and Latham was still extremely tenuous, and not one he felt prepared to pursue with Superintendent Jeffries until he had more information. Before ever broaching the subject with Jeffries, Parsons knew he would need to learn more about Lord Frederick Sayers and his ambitions in Africa. And there was only one man in London of his acquaintance whom he could turn to for that.

He returned the copy of *Hansard* to its rightful place in the reference section, walked to the Post Office in Queen Victoria Street and sent a telegram to Cheyne Walk.

21

A FEW WEARY blooms clung tenaciously to the standard roses lining the short gravel path to Sir Archibald Prosper's front door. His elegant Georgian house in Cheyne Walk faced directly onto the Thames Embankment, a situation that was something of a mixed blessing for the plants in his front garden. Facing south as it did, the garden had the benefit of whatever sunshine there might be. On the other hand, it was exposed to the river's cool breezes and chilly fogs.

Harding, Sir Archibald's elderly retainer, was delighted to see Parsons.

"I trust Miss Chapman is well, sir," he said as he showed Parsons into the study where the elderly knight of the realm was comfortably seated in a wing-backed chair beside a roaring fire drinking tea and eating buttered crumpets and jam.

"Wonderful to see you again, young man," Sir Archibald said enthusiastically, as he rose to shake Parsons' hand. "Harding, more tea and crumpets for the inspector. The poor young man looks quite famished."

Sir Archibald directed Parsons to the twin chair on the opposite side of the fireplace.

"I imagine you and your colleagues are much involved in the Sayers' business," Sir Archibald said, after the preliminary pleasantries had been completed. "Would I be correct in thinking that your visit today has something to do with that?"

Parsons had first met Sir Archibald some six months prior while investigating the Limehouse murders. Since then he had dined at Cheyne Walk with Louise on a handful of occasions, and was always delighted and flattered to find that Sir Archibald continued to take such an interest in both his private and professional life. It had been Parsons' acquaintance with such an important personage as Sir Archibald, slight though it may have been at the time, that had first persuaded Louise's parents to accept him as a possible suitor, regardless of the fact that he was a mere policeman.

"I'm not actually involved in the Sayers' investigation, sir," Parsons explained. "I've been given the task of finding General Latham's murderer. On the face of it there would seem to be no connection between the two murders. But I believe there is. Superintendent Jeffries, my superior, needless to say, will have nothing to do with this hypothesis, and before confronting him again I need to be quite sure of my ground."

Parsons described the progress of his own investigation, his doubts about the so-called

Fenian bombings, and his recent research at the Guildhall. From his own assiduous reading of the newspapers, Sir Archibald was already aware of much of the background, but he sat patiently with his fingers steepled waiting for the appeal to his wide knowledge of the world and prominent public figures that he was certain had prompted the young detective's visit. It was a situation that pleased him greatly. Even at this relatively late stage in his life, it was comforting to know that his long service as a diplomat could still be of use, especially to the young policeman for whom he felt such a fondness.

"It was only when I discovered that the page from *Hansard* found in Lord Sayers' mouth dealt with a speech about Africa and had nothing to do with Ireland that I became convinced that the two deaths were connected," Parsons explained. "That's why I came to see you. I hoped you might know more about these two men than has appeared in the newspapers. Especially, any ambitions they might have shared. I'd also value your opinion about what is actually going on in South Africa."

"When I received your telegram I imagined that you wanted something of the sort, dear boy," said Sir Archibald. "And so in the time I had available I did a little research of my own."

Sir Archibald reached for the bell-pull at the side of the mantel and tugged it.

"But before then I'll ask Harding to clear the tea tray and bring us some sherry."

He consulted his pocket watch.

"I hope it's not too early for you to imbibe," he said, with a disarming smile that rendered any disagreement impossible.

———————

AFTER CLEARING THE remains of their tea Harding returned with a tray bearing a decanter of fino, the driest of sherries, and two glasses. He placed the tray on a small intricately carved table of Chinese redwood beside Sir Archibald, and before withdrawing turned up the gas in the lamps, drew the curtains, and replenished the fire.

"Your good health, my dear boy," said Sir Archibald, raising his glass, "and to that of your charming young lady."

He clasped his hands over his chest.

"Now where shall I start," he said, with one of his charming patrician smiles. "I suppose I had better begin with a short history lesson. I know how much you enjoy them."

Sir Archibald took a sip of sherry before continuing.

"Let us start with the Sayers' family," he said. "Not too much to report there I'm afraid. The Sayers of Lincolnshire have not been a family of great distinction. The men have mostly been soldiers, a profession not exactly conducive to increasing the wealth of a family. Nor have they married well. The outcome of all this, I regret to say, was that over the years the estate in Lincolnshire became smaller as a result of successive generations of Sayers being obliged to sell off parts of their land in order to make ends meet. But it was Sayers' father, the eleventh Lord Sayers, who finally brought the family to its knees. Perhaps we should be charitable and say that it was the death of his young bride whilst giving birth to his only child that was the cause of his profligacy, because after that tragedy he abandoned all interest in his estate and turned instead to horses and cards. At neither was he successful, and he so bankrupted the estate that rather than face the consequences of his actions he chose to take his own life. And it left his son, the late Lord Frederick, with such a mountain of debts that it necessitated him selling the remainder of the estate."

Sir Archibald paused for another sip of sherry.

"But unlike his father, Lord Frederick was a man with ambition. He immediately took his seat in the House of Lords and embarked upon what turned out to be a promising political career. At first he joined the ranks of Conservative peers, but after only a short time changed his allegiance to the Liberals, no doubt thinking that if a new wind was sweeping through the corridors of power he ought to be riding it. Round about that time he also married, and in his choice of wife managed to avoid the mistakes of the earlier generations of Sayers. They had generally chosen to marry into the penniless families of the local gentry. Lord Frederick Sayers, on the other hand, married the daughter of a rich Lancastrian mill owner."

Sir Archibald chuckled.

"He foresook the old landed gentry for the *nouveau riche*," he said. "A path that many a penniless young aristocrat has been obliged to tread."

He smiled at Parsons.

"So here was Lord Frederick in his mid-twenties with all to play for. He was not only a rising political star, he was also a man with money, or should I say, access to his wife's wealth. By all accounts he was a rousing speaker, and it was doubtless that gift of rhetoric that won him his seat in the Cabinet as Colonial Secretary in the 1880 Liberal Government. But, as I'm sure you know, it was a post he did not hold for long."

Sir Archibald grinned mischievously.

"And it is the reason for that fall from grace that may be of particular interest to you, dear boy," he said. "But first, another glass of sherry."

Sir Archibald filled his guest's glass and held up his own to examine the color of wine by the light from the fire. "It's a particularly fine vintage do you not you think?"

Parsons agreed, hoping that there was nothing in his voice that betrayed his impatience. He had, after all, come to learn more about General Latham and Lord Sayers, and not to discuss the merits of Sir Archibald's sherry.

"Now, where were we?" said Sir Archibald. "Ah, yes. Lord Frederick's meteoric rise and his sudden fall. Quite a simple matter really. You see he began to dabble in affairs that were not part of his remit. And I fear he may have done that for reasons of personal gain. You see, in his privileged position as Colonial Secretary, Sayers could see in which parts of our great empire money was being made. And South Africa was one such place. There were people in South Africa making a great deal of money. One such was Cecil Rhodes. Do you know that name?"

Parsons nodded.

"I've read about him," he said. "Hasn't he made a fortune from diamond mining?"

"Quite right, dear boy," Sir Archibald replied. "But more than that he is one of the more outspoken members of the Cape Colony parliament. An ambitious young man with grandiose schemes for the increasing exploitation of the mineral wealth of Africa and an even greater British presence. From what I've read of his speeches in the English newspapers he makes a very compelling case, and unless I'm mistaken it was the inspiration for much of what Sayers had to say about Africa. Sayers was frequently alluding in Parliament to the necessity of Britain supporting men like Rhodes and for us colonizing as much of Africa as we could before other European powers realized its full potential. And, like Rhodes, he was concerned that native tribes and Boer farmers should not be allowed to stand in our path."

"I know very little about the Boers other than that they are farmers," said Parsons, "and that recently we seem to be having some territorial problems with them."

"I was coming to the Boers, dear boy," replied Sir Archibald. "But first be so kind as to put some more coal on the fire."

"The Boers," he said reflectively, after Parsons had completed his task. "Such hardworking people, and so stubborn and sure of their place in the world."

He smiled at Parsons.

"Not unlike we British," he said. "And rather like us, the Boers do not enjoy surrendering land they feel to be rightfully theirs. And in South Africa I think it's fair to say they have a fair point. You see, the South African Cape was first settled in 1652 by the Dutch East India Company as a resupply point and staging post for Dutch vessels on their way between the Netherlands and the spice islands of the East Indies. By the end of the eighteenth century there were about fifteen thousand settlers at the Cape, for the most part a mixture of Dutch Calvinists, French Huguenots and Germans. They became known as Boers, which is the Dutch word for farmer. In 1795 these Boers tried to establish their own republic at the Cape. You see, the French revolutionary armies had occupied the Dutch Netherlands, and the Boers did not wish to come under French suzerainty. And that is when we British stepped in. Like the Boers we were also fearful that the French would claim that part of southern Africa for themselves, and as a result harass our trade with the East. So we occupied the Boer territory in South Africa, and after finally defeating Napoleon in 1815 claimed it as one of the spoils of our war with France."

Sir Archibald paused to sip at his sherry.

"We never mixed well with these nomadic livestock farmers," he said with a smile. "For a start they practiced a rigid form of Calvinism that was far too extreme for our more delicate Anglican sensibilities. We even took a dislike to their way of speaking, considering their language, Afrikaner, to be a particularly ugly Dutch dialect. For their part, the Boers thoroughly objected to British rule and to the constant wars we fought with the natives on the borders of our territory. They decided we were impossible to live with, and during the eighteen-twenties and eighteen-thirties began trekking north to establish their own republics in the Orange Free State and the Transvaal. At that time we had little interest in places so far inland, but when diamonds were discovered on the border between the Cape Colony and Transvaal, matters changed dramatically. Men like Rhodes made a fortune, and spurred on by the thought that there was even more wealth to be found in the Boer republics, he and other imperial expansionists demanded that we annex their territories, and sought similarly minded politicians in Britain to goad the British government into action. One of these politicians was, of course, Lord Frederick Sayers."

"Was that why Lord Sayers lost his Cabinet post?" Parsons asked.

"Not directly, dear boy," Sir Archibald replied. "But if you are patient I'll come to that.

First let me tell you something about our wars with the natives."

Parsons took this opportunity to recharge his glass and that of Sir Archibald.

"Please continue, Sir Archibald," he said, after poking the fire.

"As you can imagine," Sir Archibald continued, "the indigenous natives, most notably the Xhosa, the Pedi, and the Zulu, objected to we British moving north from the Cape into their tribal lands, and in the late eighteen-seventies fought many fierce battles against us. Although armed with nothing more than their own primitive weapons they often proved more adept at fighting than our own soldiers. The Zulus proved especially troublesome. I'm sure you'll have read of our ignominious defeat at their hands at Isandlwana in 1879, a battle in which a British force of over a thousand was annihilated. Fortunately for the War Office, the severity of that defeat was supplanted in the public's imagination by the rousing action at Rorke's Drift shortly afterwards, when a few dozen of our soldiers bravely held out against thousands of Zulus."

"There aren't many people who haven't heard about Rorke's Drift, sir," said Parsons. "I seem to remember having a few glasses of ale with my colleagues on the day that news reached London."

"As did many others," Sir Archibald replied drily. "From what I read about that night the traffic in central London practically ground to a halt as the revelers thronged the streets."

He took a thoughtful sip of sherry.

"At my age it is far more enjoyable to take a glass by the fireside," he said. "But we are digressing. Let us return to South Africa and our gallant soldiers. Needless to say, the power of modern weapons gradually prevailed and we finally managed to subdue the native tribes and come to an agreement of sorts with each of them as to how we could peaceably occupy their lands as a stepping stone into the Boer republics. I've already mentioned the diamonds and the possibility of other important mineral finds in the Boer republics, but there was also another matter. Imperialists like Rhodes envisaged Britain eventually controlling a wide tranche of land running the whole length of Africa from Cape Colony to Egypt. They planned to build a railway along it and thereby control the commerce of the whole continent. Most people considered it thoroughly impractical, but not the likes of Rhodes and Sayers. They were convinced that such a railway was vital if Britain was to fully exploit the mineral wealth of Africa. Needless to say, they also imagined enriching themselves at the same time."

"I already know something of the war in Transvaal," Parsons explained. "I interviewed several officers in the Middlesex Light Regiment, including Captain Simpson. You may have read about him. He's shortly to be awarded the Victoria Cross for leading a patrol through Zululand in an attempt to outflank the Boers."

"I know of Simpson and the Middlesex," said Sir Archibald. "The very same regiment that was commanded by General Latham, although at the time he was still a colonel. But what you might not know, my dear boy, was that there was a rumor that the instigator of Latham's rather foolish strategy was no other than Lord Frederick Sayers, and that the purpose of this patrol was not to outflank the Boers, but to carry out a survey of land where it was rumored gold had been discovered. However, what I'm telling you may be no more than the sort of idle gossip one hears at the club. If you want to know the real truth you should talk to a journalist at the *Daily Telegraph* called Hardcastle. He was accompanying the army at the time, and from what I hear, was prevented by the authorities from reporting the full facts."

"Why was that, Sir Archibald?" Parsons asked indignantly. "Surely the public had a right to know about such things."

"The scandal, my boy," said Sir Archibald. "Think of the scandal. The Army's rather inadequate performance in South Africa has been bad enough, but if it was ever made public that one of their senior officers was colluding about the possible discovery of mineral deposits with a Cabinet Minister who had absolutely no jurisdiction in military matters, there would have been an uproar. Naturally when the Prime Minister was appraised of the truth he had no option but to ask Lord Frederick to resign from the Cabinet."

"And do you think it possible that Simpson was recommended for his award to pre-empt any criticism of Latham's tactics?"

"I think that there is every chance that was indeed the case," Sir Archibald replied. "And what is more I think that Latham's subsequent promotion and knighthood was a direct result of a promise Sayers had made whilst he was in power. It may have suited the Government to honor that promise in order to ensure Latham's silence, but Latham was nevertheless made to pay. As far as most senior figures in the military and politics were concerned his appointment as senior military commander in Ireland was the end of the line for him. He would never again be allowed the freedom to mishandle troops in the field."

Sir Archibald sipped his sherry thoughtfully.

"There is another connection between Sayers and Latham," he said, "and much to my surprise the newspapers have failed to unearth it. But that may be because Latham's wife died many years ago."

"Latham's wife!" said Parsons in amazement. "What, for heaven's sake does she have to do with all this?"

"Very little directly, poor soul," Sir Archibald replied, "except that she was the youngest daughter of Zachariah Broadstone and sister to Vespasia, the lady who later became Lady Sayers. You see, it is not widely known that Lord Frederick Sayers and General Latham were brothers-in-law. Now, how much that influenced the decision of General Latham to fall into line with Lord Sayers' ambitions is not for me to say. But perhaps Lady Sayers herself may be able to help you."

Sir Archibald rose from his seat and selected a volume from amongst the many crammed into the bookshelves on either side of his fireplace.

"Let me see if *Burke's Peerage* can be of assistance," he said, flicking through the leather-bound book until he reached the relevant page.

"Ah, yes," he said in a satisfied tone. "It's just as I imagined. Although I believe he was living in Lambeth at the time of his death, the late Lord Sayers chose to have his wife's properties in London and Lancashire listed as his principal addresses, alongside those of the House of Lords and the Reform Club. Regardless of where one actually lives, dear boy, one's image is always best promoted if one can provide a good address for the records."

"As I understand it Lady Sayers lives in Lancashire," Parsons said.

"Indeed she does, dear boy. To be precise she lives at Broadacre Hall, near Manchester," Sir Archibald replied. "As you may know it was only within the last few days that she buried her husband. Perhaps if you were to call upon her she may choose to tell you more about her sister's marriage and the relationship between her late husband and General Sir Maxwell Latham."

22

Manchester, Tuesday, 28th October

MANCHESTER'S FIRST COTTON mill was built in 1780 by Richard Arkwright. It was an invention that heralded the Industrial Revolution, and led to Britain becoming the foremost economic power in the world. By the middle of the nineteenth century there were a hundred cotton mills operating in the city. They brought untold wealth to a new industrial middle class of manufacturers and entrepreneurs, and abject misery to the thousands who labored for a pittance in these new factories and dwelt in abject misery in some of the worst slums in Europe.

It was the cotton mills that had made Zachariah Broadstone's fortune and had enabled him to build an ostentatious mansion in fifteen acres of prime countryside to the north of Manchester in keeping with his reputation as being one of the richest men in Lancashire. This Gothic manor, with its magnificent hall of English oak rivaling that of a medieval baron, was crammed from top to bottom with costly and elaborate furnishings to match those of any other member of the *nouveau riche*. Broadacre Hall, as he named it, was close enough to the city that his coach could take him to any of his mills in less than forty-five minutes, but far enough away from their tall chimneys to be spared the stifling and malevolent emissions that frequently blocked the sun and hid the stars.

But the great house and his wealth brought Zachariah little joy. His delicate and sickly wife was never comfortable in such lavish surroundings and had no heart for entertaining on the scale that Zachariah had planned for the purpose of impressing others in the county. Especially those whose money was older than his and whose titles more distinguished. Weakened by the frequent miscarriages that had followed the birth of her first daughter, Vespasia, Mrs. Broadstone had died within five years of moving to Broadacre Hall, during the long and exhausting delivery of Claudia, her second.

The lack of a son and heir to his cotton empire was a great blow to Zachariah. For all her intelligence and willingness to learn he chose not to involve Vespasia in his business affairs, especially after she had begun to lecture him about the unsatisfactory working and living conditions of his workers. In consequence it was with some satisfaction that he accepted an offer for her hand from a member of the landed aristocracy. Penniless though Lord Frederick Sayers might be, his ancestry was sufficiently long and distinguished for it to satisfy a prospective father-in-law whose main aim in his declining years was to achieve social recognition beyond the narrow world of industrial Manchester. Sayer's seat in the House of Lords and his active involvement in politics was as much as Zachariah could hope for in a son-in-law. He was visibly disappointed by the young politician's abrupt change of allegiance from Zachariah's own party, the Conservatives, to the more reform-minded Liberals, and sadly did not live to see that decision vindicated by his son-in-law becoming a Cabinet minister.

The marriage of his youngest daughter was less to Zachariah's liking. He had always regarded young men who chose to become army officers as indolent and unproductive, and was less than pleased when Claudia returned home from a rare visit to London with the unwelcome news that she intended marrying a young officer, especially when Zachariah learned that Captain Maxwell Latham possessed little money and had no family worth speaking of. So he was as surprised as anybody to find that upon meeting Latham he found something to like about the man, recognizing in him a ruthless ambition not unlike his own. As a result Zachariah not only gave a reluctant blessing to the marriage but also consented to Claudia's wish to purchase her future husband's promotion to major as an engagement present.

Zachariah spent the declining years of his life alone. Both daughters had moved to London to be near their husbands and rarely visited Manchester, so that if he was ever aware that neither were truly happy in their marriages he never spoke of it, his sole hope being that one or the other would provide him with a grandson who might one day inherit the Broadstone empire. It was not to be. The closest he came to realizing that dream was when Claudia gave birth to a premature baby boy. But neither the mother nor child survived.

———————

PARSONS HAD RISEN that morning before five, and had caught the six-ten train for Manchester, arriving at the London Road station at five minutes past eleven. He had dozed for most of the journey, waking only when the train reached its destination and he had his first sight of the rows of tall factory chimneys belching black smoke towards a sky of unremitting gloom.

The previous evening he had sent a telegram to Lady Sayers hoping that it would be convenient to call upon her. He had explained that he was a Scotland Yard detective investigating her husband's murder, and that he was in possession of some new evidence that he wished to discuss with her. He had also sent one to Scotland Yard informing Harris of this last minute change of plan. He had not explained where he was going lest Jeffries question Harris as to his whereabouts. He had simply said that he would meet Harris at Scotland Yard on Wednesday afternoon. In the meantime Harris should attend General Latham's funeral in his place before carrying out the instructions Parsons had previously given him.

Parsons had sent a third telegram to Thomas Mann, his long-suffering whist partner, apologizing yet again for failing to meet him at the Westminster Club for their regular Tuesday evening game. It was fortunately not the night of the club's monthly competition, but Parsons nevertheless knew how much Mann was irritated by these last minute changes in plan. Mann rarely had cause to miss their Tuesday appointment, his duties as a schoolmaster at Westminster School being of a far more predictable nature than those of Parsons. In consequence he had little sympathy whenever Parsons excused his frequent absences by claiming that his own profession did not always follow a routine pattern. Parsons had wondered as he had handed the telegrams to the post office clerk, how Louise would have responded. He suspected that her reaction might be not unlike that of Mann's. It was yet another reason, he decided, that should they ever become engaged, that their engagement should be a lengthy one.

———————

LADY VESPASIA SAYERS did not look at all like Parsons' idea of a titled lady. Unlike other women of her class she did not choose to rely upon tight corseting to mold her body into the sought-after hourglass figure. Instead she allowed her clothes to flow loosely around her tall angular frame. In keeping with her recent widowhood she was dressed in mourning, a blouse of black silk with puffed sleeves, a matching skirt, and a black ribbon fastening a full head of loose curls. Had Parsons been asked to describe the color of her hair he would have said that it lay somewhere between that of the sky at sunset and a decent glass of burgundy; but whereas most women would have chosen to accentuate such an unusual and vivid color by allowing it to grow, Vespasia had chosen instead to have her naturally curly hair cut short. Such a decision, Parsons considered, served only to emphasize the two large, emerald colored eyes, the fine straight nose, and the thin lips that suggested she was a woman who did not suffer fools gladly.

She received Parsons with utmost civility in a spacious south-facing drawing room, and offered him a seat in an easy chair near hers from where they could both admire the pristine flower beds and the lush green lawns that were expansive enough to accommodate several cricket fields. Until coffee arrived they made polite and inconsequential conversation about his journey and the weather.

"Well, inspector," she said, in a low voice that still bore traces of her Lancastrian roots. "What new information do you seek from me that I haven't already provided. A colleague of yours from Scotland Yard has already visited me."

"First let me apologize for arriving so soon after your husband's funeral, your ladyship," said Parsons. "It must be a distressing time for you, and had it been possible I would've delayed my visit until a later date."

"The funeral was a quiet affair, inspector," Vespasia replied. "I had no wish to allow myself to be enmeshed in the sort of charade that would have accompanied Frederick's funeral had it been held in London, with scores of politicians and other sanctimonious members of the Establishment making token appearances and offering meaningless words of sympathy. Instead I brought my husband's body here and buried him in our local parish cemetery with my father and my sister. There was really nowhere else for him to go."

Her green eyes challenged Parsons to deny that her decision had been anything but the correct one.

"And please refrain from calling me 'your ladyship'," she said. "I found it difficult to accept being called that while Frederick was alive. Now that he is dead I prefer to be the same as everyone else around here."

For the first time since his arrival she smiled, and the emeralds in her eyes sparkled.

"You may call me Vespasia or Mrs. Sayers," she said. "Whichever you are most comfortable with."

Parsons placed his empty cup on the small occasional table beside his chair. With such a plainly spoken woman it might suit his purpose better if he were completely honest about his visit.

"I have been less than truthful to you about the real purpose of my visit, Mrs. Sayers," he said.

"I am not directly involved in the investigation of your husband's murder as I claimed. I am instead investigating another. That of General Sir Maxwell Latham. But until yesterday I had no idea that the general was once your brother-in-law."

"I cannot deny that, inspector," she said, her voice suddenly cooling. "A fact is a fact. But if I was given the choice I would never wish it to be known that I was ever connected with that selfish brute in any way!"

Surprised by the intensity of her words Parsons decided to proceed with caution. He had come a long way to interview Vespasia Sayers and taken a considerable risk in deceiving her about his true involvement in the investigation of her husband's murder. It would be galling to be asked to leave before he had the chance to learn anything.

"I have no wish to upset you by recalling unhappy memories," he said solicitously. "But if it were at all possible I would like you to tell me what you feel able about your sister's marriage. I can see that you find the subject distressing, and I quite understand why, as only yesterday I learned that your sister died in childbirth."

"You are well informed, inspector," Vespasia said coldly. She laid her cup to one side and clasped her hands together. "As you say, my sister died whilst giving birth to a son. But she also died of a broken heart. You see, long before she died she had confided in me that the handsome young officer who had paid court to her so gallantly had only married her for her prospects. But what is so unusual about that, you might ask. Many men do that, and many women are willing victims. When I married my own husband I suspect his motives were no different than Latham's. Both my husband and Latham received handsome allowances from my father while he lived, and both knew that upon his death their wives would inherit a fortune. But Latham was very different from Frederick. Once assured of a generous income Latham continued with his pursuit of women. As far as I know, Frederick did not, or if he did, he was more discrete. Latham, on the other hand, made little attempt to hide his affairs, and because my sister loved him dearly it broke her heart."

She turned to Parsons with a look of abject disgust.

"Latham was even with another woman on the night my sister died," she said bitterly. "What sort of man would behave like that! When I discovered that, I made sure that Latham would never receive another penny of my father's money!"

"From what I've learned about General Latham it appears he has changed very little since then, Mrs. Sayers," Parsons said. "In fact prior to his death he was having a relationship with his half-brother's wife, whilst at the same time becoming engaged to a wealthy widow."

"That doesn't surprise me in the least," said Vespasia. "But if you know this much about Maxwell why are you here?"

Parsons declined the offer of a second cup of coffee and waited until Vespasia had poured one for herself.

"Because I am interested in the relationship between General Latham and your husband," he said. "Although my superior does not agree with me, I am convinced that there is a link between these two murders. At first I thought the connection was Ireland. Your husband was, after all, an outspoken critic of the Government's proposals to allow the Irish to govern themselves and General Latham was on the point of being sent there as military commander. But now I'm not so sure. I believe that the connection may have been Africa."

"And what makes you think that, inspector?" she asked, her eyes bright with interest.

"I would rather not go into the details, Mrs. Sayers," Parsons explained, "but suffice to say I think both men were hoping to make a great deal of money from gold or diamonds in that part of southern Africa occupied by the Boers, and they took advantage of war in the Transvaal to pursue that objective."

"I'm afraid to say that sounds just like my husband," she said. "And that scoundrel Latham. It would also explain something Frederick said to me when I last saw him about making his own fortune. You see he had never really accepted the idea of relying upon my money. I don't think it was simply a matter of honor, I think it was more a question of him having a poor opinion about the source of my family's wealth. He thought our money was tainted. In his opinion money should come from the ownership of land, and not be soiled by the wheels of industry. From the start of our marriage he let it be known that if the opportunity ever presented itself that he would make money of his own. But from what you say the money he planned to make would be no different from mine. As I understand it the gold and diamonds of this world are extracted from the earth by sweated labor. But perhaps Frederick found it easier to accept money from that source, knowing that the sweat would be on the backs of black workers."

"When did your husband tell you of these hopes of his, Mrs. Sayers?"

"Not long after he became Colonial Secretary," she said. "I had left London by then. My father had died and I took the chance of moving back here where people don't walk around with their noses in the air and talk constantly of politics."

"Did your husband ever say how he hoped to make his fortune, or whether he had any contact with Maxwell Latham?"

"I've no idea whether he and Latham ever saw one another. Frederick knew better than to ever mention his name in my presence. But I do remember him telling me to keep my eye on the price of shares in certain mining companies in Africa. I didn't take his advice and I really don't know why he bothered to tell me. He knew I'd never taken an interest in anything to do with the Stock Exchange."

"Your husband and General Latham were both ambitious men," Parsons said. "That in itself doesn't make them unusual or necessarily make anyone want to kill them. Can you think of anyone who might have wanted to do that?"

"There you have me at a loss, inspector," she said. "In the case of Latham I would think you should be looking for a cuckolded husband. But as far as Frederick is concerned I really have no idea. Perhaps your superintendent is right after all, and there really is no connection between the two murders. But if you are thinking for any reason that it was I who had a hand in either murder let me hasten to assure you of my innocence. My sister died many years ago, and although I have never forgiven Latham for what he did to her, the passage of time has tempered the bitterness of my feelings towards him. And although I was estranged from my husband I never disliked him enough to want to kill him. Whatever reason did I have? And as it happens on the night that both men died I was at a meeting of the Women's Franchise League in Manchester. There are dozens of women who can vouch for that."

23

A HEAVY DOWNPOUR ALL but drowned the mournful strains of Handel's Dead March from *Saul* as the band of the Middlesex Light Regiment preceded the gun carriage bearing General Sir Maxwell Latham's coffin into Brompton Cemetery. In spite of the rain a small crowd of curious bystanders had gathered beside the Richmond Gate attracted by the sound of the solemn music and the sight of the coffin draped in a red, white and blue Union flag, the six black horses with their nodding black plumes and glistening coats, and the squad of redcoated soldiers marching in slow time.

From an elevated and sheltered vantage point under a chestnut tree Harris watched the cortege approach the silent group of mourners huddled under large, black umbrellas on one side side of the newly dug grave. As far as he could tell the majority of the men were army officers from the Middlesex regiment. There was a sprinkling of older men, possibly former comrades of Latham or senior officers from the War Office, each with a chest full of medals and the badges of their elevated rank emblazoned proudly on their epaulettes. In contrast, the women were indistinguishable from one another, each of them dressed in heavy mourning with their faces hidden beneath thick black veils.

RSM Whitehead stood rigidly to attention on the opposite side of the grave at the end of a line of six soldiers, all of them seemingly oblivious to the rain soaking their uniforms and spilling off their helmets onto their faces and down the back of their necks. The portly figure of the vicar of Brompton Church in his long, wind-swept surplice appeared far less phlegmatic. Clutching an umbrella in one hand and a bible in the other, his was the one face reflecting the true discomfort of the occasion.

The hearse moved slowly towards Latham's final resting place, the rasping of the horses' hooves and the soldiers' boots on the gravel path accompanying the doleful notes of trombones, tubas and muffled drums. Then at a sharp, shrill word of command from Whitehead the procession came to a halt, and a pregnant silence, broken only by the shuffling of the horses' hooves, settled like a shroud. During those few seconds it seemed to Harris that he, like everyone else, was holding his breath in anticipation of what was to follow.

At a second word of command from the RSM, six soldiers marched forward from behind the gun carriage, hoisted the coffin onto their shoulders, carried it to the side of the grave, and laid it reverently on two trestles. There was a further brief silence, the vicar delivered a final wailing benediction, a volley of shots was fired by the soldiers at the graveside, and the band played *Abide with Me* and the national anthem. Then the flag was removed from the coffin and General Sir Maxwell Latham was gently laid to rest.

It was a signal for the mourners to begin drifting away, the men escorting their ladies to the waiting carriages, and the more curious members of the public who had followed the cortege into the cemetery making their way home. Only then did the RSM move from his position of attention and calmly begin supervising the departure of the band, the gun carriage, and the soldiers.

Harris had been unsure of what exactly had been expected from his presence. When Parsons had discussed the funeral the day before it had been understood that they would both attend. But Parsons had disappeared without leaving Harris with any clear instructions. He had dutifully taken note of what had taken place, and had made a list of any of the mourners he recognized. There were few enough of those. Apart from the RSM there was only Colonel Cordell and the three officers he and Parsons had previously interviewed: Arbuthnot, Holland and Simpson. And with the women it was nigh impossible to distinguish one from another. They were all dressed in mourning and their faces were hidden behind thick black veils. Harris did notice one woman with a black cane who had some difficulty when she walked. Cordell had spoken to her for a few minutes, but

Harris was too far away to hear what was said. Not for the first time it crossed his mind that were it not for Venetta Cordell's distinctive accent and her admission to being in General Latham's house, there was no way that anyone could ever have been certain that she had been present on the night he was murdered.

Harris remained under the tree waiting for the cemetery to clear before embarking upon the other tasks that Parsons had left him. He was on the point of leaving when one of the soldiers approached him and saluted.

"RSM's compliments, sir," he said. "Mr. Whitehead would like you to join him in the Sergeants' Mess for a drink."

Harris' first inclination had been to refuse. He had more important things to do, and did not imagine that he would feel at ease drinking in the Sergeants' Mess. Especially in his wet clothes. But then he changed his mind. Parsons always maintained that a good detective made the most of chance encounters and unexpected invitations. "You never know where they might lead, Harris," he had said on frequent occasions.

ALTHOUGH THE DISPLAY of military memorabilia in the entrance hall of the Sergeants' Mess was less ostentatious than that in the Officers' Mess, as far as Harris was concerned there were enough sabres, lances, flags and guidons to convince any visitor of the nature of the establishment he had entered. It had taken him a little time to persuade a suspicious mess servant that he had indeed been invited to the Mess by the RSM, but eventually he was led through a raucous crowd of men with three gold stripes on the arms of their red jackets to that part of the long bar where Whitehead was holding court. As far as he could see there were no other civilians present, and Harris felt distinctly uncomfortable in his wet suit.

The noise was deafening, the air thick with the smoke of pipes and cigarettes, and, much to Harris' dismay there was an overpowering smell of alcohol. But it was evident even to his jaundiced eyes that the sergeants of the Middlesex Light Regiment were enjoying themselves. Whatever they might really think about their former commanding officer they were not going to forego the opportunity of making themselves thoroughly drunk in his honor.

"So glad you could join us to drink the general's health, Sergeant Harris," said Whitehead, a tumbler of brandy grasped firmly in his hand. He had changed into a dry uniform, and though he made an effort to hide it, Harris detected the expression of smug superiority on the RSM's face as he scrutinized Harris' appearance.

"I believe that inspector of yours wanted this." Whitehead handed Harris a folded sheet of paper. "It's a list of the people who have a key to the back gate. I don't think you'll find any names there you wouldn't expect."

Much to Harris' surprise Whitehead nudged his arm and winked.

"I'm glad that inspector of yours didn't come to the funeral. I wouldn't have felt comfortable inviting him here. As far as I can see he comes from a similarly privileged background to that of the young officers in this regiment. But you're different. You're one of us."

The RSM gave Harris a hearty slap on the back.

"Now what's your poison?" he said.

"A glass of lemonade would be fine, Mr. Whitehead," Harris replied. "I never touch alcohol."

At a nod from Whitehead the two sergeants with whom he had been speaking when Harris arrived moved away, a facetious grin on each of their faces.

"I see the Temperance Society's arrived, sir," said one. "I'm going before I'm asked to sign the pledge!"

"Don't mind them, sergeant," said Whitehead, who seemed equally surprised by Harris' request. "The Sergeants' Mess is never known for its good manners. More's the pity. But what can you expect. Most of these men started off in life much like me. They come from the slums and back streets of this great country, and if any of them had parents that loved them they were luckier than most."

Harris had always known that the army recruited from the dregs of society. There had been enough drunken soldiers in the East End of

London for him to have seen the full extent of their depravities. He had assumed that with promotion and responsibility that that type of behavior would have mellowed. But from the raucous voices and coarse language around him, he could see that he was mistaken.

As Whitehead turned to the bar to order the lemonade Harris was able to take his first close look at him. Without his helmet, silver-topped cane, and parade ground manner the RSM appeared a very different person. He was far shorter than Harris remembered, in fact he was one of the smallest men in the room, scarcely taller than Harris himself. Whitehead was also clean shaven, unlike most other men in the room, who chose to accentuate their gender and masculinity with an a generous display of facial growth. But the RSM was no weakling, of that Harris was sure. Beneath the immaculate red jacket Harris detected a strong, wiry frame.

"So how was it *you* came to join the army, Mr. Whitehead?" Harris asked, and listened with growing interest to the story of the RSM's wretched childhood and adolescence and his choice of the army as a way of improving himself and seeing the world.

"I must congratulate you on your obvious success," Harris said, after Whitehead had concluded. "Even from what little I know about the army it's obviously no mean achievement to become RSM."

"Ah, but I haven't finished yet, sergeant," said Whitehead lowering his head towards Harris and tapping the side of his nose confidentially with his index finger. "I want to be over there."

He nodded his head in the direction of the Officers' Mess.

"I've more military experience than any of those faint-hearted, pussyfooting dilettantes," he said in a low voice, "and I'm a better man than any of 'em. They might have the advantage of an expensive education, but by God I know more about life."

Harris was beginning to think that the brandy was loosening Whitehead's tongue. In normal circumstance he could not imagine the RSM speaking so disrespectfully about the officers in his regiment.

"But more than anything I want to command this regiment," said Whitehead, poking Harris in the ribs with his elbow before taking another long swill of brandy. "If Plumb can make it to major, then why shouldn't I become a colonel!"

The look in Whitehead's steely blue eyes had grown more intense. Harris began to feel uncomfortable, especially whenever Whitehead leaned towards him and he smelt the alcohol on his breath. Together with the noise and the tobacco smoke it was beginning to make him feel nauseous. But there was one question he wanted to ask before he left.

"Were you here when the Fenians bombed the barracks, sir?" he asked.

For a moment the RSM seemed unsure of an answer. He swayed a little and his eyes appeared to lose their focus, confirming Harris' certainty about him becoming inebriated.

"As a matter of fact I wasn't," he slurred. "I was in a pub with one of my colleagues. Why do you ask?"

"Oh, just my curiosity," said Harris. "I don't know much about what actually happened other than what I've read in the papers. And that was little enough. But I didn't notice signs of any damage when I was here before."

"That's because there was little to speak of. If you ask me it was a rather pathetic attempt. It wasn't until I arrived back in barracks later that evening and checked the guard commander's report that I knew anything had happened."

"So you don't think there was any connection between the bomb and General Latham's murder?"

Whitehead threw back his head and laughed loudly, attracting the attention of several of the men standing nearby.

"You can't be serious, sergeant," he said.

Whitehead leant forward until their noses were almost touching and Harris could smell his stale breath.

"We all know what that was about," Whitehead said, once more tapping the side of his nose and winking. "The general was a fine man, but he was always one for the ladies. Especially if they were young and pretty and spoke with a French accent."

The strong smell of the brandy on Whitehead's breath was becoming more than

Harris could bear, and he knew that if he stayed in the room any longer he might disgrace himself and be sick.

"You'll have to excuse me, Mr. Whitehead," he said hurriedly. "But I have other things to attend to today. Thank you for your hospitality."

And before the RSM could stop him Harris had wriggled through the crowded room and had made good his escape.

———————

IN CONTRAST TO the exuberant mood in the Sergeants' Mess, that in the anteroom of the Officers' Mess was as somber and subdued as the portraits of the Queen and the late Prince Albert hanging over the fireplace. In spite of his German ancestry the regiment had been proud to have formerly had the prince as its colonel-in-chief, and at his death had been disappointed when that honor had been bestowed upon one of her majesty's younger children. They had been hoping that the Prince of Wales himself would have succeeded his father, the Prince of Wales being especially popular in military circles for his interest in field sports and his outgoing personality.

In view of the fact that the regiment was mourning the loss of one of its most distinguished sons, the solemn mood was understandable. The presence of Lady Cordelia Arbuthnot and other equally distinguished wives of senior officers from the War Office had also served to dampen the usual boisterous spirits of the younger officers.

In normal circumstances the occasion would have been one for reminiscences about the late General Latham's gallantry and his illustrious career. But this was not proving to be such an occasion. Instead a subject that had hitherto been only the subject of whispered conversations in withdrawing rooms or in the more remote corners of the Mess was now being given free rein. General Latham's soldierly qualities had become secondary to his reputation as a philanderer, and the scandalous fact that he had stooped so low as to seduce the wife of his half-brother, the man who had succeeded the general as the regiment's commanding officer. And if that were not outrageous enough, Venetta Cordell, whom most in the room were inclined to regard more as a brazen vixen than an innocent victim, had been arrested for the general's murder. And if the rumors were to be believed, the likely motive for this murder was Latham's recent, almost clandestine, engagement to an Irish heiress that scarcely anyone had ever heard of. It was altogether a disgraceful situation, and one without precedence in the annals of the illustrious regiment.

There was little sympathy for Cordell. The general opinion of him shared by the senior officers from the War Office and even those of his own regiment was anything but flattering. It seemed scarcely believable that a man in his position should have been foolish enough to have chosen such an unsuitable wife, and have then allowed himself to be cuckolded by his own brother. Such a state of affairs had made the regiment and its commanding officer a laughing stock.

The feelings of the ladies were more ambivalent. There were those who said that it should have been obvious to Cordell from the start, as in retrospect it had been to them, that Venetta was no more than an adventuress. A few had some sympathy for him and were even prepared to admire him for putting on a brave face by attending the funeral and coming to the Mess. But there were others who were far less sympathetic and said that he had little choice. And among that group there were those, among whom Lady Cordelia was prominent, who said that Cordell was a pathetic creature with unnatural tendencies. One lady had even ventured to say that he wore a corset.

Lady Cordelia had gone as far as to actually snub Cordell when he had attempted to speak with her, sweeping past him without as much as acknowledging his presence to a corner of the room where she had become deeply engaged in conversation with a young officer with a broken nose, who had recently become the Army heavyweight boxing champion. She had decided on a previous visit to the Mess that the broad-shouldered young man had distinct possibilities, and in her dreams had fondly imagined her coachman and the young officer wrestling naked for her honor before finally deciding to jointly bed her. It was unlikely ever to occur, she mused, as she smiled coquettishly into the young officer's dark eyes, but one could always dream. After all, her money had been able to purchase most things she had ever wanted in life. It had been a matter of great regret that it had not purchased her husband's promotion, but even that, she felt might now be within her grasp.

Cordell had retreated into another corner of the anteroom, embarrassed and humiliated by Lady Cordelia's rebuff, where he was joined almost immediately by a suitably commiserative Major Holland.

"I saw what happened, colonel," he said. "Everyone knows that woman's behavior is disgraceful. It's just unfortunate that Arbuthnot is incapable of exerting any sort of control over her. But what else can you expect from Charles? Even his soldiers have little that's good to say about him."

"Enough of that, Mark," said Cordell. "I'm not in the mood for your sort of spiteful remarks. I just want to get this bloody thing over and done with. Then I want to go home. This isn't easy, you know. Here we are allegedly mourning the death of my half-brother, and most of these people are instead talking about Venetta and me."

"I'm sure the police have made a terrible mistake, sir," Holland said ingratiatingly. "That foolish young inspector doesn't know what he's doing. Everyone knows that Venetta could never have murdered the general."

Cordell swung on Holland.

"For God's sake, Major Holland," he said angrily. "Can't you leave me alone. I don't want to hear anything more from you about Maxwell or my wife."

Audley Simpson had also noticed Lady Cordelia's sleight and Cordell's subsequent animated conversation with Holland. He had been drinking steadily since breakfast, and had instructed the waiters bringing the silver salvers of sherry to the mourners that they should ensure that there was always a glass of whiskey on each of their trays.

Grabbing a fresh tumbler from a passing waiter he shouldered his way rudely through a huddle of whispering women and headed straight towards his commanding officer.

"Don't take any notice of any of them, Hector," he said in a voice loud enough to silence the conversation of those nearby. His voice was heavy with emotion, and there were tears in his eyes as he attempted to place an arm around Cordell's shoulders.

"When you met that woman I told you that I'd always be here. You know that, Hector, don't you. Well, she's gone now. It's just you and me again. Just like it was in Africa."

Cordell backed away from Simpson in horror. But Simpson was too drunk to notice the expression on the colonel's face.

Holland and those around were horrified by what they had witnessed. Simpson was not only disgustingly drunk in the presence of ladies, he had committed a cardinal sin for a young officer by behaving in public in such an inappropriate fashion with his commanding officer. Holland attempted to defuse the situation by grabbing Simpson's arm and pulling him away. But Cordell pre-empted him, his initial shock at Simpson's unexpected outburst giving way to fury.

"Get out of my sight, Captain Simpson," Cordell shouted in a shrill voice bordering on hysteria.

He paused, as though struggling to find the right words. And when he finally spoke his bitter words of condemnation echoed around the now-silent room.

"I wish to God we'd never recommended you for that medal," he said. "God knows you never deserved it."

24

AFTER DRIVING THE Arbuthnots back from the Officers' Mess, Cooper decided to take the evening off. Unlike other servants in the household he was free to come and go as he chose in the evenings, provided his services were no longer required. It was seldom that they were. More often than not Major Arbuthnot spent his evenings in Mayfair at his club, and when he went he either walked or took a cab. If anyone was to call upon Cooper it would be Lady Cordelia, although the services she required her coachman to perform were generally in the afternoons. Consequently, provided the horses and carriages were ready for the next day there was little reason for Cooper to remain at Eaton Square unless he chose. And this evening he chose to go out. If Lady Cordelia wanted him she would have to do without.

The Cruelty to Animals Act of 1835 had been intended to put an end to the brutal blood sports that had so delighted Londoners in Hogarth's day.

Bearbaiting, bull-baiting and dogfighting had become illegal. But regardless of the Act there were still many places in London where it was still possible to see dogs killing rats, or even to watch one dog set upon another. These cruel pursuits were often held in the most unlikely places, like the small terraced house to which Cooper was heading that was situated in a dark back street just north of Wandsworth Road, less than two miles from the elegant houses in Eaton Square.

Cooper's brisk infantryman's stride covered the distance in less than half an hour, and by nine o'clock he was one of a crowd of fifty excited aficionados crammed into one of two tiny bedrooms in the house of the most notorious dog-trainer south of the Thames. Every window had been boarded up, and the policeman on duty in that area had been paid a few pounds to ensure that he kept well away. Even so there was strict security on the front door. Regardless of a person's wealth or position, only those faces that were recognized were admitted. It was a motley cross section of society, ranging from lower working class men like Cooper to members of the aristocracy. They had little in common other than a lust for blood and the desire to bet on the prowess with which one animal could kill another.

Two dim gas lamps provided barely enough light for those at the back of the excited crowd to see inside the circular wire enclosure in the center of the room. Measuring only six feet in diameter this enclosure served as the 'pit' in which terriers and rats met in mortal combat. A wire cage containing rats was connected to the 'pit', and from it twelve rats at a time were prodded into the 'pit' to be set upon and eventually killed by a terrier. The noise inside the small room was deafening, a hideous blend of shrieking rats, yelping dogs, and sweating men and women howling for blood.

Not everyone had come solely to witness a blood spectacle. Some were there to admire the dexterity and speed with which the dogs despatched the rats. Most of these were owners and trainers of the terriers, hoping to make a profitable sale at the end of the evening. A strong and agile ratter would always command a good price. But for the majority as much as the bloodletting it was the fever of betting, and during the course of the evening large sums would be wagered on the time it took for each dog to slaughter its allotment of rats.

It was an especially lucrative evening for the owner of the house. Apart from the admission fee, he received a ten per cent commission on all bets placed, and a five per cent commission on each dog sold. Cooper had once calculated that in the course of an evening the owner of the house stood to take between twenty and thirty pounds. With fights taking place twice a week, he estimated the owner's annual income to be around two thousand five hundred pounds, a sum in excess of six times the annual salary of the Governor of the Bank of England. It was no wonder he could afford to buy twenty thousand live rats each year at three pence each.

Cooper had spent much of his life around animals. His father had worked with the foxhounds on a large estate in Wiltshire, and Cooper reckoned he knew a good dog when he saw one. Admittedly there was a difference between a foxhound and a terrier, but there was something about the look in a dog's eye and the way it held its head that told you whether it was up to the job.

It normally took a good ratter less than two minutes to kill a dozen rats, and bets were placed on the length of time each dog would take to despatch three, six, nine or all twelve of its rats. Different odds were offered for each dog, and no sooner had the bookmaker called the odds than fistfuls of money were thrust towards him. Alcohol flowed freely, either brought into the house in a coat pocket or sold by the glass at exorbitant rates. Cooper never drank on such occasions. There would be time enough for that later. From experience he knew that the better dogs were frequently held back until the end of the evening. By that time many in the crowd were thoroughly intoxicated, and spurred on by the noise, the smell of human sweat, and the scent of blood became increasingly reckless in their betting. It was only then that Cooper made his move.

By the time the last rat had died Cooper was eight pounds in pocket. It was by no means a fortune, but to a man whose annual wage was twenty pounds it represented a tidy sum. It was certainly enough for him to treat himself to a few stiff drinks and find a woman. A woman who would do more than just lie on her back and let him do all the work.

25

London, Wednesday, 29th October

IT WAS ALMOST midday before Parsons arrived back at Scotland Yard. To his relief he found Harris at his desk and the fire in his office still alight. Since leaving Lady Sayers very little else had gone right.

He had decided to spend the night in Manchester, and to be sure of catching the first train had booked into a hotel near the railway station, only to discover subsequently that it refused to sell alcohol on religious grounds. As a result he had been obliged to tramp back into the City Centre to find somewhere suitable to eat. The following morning the departure of the early train had been delayed because of a faulty carriage door, and when he had eventually arrived at Euston heavy rain had meant a long wait in line for a cab, and the ensuing journey to Whitehall had taken almost an hour.

Harris had little sympathy for Parsons' plight. Apart from a telegram instructing him to attend General Latham's funeral he had had no contact with the inspector, nor had he the slightest idea where he had gone. It could have proved embarrassing should Superintendent Jeffries have asked. Fortunately Harris had managed to avoid the superintendent, but he was far from being impressed when he heard where Parsons had been.

"I hope you learned something useful while I was traipsing around London, sir," he said, after the two men had taken their tea to Parsons' office.

That had not been the case, Parsons reflected sadly. Lady Sayers had told him little that was germane to the investigation.

"Maxwell Latham and Frederick Sayers were brothers-in-law," he explained, in an attempt to soothe Harris' wounded feelings and offer an excuse for his unheralded absence. "I only discovered that after leaving you on Monday, and couldn't tell you where I was going in case Jeffries asked you. He'd have had a fit if he knew I was still asking questions about Sayers. Regardless of that I still felt justified in going to Manchester. Lady Sayers could well have had knowledge of some aspect of the relationship between the two men to explain why they were both murdered on the same night. But all she said that was relevant was that she thought her husband had an interest in mineral exploration in Africa."

"But I thought you said there was a family connection," said Harris. "Surely you asked her about that."

"Of course I did," said Parsons irritably. "But it didn't get me very far. It turns out that Latham married Lady Sayers' younger sister; who, if you remember what Arbuthnot told us, died in childbirth. And from what Lady Sayers told me, Latham only married her sister for her money."

"And what's so unusual about that, sir?" Harris asked morosely. "As far as I can see people like Latham and Sayers do that all the time."

"There's nothing at all unusual about it, Harris," Parsons snapped. "Although there was plenty of money available judging by the size of Lady Sayers' house. Her father had made his fortune from cotton mills, and the two daughters were his only family. So Latham knew that he was on to a good thing. As did Sayers, of course, but from what Lady Sayers told me her husband was always intent on making his own money. I'm not sure that Latham had that sort of ambition. He appears to have been more interested in promotion and chasing the ladies. I learned that the purchase of his majority was an engagement present; and once assured of that and the prospect of the further promotion that his new young wife's money might bring him, Latham appears to have returned to his womanizing. As it happened Cardwell's reforms made it possible for him to gain promotion from his own endeavors, so he made little attempt to hide his indiscretions. According to Lady Sayers he was even with another woman on the night her sister died. So much for Arbuthnot's story about Latham being heartbroken by his wife's death."

253

"Do you think Lady Sayers could have murdered Latham?"

"It crossed my mind that she might have, Harris," said Parsons. "But only briefly. Although she readily admitted that she hated Latham at the time of her sister's death and made a point of seeing that he never got another penny of her father's money, she said that her feelings towards him had mellowed over the years. And after all, why would she wait all this time before killing him? But she must have thought I suspected her when she learned I was investigating Latham's murder. Why else would I have traveled all the way to Manchester? As it happened she had an alibi. On the night he died she was at a women's political meeting in Manchester and there are scores of witnesses."

"Women and politics," said Harris in disgust. "That's one subject on which Mrs. Harris and I are in full agreement. She says a woman's place is in the home."

Parsons knew his own mother would have shared Mrs. Harris' opinion. Amelia Parsons firmly believed that a married woman's role in life was to care for her husband and family and ensure the smooth running of the home. It was one of the few subjects on which she and her son did not agree. As far as Parsons was concerned there was no reason why an educated woman with sufficient money to ensure that her children were adequately cared for should not interest herself in public affairs and good works. But he also had some sympathy with Mrs. Harris' point of view. As a mother of small children living in a rough working class area of London it was obvious that her duty was to remain home and see to their welfare.

Parsons got up from his desk and shoveled more coal on the fire.

"Well, I hope your time was spent more fruitfully than mine, Harris," he said.

"That depends on what you mean by fruitful, sir," said Harris. "I went to the general's funeral as you instructed, but I didn't learn much other than that one woman dressed in a long black coat and a thick veil looks much like any other woman dressed in a similar fashion."

"That's a very helpful observation, Harris," said Parsons. "And one that we were already aware of. But what about the mourners? Were there any people at the funeral you think worth talking to?"

"Not as far as I could see. There were a few senior officers and their wives, and a lady with a walking stick. I saw her talking to Colonel Cordell. But I've no idea who she might be."

"And that was it!" said Parsons irritably. "You learned nothing more than that!"

"Well, as a matter of a fact I did, sir," Harris said indignantly. "After the funeral the RSM invited me to the Sergeants' Mess to join him for a drink. He said it was to honor the general, but I really think he wanted the opportunity of telling me what a fine fellow he was, and about the obstacles he'd had to overcome to reach his present position. And I have to admit that I was impressed by what I heard. The more I learned about his early life the more it seemed the two of us had in common. As you know I had a rough upbringing, and it's been a struggle for me to get where I am. But what I went through and what I've achieved is nothing compared to Whitehead. From what he told me he practically runs that regiment single handed."

"And that's exactly what RSMs are for, Harris," said Parsons impatiently. "At least that's what my father told me. They're responsible for discipline, and any regiment worth its salt has a good man as RSM."

"Well, it seems I'm not telling you anything you don't already know," said Harris sullenly. "It sounds like I wasted my morning in much the same way you wasted your time in Manchester."

Parsons knew he was being unfair. If anyone should feel guilty for misuse of time it was him.

"I'm sorry, Harris," he said. "I shouldn't let my frustration rub off on you. But what about the list of key-holders the RSM was supposed to give you? Did he remember that in between telling you what a splendid fellow he is?"

"As a matter of fact he did, sir. And you can see for yourself that it's pretty much as Colonel Cordell said."

Parsons glanced down the names on the list that Harris gave him. Harris was right. For the most part the names were those of the officers and senior noncommissioned officers living in the barracks. The only exceptions were the two married company commanders, Arbuthnot and Plumb. Both of them had keys although they lived in their own houses.

"What about the other things I asked you to do?" Parsons asked "Did you check the statements made by the cab drivers and the policeman who claimed to see Mrs. Cordell in Chester Place? And what about Lady Cordelia?"

To Parsons' irritation Harris confessed that he had not had the time to complete his enquiries.

"But you managed to find time for a drink in the Sergeants' Mess," Parsons said irritably. "And that wasn't especially productive. Haven't you learned anything useful at all?"

Parsons' temper rarely got the better of him, and Harris sensed that his unusually bad mood was more than likely a result of confusion. Parsons had initially considered the Latham enquiry to be relatively straight forward. Harris was still inclined to think that it was, and from what he could see Parsons was intent upon making matters unnecessarily complicated by attempting to link Latham's murder with that of Sayers. And as a result of that he no longer seemed to know in which direction he was heading. The signs were inauspicious, especially if Superintendent Jeffries ever got wind of the game that Parsons was playing. It was at times like this that Harris was relieved to be a mere sergeant.

"As it happens I did, sir," he replied resolutely. "But I'm not sure you'll want to hear what I have to say."

"Then for Heaven's sake tell me, Harris," said Parsons, who was beginning to think that nothing was turning out as he planned. "Let's get it over with and then we can go for a drink!"

Harris explained that he had eventually tracked down the two cab drivers.

"It took me most of the day, I can tell you, sir. I had to chase them from one cab shelter to the next."

"And hopefully they had something worthwhile to say," said Parsons.

"I'm afraid not, sir," said Harris, with a wry smile. "They stuck to their original stories. It was Constable Matthews who changed his."

"You mean the policeman who said he'd seen a veiled woman arrive at General Latham's house at quarter past midnight?"

"The very same man, sir," said Harris.

"Well, go on Harris," Parsons said, beginning to fear the worse. "What did he have say?"

"He admitted to making a mistake, sir. He said that it was at quarter to twelve that he saw the veiled woman in Chester Place and not at quarter past. When he thought about it afterwards he realized that when he heard the clock strike the quarter hour he was several hundred yards away in Westbourne Street. But he was still certain about one thing. He said that the woman he saw in Chester Place before midnight spoke to the cab driver in a foreign accent. He didn't hear what she actually said, but he's certain she was foreign."

"Is Matthews quite certain of this, Harris?" Parsons asked. "After all, he gave us the wrong information the first time. Why is he so sure that what he's telling us now is the truth?"

"Because when he was in Westbourne Street and he heard the clock strike he checked his own watch to see if he had enough time for a cigarette."

"So why did he ever say he was in Chester Place at quarter to twelve?"

Harris looked a little crestfallen.

"That's probably my fault, sir," he admitted. "When I questioned him the first time I may've given him too much information before asking him questions. I could've put ideas in his head. If you remember at the time I spoke with him everything was at sixes and sevens in F Division, and most men like Matthews who'd been working the night shift had been kept on duty because of Lord Sayers' murder. Matthews was tired when I saw him and he may have just given me the answer he thought I wanted to hear."

"And look what a mess it's got us into, Harris," said Parsons angrily. "We've arrested the wrong woman! Venetta Cordell is in all probability as innocent as she claims!"

"Do you want to hear what my wife and her mother think about that, sir?" Harris asked.

"If you really insist, Harris," Parsons said angrily. "But I really can't imagine what your good lady and her mother would have to say that is at all relevant!"

Parsons bitterly regretted the words as soon as he had spoken them. There was no excuse for such bad manners, especially when speaking to a subordinate; and Harris would have been perfectly at liberty to refrain from any further comment.

"You must forgive me, Harris," he said disconsolately. "I'm tired after my journey."

Harris gave him a long cool look before continuing.

"Well, sir," he said at last. "When I told them about General Latham being stabbed they said it didn't sound like a woman."

"Whatever are you talking about, Harris?"

"They said that if a woman was going to kill someone with a spear she would stab him downwards. Not the way the surgeon said. If you remember he said the general was stabbed the other way. Here let me show you."

Harris rose to his feet, picked up the poker from the side of the fire, and approached Parsons' desk.

"Telegram for you, Sergeant Harris," said a clerk, who at the point at which Harris was raising the poker, put his head around Parsons' office door. "From Kensington Barracks."

"It's probably Colonel Cordell demanding my resignation," said Parsons gloomily. "And from what I've just heard he has every justification. Though it beats me why he should be contacting you and not the Commissioner."

Parsons handed Harris a paper knife and slumped back into his chair disconsolately as he watched the sergeant open the envelope.

"It's not from the colonel, sir," Harris said quietly. "It's from the RSM. And I don't think you need worry about Colonel Cordell asking for your resignation just at present. Just listen to this. *Regret to say Colonel Cordell took his own life last night. Thought you and your inspector should know. Whitehead.*"

26

I T WAS SHORTLY before two when the cab
dropped Parsons and Harris outside the main
gate of Kensington Barracks. They had spoken
little during the journey. Parsons was distracted
and lost in thought, mindful that the decision to
arrest Venetta Cordell, although not entirely his,
could well have caused her husband to take his
life. And such a tragedy could have been avoided.
Had Constable Matthews told Harris the truth in
the first place it would have been obvious that
Venetta was as innocent as she had claimed all
along, and that Latham was already dead when she
arrived at his house. He had been murdered by a
woman arriving a half hour before Venetta.

"I've orders to take you straight to the RSM's
office, gentlemen," the guard commander said.
"Please follow me."

The sergeant led them along the side of the
parade ground, where much to Parsons' surprise
soldiers were drilling noisily. He had imagined
that the tragic death of their commanding officer

might, at least temporarily, have silenced the loud words of command and the stamping of boots.

He recognized the building from an earlier visit. The words 'Regimental Headquarters' and 'Orderly Room' were stenciled in white paint on a large wooden sign painted in the red, yellow and blue colors of the regiment. The same white paint appeared to have been used on the row of smooth rounded stones on each side of the immaculate gravel path leading to a flight of three steps and an open door.

"Two gentlemen to see the RSM," the guard commander said to one of the four clerks in the main office. Then he saluted and marched smartly back to the Guard Room.

"This way, gentlemen," said the clerk, leading Parsons and Harris along a corridor with bare white walls and scrubbed wooden floors past one closed door with a polished brass plate announcing that it was the office of the 'Chief Clerk' to a second with a similar brass plate saying 'Regimental Sergeant Major'.

This door was open. Whitehead, it seemed, had been expecting them.

"Good afternoon, gentlemen," he said solemnly as he rose to greet them. "Dreadful news I'm sure you'll agree. Especially coming so soon after the general's death."

"I'm obliged to you for sending a telegram to Sergeant Harris, Mr. Whitehead," said Parsons. "Not everyone would think of informing the police."

"Only my duty, sir. Suicide's a serious business. A crime if I'm not mistaken."

"You're quite correct in thinking that, Mr. Whitehead," Parsons said, as he took a seat in one of the two chairs set in front of the RSM's desk. "The law of England is very explicit on the subject. It treats suicide and attempted suicide as a felony, and if anyone is found to have assisted the victim in taking their life that person would be guilty of murder."

As he spoke Parsons examined his surroundings. A man's office, he maintained, said much about the man himself; and if the methodical tidiness of the RSM's room and his desk was any indication, Whitehead was one of the most meticulous men he had ever met. His desk was positioned exactly opposite the door, allowing the light from the two windows facing onto the parade ground to fall equally upon the surface of the desk. A large spotless blotting pad had been placed precisely opposite Whitehead's seat, with an ivory pen holder slightly to one side. Judging by the position of the pen, the RSM was right-handed. Two wooden trays for correspondence occupied the corners of the desk nearest the door, the sides of each tray arranged to align precisely with the edges of the desk. Neat lettering on these labels indicated the nature of the correspondence in each tray. One label said 'IN', the other 'OUT'. Highly polished floor boards, blemish-free white walls, and a solitary pine cabinet completed a picture of spotless efficiency.

Yet there was nothing in the room to reveal anything of the RSM's personal or military life. There were no photographs or memorabilia of any kind. Whitehead, it appeared, was not a man to dwell on the past.

"I normally do not take tea until later in the afternoon," he said, as he watched Parson's reflective examination of his office with some amusement. He ignored Parsons' remark about tea being unnecessary at such a time, and instead spoke directly to the clerk who had remained waiting at the door.

"Jenkinson, my pot and three cups," he instructed. "Be quick about it, and close the door behind you."

Whitehead returned his attention to Parsons.

"What you have just said may well be true, inspector," he said after the clerk had closed the door. "But in this instance I'm sure you'll find that Colonel Cordell acted alone. The facts surely speak for themselves. The colonel was under tremendous emotional strain. His wife had been arrested for murdering a former commanding officer, and I regret to say that his own authority was being seriously undermined by the behavior of some of the officers."

"Are others of the same opinion?" Parsons asked.

"Those I've spoken to," said Whitehead. "And by that I mean the officers who were in the Mess yesterday afternoon. But I'm sure you'll soon discover that for yourself when you question them."

"You seem remarkably well informed about all that has happened, Mr. Whitehead," said Parsons.

"Nothing goes on in this regiment without me knowing, sir. I have eyes and ears everywhere. How else could I do my job as RSM?"

Jenkinson returned just then with a tray bearing a pot of tea, three cups and saucers, a jug of milk, and a small bowl of sugar, and placed it on the desk in front of the RSM. To his surprise Parsons saw that the tea set was made of delicate bone china. No one at Scotland Yard, to his knowledge, drank tea in such style. As Harris had said, the RSM was a remarkable man.

"Who is now commanding the regiment?" Parsons asked.

"For the moment it is Major Arbuthnot," replied the RSM as he began pouring the tea into the three cups. "He is the senior major. No doubt that will please his wife. It's well known in the regiment that she has always wanted to be the colonel's lady. But she may yet be disappointed. The appointment is only temporary, and the War Office may yet appoint someone else."

Whitehead's face seemed to light up.

"Who knows how these things work," he said with a smile. "Perhaps the new commanding officer will be someone quite unexpected."

He lifted his cup and took a sip of tea.

"But I'm sure you'll be wanting to speak to Colonel Arbuthnot as soon as possible. I believe he's in the Officers' Mess at present along with most of the other officers. I'll send word to him of your arrival."

"That's most considerate of you, Mr. Whitehead," said Parsons. "But in the meantime perhaps you will be kind enough to tell me your understanding of what happened."

The RSM set his cup down and rested his clasped hands on the edge of the desk. They were hands, Parsons mused, that, like everything else about the man, displayed both strength and order. There was strength in his grip and order in his neatly trimmed nails.

"Much of what I'm telling you is, of course, only hearsay, gentlemen," he said, lowering his voice as though one of the clerks might be listening at his door. "It's merely what I've learned from some of the officers, the servants in the Officers' Mess, and the colonel's own domestic staff. All I can say for sure is that Pound, the colonel's servant, came to me this morning while I was inspecting the men's breakfast to tell me the tragic news. Naturally, I went straight to the colonel's house, and when I saw with my own eyes what had happened I immediately sent for Major Arbuthnot. As soon as he arrived I took him to see the colonel's body. It was after that that I notified Sergeant Harris."

Whitehead unfolded his hands, leaned back in his chair and smiled.

"Sergeant Harris may have told you, inspector," he said, "that the two of us had a few drinks together after the funeral yesterday. I thought he might want to see how we in the

Sergeants' Mess paid our respects to the general. The Officers' Mess, of course, has its own way of dealing with such matters. And whereas our wake was, shall I say, a lively affair; the party in the Officers' Mess was, by all accounts, quite the opposite. It appears that many of the officers and their ladies were less than supportive of Colonel Cordell over the loss of his half-brother and the unfortunate circumstances surrounding his death. He even appears to have been ostracized by some. Perhaps you gentlemen may think it understandable in the circumstances; but, believe me, it is most unusual for any commanding officer to lose the respect of his officers in that way. And for such a thing to happen in a proud regiment like ours is, in my experience, quite unprecedented."

"Yet that seems hardly a good reason for Colonel Cordell to commit suicide," said Harris. "If he was that upset by the way he was treated by other officers he could simply have resigned his commission."

"No one could argue with that logic, sergeant," Whitehead said. "But there was more than what I've told you so far. It wasn't just the way in which many of his officers treated the colonel that seems to have affected him as much as what happened between he and Captain Simpson."

Whitehead paused, turning his head towards the sounds on the parade, as though hearing them for the first time. His eyes gleamed for a moment, but they clouded when he began talking again.

"From what I hear Captain Simpson was extremely drunk," he said in disgust. "He even tried to put his arm round the colonel. I've never heard of such a thing. Never! Naturally the colonel was furious, and unfortunately chose that moment to tell Captain Simpson something that should never have been said in public, whether it was true or not. Especially in the anteroom of the Officers' Mess."

Whitehead pursed his lips in disapproval.

"The colonel told Captain Simpson that he wished he'd never supported his recommendation for the Victoria Cross. He said it was never deserved."

"What happened then?" Parsons asked, surprised by what he had just heard. He had been brought up to believe that, in public at least, a gentleman kept his feelings to himself.

"It seems that Captain Simpson was escorted from the room, and that for the rest of the afternoon very few people spoke with the colonel. And from all accounts he drank far more than usual."

"What happened when the colonel went home?" Parsons asked. "Did Pound tell you how he behaved?"

"Pound told me that the colonel went straight to his study and stayed there for the rest of the evening. He was heard going upstairs at about eleven, and later one of the servants heard a bath running. That was all anyone knew until Pound took him his morning tea. That's when he found the body."

"Was there a suicide note?" Parsons asked.

"There was," said Whitehead. "It was on a table in the colonel's bedroom. I told Pound not to touch it, so it should still be there."

"Has anyone informed Mrs. Cordell?" asked Harris.

"Not as far as I know, sergeant," Whitehead replied. "But now that you gentlemen are here you will doubtless ensure that that is taken care of."

———————

PARSONS RECOGNIZED THE servant who answered the Cordell's door as the one who had done so on each of his previous visits.

"You must be Mr. Pound," he said, as Harris and he were escorted to the colonel's study.

"That's right, sir," Pound answered. There were dark rings under his nervous eyes and his face was ashen. The poor fellow looked as though he were on the point of a nervous collapse.

"Are the other servants in the house?" Parsons asked.

Pound replied with a nod, as though he had temporarily lost the power of speech.

"Then I'd like you to bring them here," instructed Parsons. "I want to ask them a few questions."

———————

WITHIN FIVE MINUTES the three other servants had assembled and were standing alongside Pound in an apprehensive line. Pound introduced each in turn: his wife, whom he said was the cook; the housemaid, Jenny Blake; and Mrs. Cordell's lady's maid, Edith Arnaud. Each of them confirmed they had been in the house during the previous evening and throughout the night.

"I'd like each of you to tell me exactly what you remember of last evening," said Parsons quietly. "Perhaps you'd care to start, Mr. Pound, by explaining what happened after the colonel arrived back from the Mess, and the rest of you can add your comments as you see fit."

Pound cleared his throat with a nervous cough.

"The colonel came back at around five-thirty, sir," he said. "He came straight here to his study, and as far as I know he didn't go anywhere else until he went to bed."

"Did he take his supper here?" Parsons asked.

"He did, sir," Pound replied. "He said he didn't want to eat in the dining room."

Mrs. Pound interrupted he husband.

"A nice fried sole, it was, sir, with Brussels sprouts and mashed potatoes. And some of my best cheddar. But he never done more than picked at it."

"Did you notice anything significantly different about the colonel when he returned, Mr. Pound?" Parsons asked. "I've heard he had been drinking rather excessively."

"Oh, he had, sir," Pound said. "There was no doubt about that. He could hardly walk straight. The colonel was not normally one for drinking, sir, unlike some officers I could name. As soon as I saw the state he was in I brought him a pot of tea thinking that it might sober him up. But he said he didn't want it. Instead he told me to bring a decanter of sherry. He drank most of that, sir, as well as a carafe of wine with his supper."

"How did he appear to you?" Parsons asked.

"His spirits seemed very low, sir. I said as much to Mrs. Pound. I can't say I'd ever seen him like that before."

"Did you see or speak to him again after you cleared the supper dishes?" Parsons asked.

"No, sir," Pound said.

"Did any of you?" Parsons asked the other servants.

"I heard him going upstairs at about eleven o'clock, sir," said Mrs. Pound. "I was still in the kitchen then."

"And where were the rest of you at that time?" asked Parsons.

Pound and the other two servants explained that they were in their bedrooms on the top floor of the house. None of them had heard Colonel Cordell going upstairs to his room.

"But I thought I heard him running his bath, sir," said Jenny Blake, the housemaid. She blushed. "My bedroom's above his and I was reading in bed at the time."

"One of those foolish romances," Mrs. Pound interjected. "I'm always telling her it gives her ideas."

Parsons ignored the interruption.

"What time would that be, Jenny?' he asked.

"It was well after twelve," she said. "More like half past, I think."

"How can you be sure of that?" asked Parsons.

"Because I've got an alarm clock," the housemaid said proudly. "And when I saw how late it was I stopped reading. Otherwise I knew I'd have trouble getting up in the morning."

"And you heard nothing afterwards?"

"No, sir."

Parsons turned to Pound.

"Was the house locked last night?"

Pound appeared flustered by the question.

"I can't honestly say, sir," he said. "To be honest with you I was so concerned about the colonel that I don't remember doing it."

"Is it normally locked?" Parsons asked.

"It is, sir."

"And who has the keys?"

"There's only one set, sir. And I have that," Pound said, taking a set of keys from his pocket and showing them to Parsons. "These two large ones are for the front and back doors, sir, and the small one is for the wine cellar."

"Just one set," Parsons said in surprise. "So what would happen if Colonel or Mrs. Cordell were out late? Would the door be left unlocked until they returned?"

"One of us, normally me, would wait up for them to return, sir," Pound explained.

"Did that happen on the night General Latham was murdered?" Parsons asked. "It has already been established that Mrs. Cordell went out that night. Did anyone hear her return?"

"No, sir. But that night Mrs. Cordell had given instructions that no one should wait up. Not even Edith."

"Was that usual?"

"No, sir," Pound replied.

"Excuse me for interrupting, sir," said Mrs. Pound, her apology directed as much to her husband as to Parsons. "But there is another set of keys."

Pound was clearly embarrassed by his wife's interruption.

"Mrs. Pound's right, sir," he said reluctantly. "There is a spare set. They're kept in the Orderly Room.

Parsons exchanged a swift glance with Harris. That would mean that anyone with access to the Orderly Room could have taken the keys to the colonel's house.

"I believed that it was you, Mr. Pound, who discovered the colonel's body?' Parsons said.

"I did, sir," Pound replied. "I took him his morning tea as usual, but his bed was empty. I could see it had been slept in, so I assumed that the colonel was already up and had gone into his bathroom. I thought at the time that that was strange, because the colonel doesn't normally rise until I bring him his tea. And after the amount he'd had to drink the previous night I couldn't imagine him getting up without a nice strong cup of tea."

"Does his bathroom adjoin the bedroom?"

"Yes, sir. The colonel and his wife both have their own bathrooms."

"What did you do next?" Parsons asked.

"I knocked on the bathroom door to inform the colonel that his tea was ready. I didn't want it to get cold. But he didn't answer and I couldn't hear any noise inside. So I opened the door, and that's when I saw his body."

"Tell me exactly what you saw, Mr. Pound," said Parsons. "I realize that it's difficult for you. But I have to know."

Pound glanced at the other three servants, whose tense faces were turned towards him in anticipation. His wife, who was standing beside him gave his arm a reassuring squeeze.

"It was terrible, sir," Pound explained. "There was blood everywhere. On the floor. In the bath. Everywhere."

"What did you do?"

"Nothing, sir. What could I do? I could see the colonel was dead. So I came downstairs and told the wife."

"And I told him to go to the RSM," Mrs. Pound said. "Mr. Whitehead always knows what's best to do."

"Did the RSM come here?"

"He did, sir. He came right away. And when he saw what had happened he said he would send for Major Arbuthnot."

Has anyone else been here, other than the RSM and Colonel Arbuthnot?"

"No, sir."

Parsons turned to Harris.

"Harris, I want you to find out if you can send a telegram directly from the Orderly Room. If not find the nearest Post Office. Ask Chelsea Division to send their police surgeon over here. Tell them it's urgent. Then inform the RSM and ask him to have the surgeon brought here as soon as he arrives. After you've done that come back here and wait for the surgeon. And send for me when he arrives. I'll probably be in the Officers' Mess."

"What about Mrs. Cordell, sir?" Harris asked. "Do you want me to ask someone at Chelsea Division to tell her what has happened?"

"Not yet, Harris, I'll deal with that later."

Parsons turned again to Pound.

"Now I'd like you to show me Colonel Cordell's room," he said.

27

THE BEDROOMS ON the first floor had been arranged in perfect symmetry. There were two in the west wing and two in the east, and a bathroom in each wing.

"Colonel and Mrs. Cordell occupied separate wings of the house," Pound said as he explained the geography of the first floor. "It was an arrangement that Mrs. Pound and I could never understand. Especially as the colonel and Mrs. Cordell had not long been married."

"Do you like Mrs. Cordell?" Parsons asked.

Pound was unsettled by the question. It was clear that he was not in the habit of being asked questions of a personal nature about his employers.

"I can't say I do, sir," he said after a few moments hesitation. "She's rather a highly strung young lady. Rather like that little dog of hers, if you don't mind me saying, sir. She's not at all like any other officer's wife I've ever met. But there again she's French, and I suppose that it explains it."

——— — —

BY THE STANDARDS of Parsons' more humble accommodation the colonel's bedroom was large, but he found that to be true of the bedrooms in many middle and upper class houses. It was probably the result of his living in cramped dormitory accommodation whilst at school, in an attic bedroom whilst a student at London University, and more recently in his rented rooms in Camberwell and Chelsea.

As he had imagined, the furniture was plain and functional: a large mahogany bedstead, a matching wardrobe, a chest, a table and chair, a bookcase, and a low cupboard with a sideboard top that Venetta Cordell would doubtless have called a *chiffonier*. Of the three windows, one overlooked the parade ground, and the other two faced towards the Officers' Mess.

"Did you open the curtains this morning?" Parsons asked.

"I did, sir. That's part of my normal routine. I put the tray with the colonel's tea on the table, then I draw the curtains. That's when I saw the note."

A single sheet of good quality white note paper lay on a blotting pad in the center of the table with an inkstand and pen tray set to the right hand side. The Cordell's address was embossed upon the note paper in an elaborate flowing script. As he bent over to examine it with his magnifying glass, from the corner of his eye Parsons could see the squads of soldiers drilling on the parade ground. Regardless of the commanding officer's death, the routine of life in the barracks appeared to be continuing as normal. A decision, Parsons imagined that had been taken by the RSM and not the acting colonel.

A short ambiguous sentence had been printed in the center of the paper in large ungainly capitals.

Parsons read: *'I CAN NO LONGER LIVE WITH THAT LIE AUDLEY'*

"I notice that the colonel was right handed," said Parsons.

"That's correct, sir."

"Is this the colonel's writing?" he asked.

"It could be, sir," said Pound. "But I can't be sure, seeing that the words have been printed. I don't think I can ever recollect the colonel writing like that. But it looks as though it was written with his pen, and as you can see the note paper is his. There's more of it in the drawer."

Parsons opened the drawer. As Pound had said there was a neat pile of embossed note paper inside together with some matching envelopes.

He picked up the suicide note and examined it again. Presumably, the 'Audley' to whom the note was addressed was Captain Simpson. Cordell's last thoughts, it appeared, were not for his wife, but for the young officer with whom he had argued only a matter of hours before he died. How, Parsons wondered, would Simpson react when he learned of the note? How would he feel when he discovered that Cordell had, in one way or another, implicated him in his untimely death? Had he been in Simpson's position, Parsons thought, there was little doubt that he would consider himself in some way culpable for what had occurred.

And what did the words mean? *'I can no longer live'* was self-explanatory. But what was the 'lie' mentioned in the note? And why *'that'* lie, and not *'this'* one. Had the note said *'this'* lie it would have suggested a lie that was still extant at the time of Cordell's death. But the use of the word *'that'* suggested something that had happened in the past. Perhaps, Parsons thought, he was being too pedantic by splitting hairs in this way. On the other hand the words might indicate something of Cordell's state of mind at the terrible moment he had decided to take his own life. There was probably only one person who could explain the meaning of the note, and that was Audley Simpson.

There was another confusing aspect about the note. Why had Cordell chosen to print it? It was also difficult to tell whether he had written it with his left or his right hand. Had the words not suggested otherwise the note might even have been the work of a person who was barely literate. But only an educated person would have chosen such words.

Admittedly Cordell was drunk when he wrote the note. But in that case Parsons considered it even less likely that he would have chosen to print his final words. A person who was drunk would surely scrawl the words in a way that came most naturally. And for most people that would be to write them. Parsons felt that his first instinct had been correct. Whoever had written the note had been attempting to disguise their hand, in much the same way that the person who had sent the last note to Venetta Cordell had done.

"I'll take this," Parsons said, taking a final look at the desk before folding the suicide note and placing it in the inside pocket of his jacket.

He turned in the direction of the bed.

"If I remember correctly you said that the colonel did not normally get up before you brought him his morning tea."

"That's correct, sir. More often than not he was asleep when I came into his bedroom. He was always a good sleeper, although you could tell from the state of his bed sheets that he tossed and turned a lot during the night."

"But this morning he wasn't in his bed when you arrived."

"No, sir. And as I said, I was surprised by that. Seeing that he'd gone to bed late, well, late for him, and that he'd drunk so much. From what Jenny Blake said it was well after midnight when he ran his bath."

Parsons had no wish to discuss his suspicions with Pound. As far as he was concerned at the time Jenny Blake heard the bath running Cordell was more than likely already dead.

"Take a look around the room and tell me if you see anything out of the ordinary, Mr. Pound," Parsons said. "Anything at all, no matter how trivial it may appear."

Pound walked slowly around the room, examining each piece of furniture. He opened the wardrobe and each drawer of the chest.

"Everything looks just the same as usual, sir," he said.

"And what about the bed? Is this how you would expect to see it if the colonel had got up before you arrived with his morning tea?"

"Yes, sir. I'd say it was. It looks just as it would if the colonel had been sleeping in it."

Parsons said nothing, but he found it difficult to imagine why any man seriously contemplating suicide would choose to go to bed. Especially a man who had been drinking as heavily as Cordell. From his own experience of such things, he knew that whenever he went to bed after a heavy night of drinking he immediately fell into a deep sleep, and got up only with the greatest reluctance when it was necessary to answer a call of nature. On the other hand, there was always the chance that Cordell's state of mind had been such that, regardless of how much he had drunk, he had not gone to sleep straight away, but had lain awake agonizing about the terrible act he was contemplating. But Parsons did not think that that had happened.

CORDELL'S BODY LAY slumped inside a large cast-iron bath. His left arm, the one nearest the door into his bedroom, hung limply over the side of the bath. His right arm was inside the bath, resting against his right thigh. The deep lacerations on each of his wrists were clearly visible, as was the razor that had been used to make them. It lay on a rug beside the bath, beside an almost empty bottle of Jameson Irish whiskey.

There was no longer water in the bath. Any that had been present at the time of Cordell's death had seeped away during the night, leaving a rust-colored stain around the body.

Parsons' first impression was that there was something familiar about the scene. He felt he had seen it before, although he knew he had never dealt with a similar suicide. And then he remembered. During a recent visit to the National Gallery he had seen David's dramatic painting of the death of Jean-Paul Marat. Marat had been a leading political figure during the French Revolution. And he had been assassinated whilst taking a bath.

Pound had not followed Parsons into the bathroom but remained standing uncomfortably at the threshold.

"Come closer, Mr. Pound," Parsons said. "I need you to tell me if you see anything unusual here."

Parsons took a few reluctant steps towards the bath.

"Only the bottle, sir. The colonel never drank whiskey. Well, not to my knowledge. I've only ever seen him drink a little sherry, wine or port."

"And I notice that this is Irish whiskey," Parsons said, wondering, not for the first time, why it was that Scotch whisky was spelt in one way and Irish whiskey in another. "Does that mean anything, do you think?"

Pound shook his head.

"Not as far as the colonel was concerned," he said. "Although I do believe that Captain Simpson drank it. I know that because the colonel ordered a bottle for him when he had his dinner party. The captain must've drunk nearly half the bottle before dinner. And if my memory serves me correctly that bottle's still in the drinks cabinet."

"Then I would be grateful when you have a moment if you can confirm that," said Parsons.

Parsons picked up the razor.

"Is this the colonel's?" he asked.

"It looks like it, sir. I think it's the one that's normally on his washstand."

Parsons examined the other items on the washstand: a shaving brush, a bowl of shaving soap, a bottle of cologne, a tooth brush, some tooth powder, and two hair brushes. Only the razor seemed to be missing. He opened the cupboard under the washstand. It revealed nothing out of the ordinary: spare toilet accessories and paper for the lavatory.

"Where does that door lead?" Parsons asked, pointing to a door on the other side of the bathroom.

"To another bedroom, sir. As I explained there are two bathrooms on this floor. If there were ever guests it would be necessary for them to share a bathroom either with the colonel or with Mrs. Cordell."

Parsons tried the door. It was locked.

"It was always locked, sir. Colonel and Mrs. Cordell never had guests."

———————

PARSONS CARRIED OUT a cursory examination of the other three bedrooms. There was a similarity about each of them, although there was less furniture in the guests' rooms, and in the room belonging to Mrs. Cordell, there was an attractive *chaise longue* in front of the window overlooking Church Street and a wicker basket with a soft wool blanket that must have been the poodle's bed. The only other room on the first floor was a large walk-in cupboard containing bedding and towels.

"I expect the police surgeon to be here soon, Pound," Parsons said, after they had returned to the ground floor and were standing in the entrance hall. "When he's inspected the body he'll arrange to have it removed."

Pound looked relieved.

"Thank you, sir," he said. "I'm sure you can appreciate that this has been a terrible shock for us all. But if you will wait just one minute I will check on that whiskey for you."

Pound returned with a half empty bottle of Jameson whiskey.

"This is the bottle, sir," he said. "it doesn't look to me as though anyone has touched it since the night of the colonel's dinner party."

"Thank you, Pound," said Parsons. It was yet another reason to suspect that Cordell had been

murdered, and that the murderer had brought a
bottle of whiskey with him. A bottle of Irish
whiskey.

———

THERE WAS A far less superior expression on the
mess steward's face when he saw Parsons than on
the previous occasion he and Harris had visited the
Officers' Mess.

"I'll fetch Colonel Arbuthnot at once," he
said, as he escorted Parsons to a small library
filled with leather-bound books. "You'll be more
comfortable here. May I get you some tea or a
drink?"

Parsons declined the offer, and spent the short
time awaiting Arbuthnot in examining the book
titles. The library appeared to be little used. Dust
had gathered on the top of the books, and many
had been placed in the shelves upside down. The
residents of the Mess, it was clear, were not avid
readers.

———

"AH, INSPECTOR," SAID Arbuthnot effusively,
offering Parsons his hand. "Thank you for coming.
It helps to have a familiar face at a time like this."

"I've just been to the Cordell's house,
colonel," Parsons explained. "I've examined his
body, but I'd still like the police surgeon to see it
before I have it moved to the dead house. He
should, hopefully, be here soon. But in the

meantime I'd like you to give me your impression of what happened in the Mess after General Latham's funeral. Especially anything that could have accounted for the colonel taking his own life."

Arbuthnot described the uncomfortable atmosphere in the Mess: how Cordell had been snubbed by many of the guests, including his own wife, and the confrontation between he and Simpson.

"It was nothing short of a disgrace," he said. "A young officer like Simpson behaving in that manner. Calling the commanding officer by his Christian name and attempting to put his arm around him. It's not surprising the colonel reacted in the way he did. Mind you, he should not have spoken to Simpson in the way he did. At least not in public."

"Can you tell me what was said?" Parsons asked

"The long and short of it, inspector, was that Simpson and Cordell had a real set to, which ended in Cordell telling Simpson that he was a disgrace to the regiment and unworthy of his medal. It was all very embarrassing. I thought the argument had ended when Mark Holland escorted Simpson out of the anteroom, but Sergeant Barnard told me this morning that he saw the two men quarreling again in the corridor sometime afterwards."

"I can well understand how Colonel Cordell would be upset by such a serious and public breach of etiquette, and how he would feel about being made to look foolish in front of the junior officers and his guests," said Parsons, "but I find it hard to believe that the incident in itself would be sufficient to drive him to suicide. I can't help thinking that there were other reasons. What, for instance, do you make of this note?"

Parsons handed Arbuthnot the suicide note. He read it several times before answering.

"You're right, inspector," he said. "The colonel must have been dwelling on something for more time than any of us realized. What's the lie he's referring to? Was it his marriage, d'you suppose, or perhaps something that happened before that?"

"I was rather hoping that you might tell me, sir," said Parsons. He was irritated by Arbuthnot's inconsequential response. For all his social graces, Arbuthnot did not appear to have much sympathy for the feelings of others. "Had you, for instance, noticed anything different about the colonel's behavior during the past few weeks."

"Well, I can't say that Cordell was ever what you might call a cheerful sort, inspector. Never the life and soul of the party, if you know what I mean. Apart from Simpson he had few enough friends in the regiment before he became colonel. And after he was made commanding officer he couldn't expect to have any. Well, not at least from among the other officers in the regiment. A colonel must keep his distance and retain a sense of dignity, don't you know."

If Parsons had been hoping for any information about Cordell's marriage or anything about his past relationship with Simpson that might have unbalanced his mind he was disappointed. Arbuthnot seemed to be a man drifting through life with little awareness of what was going on around him. It was little wonder that his wife found him so infuriating.

"Where is Captain Simpson now?" he asked.

"Blest if I know, inspector. I was looking for him myself earlier on. His servant told me he went out soon after breakfast and hasn't been seen since."

"So he probably knows nothing of Colonel Cordell's death."

Arbuthnot shrugged his shoulders.

"Probably not," he said. "I don't think the news had reached the Mess before he left."

"What of Mrs. Fitzgerald, General Latham's future wife? Did she not attend the funeral?"

"Now you come to mention it I did see Colonel Cordell talking to a lady at the funeral who was unfamiliar to me. Perhaps that was Mrs. Fitzgerald. Cordell was probably inviting her to the Mess, and she obviously declined. I can't say I blame her. She would only have been an object of curiosity for the rest of the ladies. As far as I'm concerned she's rather a mystery woman. If it weren't for my wife telling you the other day about General Latham's engagement I wouldn't have known anything about her. And I'm not the only one. As far as I know no one else in the regiment has ever met her."

At this juncture the mess steward arrived with news that the police surgeon was awaiting Parsons at the Cordell's house.

"Thank you for sparing me your valuable time, Colonel Arbuthnot," Parsons said, as they shook hands. "Especially as I believe you now have the additional responsibilities of being the commanding officer."

"Don't mention it, inspector," Arbuthnot drawled as they strolled along the corridor. "I'm only too pleased to have been of assistance."

"One last question, sir. Do you take the *Daily Chronicle* in the Mess.

Arbuthnot could not have looked more disgusted had Parsons broken wind.

"Good God no," he said. "You might find a newspaper like that in the soldiers' barrack rooms or even in the Sergeants' Mess. But we don't allow the gutter press in here."

Arbuthnot followed this vehement denunciation of the *Chronicle* by wishing Parsons an abrupt 'Good Day', and instead of accompanying him to the entrance hall, turned instead into an anteroom. To Parsons' surprise he headed straight for a comfortable armchair by the fire and the newspaper he had obviously been reading before their interview. The burden of command, Parsons mused, did not seem to be weighing too heavily on the new commanding officer's shoulders.

PARSONS WAS PLEASED to see that both Brompton and Chelsea Divisions employed the same police surgeon, as during his earlier encounter with Doctor Grainger he had found him more helpful than most of doctors he had previously dealt with.

"Whatever is happening to the British Army, inspector?" Grainger said genially. "Not only has one of our gallant generals been speared, by no less than a woman, if what I read in the newspapers is true; but now, from what I've just learned from Sergeant Harris, the commanding officer of one of the country's finest regiments appears to have taken his own life."

"I'd rather you reserved your judgment on the nature of Colonel Cordell's death until you examine his body, doctor," said Parsons. "I still have an open mind myself."

The two men were standing by the side of Cordell's bath.

"Slashed wrists, I see," said Grainger. "In my experience the most common form of suicide. A sharp razor, a hot bath, and a bottle of Irish whiskey to ease the passage into the next world. A familiar pattern, inspector. I must have seen it several dozen times. There must be something about sharp weapons and military suicides. Hannibal, Brutus, and Mark Antony all chose to take their lives by the sword. Perhaps that was what General Latham was doing. Falling on his sword, or in his case, on his *iklwa*."

"I can't believe it happened quite as you suggest, doctor," said Parsons. "As you know, in the general's case the *iklwa* was found lying by his side. Had he chosen to die by his own hand I don't think he would've managed to be quite so tidy."

Doctor Grainger stroked his beard. His eyes twinkled.

"Just my little joke, inspector," he said. "We medical men try to maintain a sense of humor. It helps us in situations like this."

After the rather fruitless interview with Arbuthnot, Parsons was in no mood for jokes.

"What can you tell me about the wounds, doctor? Can you say whether they were inflicted by a right or left handed person?"

Grainger lifted each of Cordell's arms and examined each of the lacerations.

"I see what you're getting at, Parsons," he said. "The cut on the left wrist is deeper than that on the right. But, frankly, I don't think that means anything. Even if Cordell was right handed it wouldn't necessarily follow that he cut his left wrist first or that the cut would be any deeper than that on the right. Think of the poor fellow's state of mind. Especially after drinking all that whiskey."

"He'd drunk even more than that during the course of the day. From what I've heard I'm amazed he managed to walk upstairs unaided."

"My very point," said Grainger. "How can we make any sensible judgment about how any man behaves when he's in that state."

The two men returned to the bedroom.

"In your experience, doctor," Parsons asked, "is it at all likely that a person contemplating suicide would go to bed for a few hours before deciding to have a bath and cut his wrists?"

"How can one decide what passes through a person's mind when they are thinking of taking their own life?" said Grainger. "Who are we to say what is normal behavior at such a time. If the individual concerned has a moral conscience he or she will know they are committing a crime, and if they are at all religious they will know that they are facing eternal damnation. Faced with the consequences of an act of that magnitude, is it not possible that a man would seek refuge in his bed before taking the final step. A return to the womb before the last terrible act. From what you've told me about Colonel Cordell he was suffering from melancholia. And if he was wrestling with that demon his behavior would have been completely irrational as far as you and I are concerned."

"So you are satisfied that the colonel took his own life, doctor," Parsons said.

"That's what I will say to the Coroner should I be called to give evidence, young man," Grainger replied. "I see nothing to suggest anything to the contrary."

28

VENETTA CORDELL'S TURQUOISE blouse added an unexpected touch of color to her otherwise gloomy cell, although like the black skirt with narrow flounces that she wore it sorely needed the application of a hot iron, in much the same way that her disheveled hair required the attention of her French maid. Yet judging by the fierce intensity in her dark eyes, she had lost none of her former passion.

"Well, Inspector Parsons," she snapped. "What do you want with me now? 'ave you come to take me to the guillotine?"

"We do not execute people like that in this country, madame," replied Parsons, "and, in any case, we are a long way yet from any English jury deciding whether or not you are guilty."

"So you are 'ere to ask me more questions?"

"That is only partly correct, madame," said Parsons. "I regret to say that I am also the bearer of some very sad news."

Venetta raised her hands to her face in alarm.

293

"Something 'as 'appened to my darling Phooby," she said in dismay. "Don't tell me that 'ector ' as done something cruel to 'er."

"Your darling Phooby?" said Parsons in surprise. "I'm afraid you have me at a loss, madame. Who is this Phooby?"

"The dog, sir," Harris said from the corner of his mouth. "Mrs. Cordell's poodle."

"*Oui, c'est vrai.* Phooby is my poodle, inspector. Surely you remember my sweet little dog."

Parsons had not forgotten the dog, it was simply that he had not expected to hear it referred to within the context of the unhappy news he had brought.

"As far as I know Phooby is well, madame," he said. "It is not Phooby that has suffered a misfortune. It is your husband."

Venetta tossed her head scornfully.

"What do I care about 'im," she said. "Since I am 'ere, not once 'as 'e or anyone else been to visit me. *Quel homme.* 'ow did I ever choose 'im for my 'usband. What can 'e 'ave done that could possibly be of interest to me?"

"I regret to say that Colonel Cordell is dead, ma'am. It's possible that he took his own life."

There was but a momentary pause before Venetta continued the vitriolic attack on her late husband.

"Suicide!" she exclaimed. "I should 'ave known that such a man would choose a coward's death."

Parsons was amazed by Venetta's cold response to the news of her husband's suicide. Doubtless there would have been tears and cries of anguish had he brought news of the death of her poodle. Yet she had nothing but scorn for a husband who could well have taken his own life as a result of the melancholia that her own actions may have caused. He had rarely encountered such indifference and lack of feeling in a woman.

Parsons took the suicide note from his pocket and gave it to Venetta. She read it once briefly and handed it back without comment.

"Is that your husband's writing?" Parsons asked.

She shrugged.

"Peut etre."

"Are you sure, madame."

She shrugged again.

"Je suppose si. 'Ow can I tell, inspector. The words are printed. I 'ave not seen my 'usband write like that."

"And what about the message. What do you think your husband meant by those words?"

Venetta held out her hand for the note. This time she read it more carefully.

"What was the lie your husband was referring to, madame?" Parsons asked.

"I cannot be sure, inspector. But per'aps 'e was referring to our marriage. That was a lie from the start."

"And what exactly do you mean by that, madame?"

Venetta's dark eyes flashed as they engaged those of Parsons.

"Because 'e prefer men to women, inspector. Especially that silly drunken young man, Audley Simpson. I should 'ave known that when I saw them together at Rochefort, an' from the way that Audley be'ave after 'ector told 'im we were to be married. 'E began to drink 'eavily then, and 'e 'as been drunk ever since."

PARSONS HAD, AT first, intended releasing Venetta after learning that Constable Matthews had made a mistake about the time he had seen a veiled woman in Chester Place, as she was clearly not that woman. But then he had changed his mind. Matthews may have had his doubts about the times, but the two cab drivers had not. Who was to say which of them was telling the truth? Perhaps there had been two women with foreign accents in Chester Place that night, perhaps only one.

He considered it better to leave Venetta where she was, at least for the time being. Even were she innocent there were excellent reasons for it to appear that the police still considered her to be guilty. In the first place, if another woman was guilty of the murder she might feel an unwarranted confidence that she had managed to escape justice. And that could lead to her becoming careless. And secondly, there was still the telegram he had sent to Paris. As yet he knew little about Venetta's life before she became Mrs. Cordell.

"One last question, madame," Parsons said. "You told me earlier that the messages from General Latham were always sent by way of a newsagent's shop near the barracks. If I remember correctly it was in Silver Street. And you told me that you always sent your maid, Edith, to collect these messages for you. Do you know who it was that delivered the general's messages?"

"*Oui. Naturelment.* It was Bradley, Maxwell's man servant. Maxwell said 'e was a man 'e could trust."

"I WANT YOU to visit that newsagent, Harris," Parsons said as they left the police station. "For a start I'd like to know how this unofficial postal system of his works. But more specifically I'd like descriptions of the people who delivered and collected these notes between the general and Mrs. Cordell. Especially the last note."

"And where will you be, sir?"

"I'm going to question Bradley again. I want to hear what he has to say about these notes. And if another woman was at Chester Place on the night the general was murdered, I want to know why Bradley hasn't seen fit to mention it before."

29

A CHEAP WREATH was hanging on the front door of General Latham's house in Chester Place and the curtains were drawn. Although it appeared that Bradley had made a gesture of sorts to mark the passing of his employer his own appearance, had, if anything, deteriorated. He was unshaven, his clothing was disheveled, and there was a strong smell of alcohol on his breath.

"Why did you not tell me that another woman had visited the general shortly before Mrs. Cordell?" Parsons demanded, after Bradley had opened the curtains in the study and the two men stood facing each other across the stained brown rug.

Bradley's unkempt features creased into a frown.

"I don' know what you mean, sir," he said rudely. "There weren't no other woman 'ere that night."

"Then what would you say if I told you that a reliable witness saw a cab drawing up outside this house at a quarter to twelve with a woman passenger, and saw that woman enter this house. The witness also said that the woman was dressed in black, wore a heavy veil, and spoke with a foreign accent."

"Then I'd say 'e were a bloody liar, sir. There were only one woman 'ere that night. Colonel Cordell's bloody French wife. She were the only one that come 'ere. No one else. I swear that on my mother's grave."

"Regardless of what you say, Bradley," Parsons said sternly, "it's still possible that you could've been mistaken. After all, as I recall you had been drinking heavily."

"I can't deny that, sir," Bradley said indignantly. "But I know I weren't mistaken. Not about that. An' 'ow come I managed to remember one woman and forgot the other?"

"Then what possible other explanation can there be?" Parsons demanded. "How could someone get into this house without you knowing unless they had a key?"

Bradley shook his head.

"There were only one set of keys," he said. "Look, I'll show 'em to you."

Bradley led the way to a hat and umbrella stand in the hall and opened a small drawer below the mirror.

"'ere you are, sir," he said with a self-satisfied expression on his face. "Keys for all the downstairs rooms. An' one for the front door. I always kep' 'em 'ere. Then I knew where to find 'em. An' they was 'ere that night."

"How do you know, Bradley? Did you have any reason to use them?"

A smug, self satisfied look appeared on Bradley's face.

"Yes, sir," he said. "I used them to let Mrs. Cordell in."

Confounded by Bradley's assurance, Parsons decided to pursue another angle.

"Let us forget the keys for one moment, Bradley," he said. "Tell me about the notes you delivered to the newsagent in Silver Street."

Bradley was visibly shaken by the question.

"Who's been telling you 'bout them, sir?" he mumbled, shuffling his feet and examining his unpolished shoes.

"Don't concern yourself about that, Bradley. That's my business. I just want you to confirm that you carried out this task on behalf of the general. I also want to know whether you delivered any notes during the week prior to the general's death."

Bradley raised his head, and his brow creased in concentration.

"No, sir. I didn't," he said, after a lengthy deliberation. I never went to Silver Street that week. The las' time I went there was on the Monday of the week before."

"And did Mrs. Cordell visit General Latham shortly after that?"

"She did, sir. She come 'ere on the Thursday. It were not long after dark. I remember I 'ad jus' finished putting the ash bin outside ready for the dustman. An' as I told you before, I recognized 'er 'cause she come 'ere so often. If I took those notes to Silver Street for Mrs. Cordell an' then I seen 'er when she come 'ere, don' you think I'd know that it was 'er that was 'ere on the night the general was murdered?"

Parsons could see that Bradley's conviction remained unshaken. For his part, he began to feel he was going round in circles. There was little doubt that Venetta Cordell had visited the house on the night the general was murdered. But who was the other woman? And why had Bradley failed to see her?

"Now I want you to think carefully before answering this question, Bradley," he said. "Did anyone ever recognize you when you were delivering these notes?"

"Course they did, sir. Silver Street being so near the barracks there were nearly always soldiers around, both in the street and in the shop. They go to the newsagent for their newspapers an' tobacco. I must've seen dozens of men I knew, who would've recognized me. Don't forget I were once a Middlesex man m'self."

"One last question, Bradley. Did General Latham read any particular daily newspaper?"

"Yes, sir. 'E always read the *Times*."

"What about the *Daily Chronicle*?"

Bradley looked at Parsons in surprise.

"Bless you, sir," he said. "The general wouldn't wipe 'is arse with a rag like that."

———

PARSONS HAD ARRANGED to meet Harris at a coffee house in the Bayswater Road to compare notes and to make plans for the following day. He arrived before Harris and was fortunate to find a vacant table, as the coffee house was already beginning to fill with workers from the local offices and shops.

Parsons ordered a pot of tea and two rounds of toast. He did not have to wait long for Harris. Within ten minutes the sergeant's genial face appeared at the door, and the dapper figure in the brown check suit made its way through the crowded tables to the corner where Parsons was sitting.

"Tea and toast, Harris?" asked Parsons cheerfully.

"Nothing for me, thank you, sir. The missus will have my supper waiting when I get home. Her mother's coming round tonight and that normally means something special. So I'd better not be late."

"Then I won't keep you from the bosom of your family overlong, Harris. As soon as you tell me what you learned at the newsagent you can be on your way rejoicing."

Parsons spread a generous helping of raspberry jam on his second piece of toast and replenished his cup.

"It was just like Mrs. Cordell said when we first interviewed her, sir," Harris said. "The newsagent has an arrangement whereby his customers can rent post boxes, either by the day, the week or the month. He said it was a common practice amongst newsagents. In the case of General Latham and Mrs. Cordell a box was rented by the month. The general, or should I say, his manservant, Bradley, paid for it."

"And who delivered and collected the notes?"

"From the descriptions the newsagent gave me it was Bradley and Mrs. Cordell's French maid. The newsagent remembered the maid in particular. He said she was a very attractive young lady. In particular he remembered her pretty accent. He said she was always the center of attention whenever she was in the shop, especially amongst any soldiers who might be there."

"I'm particularly interested in the last note Venetta Cordell received, Harris. Did the newsagent remember who delivered that?"

"He did, sir. He remembered it being a Sunday evening. It was well after dark, probably about seven, and he was just thinking about closing the shop. He said he stays open much later during the week, but Sunday evenings are generally quiet. The note was delivered by someone he'd never seen before. A woman in a long black dress and wearing a heavy veil. He said the woman spoke with a foreign accent. The newsagent thought it might've been French, but he couldn't be certain. All he could say was that it didn't sound quite like the accent of the young woman who normally collected the notes. He said the other woman's voice sounded much coarser, and he thought she was probably older."

"What did this woman say?" Parsons asked, his toast for the moment forgotten.

"She said she was delivering a note for the young French woman, and she asked if the newsagent could be sure she received it. Naturally the newsagent understood who she meant."

"And that was it? You mean the newsagent just took this note without question and put it in the post box for Mrs. Cordell's maid to collect without ever questioning the woman's right to use the box."

Parsons was surprised by what Harris had said. He had assumed that by renting a post box a customer would be entitled to the newsagent exercising a degree of discretion as to who should be allowed to use it.

"That's right, sir. I asked him about that, but he said he wasn't paid to decide who was allowed access to his post boxes. As far as he was concerned it was for the use of anyone who wanted to communicate with either of the two parties. As long as the rent was paid he didn't care who used the boxes. Sounds a bit fishy doesn't it, sir. But it certainly gives us another reason to believe Mrs. Cordell may not have murdered the general. It might have been this older woman. The one who took the last note to Silver Street. If Mrs. Cordell hadn't received that note she wouldn't have chosen to go to Chester Place when she did. And then she wouldn't have been arrested for murdering General Latham."

30

PARSONS HAD ONE more call to make that evening. Although she might well have been present at General Latham's funeral, little else had been seen of Mrs. Fitzgerald, the wealthy Irish lady the general was proposing to marry, and very little was known about her. It was time, Parsons felt, to make her acquaintance. After all, if Venetta Cordell, a lover the general had decided to abandon, had a strong motive for murdering him, did it not also follow that his future wife might feel equally aggrieved at the thought of him deceiving her?

Whilst at the Guildhall Library Parsons had searched through back copies of the *Court and Society Review* until he had found the announcement of an engagement between General Sir Maxwell Latham of 17 Chester Place and Mrs. Edwina Fitzgerald of 48 Portman Square. The information given in the announcement had been brief. It had said only that the marriage was to take place quietly in Dublin. No date had been given.

Portman Square was within a comfortable walking distance of some of the finest parks in London. Regents Park and the grounds of the Zoological and Botanical Societies lay to the north, and to the south the parks bordering Buckingham Palace: Green Park and St. James's Park. It was also within a few hundred yards of the three hundred acres of Hyde Park, although any pedestrian choosing to walk in that direction from Portman Square would have to brave some of the heaviest traffic in London in the area around Marble Arch.

Parsons had chosen to walk to Portman Square from the coffee shop in Bayswater Road by way of Chester Place. Even allowing for the lengthy time it had taken him to cross Edgeware Road the journey between the two houses had taken less than twenty minutes. A cab or carriage ride at the late hour the general was murdered would have taken far less time.

Like many squares in this privileged corner of London, Portman Square had been built during the eighteenth century in the classical style that had then been fashionable. Many houses in the square were owned by members of the nobility, although they had not chosen to advertise that fact by being vulgar enough to put their names on brass plaques outside their front doors. But it said much about the fortune and social standing of Mrs. Fitzgerald that she should be living in such select company.

Like the other houses in the square, the large black double-door of number forty-eight with its gleaming brass knocker, was approached by a flight of wide stone steps and protected from the weather by an open porch supported by two Doric columns. Even at an hour when countless thousands were wending their way home from their places of work the square maintained a dignified silence: a peaceful oasis only a short distance from the hurly-burly of the London traffic.

As he waited for a response to his loud knock Parsons basked in this unaccustomed tranquility and the agreeable sensation of feeling the warmth of the last rays of the setting sun on his back. Doubtless there was a delightfully secluded garden at the rear of the house that would enjoy the benefits of the morning sun and provide an ideal spot on a summer's day to breakfast at leisure and peruse the morning paper. Portman Square was indeed a most enviable place in which to live.

Parsons did not have long to wait before a tall, handsome manservant in green livery opened the door.

"Good afternoon, sir," he said, in a soft Irish burr. In a city in which most servants were native Londoners the accent was a pleasant surprise, and it perfectly complemented the man's fine head of copper-colored hair. There was little doubting that he came from Ireland.

"Mrs. Fitzgerald has been expecting a visit from the police," the manservant said, after Parsons had introduced himself and explained the nature of his business. "Please be so good as to follow me."

The servant led Parsons up a wide spiral staircase past gilt-framed portraits of distinguished men and women whom Parsons presumed to be family antecedents, each succeeding generation dressed in a manner and painted in a context in keeping with their obvious wealth. Paintings of idyllic rural scenes - Parsons recognized a Turner and a Constable amongst them - lined the walls of the circular balustraded first floor landing, interspersed at regular intervals with fluted pedestals bearing busts of heroic figures from the classical worlds of Greece and Rome.

Parsons followed the servant along a long corridor with yet more paintings of rural scenes, this time of Ireland, until he stopped in front of one of the doors and knocked politely.

"Enter," a woman's soft voice said from within.

"Inspector Parsons of Scotland Yard, ma'am," said the servant as he opened the door and preceded Parsons into the room.

"Thank you, Dwyer, that will be all."

The accent, although more refined than that of the departing servant, nevertheless betrayed the woman's Irish roots. But until she spoke for a second time Parsons had some difficulty in locating the source of the voice in the large, richly furnished drawing room.

"I'm over here by the window, inspector."

A small woman with dark-green, intelligent eyes and gentle features sat in a wing-backed chair facing towards the street. It was likely, Parsons thought, that she would have witnessed his arrival.

Out of respect for the man she had hoped to marry she wore a simple dress of black sateen. It was a color that served to accentuate the luster of auburn hair that in the last rays of the setting sun seemed especially vibrant. Parsons noted that she made no attempt to hide any flecks of gray. Had she chosen to do so, he considered she would look many years younger than her present age, which he estimated at being in the early to mid fifties. She wore a simple gold locket and two rings: a wedding band on her right hand and a diamond on her left. Parsons surmised that the first ring represented an earlier marriage, the second her engagement to General Latham.

"Edwina Fitzgerald," she said as she offered a delicate hand for Parsons to shake. "Please help yourself to a glass of sherry, inspector. You'll forgive me if I do not join you, but I have already enjoyed my singular glass. I find that one glass of wine before dinner to be quite sufficient for a woman of my years."

Her virescent eyes twinkled and her mouth widened into a grin.

"I've been expecting a visit from the police ever since poor Maxwell was murdered," she said softly. "I'm only surprised it has taken so long. But no doubt there have been more pressing demands upon your time such as finding the fiends who were responsible for the assassination of Lord Sayers."

Parsons was surprised by what she had said. If he understood her correctly she was implying that the pursuit of those responsible for Lord Sayers' death was more important than finding the murderer of her future husband.

"Please do not misunderstand me, inspector," she said, as though sensing the confusion her words had caused. "Of course, I want to see Maxwell's murderer brought to justice. And from what I read in the newspapers you are well on your way to doing that. It is simply that I feel I have a larger score to settle with the Fenians."

She stooped to pick up a black ebony cane that, unseen to Parsons, had been lying on the floor beside her chair.

"They not only killed my husband," she said with unexpected bitterness. "They were also responsible for scarring and crippling me for life."

"I am most sorry to hear that, ma'am," Parsons said, "and if it is not too distressing I would like you to tell me how that occurred."

"I'm only too pleased to oblige, inspector," she said. "But I see that you're neglecting your sherry."

Mrs. Fitzgerald waited until Parsons had taken a sip from his glass before continuing.

"My late husband's family can trace its roots to the twelfth century Norman conquest of Ireland," she said. "But over the centuries the family intermarried with the native Irish and became thoroughly assimilated into their culture. As a result they developed a strong love for the country and its people, and indeed, after a few generations, considered themselves to be no longer anything but Irish. My husband's marriage to me, an O'Shaughnessy, was a small part of that evolution. However, as strong as our allegiance to Ireland might be, neither my late husband nor I could ever empathize with the men and woman of violence who in more recent years have chosen the gun and the bomb as a way of attempting to gain Ireland's independence. Indeed, my husband spoke out strongly and frequently against them. And for that he was punished. Those fiends burned our home in Wicklow and my husband within it. I escaped with my life, but the scars on my body will always remain with me and remind me of that truly dreadful night."

"How long ago did this happen?" Parsons asked.

"Three years, inspector. Since then I have been living here in fear of returning to my native land. My husband's family have owned this house for generations. But when he was alive we rarely came to England. We far preferred that wild and beautiful country across the sea. I choose to live a solitary life here, so as you may imagine, I have few friends. You see, in spite of all that has happened, my heart is still in Ireland."

She smiled wistfully at Parsons.

"I met Maxwell only a few weeks ago in Hyde Park," she said. "I was taking the air in my carriage and he was riding. He was a fine figure on a horse, and in my rather grand carriage I no doubt presented an attractive proposition for him. We talked for a while and I learned that he was shortly to be taking up a senior post in Ireland. For my part I told him about my widowhood and my estates in that country."

She reached across and gently touched Parsons' hand.

"I could see his eyes light up when he heard that," she said. "And I could see at once that he was interested in me. I am not a foolish woman, and I knew that such a man could not possibly love me. You see, I have since made a few discrete enquiries, so I knew of Maxwell's reputation. I also learned that he continued with his liaisons even after he had asked me to marry him. But I was prepared to ignore all that. As far as I could see we both had a need for one another. If he was to entertain in the manner expected of the senior military officer in Ireland he would need money. He had told me he had little, and I had more than enough for us both. And for his part he could offer me the sort of security and protection I needed if ever I was to feel safe again in the country I loved. What need did either of us have for romance when we would have everything else we wanted?"

"From what you said earlier it seems that you don't believe the Fenians guilty of murdering General Latham," said Parsons.

"I have no doubt about that, inspector," she replied. "I know their methods. Maxwell was, of course, an obvious target, once his appointment had been announced; and who knows, the devils may have attempted to kill him at a later date. In my opinion you've arrested the right person. If I was a young woman I think it very possible I would have reacted in much the same way as Mrs. Cordell did after learning that her lover had abandoned her for another. Especially if the other woman was older and less attractive. You see, we Irish can be every bit as passionate as the French. That is probably why you English will never understand either of us."

"You're probably right about that, ma'am," Parsons said. "We English often appear lacking in emotion. But in view of this Irish passion that you speak of I hope you will forgive me for asking my next question. Where were you on the night General Latham was murdered?"

Mrs. Fitzgerald's charming smile made plain that she had not taken offense.

"I perfectly understand your reason for asking me that, inspector. You would be failing in your duty had you not done so. But you cannot honestly believe that I would do anything to destroy my one hope of returning to Ireland. Especially as I was already aware of Maxwell's past liaisons when I accepted his proposal of marriage. I did not kill him, inspector. I was here the night he was murdered. Dwyer can vouch for that. Well, at least he can vouch for me until I went to bed at ten thirty. After that you will just have to accept my word. But as it happens I have never visited Maxwell's house, nor had he ever come here. We wanted our relationship to remain a secret until Maxwell's appointment was made official. Only then did we announce our engagement and begin making plans for the wedding."

Edwina Fitzgerald gazed wistfully towards the silent street outside her window.

"But that was not to be," she said sadly. "And now I do not know when I shall ever see my beloved Ireland again."

Parsons saw the tears gathering in her beautiful green eyes. Only she could know if they were tears for the death of her future husband, or because her return to the country she loved had been indefinitely delayed.

"You may be surprised to learn that few people I've spoken to know much about you, Mrs. Fitzgerald," Parsons said. "Although I believe you were present at the general's funeral and were perhaps even invited to join the other mourners in the Officers' Mess."

"Both of those are true, inspector. It was only right that I should attend Maxwell's funeral, although I have refrained from mourning him in the manner that many people would consider appropriate. I am sure it will not have escaped your notice that there is no wreath on the door, nor have I felt it necessary to have sand scattered in the street, stop the clocks in the house, or cover the mirrors. I also declined Colonel Cordell's kind invitation to join him in the Mess. I dislike crowds and social gatherings such as that. Apart from the fact that I knew nobody, my recent engagement to Maxwell and my obvious physical impairment would have made me something of a curiosity. And that was a situation I wished to avoid.

31

PARSONS WAS DELIGHTED to find a letter from Louise on Mrs. Oakley's hall table. Knowing the good lady as he did he knew that as soon as she had seen the post mark she would have made a point of placing the letter in a prominent position where he would be sure to see it when he came in. She had chosen to lean it against the large cut-glass vase of fresh flowers she regularly replenished from her large south-facing garden. Even in late October she could still muster a charming display of violet grandiflorus and white tradescanti. It was a charming and romantic gesture.

Louise and her family, he read, after climbing the stairs to his sitting room with the sandwich and bottle of port he had bought on the way from Portman Square, would be leaving Keswick at the end of the week. Amelia Parsons would be accompanying the Chapmans to London and would stay with them overnight on Saturday, as their train would reach Euston far too late for her to contemplate a further tiring journey to her home in Hampstead. Louise therefore hoped that Parsons could make himself available on Sunday to escort his mother to King's Cross Station. That was, she wrote, if it were not too much trouble.

Parsons found himself unexpectedly irritated by the implication that it would ever be inconvenient or too much trouble for him to escort his mother anywhere. He was also dismayed to read that Louise had been disappointed at receiving only one letter from him since his return to London. Her parents, she wrote, had commented several times on his neglect, and even his own mother had said that under the circumstances she would have expected him to have written more often.

It was all very well for them to say that, Parsons thought gloomily. After all Louise had written to him only once. And she was not in the middle of a increasingly complex murder investigation. Compared to him she had all the time in the world. Was this, he wondered, an early indication of how difficult she would find it being married to a man who was frequently obliged to work long and unpredictable hours. She was, after all, accustomed to seeing her father work the leisurely hours of a wealthy banker and watching her indolent brother enjoy the lengthy periods of leave he was entitled to as a cavalry officer.

With other more important things on his mind Parsons had little wish to dwell on the matter, and scribbled a hasty reply saying that he would be at the Chapman's house in Kensington at ten thirty on Sunday. Then he found a clean plate for his sandwich, opened the bottle of port and poured himself a generous measure.

———————

IN SPITE OF the existence of a suicide note and Doctor Grainger's conviction about the nature of Cordell's death, Parsons was far from being convinced that the colonel had taken his own life. For a start, the note had been printed in a clumsy fashion. Admittedly the colonel had drunk to excess, a situation that would doubtless have affected his handwriting, but even in those circumstances Parsons could not imagine him resorting to printing his final words. The more he thought of it the more unreasonable it seemed. The voice of Reason was soft, but it was nevertheless persistent. And Parsons flattered himself on being persistent.

Parsons envisaged that something more sinister than suicide had occurred that night. He imagined Cordell going to his room much the worse for drink, and, as most men in his condition would have done, falling onto his bed into a deep sleep. Sometime later, probably between twelve and half past, his murderer had come into the bedroom, smothered him with one of his pillows, and run the bath. Then he had dragged Cordell into the bathroom, slit his wrists and left him to bleed to death.

Whoever the murderer was must have known something of Cordell's state of mind. He must have been aware of the quarrel with Simpson, and have known that Cordell had been drinking to excess. And as far as Parsons could see that could only be one of two groups of people. Either Cordell's servants or the men and women in the Officers' Mess on the afternoon before he died. But which of these people would have decided to write such an unusual suicide note to Audley Simpson? And for what possible reason?

Parsons finished his sandwich, poured himself another large glass of port and allowed his imagination free rein. It was the part of detection that gave him the most pleasure.

If, as he suspected, Cordell had been murdered, was it not also possible that the person or persons involved had murdered Latham? It seemed too great a coincidence that both deaths had taken place within such a short space of time for there not be a link between them. The two men were half-brothers, had served together in the same regiment, and one man's wife was the other's mistress. There was also a similarity between Cordell's suicide note and the last note Venetta Cordell had received.

Parsons took a long and thoughtful sip of port. Who were the possible suspects and should Venetta Cordell still be considered as one? The evidence against her for Latham's death looked increasingly less convincing; and without an accomplice there was no possibility of her being involved in the murder of her husband. But if she had an accomplice was she part of a conspiracy to murder prominent military and civilian figures?

Were she and her maid, Edith, working together? Had one of them murdered Latham, and the other, Cordell?

Parsons considered that possibility and then dismissed it. Venetta Cordell might well have murdered Latham, but Edith could not have killed Cordell without herself having an accomplice. There was no way a slim young woman such as she could have managed single-handedly to smother Cordell, drag him into the bathroom, and lift him into the bath.

In Parsons' opinion there was only one person with both motive and opportunity for both deaths. Lady Cordelia Arbuthnot. By general consensus she was an ambitious woman who considered her husband to be the rightful commanding officer. If Venetta Cordell was to be believed, Cordelia had attempted to secure that promotion by offering to become Latham's mistress. And Latham had turned her down, and then proceeded to add insult to injury by having his incompetent half-brother promoted in Arbuthnot's place. But now, with both men dead, Arbuthnot was again an obvious candidate to be commanding officer.

If Venetta could be in Chester Place on the night Latham was murdered, then so indeed could Cordelia? If Venetta had access to Cordell's *iklwas*, then surely so had Cordelia. Cordelia could also have been the older woman seen in the newsagent's shop delivering the last note for Venetta. The note that had prompted her to visit Chester Place, and thereby become the prime suspect for Latham's death. It was also Cordelia who had fired Venetta's passions by informing her of Latham's engagement, and of his decision to abandon her for an older and richer woman.

Cordelia had also been present in the Officers' Mess to witness the scene between Cordell and Simpson. She would have been aware of Cordell's fragile state of mind; indeed she had contributed to it by publicly snubbing him. And she would have seen Cordell become increasingly drunk. It was not something she could have planned, but it, nevertheless, provided her with an excellent opportunity to murder him. But would she have chosen to act alone? Would it not have made more sense for her to have an accomplice? Perhaps the same accomplice who had taken her to Chester Place on the night she murdered Latham.

Parsons poured himself another glass of port. He was warming to the task, and the more he thought of Cordelia as a suspect the more he considered it likely. If any woman was capable of thrusting an *iklwa* into Latham's chest or slashing Cordell's wrists it was she.

An accomplice would also explain the conflicting evidence provided by Constable Matthews and the two cabmen. If Cordelia had been the veiled woman seen before midnight in Chester Place by Matthews it would explain why no hansom driver had ever reported having her as a passenger. She had no need of a cab when she had a carriage of her own and a coachman to act as her accomplice. And the accent that had deceived both the newsagent and Matthews would have been easy enough to contrive. It would have been a relatively simple matter for Cordelia to have summoned up a few words of French.

There was the small matter of how Cordelia had gained access to Chester Place without a key. But Parsons doubted whether that had presented much of a problem to such a determined and resourceful woman. What was of far greater significance and was now of critical importance to the investigation, was knowledge of her whereabouts on the nights that Latham and Cordell were murdered. And that was an issue that Harris was at present addressing.

Parsons was pleased with his evening's work, and was tempted to celebrate by refilling his empty glass. But then he realized that he had already drunk more than half the bottle. It was high time to exert some self-control. He had no wish to wake up in the morning with a sore head. Tomorrow promised to be another busy day.

32

A PALL OF EXPENSIVE cigar smoke blanketed the oval faro table at *Lasiters*, the exclusive Mayfair gambling club. Men in elegant evening dress gathered in small groups, the glow of the gas lamps in the chandelier above the table reflected a thousand fold in the cut glass of their brandy glasses and the pearl and diamond studs of their starched white shirt fronts.

Charles Arbuthnot toyed nervously with the stack of wooden betting counters in front of him and contemplated his next move. There were eighteen black counters each worth a pound, seven brown fives, five blue tens, four red twenties and two purple fifties. Two hundred and eighty-three pounds. It was a tidy sum, and one which on most nights he would readily have settled for. But not tonight. He needed far more than that to settle his monthly account, and Cordelia could no longer be relied upon to bail him out.

As the news of his good fortune had spread, the crowd around the table had thickened. Charles was a popular member of the club, although his gaming technique was considered by many to be reckless and unsystematic. But no one could deny that Charles had style. Who could fail to admire a man who played with such careless abandon, and at the same time could accept his losses with such insouciance.

It was good to see Charles enjoying a winning streak after his recent run of bad luck. His total losses for the month were, of course, a matter between Charles and the club management, but the general consensus was that he needed somewhere in the region of a thousand pounds to avoid the indignity of being named. That was not an event to be taken lightly. To be named for failing to honor a gambling debt could bring shame, ostracism, and, in the worst of cases, an appearance in court. For those unfortunate few it was a fate worse than death.

Of course, it was always assumed that Charles' wealthy wife honored his debts. That was until now. There was an ugly rumor circulating that Lady Cordelia had refused her husband further money; and judging by the beads of perspiration on Charles' forehead and the nervous way in which he fingered his chips more was at stake than usual. It was clear that Charles' evening had reached a critical stage.

The conversation around the table had fallen to a whisper, each man sensing that the next play would decide matters one way or another. Every sportsman knew the thrill of the chase. But there was nothing quite like being in at the kill.

The wooden faro board between Charles and the dealer had the thirteen cards of the spade suit painted on its surface. It was a tradition of the game that the spade suit was used, although hearts, diamonds or clubs could equally well have been used. It was only the face value of each card that counted. There were two rows of six cards: the row nearest the dealer contained those between the ace and six, the row nearest Charles the cards between eight and the king. The thirteenth card, the seven, was on the dealer's right, at the end of the two rows of cards and midway between them.

It was the simplicity of faro that had always appealed to Charles. He had never favored games that required intellect and mental agility. His idea of an exhilarating game was one in which a large sum of money could be staked on the turn of a single card.

In faro, wagers can be made on one or more of the thirteen cards on the board. The dealer, who was also the bank, then deals face up from a new deck, discarding the first of the fifty-two cards, and dealing the remainder in pairs. The first card of any pair is the 'banker's card', and all bets placed upon that card become the dealer's. The bank pays out on the second card: the 'player's card' or the *carte anglais*.

The nature of the game changes when the dealer retains only three cards. At this stage the odds are increased, and there is a greater chance of winning or losing large sums of money. And it was precisely at this stage that Charles had earned his reputation as a man who took the sort of wild and unnecessary risks that more often than not led to him losing his entire evening's winnings. At this stage any player who has kept a careful note of the forty-nine cards already played will know exactly which cards the dealer has remaining in his hand. All that is necessary is for the player to decide the order in which those three cards are to be dealt.

The dealer had just offered Charles and the five other players remaining in the game the opportunity of making a wager on these last three cards. There was no obligation to accept this challenge; so that Charles, had he chosen, could have withdrawn from the game with his winnings intact. But the odds were irresistible, for were he to guess the order in which the last three cards were dealt he would receive four times his stake.

Charles knew that the three cards remaining were the two, the eight and the queen. It was just a matter of deciding the order in which they would be played. Normally he made the decision in a cavalier fashion with little apparent thought. But tonight there was far more was at stake. His reputation at the club and even his good name could be riding on the next few minutes; and he could sense a feverish anticipation growing amongst the onlookers pressed around the table.

Finally he reached a decision. The queen, he decided, would come first, the deuce last. He scrawled the numbers on a paper, signed it, folded it, and passed it to the man acting as the dealer's assistant. Then he pushed the whole of his winnings onto the table.

There was a palpable gasp of surprise, and from the darkness around him Charles could hear whispers of both admiration and derision.

"The man's a fool," said one.

"Good for you, old boy," said another.

"We'll probably see him next in the High Court," said a third.

A silence fell as the cards were played. Men craned forward, some to see the fall of the cards, but most to watch the expression on Charles' face.

Charles had eyes only for the cards. His hands were clasped tightly, the knuckles showing white, and perspiration trickled down his ashen face and soaked the back of his silk shirt.

His heart missed a beat when the queen was played, but when it was followed by the eight Charles sprang to his feet, his renowned composure and equanimity abandoned.

"My God," he shouted, "I've won! I've bloody won!"

None of the remaining players had guessed the correct sequence. Charles was the sole winner of eleven hundred and thirty-two pounds. Fourteen hundred and fifteen pounds, if he included his stake. Enough to pay his debts and still have plenty to spare. It was a cause for celebration.

THE DINNER WITH two of his fellow gamblers at the Cafe Royal in Piccadilly was a riotous affair.

They dined on hare soup, oyster patties, a saddle of mutton and a cheese fondue, and consumed five bottles of vintage champagne. Charles had insisted on paying, his mood one of boundless magnanimity.

It was after two in the the morning when the three men parted. Charles headed for Bayswater. After the thrill and relief of his great win, followed by an excellent dinner, he felt the need to satisfy another appetite. He needed a woman. He had been too long without one.

———————

A CRESCENT MOON flirted with the flurrying fog as the cab turned off Westbourne Grove into Newton Terrace and stopped outside one of the large houses in the short *cul de sac*. The street was silent at this late hour, the more respectable inhabitants of Newton Terrace having long since gone to their beds. That was not the rule in the house Charles entered. In Kate Hamilton's house the residents slept mainly during the day.

Kate had chosen the house carefully. Apart from its relative seclusion it was close enough to the barracks in Chelsea, Knightsbridge, Kensington and Hyde Park to ensure a steady flow of respectable clientele. Young, unmarried army officers had a need that was unlikely to be satisfied by well-bred single ladies of their own class, for whom the slightest sign of impropriety meant losing the chance of a respectable marriage. And such were the strictures of the officer corps that captains and lieutenants were strongly discouraged from marrying, and even those majors who were actively seeking a suitable bride were unlikely to satisfy their sexual appetites much beyond that of exchanging a few clumsy kisses. There were also married officers like Charles. Men whose intimate relations with their wives were only a distant memory. It was military patrons such as these that Kate provided for. She offered her exclusive clientele a service that was discrete, and an assurance that her girls were regularly inspected to ensure they were free of disease.

In addition to Kate, the house was large enough to accommodate four girls. For her part Kate provided free board and suitably fashionable clothing for them, and in return kept the bulk of their earnings. She chose her girls carefully. Good looks and an attractive figure were, of course, essential to attract the virile young men who frequented her establishment. But Kate considered it equally important that the young women were desperate enough to accept the one-sided arrangement she imposed in return for being well fed and having a roof over their heads. Typically they were women who had previously been employed in domestic service, as sales assistants, or as dress makers, and had lost these positions by embarking upon relationships that their employers considered unsuitable.

Charles was hoping to avoid meeting other officers from the regiment. He was, after all, now their commanding officer. The last thing he wanted was to be seen by one of the young officers he would later encounter in the Mess. He was not a regular client of Kate's. For the most part he preferred the excitement of the faro table to the pleasures of the bedroom, but the thrill of his victory and an excess of champagne had rekindled his libido.

"Good evening, Major Arbuthnot," Kate said when she answered the door. "Or should I say 'colonel'. My heartiest congratulations. And may I say how pleased I am to see that, in spite of your promotion, you continue to honor us with your company."

Charles was surprised that Kate knew of his promotion. It had been so recent that she could only have heard about it from another officer in the regiment. Perhaps that officer was still in the house. For a moment Charles thought of leaving. But the evening had been such a great triumph that he was reluctant to deprive himself of one last pleasure. He was relieved, nevertheless, to find the drawing room, with its cheap glass chandeliers, its collection of gilt-framed mirrors, and its dark draperies, occupied only by three attractive young women seated demurely on red velvet sofas.

"Allow me to introduce my girls," Kate said. "I think they are all new since you were last here."

This is Eustace," she said, indicating a dark eyed girl with long brown hair. "Victoria is the beautiful blonde, and Roselinda my exquisite redhead. But allow me to get you a drink while you are making up your mind. A glass of champagne, perhaps."

Charles bowed to each of the young women. He had already decided which one he wanted. The dark one in the low-cut black dress reminded him of the Queen of Spades on the faro table. And she had proved lucky for him.

He took the glass offered by Kate and took a seat beside Eustace. But before he had opportunity to start a conversation Mark Holland entered the room with a fourth woman.

"Charles," he said in delight. "You old devil. I didn't expect to see you here."

Holland was obviously the worse for drink. He had his arm around the woman's shoulders and was leaning heavily against her to avoid staggering.

"I can recommend any of Kate's girls," he said expansively. "I should know. I'm one of Kate's best customers. But this is my favorite. Leastwise, she is tonight."

Holland giggled like a naughty schoolboy and gave the woman a clumsy kiss on her cheek.

"Charles," he said. "Allow me to introduce Bernadette, my little French girl. She's come all the way from gay Paree."

33

Thursday, 30th October

FOLLOWING HIS EARLIER reprimand, Parsons had managed to avoid Jeffries, and had hoped that the superintendent was too involved with his own problems to take an undue interest in whatever Parsons was doing. But that situation, he knew, could not last.

As he filled his mug from the tea pot in the General Office, Parsons learned that during the past few days much of the heat had been taken off Jeffries. Although no one had actually been arrested and charged with Lord Frederick Sayers' murder, the nationwide hue and cry led by Jeffries had achieved a modicum of success. Weapons had been discovered in the Irish neighborhoods of London and Liverpool, leading to several arrests and the promise of long prison sentences. In addition, the feared attacks on other senior Establishment figures had failed to materialize, and the general consensus in the corridors of power was that although the CID had failed to arrest Sayers' murderer it had, nevertheless, performed adequately.

The public had also begun to grow weary of the subject, as a result of which newspaper editors had concluded that their constant criticism of the police was no longer serving its purpose, and that fresh material was needed to titillate their readers. And as fortune would have it a suitable alternative presented itself. A junior member of the Cabinet was caught with his trousers down in an East End bordello, a situation that not only afforded the public much amusement but also enabled the press to speculate at great length upon the quality of men who were running the country. It was yet another reason why the politicians had chosen to refrain for raising the subject of police incompetence in Parliament.

It was, in consequence, a somewhat rejuvenated Jeffries who summoned Parsons to his office for a progress report.

"For what it's worth I think you've got the right woman, Parsons," he said, tapping the stem of his pipe against his tobacco-stained teeth. "This French woman seems just the sort to have carried out a demented attack on her lover. Isn't that what the French call a crime of passion?"

"But the evidence against her isn't as strong as it first appeared, sir," Parsons said. "Not after the police constable changed his mind about the time he saw the veiled woman arrive at the general's house."

Jeffries puffed hard on his pipe and exhaled a long plume of smoke.

"That's as may be," he said. "And I've no objection to you checking on this Arbuthnot woman. But whatever you do you're not to release Mrs. Cordell until you're convinced of her innocence and have cast iron evidence against the other woman. I take it you've charged Mrs. Cordell."

"Yes, sir. I did that at the time she was arrested."

"Good work. Now what's this I hear about her husband committing suicide?"

Parsons outlined the series of events that had led up to the Colonel Cordell's death and his own subsequent investigation.

"You say he was a highly strung man, Parsons," Jeffries said.

"That was my opinion when we first met, sir. I thought at the time that he was a most unlikely person to be commanding an infantry regiment."

"Well, that's nepotism for you, Parsons. The general was his half-brother, wasn't he? He probably arranged Cordell's promotion. It happens all the time. Just take a look at the so-called leaders of this great country of ours. Most of them wouldn't be where they are without a helping hand from someone in their family. And we all know that the higher echelons of the police forces throughout the country are riddled with retired senior army officers."

Parsons was not surprised by Jeffries' outburst. The superintendent's opinion of the

methods used to fill the senior ranks of the
Metropolitan Police were well known, although he
was not usually so scathing with his remarks in
front of a junior officer like Parsons. It was,
thought Parsons, an understandable reaction to the
pressure Jeffries had experienced during the
Sayers' investigation from Colonel Wilson, the
Police Commissioner. On the other hand, Jeffries
could well have been having a dig at Parsons
himself. It was common knowledge in the
department that Parsons' father, a retired Indian
Army colonel, had prevailed upon the
Commissioner to accept his son into the CID even
though he fell short of the minimum height
requirements. Although Parsons had subsequently
more than proved his worth as a detective, the
charge of nepotism would always remain.

Parsons was not, therefore, displeased when
Jeffries decided to change the subject.

"Does the police surgeon think it's suicide?"
Jeffries asked.

"Yes, sir," Parsons said unenthusiastically. "I
received Doctor Grainger's report only this
morning. He confirms that Colonel Cordell died
somewhere between midnight and two in the
morning, which agrees with what the colonel's
servants said. And he hasn't changed his mind
about the cause of death."

"You don't sound convinced, Parsons. Didn't
you say there was a suicide note? Something about
not living any longer with a lie. What do you
suppose that was all about?"

"Before Colonel Cordell died he and Captain Simpson were seen having a very loud and public row in the Officers' Mess. The lie referred to in Cordell's note may well have had something to do with his marriage, but on the other hand it could refer to the relationship he had with Simpson. You see, before he was promoted and married, Cordell and young Simpson had a very close friendship."

Jeffries considered the implication of what Parsons had said for several minutes, during which he puffed forcefully on his pipe.

"Are you suggesting that their relationship was homosexual, Parsons?" he said finally. "If so you had better watch your step. You'll be skating on pretty thin ice if you try to prove that one. And hadn't Cordell just got married? Doesn't that say something about his sexual inclinations?"

"Not really, sir," Parsons explained. "For social reasons, if for no other, commanding officers in the army are expected to marry. But even if we assume that Cordell had chosen to marry out of necessity, his marriage nevertheless seems to have come as a complete surprise to most people. Especially to Simpson. The two men were holidaying together in France when Cordell met his future wife, and if the rumors are true it was she who took the initiative when she realized his predicament."

"What exactly do you mean by *his predicament*, Parsons?"

"I mean that Cordell must have told her that he was in need of a wife, and it appears that she didn't waste time in persuading him to marry her.

From what I've learned it was a marriage that was doomed from the start. They were obviously ill-matched, and Mrs. Cordell, for one, never made any attempt to hide that from Sergeant Harris and me. She as good as told us that her husband had been less than intimate with her, a fact that is supported by their bedrooms being in separate wings of the house. Mrs. Cordell claimed that this lack of intimacy was the main reason for her entering upon a relationship with General Latham. So although Cordell's suicide note may make some sense in the wider context of his marriage, I'm afraid it makes little sense to me. As far as I'm concerned his death was not suicide."

"Far be it for me to criticize you for keeping an open mind, Parsons." said Jeffries thoughtfully. "But just you keep your eye on the ball. Your job at the moment is to get a successful conviction for General Latham's murder. All this speculating about what may or may not be behind Colonel Cordell's death can wait."

The superintendent began emptying the bowl of his pipe into his ashtray. It was his signal that the interview was over.

"And one final warning, Parsons," he said. "I'm sure you must be aware that Colonel Cordell's death and his wife's arrest for murdering General Latham has already attracted considerable interest in the Commissioner's office. So if you know what's good for you I wouldn't start leveling charges of homosexuality against anyone. Even if they subsequently prove to be false, accusations like that can ruin a man's reputation.

It doesn't do the army much good either. And there are plenty of senior officers, including Colonel Wilson, who would not take kindly to that."

"WELL, HARRIS, WHAT news have you got about Lady Arbuthnot?" Parsons asked when he and Harris were drinking tea together in Parsons' office. "I'm convinced she's involved in Latham's death. Perhaps Cordell's as well."

"I'm sorry, sir, but I've got nothing to report yet. I'm still trying to find a way to get one of Arbuthnot's servants to talk openly about his employer. I don't want to approach any of them directly so I've asked the desk sergeant at Chelsea Division to question the constables who regularly patrol the area around Eaton Square to see what they know about the Arbuthnots and their servants. And that may take a day or two."

Parsons was far from pleased. After his deliberations the previous night he was convinced that his suspicions about Cordelia Arbuthnot were well founded. But he needed something more than speculation. And he had relied upon Harris to get it for him.

"Well, that's just not good enough, Harris," he said irritably.

Almost at once he regretted his tone. If he was honest he was still vexed by what Louise had said in her letter, and it was unfair of him to make Harris suffer for that. Harris, he knew, was only doing what he felt was best. And if that took longer than Parsons had anticipated he would just have to be patient.

"Let me know the moment you discover anything, Harris," he said lamely. "Especially if you find out who used the Arbuthnot's carriage on the nights Latham and Cordell died. As I said before, I think the coachman is your best bet. If anyone knows about the Arbuthnot's nocturnal movements it'll be him. And for all we know he could even be Lady Cordelia's accomplice."

"How long have I got, sir?"

"Let's aim to meet here on Saturday morning, Harris. That gives you another two days."

Parsons knew that the next few days were crucial if he was hoping to arrest Lady Cordelia. He considered interviewing the Arbuthnots again, but for the moment could not think of a good enough reason."

As Harris was leaving the office one of the clerks entered.

"Telegram for you, inspector," he said.

"Wait a minute, Harris," Parsons said, reaching for his paper knife. "This may be important."

At first Parsons could not believe his eyes. It was the last thing he had been expecting.

"It's from Whitehead," he said, his eyes still fixed on the words before him. "There's been another suicide at the barracks. It's Captain Simpson this time. That wretched young man has shot himself."

34

"I'LL TELL YOU what I already know, inspector," RSM Whitehead explained, as he and Parsons set off at a brisk march around the edge of the parade ground towards the Officers' Mess. After sending word for the police surgeon Parsons had come to the barracks alone. Harris' own investigation was far too important to be interrupted, even by a second suicide in the barracks within the space of twenty four hours.

"Captain Simpson's servant found his body this morning before breakfast. It looks very much as though the captain shot himself in his room sometime late last night."

"How do you know it wasn't early this morning, RSM," asked Parsons.

"Of course, I can't be certain, sir. I'm not a doctor, but I've seen a few dead bodies in my time. And from the state of Simpson's when I saw it I'd say he'd been dead for several hours."

"And what time was that?"

"Just after eight. I'd just finished my breakfast when I heard the news."

"Who else knows about this?" asked Parsons.

Whitehead barely checked his step, but from his expression Parsons could tell that he considered the question to have been foolish.

"It's common knowledge by now," he said impatiently. "This is a military barracks, Inspector Parsons. News travels around here faster than a bush fire."

"What about Colonel Arbuthnot? Has he been informed?"

"He's already here. I believe Major Holland sent for him as soon as he was told about Captain Simpson's death."

———————

EVEN THE NORMALLY languid Arbuthnot appeared shaken by events. His handsome features were more haggard than usual, and he looked short of sleep. It was also apparent that he had been summoned from his house before he was ready to leave, as his hair showed signs of being hastily brushed and his face was unshaven.

"This is absolutely shocking news," he said as the three men made their way upstairs to the bachelor officers' bedrooms. "In all my years in the army I've never seen anything quite like this. First the commanding officer, and now one of our best young officers. Heaven knows what it will do for the regiment's reputation. If you also include the fact that one of our wives has been arrested for murdering a general, it won't be surprising if the rest of the army considers us to quite beyond the pale."

It was unlikely that many would even know the meaning of the expression, thought Parsons. 'Beyond the Pale' was an epithet used by many people, but few knew its origin, 'The Pale' had been the only area of Ireland controlled by England during the late Middle Ages. Everything beyond the Pale was considered to be inhabited by a wild and uncivilized people: the Irish. In many people's opinion little had changed since then.

A mess servant in a white shirt, a black bow tie, and navy serge trousers was standing outside one of the doors on the first floor.

"Major Holland ordered Sergeant Barnard to keep a servant posted outside Captain Simpson's door," Arbuthnot explained. "As you probably know Holland's the senior officer living in the Mess. So other than him, the RSM and myself no one's been in the room since Simpson's servant found the body at half past seven this morning. That's when he brought Simpson his morning tea."

"Sergeant Barnard is, I assume, the mess sergeant," Parsons said.

"That's correct, inspector," Arbuthnot replied.

"I hope that means that nothing in the room has been touched."

"To the best of my knowledge that is correct."

"And where is Captain Simpson's servant now?"

"He's downstairs with the other mess servants," said Arbuthnot. "I imagine they're all in the kitchen. No one's been allowed to leave the building. But that doesn't mean that the news hasn't got out. The gate sentry asked me whether it was true that Captain Simpson was dead when I arrived this morning."

From the corner of his eye Parsons detected the smug expression on Whitehead's face. As the RSM had said, news traveled fast in the close confines of the barracks.

"I'll want to speak with Captain Simpson's servant after I've examined his body," Parsons said. "I'll also want to see the rest of the servants and each of the officers who were in the Mess last night. Can you arrange that for me, colonel?"

Arbuthnot nodded.

"My compliments to Major Holland and Sergeant Barnard," he said to the servant. "Ask Major Holland to assemble all the officers in the ante room, and then tell Sergeant Barnard that Inspector Parsons wants to see Captain Simpson's servant immediately. Tell him the other mess servants are to remain in the kitchen, and remind him that no one is to leave the building without my authority."

"And what exactly would you like Mr. Whitehead and me to do, inspector?" said Arbuthnot frostily. The new commanding officer had not relished being given instructions by the bumptious young policeman he considered to be his social inferior.

"I'd appreciate it, gentlemen," Parsons said, "if you will leave me to examine the room alone, and I would be grateful if you will have Doctor Grainger escorted upstairs as soon as he arrives."

PARSONS' FIRST IMPRESSIONS of Simpson's room was that it provided a stark contrast to the ostentatious display of military memorabilia on the floor below. At best, with its simple furniture of cheap pine, the room could be described as a picture of disheveled unpretentiousness. Even his humble rooms in Elm Park Avenue were more lavishly furnished; and he did not imagine that his income matched the private means that Simpson, like most other army officers, possessed.

A large wardrobe, with one door hanging ajar occupied much of the wall to the left of the door. To the right stood a pine chest with two of its four drawers partially open. Each had items of clothing draped over the edge. Parsons could only imagine what the RSM had thought when he saw the room earlier.

A tray with a teapot, a jar of milk, and a cup rested on top of the chest, and as Parsons moved further into the room he could see that beyond the chest was a washstand with a mirror and a freestanding towel rail. Simpson's narrow bed flanked the third wall, with a small locker beside it on which there were a set of keys. The covers of his bed had not been drawn down, but there was an indentation in the pillow and along the counterpane that suggested that at sometime prior to his death he had been lying there.

At the time of his death, Simpson appeared to have been sitting at his desk facing the window. The curtains were open, so that had he still been alive, he would have seen the soldiers on the parade ground below him, performing the routine drills that he would doubtless have seen countless times before.

The young man's torso had slumped forward onto the desk. It was lying in a pool of blood, that before it had dried had spilled out across the desk and onto the floor. Simpson's head was twisted to the right, and were it not for the blood Parsons might well have thought he was resting. His left arm hung loosely at his side, its outstretched fingers stretching towards the floor. The other arm rested on the desk, forming an almost perfect right angle from Simpson's shoulder to the revolver in his hand, his four fingers wrapped around the stock and his thumb on the trigger. An almost empty bottle of Jameson Irish whiskey was perched on one corner of the desk and two photographs in silver frames on the other.

Parsons was immediately struck by two things. The first was that the position of the body, the whiskey bottle and the photographs gave the impression of having been carefully arranged in what was almost a theatrical fashion. The second was that the brand of whiskey was the same that had been found in Cordell's bathroom.

He bent to look at the two photographs. One was of an older couple: the man tall and slim like

Simpson, but with a mass of hair and a beard; the woman small and delicate. He was dressed as a minister of the church, she in a simple floral dress. These were, no doubt, Simpson's parents. The other photo showed two men on horseback. One of the men was Simpson himself. The other was Hector Cordell. They were both dressed in uniform and were smiling, and looking more carefree than Parsons would ever have imagined them capable. He picked up the frame to examine the photograph more closely, noticing as he did, that apart from a single fragment in the corner of the frame, the glass was missing.

A bloodstained sheet of cheap note paper lay almost equidistant between the two photographs, on which a single sentence had been printed in a clumsy hand. Parsons read: *'THAT LIE DESTROYED US BOTH'*. Unlike Cordell, Simpson's suicide note did not appear to have been addressed to anyone in particular. At first sight these final words did not seem intended for the young man's parents, and Parsons could only imagine how sad that would make them feel. There was also no indication as to what the lie might be, but it took no great leap of the imagination to see a link between the lie referred to in this note and that in Cordell's.

There was no sign of a pen or ink. If Simpson had written the note and then placed the pen and ink in one of the desk drawers before shooting himself, Parsons mused, he was exhibiting a degree of tidiness that was not obvious in other parts of the room.

The position of Simpson's head also struck Parsons as unusual. Had Simpson placed the barrel of the revolver in his mouth, held the stock in the fingers of his right hand and pulled the trigger with his thumb, Parsons would have expected Simpson's head to have been thrown backwards by the impact of the bullet entering his head. The impact might even have been great enough to have overturned the chair, in which case Parsons would have expected to find Simpson lying on the floor on his back instead of resting on his desk.

The revolver was a Webley, a type popular with army officers. It was also a weapon similar to that used to kill Lord Frederick Sayers.

In spite of the onset of *rigor mortis* Parsons was able to remove the weapon from Simpson's hand and open the cylinder. Only one shot had been fired. The remaining five bullets were still in place. Was that normally the case, he wondered? Would someone contemplating suicide fully load the cylinder when one shot was intended to be sufficient? But perhaps Simpson always kept his weapon fully loaded.

Parsons had noticed Simpson's badly bitten nails at their previous interview. Now that he was dead they looked even more pitiful. There was bruising on his right thumb that had not been there a few days ago. Parsons doubted it was a result of firing the revolver, but hopefully Doctor Grainger would be able to answer that.

Parsons' deliberations were interrupted by the arrival of a small, clean-shaven, middle-aged man with thinning straw-colored hair. He was wearing the uniform of a mess servant.

"You must be Captain Simpson's servant," Parsons said.

"Yes sir," the man replied nervously, with an apprehensive look towards the desk. "My name's Henderson."

"Have you been the captain's servant for long, Henderson?" Parsons asked.

"Only a few months, sir," Henderson explained, his words almost tripping over themselves as they spilled from his mouth. "Ever since the regiment come back from Africa. I weren't there, sir. Most of the officers' servants are soldiers. But there are some like me, who ain't no more. I was a soldier once. But not no more. When the regiment goes overseas a few of us stays 'ere. They keeps us on to make sure evry'thin's shipshape when they come 'ome."

"How would you describe Captain Simpson's mood during those months, Henderson."

"It were variable, sir. When he come 'ome first 'e were full o' life. Told me 'e were pleased to be back in the old country in one piece where there weren't no bloody natives tryin' to kill 'im. An' when he 'eard 'e were goin' ter get a medal for what 'e done 'e were on top o' the world. But round 'bout the time Major Cordell got made colonel things changed, sir. From what I 'eard Captain Simpson an' 'e were good friends in Africa. But naturally when the major become colonel 'e 'ad to put some distance between 'imself and the other officers. That's 'ow it should be. Ev'ry commandin' officer I've known 'as been like that. But Captain Simpson didn' like it one bit. 'E thought seein' that they been so friendly in Africa that Colonel Cordell would make an exception with 'im. But then 'e told me they was goin' away together. Somewhere in France I think it was."

"Rochefort?" Parsons asked.

"That's it, sir. It were Rochefort. Funny sort o' name ain't it. But what else would you expect from them Frenchies?"

"Did he speak about anything that happened in Rochefort? For instance did he say that Colonel Cordell had met someone he intended to marry?"

"No, sir. An' I wouldn' expect 'im to. Me bein' 'is servant like. All I can say is that when 'e come back 'e started drinkin' in a big way. I never seen anyone drink like that before. An' I seen plenty of drunks in my time in the army. It were a pity. 'E were such a nice young man. After a time none of the other officers wanted much to do wiv 'im, 'part from Major Holland. But if you were to ask me 'e were only friendly with the captain 'cause 'e were goin' to get a bleedin' medal."

"Did you ever hear any gossip in the Mess about the colonel and Captain Simpson?"

Henderson looked uncomfortable. It was clearly a subject he was reluctant to discuss.

"Some of the officers weren't at all 'appy about their relationship," he said. "Especially those who'd been in Africa. They called the captain 'Mrs. Cordell' behind 'is back. But if you ask me the captain were more of a man then the colonel ever was."

"How did Captain Simpson react to the colonel being married?"

"'Is drinkin' got worse, sir. 'E 'it the bottle first thing in the mornin' and 'e carried on most o' the day. If it 'ad been anywhere else but the army I reckon 'e been out on 'is ear. But the army seems to put up with drunks, 'specially if they got a medal or two. An' 'ow would it look if the regiment got rid of a man who bin awarded the bleedin' Victoria Cross?"

"Do you know when this photograph was taken, Henderson?" Parsons asked, pointing to the two men on horseback.

"Sometime when the regiment was in Africa, sir. The colonel was a major then and Captain Simpson was a lieutenant. I never seen either of them look that 'appy since."

"I notice that there was once glass in the frame. Do you know how it happened to break?"

"Yes, sir. Captain Simpson did it."

Henderson thought for a moment.

"It were las' Saturday," he said. "That were the day of the barrack inspection. The captain were in a rare state that mornin'. 'E 'ated barrack inspections. 'Specially if the RSM was there. When I come to tidy the room after 'e'd gone I found the photograph lyin' on the floor. Reckon 'e threw it against the wall."

"Do you know when Captain Simpson learned about the colonel's death?"

"Not 'til 'e come back to the Mess. That would be not long before dinner last night, sir."

"Do you know where he'd been?"

"No, sir. All I can tell you is that 'e disappeared before breakfast the day a'ter General Latham's funeral."

"And how did he act when he heard that Colonel Cordell had taken his own life?"

" 'E were shocked, sir, 'specially when I told 'im what the colonel 'ad written in 'is note. 'E didn't 'ave no dinner. 'E come straight to 'is room with a bottle, sir. When I come to turn down the bed around nine last evening 'e was in a rare state. 'E were lyin' on 'is bed, an' I thought 'e been cryin'. That's when 'e sent me to get another bottle."

"I notice that the bottle on the desk is Irish whiskey. Was that Captain Simpson's regular drink?"

"Ever since I known 'im, sir."

"And what about the colonel? Did he like Irish whiskey?"

"Blest if I know, sir. As far as I know the colonel wasn't one for drinkin'."

"Tell me about this morning, Henderson," said Parsons. "I believe you brought him a cup of tea as usual."

Henderson turned his head towards the chest.

"I put the tray there as usual before I opened the curtains. That's when I saw Captain Simpson sittin in 'is chair with 'is 'ead on the desk. I seen the bottle and I reckon'd 'e'd fallen asleep at 'is desk. It weren't 'til I drew the curtains that I seen the blood. Then I seen the gun, an' I knew what 'e'd done."

"Did you touch anything else in the room other than the curtains?"

"No, sir."

"You're sure you didn't move the chair?"

"No, sir. The chair was jus' like it is now."

Parsons picked up the note and showed it to Henderson.

"Is this the captain's writing?" he said.

Henderson examined the bloodstained note.

"It could be, sir," he said. "But if it is 'e weren't usin' is usual pen."

"What do you mean by that?"

"Well sir, the captain weren't much a writer, but 'e were very proud of 'is fountain pen. 'E told me no one 'e knew 'ad one quite like it. It were American, 'e said. 'E tol' me 'is parents brought it back fr'm America as a present. 'E normally kept it in the drawer in 'is desk. An' I 'appen to know 'e liked blue ink. This 'ere note's written in black ink."

"Thank you, Henderson. I'll check that later. Is there anything else you want to tell me?"

"No, sir. I reckon that's all."

"One last thing, Henderson. The keys on the bedside locker. Are they Captain Simpson's?"

Henderson crossed the room and picked up the keys.

"Yes, sir. They're 'is. One's for the back gate of the barracks. All the officers 'ave one. The other key's for 'is parents 'ouse. 'E told me once that they live out 'o town."

DOCTOR GRAINGER ARRIVED as Parsons was examining the contents of the chest and the wardrobe. Other than the military uniforms there were six fashionable bespoke suits, expensive linen, silk socks, and handmade boots and shoes. It was a wardrobe way beyond Parsons' means; confirming that, like most army officers, Simpson had a private income.

"This is becoming a serious habit," said Grainger grimly, as he bent to examine Simpson's head. "Two suicides in the space of twenty-four hours is hardly going to encourage the next batch of cannon fodder to join this regiment."

"Then you think that, like Colonel Cordell's death, this was suicide," Parsons said. "Don't you think that if that was the case the impact of the bullet would've thrown Simpson's head backwards?"

"You have a fair point, Parsons," Grainger conceded. "But on the other hand these things don't always work to a formula. The body's response to a trauma such as this is never predictable."

"But what about the revolver? Surely if the impact of the bullet first jerked the body backwards, then there must have been some sort of reaction to propel it forwards again. If that was the case wouldn't you expect Simpson's grip on the revolver to have been loosened?"

"In most cases I would agree with you, Parsons. But as I said we are not dealing with a precise science."

"I noticed that there is some heavy bruising on the right thumb, doctor. The thumb that was used to pull the trigger. Would you say that had been caused at the time of death?"

The doctor bent to examine Simpson's right hand.

"Probably not," he said. "Judging by the severity and coloration of the bruise I'd say that had been caused by some incident sometime before his death."

"And what about a time of death, doctor. Can you hazard a guess as to when that might have been? As we can both see *rigor mortis* has set in."

"That certainly suggests that he died sometime in the early hours of the night, but I'll know more when I've examined the body. I'll be able to tell you more about that bruise then. My assistant will bring my report to Scotland Yard as soon as it's ready."

————

AFTER DOCTOR GRAINGER had left to make arrangements for moving the body, Parsons dragged the chair and Simpson's body away from the desk in order to examine the contents of the drawer. As Henderson had said, there was a fountain pen inside, along with a half empty bottle of blue ink, and some note paper and envelopes. If Simpson had used his own fountain pen to write

the suicide note he had been remarkably
meticulous in replacing it in the drawer before
shooting himself. But Simpson had clearly not
used his fountain pen. The ink in the pen was blue.
The same color as the ink in the bottle. And the
note had been written in black ink on paper quite
unlike any found in Simpson's desk.

Parsons had little doubt that Simpson, like
Cordell, had been murdered. Both deaths had been
elaborately staged by a person who knew that both
men were the worse for drink. And in each case
the suicide note had been crudely printed. But
there was a significant difference between the two
notes. In Cordell's case note paper from the
colonel's desk had been used, whereas with
Simpson the paper in his desk had been ignored
and the murderer had instead decided to use a
sheet of paper torn from a cheap exercise book.
That suggested that Cordell's note had been
written at the time he was murdered, but
Simpson's had been written in advance.

There was, nevertheless, a distinct similarity
between the two notes. In both cases the murderer
had made a deliberate attempt to hide his identity
by printing the notes in a clumsy fashion, and they
had both been written in black ink with a broad
nib pen similar to the one on Cordell's desk. It
was a pen similar to thousands of others in use
throughout the country. And then there was the
whiskey. A bottle of Jameson's had been found at
the scene of each death. It may have been
Simpson's favorite tipple, but it was not Cordell's.

PARSONS LEARNED LITTLE that was new from the other officers or the mess servants. If Simpson had returned to the Mess before dinner the previous night then no one claimed to have seen him. Colonel Arbuthnot had said that he was at home all evening, Major Holland that he had been reading in his room until he went to bed at eleven apart from the time he was at dinner. The younger officers had all been playing billiards, a fact that was later verified by the servant who had been serving them drinks. The servant also confirmed that the same group of officers had continued playing billiards after dinner, and that by the time they had gone to bed around midnight they had been well and truly drunk. It was, the servant had said ruefully, the way in which the young officers spent most of their evenings.

No one could identify the revolver as being Simpson's. Arbuthnot confirmed that it was of a type used by most officers, and suggested that Parsons check the serial number against the records kept by the Armoury Sergeant. It was against regimental standing orders, Arbuthnot explained, for Simpson to have kept a weapon in his room. But of late, Arbuthnot said wearily, Captain Simpson had not been behaving normally.

None of the mess servants slept in the Officers' Mess. Sergeant Barnard, the senior mess steward, was a bachelor, and had accommodation in the Sergeants' Mess; the other servants had a separate dormitory in the one of the soldiers' accommodation blocks. The last servant to leave the Mess on the previous night had been the duty barman. After clearing the dirty glasses from the billiard room he had finally managed to close the bar around midnight, and had finally left the Mess at about half past twelve. When asked by Parsons whether there were lights in any of the officers' bedrooms at that time he had said that there had been, but he really couldn't be sure in which of the rooms. He had been more anxious to get to bed, as he had to report back for duty at six.

Parsons discovered, that like the majority of the buildings in the barracks, the Officers' Mess was unlocked at night. Arbuthnot pointed out that security inside the barracks had never previously been considered a problem. As a consequence, Parsons reflected ruefully, practically anybody living in the barracks could have entered the Mess at any time during the night.

If everyone was telling the truth, then it appeared that, with the exception of Henderson, no one had seen Simpson during the course of the previous evening. Nor did anyone living in the Mess claim to have heard a shot during the night. It said much about the vigilance of the officers of the regiment, Parsons reflected, that at a time when a murderer was stalking the corridors of their Mess, they were all, with the possible exception of Major Holland, the worse for drink.

35

A S SOON AS the first rumors of Captain Simpson's suicide began to spread through the barracks Whitehead knew that he would have to act. He was, after all, the man responsible for regiment's discipline, and his first concern was for the men's morale. Every infantry regiment grows accustomed to losing its officers in battle, but in Whitehead's long career as a soldier it was unprecedented for two officers in the same regiment to take their own lives within the space of twenty-four hours.

Colonel Cordell's suicide had been the major topic of discussion in every mess and barrack block during the previous day, and with the news of Simpson's death there was a real danger that cracks would appear in the ordered regime that Whitehead had carefully nurtured since becoming RSM. Already the men were starting to behave more like gossiping fishwives than professional soldiers, and something would have to be done to put a stop to that.

As soon as he returned from the Officers' Mess, Whitehead ordered the three company sergeant majors to assemble their companies on the parade ground in full battle order. His instructions were explicit. The men were to be drilled until they dropped. Every soldier, with the exception of those who were genuinely sick or on fatigue duties, was to be employed in this manner until their dinner at one o'clock. The same routine was to continue in the afternoon, on the following day, and until such time as Whitehead decided otherwise. He was not going to allow his soldiers time for idle gossip. These instructions, naturally, did not include the officers. It was just possible that, out of curiosity, they might appear at the edge of the parade ground from time to time, but if past experience was anything to go by the majority would choose to spend their day idling in the Mess.

Whitehead also decided to confine the regiment to barracks and ban the sale of alcohol in the soldiers' club. With their weekly pay due the next day, he had no wish to be burdened with the routine disciplinary problems that inevitably arose from the fighting, insubordination and damage to military property that invariably followed a night of heavy drinking. It was his duty to ensure that the regiment did not fall apart. He would, naturally, have to seek the commanding officer's permission before implementing these instructions, but he suspected that Colonel Arbuthnot would be more than content to agree with anything he suggested.

AS HE PACED the soldiers' mess halls during their dinner break Whitehead could sense the hostility that his instructions had engendered. It was not something he had ever experienced since becoming RSM, and he had to admit that it was not a pleasant feeling. But, in his opinion, it was better for the men's anger to be directed towards him than for them to feel that their officers had, in any way, failed them. And after a few days, when the initial shock of the two deaths had passed and the regiment had returned to a normal routine, Whitehead was confident that he would quickly reestablish his customary good relations with the men.

Whitehead knew that, with a few exceptions, soldiers had a poor opinion of their officers. From their point of view these were rich men merely playing at being soldiers. As far as they could see their officers came and went as they pleased, avoiding the drudgery and dull routine that was part of each soldier's day. This was especially true when a regiment returned from active service. During such times officers could choose to absent themselves on leave for several months at a time. That would never be the case were he ever to become one of their number, Whitehead determined, as he walked between the long dining tables with his shoulders pulled back and his head held high. He had too much affection for the regiment and its men to ever want to be away from them for long. And in any case, where had he to go?

There was little that Whitehead heard about the late Colonel Cordell in the soldiers' whispered conversations that was complimentary. Those soldiers who had served in his company in Africa recalled only his weak leadership, and even the most junior soldier knew that Cordell owed his promotion to his family ties with the late General Latham rather than to any qualities of his own. Latham's death was a different matter. Although the majority of those who had served with him in Africa admired him, there were a few dissenting voices. One bitter old soldier, who had lost his corporal's stripes under Latham's strict regime, and was unaware that Whitehead was close enough to hear what he said, even referred to the late general as a heartless bastard who deserved all he got for taking risks with other men's lives.

The comments that Whitehead heard about Simpson were mixed. His relationship with Cordell was the subject of many a crude remark, but there was a general consensus that the award of the Victoria Cross was something for which the regiment should be proud regardless of the nature of the recipient. But there were dissenting voices even about that. Whitehead heard more than one comment about the award being no more than a cover-up for a badly bungled operation. An operation from which few soldiers had returned, and of those few, all but one had chosen to leave the regiment. There had to be a reason for that.

"If you want to learn the truth about what happened on that patrol," Whitehead heard one soldier say, "you want to speak to Sergeant Oakes."

———————

AS WAS HIS custom Sergeant Oakes had already consumed three pints of beer before his dinner and had taken a fourth with him to the table. Whitehead had not placed any restriction on the sale of alcohol in the Sergeants' Mess. The RSM knew better than to try to enforce such an unpopular measure amongst his peers. After all, he relied upon his senior noncommissioned officers to enforce his unwelcome instructions on the remainder of the regiment.

Oakes was one of the more junior and least popular sergeants in the Mess. To many his recent promotion had been both unexpected and unwarranted, and it was one of the few criticisms of the RSM from within the Sergeants' Mess that it had been he who had recommended Oakes' promotion to the commanding officer. Few other sergeants had supported it. Whitehead's contention that Oakes had fully deserved his promotion for his gallantry whilst on Simpson's patrol had always been met with a degree of scepticism, regardless of the RSM's contention that if Simpson had been promoted and awarded a medal for bravery, then a corporal like Oakes who had shared his perils was entitled to be made a sergeant.

It was an argument that had been grudgingly accepted, although Oakes' subsequent appointment as Provost Sergeant had met with general condemnation. Colonel Cordell might have been content to endorse the RSM's recommendation, but it was a bitter pill for the Sergeants' Mess as a whole to swallow. The position of Provost Sergeant was one that was much sought after. Not only did a Provost Sergeant have the relatively undemanding task of supervising the Guard Room and the prisoners, he was also excused from the arduous and unpopular field exercises.

It had been a tradition for more years than anyone in the regiment could remember that the Provost Sergeant was appointed either from one of the ambitious young sergeants who were earmarked for rapid promotion or from the more senior sergeants who were unlikely to progress further. Oakes fitted neither category, and furthermore had few personal qualities to endear him to his fellow sergeants. As a result Oakes had become something of a pariah. His promotion and subsequent appointment were generally regarded as a serious misjudgment by Whitehead, and only the hard-won respect that the RSM had earned over many years enabled him to ride out the storm.

On most days few were willing to share a table with Oakes. Apart from his unpopular promotion he was a man whose personal attributes left much to be desired. Even by the crapulent standards of the Sergeants' Mess it was considered that Oakes drank too much, his speech was more vulgar than most, and his body odor was noticeably offensive even amongst men whose personal hygiene was not of the highest.

But on the afternoon following Simpson's suicide, two of the junior sergeants less familiar with the details of Simpson's fateful patrol had joined Oakes as he sat morosely spooning large mouthfuls of Irish stew and dumplings into his mouth.

"You were with 'im that day, Oakesy," one said. "Did you ever think 'e'd top 'imself?"

Oakes set down his glass, wiped his mouth with the back of his hand, turned his bloodshot eyes upon the questioner, and laughed humorlessly.

"We all thought we was goin' to die that day, mate," he said. "An' we'd all want a bullet to put through our brains rather than let them bloody savages get their 'ands on us. We knew what to expect. We seen what they done to others. Skewered 'em on bloody stakes an' left 'em fer the bloody animals. We seen it, mate. Don't you think it gives me nightmares still?"

"You think that's why Captain Simpson shot himself?" the second sergeant asked. "But what about the colonel?"

"What I'm saying, mate," Oakes answered, "is that if that bloody Simpson 'ad the same dreams as me it might've turned 'is 'ead. Anyone could see 'e were drinkin' imself to death. An' I know why. If 'e 'ad any conscience at all, 'e would've topped 'imself long before now. An' that goes for that bloody colonel of ours. They both got blood on their 'ands."

"What d'you mean by that, Oakesy?"

But Sergeant Oakes realized he had said more than he intended. He had seen Whitehead watching him from across the mess hall. The RSM had told him never to talk about it. That was part of the deal they made when he was promoted. He drained the last of his ale, belched loudly, and hurriedly left the table.

36

PARSONS HAD TO wait fifteen minutes for Whitehead to return to his office from the Sergeants' Mess. There were signs of strain on the RSM's face, a weariness in his eyes, and a general irritability in his demeanor that Parsons had not seen before. Doubtless the pressures of keeping a regiment of nearly one thousand men under control almost single handed at such a time were beginning to have an effect even on a man of Whitehead's iron constitution.

"If it's convenient I'd like to see the Armoury, Mr. Whitehead," Parsons said. "I assume there are records there of all the regimental weapons, and if your system is anything like that of the police each weapon will have to be personally signed for before it's ever allowed to leave."

"Quite correct, sir," said Whitehead. "If you will be so kind as to follow me I'll collect the Armoury keys from the key cabinet in the Orderly Room."

Whitehead obtained the key to a shallow steel key cabinet from one of the Orderly Room clerks and opened it. Inside were rows of neatly labeled keys hanging on hooks.

"There is a duplicate here for every door and every lock in the barracks," Whitehead said, as he selected the Armoury keys.

"Including the colonel's house and the Officers' Mess?" Parsons asked.

"That's correct, inspector. But I'm sure you will know by now that most of the buildings inside the barracks are rarely locked. Until recently that has never presented a problem. Of course, it's a different matter for the Armoury. There is no question of it ever being left unlocked if it is unattended. The Armourer has one set of keys. The other set is kept here, and anyone taking them must sign for them."

"Does that apply to all the keys?" Parsons asked.

"Indeed it does," said Whitehead, signing his name in a neatly lined book that one of the clerks handed him. "You can see for yourself."

Parsons spent a few moments examining the book. No keys had been signed for in the past few days, but that meant very little. As far as he could see the perfectly satisfactory arrangements for their safe custody were largely redundant, as most of the doors in the barracks were never locked.

PARSONS WAS RELIEVED to find that it was only a short distance from the RSM's office to the Armoury, and that Whitehead chose to walk there at a relatively sedate pace, pausing frequently to watch the intricate regimental drills that were being executed on the parade ground.

"What a splendid sight," he said, as much to himself as to Parsons. "One should never underestimate the importance of what a soldier learns on the parade ground. The discipline he learns there can save his life on the battlefield."

Parsons did not reply. But he could see that the RSM had a valid point. If history was any judge, the way in which British soldiers responded instinctively to the words of command they received in action had been the reason for some of the country's most celebrated victories. How else had the squares of British infantry held firm at Waterloo against Napoleon's desperate cavalry charges? But modern warfare was not proving to be that simple. The Boers and Zulus might not have the benefit of a parade ground education such as that Parsons was witnessing, but each in their own way had proved themselves to be more than a match for the British army.

THE ARMOURY WAS a rectangular-shaped building that had been whitewashed in a fashion similar to the Guard Room and Regimental Headquarters. Vertical steel bars protected a row of three small windows on each side; and the only entrance, a thick wooden door reinforced by steel plates, was secured by three bolts, each of which had a heavy padlock.

There was no one inside. The Armourer, Whitehead explained, had been ordered to drill with the rest of the regiment.

"Is that why the men do not have their weapons with them on the parade ground?" Parsons asked.

"Correct, sir. That was my decision. I want the men fully occupied until things quieten down, so I ordered full regimental drills today. But I didn't want every soldier drawing his weapon from the Armoury before each parade and having to hand it back in afterwards. Weapons are not permitted in the barrack rooms or in the soldiers' mess halls, so you can imagine how much time would have been wasted if we had to go through that process twice in one day."

Whitehead struck a match and lit a paraffin lamp, enabling Parsons to see the hundreds of rifles stacked vertically in wooden racks running down the center and along the sides of the building. Lengths of thick chain, secured at each end by a heavy padlock, passed through the trigger guard of each weapon.

"Each weapon is identified by a serial number," explained Whitehead, "and that number is recorded in the Armourer's book. Whenever a soldier removes his rifle he signs for it, and when it is returned the Armourer signs it back in."

The RSM picked up a stiff-backed book with a well-worn cover from a table by the door.

"You can see for yourself, inspector," he said, as he opened the book at random and showed Parsons.

"That seems quite straight forward, Mr. Whitehead," said Parsons, after taking a cursory glance at a few of the entries. "We have much the same sort of procedure in the police. But where are the revolvers?"

The RSM selected another key and opened a steel cabinet near the door. Inside Parsons counted twenty four revolvers, secured by a chain in a similar fashion to the rifles.

"If you care to turn to the section for 'Revolvers' in the Armourer's book I'm sure you will find that they're all accounted for," Whitehead said. "If they're not, I'll want to know why."

Parsons compared the serial numbers of the revolvers in the case to the list in the Armourer's book. The two agreed exactly.

"If they didn't the Armourer would be looking for a new job," Whitehead said.

"Then how do you account for the revolver in Captain Simpson's room?" Parsons asked.

"I have to admit that we do not have a record of every weapon in the barracks," Whitehead said. "Most of the officers brought back revolvers from South Africa. Some of the sergeants as well. As a matter of fact I have two in my room. After every skirmish there were always weapons lying around. Their previous owners were more than likely dead. When the Zulus wiped us out at Isandlwana there were hundreds on the battlefield. Naturally the

Zulus took most of those, but we retrieved them later when we took our revenge on those bloody heathen."

"And you say these are unaccounted for," Parsons said in dismay.

"I'm afraid so, sir," Whitehead said. "I'm sure you've made a note of the serial number of the revolver that Captain Simpson used, and I'm willing to bet it was one he brought back from Africa. One that probably belonged to some poor bastard who didn't come home. You won't find any record of that revolver here and I doubt you'll find it anywhere else unless you're prepared to spend a few weeks trawling through the records of all the regiments who were in South Africa. And I'm not sure what good that would do you."

———

"DO YOU THINK it's possible there may have been an intruder during the night?" Parsons asked after they had left the Armoury and were standing at the edge of the parade ground. The RSM turned his attention from the squads of redcoated soldiers marching in close order and regarded Parsons with surprise.

"Are you seriously suggesting that Captain Simpson was murdered, sir?"

"I have to consider every possibility," Parsons replied. "I'd be failing in my duty if I didn't."

"You must forgive me, sir," Whitehead said apologetically. "I spoke out of turn. It's just that I find it difficult to accept the idea of someone from outside entering the barracks and murdering one of our officers."

Then we agree to differ, thought Parsons. There are people who can come and go through the back gate at any time of night or day provided they have a key.

"If anyone had attempted to enter the barracks during the night," Whitehead continued, "there will be a record of it in last night's guard report. Not only that, but the Guard Commander would have informed me."

Whitehead's eyes narrowed.

"But on the other hand," he said grimly, "if there *was* an intruder last night, and the Guard Commander failed to tell me, I'll want to know why. And now that you've raised my curiosity I suggest we go to the Guard Room and check the report."

————————

SERGEANT OAKES WAS halfheartedly supervising a prisoner scrubbing the Guard Room floor when the two men entered. With the whole regiment on the parade ground Oakes had clearly not been expecting visitors. He was slouched in a chair with his jacket undone and his feet on the table, and at the sight of the RSM almost fell onto the floor in his attempt to stand up. In a desperate attempt to recover his dignity he sprang to a position of attention and began buttoning his tunic, at the same time bellowing a sharp word of command to the prisoner, who also scrambled to his feet and stood motionless with his arms pinned to his sides.

"At ease, Sergeant Oakes," said Whitehead sharply, making little attempt to conceal his displeasure at the state of Oakes' dress. Parsons could only imagine what the RSM would say to the unfortunate sergeant after he had gone.

Whitehead eventually turned his attention to the prisoner. "What are you here for, Blackwood?" he demanded.

"Striking a superior officer, sir," said the young soldier, with his eyes fixed firmly to his front.

"Striking a superior officer," the RSM repeated, standing squarely in front of Blackwood and staring fiercely into his eyes. "And how did you manage to do that?"

"I was drunk, sir,"

The RSM paced slowly behind the prisoner and spoke so softly that Parsons could barely hear what he said.

"Were you in Africa, Blackwood?"

"No, sir," said the trembling soldier. "I only joined the regiment two months ago."

"And you've already struck a superior officer!" Whitehead said furiously. "By God, if you'd have done that in Africa you'd have been flogged. And if you'd been in my company I'd have had the pleasure of doing that myself."

THERE WAS NOTHING in the Guard Report to indicate that an intruder had been in the barracks during the night. Parsons had not expected that there would be. Had anyone decided to climb over the high barrack railings they would surely not have chosen to do so when there was a sentry patrolling nearby.

Parsons flicked through the pages of the report until he came to the the the entry relating to the bomb attack on the barracks. As he had expected it merited only a few lines.

"I notice that the bomb attack wasn't as serious as I had imagined," he said to Whitehead.

"Storm in a teacup, sir," the RSM replied. "The newspapers blew it completely out of proportion. Diversionary tactics, if you ask me. The bloody Fenians were just trying to distract the authorities from their main business of the night. And that was to murder Lord Frederick Sayers. Nevertheless I wasn't pleased with the way the Guard Commander handled the situation, and I took disciplinary action against him."

Parsons did not answer. What Whitehead had said about the bombing of the barracks sounded plausible enough, but it was not a theory that he subscribed to. It might well have been that the bombs at the barracks and at the residence of the local Member of Parliament had been intended as a diversion. But he was not convinced that they were the work of the Fenians.

But he had learned something of interest. One of Cardwell's reforms had been to abolish flogging in the army. And yet the RSM had openly admitted to flogging soldiers in Africa. It was in Parsons' opinion a barbarous punishment, and one that he imagined only a senior officer could sanction for a serious breach of discipline. But doubtless it would leave a victim with a serious grudge against whoever he felt was responsible.

Perhaps that was what lay behind the deaths of Colonel Cordell, Captain Simpson, and even General Latham. If any or all of them had been instrumental in a soldier being flogged, would not the victim of that punishment have felt aggrieved. But would it have been motive enough for murder? In most circumstances Parsons did not believe that it would; unless, of course, the soldier concerned considered himself to be the victim of a miscarriage of justice.

37

AFTER LEAVING THE barracks Parsons headed towards South Kensington in search of a quiet pub. He imagined that on most days that could prove to be difficult with hundreds of soldiers living only a short distance away. But today the Middlesex Light Regiment was confined to barracks and there was not a single red jacket to be seen on the streets.

The handsome oak door and bay windows of the *Queen Adelaide* beckoned welcomingly from across Victoria Road, and once inside Parsons was gratified to find only a handful of people seeking a late lunch like himself and two old men sitting by the fire nursing their drinks.

"You're unusually quiet today," Parsons said to the solitary barman absent-mindedly burnishing empty beer glasses. "Where are the soldiers? Are the Middlesex on manoeuvres?"

"Rumor has it they're confined to barracks," the barman replied. "Seems there's been another suicide in the barracks. Second in a matter of days.

First the colonel and now the young officer who won the Victoria Cross. Can't make it out myself. You'd think they both had everything to live for."

Parsons was surprised to discover that the news of the latest tragedy had spread so quickly. But when he thought about it, it was obvious. The soldiers might be confined to barracks, but that wouldn't stop the information spreading by way of the postman or a tradesman delivering supplies to the barrack kitchens.

"They're generally packed in here like sardines," the barman continued. "Especially in the evenings. Even the sergeants come here. Not that they mix with the rabble. They normally use the snug."

With an almost imperceptible move of his head the barman indicated a smaller bar at one end of the room.

"That's where most of our civilian customers generally go in the evenings as well. It works out better that way. Then the privates and corporals can let their hair down in here without upsetting anyone else."

"What about the more senior noncommissioned officers?" asked Parsons. "Do they come here as well?"

"Those that live in the barracks. Even the RSM himself is one of our regulars. We're always pleased to see Mr. Whitehead drop in. It keeps the lads in order. No one wants to get on the wrong side of the RSM."

Parsons did not comment, but after what he had just seen in the Guard Room he could well imagine that it was in the best interests of any soldier to keep in the RSM's good books. Instead he asked what was available to eat, and after ordering fried sole with mashed potatoes and carrots took his pint of ale to a quiet corner table where even the muffled voices of the few customers would not disturb him.

———

ON THE FACE of it, both Cordell and Simpson had reason enough to take their own lives. They had both been through a harrowing campaign in Africa. Especially Simpson. And both men had other problems.

Cordell's promotion had brought with it an obligation to marry, and in his haste to the altar he had made an unfortunate choice. A fiery and passionate Frenchwoman was the last thing a man of his temperament needed, and from all accounts the marriage had been a disaster for both parties.

Venetta Cordell's motives for marrying her husband were still a matter of conjecture. Parsons had yet to receive any word of her from the Paris police, but if Lady Cordelia was to be believed, Venetta was the sort of woman who would consider marriage to a senior British army officer to be a step up the social scale. That was, of course, if Cordelia's opinions were worth considering. But whatever her reasons might have been, Venetta had soon tired of the marriage. She had found her husband to be dull and unwilling to satisfy her sexual demands, and as a result had transferred her affections to another man. It just so happened that this man was a more senior officer, a notorious womanizer, and her own husband's half-brother.

A betrayal like that would have been more than enough to drive some men to take their own lives. And in Cordell's case it was not his only problem. There was also his tortured relationship with Simpson: a relationship, that by all accounts had flourished whilst the two men were in South Africa, but had floundered after Cordell's promotion and his subsequent marriage. This relationship had seemingly reached a nadir on the day of General Latham's funeral. The two men had quarreled bitterly in public, after which Cordell had become uncharacteristically drunk. Cordell must also have felt that his position as commanding officer was being undermined. By common consent he had only achieved that promotion because his half-brother was both a general and a former commanding officer. In the process Cordell had lost the respect of his fellow officers, and possibly even that of the soldiers themselves, and to cap it all his half-brother had slept with his wife.

Simpson had returned from Africa a hero, and at a time in his life when he should have been riding the crest of a wave he had instead turned to drink. That in itself might have been the result of his experiences in Africa. He had doubtless seen many dreadful things, the like of which Parsons could only imagine. But it seemed that much of Simpson's unhappiness and consequent heavy drinking had stemmed from a worsening relationship with Cordell that had followed his promotion and marriage. Cordell had even rejected Simpson's misguided attempts to console him after his public humiliation in the Officers' Mess following Latham's funeral. And what must have been especially hurtful for Simpson during this final quarrel was to hear Cordell say that he was unworthy of his Victoria Cross.

Simpson had left the barracks soon after breakfast the next day, knowing nothing of Cordell's death, or of the suicide note addressed to him. A note that implied that Cordell had taken his life as a result of a lie that Simpson must have been aware of. It was not clear whether this lie referred to Cordell's marriage, his relationship with Simpson, or to something else. But whatever the lie might have been, the news of Cordell's suicide could well have been enough to unbalance the mind of an already disturbed young man like Simpson. Especially if he felt in any way responsible for what Cordell had done. In that situation it was easy to imagine why Simpson might have chosen to end his life.

———

PARSONS SWALLOWED THE last of his ale and wiped his mouth with his napkin.

Presented with these facts a coroner would find the explanations for both suicides to be perfectly plausible. The police surgeon seemed of the same opinion. But Parsons was far from convinced. There were details that might seem insignificant to a coroner, which he considered to be relevant. Both suicide notes had been printed in black ink in a purposefully clumsy hand intended to hide the identity of the writer, and a bottle of Jameson Irish whiskey had been found with both bodies. The whiskey might have been an attempt to link the two deaths; but if that was what had been intended, as far as Parsons was concerned it was unconvincing. Jameson was, admittedly, Simpson's drink of choice, but it was not Cordell's.

In Parson's opinion the two men had been murdered, with a distinct possibility that the two deaths were linked to General Sir Maxwell Latham's murder, and possibly even to that of Lord Frederick Sayers. Taken as a whole that made perfect sense. Sayers' death had conveniently been blamed on the Fenians, and the prime suspect for Latham's murder was in prison. But, if in fact someone else had committed both crimes, did it not make perfect sense for that person to make it appear that both Cordell and Simpson had committed suicide.

Both suicides had been staged unconvincingly. They had all the hallmarks of someone acting in haste, possibly because a suitable opportunity had presented itself. In this case that opportunity that followed hard upon the heels of the public quarrel between the two intended victims. Following that quarrel Cordell had proceeded to drink to excess, thereby making it relatively easy to murder him and stage a suicide. Simpson was a heavy drinker at the best of times, and the news of Cordell's death would only have made matters worse and, in consequence, have made his murder even simpler to arrange.

But in his haste the murderer had been careless. He or she had made mistakes. And one in particular was especially germane. Whoever had murdered Cordell and Simpson must have been privy to their quarrel. And that narrowed the list of suspects considerably.

38

NUMBER THIRTY EIGHT Home Road, the Battersea home of Major Albert Plumb, was a far cry from the Arbuthnot's elegant mansion in Eaton Square. Plumb had been, until Cordell's death, an officer of equal rank to Arbuthnot; but according to Major Holland, he was a man whose social position was far inferior.

Parsons had obtained the address from Sergeant Barnard before leaving the Officers' Mess. His brother officers might not deign to visit the Plumb's humble abode, but Simpson had gone there frequently. From what he had said Simpson had not only enjoyed Mrs. Plumb's homely cooking, he had also discovered a solace there that he had not found amongst his brother officers.

The walk to the Plumb's house had taken Parsons less than half an hour, but it was long enough for him to cross the Thames to its south bank, leaving the genteel houses of the professional and monied classes of Kensington and Chelsea to enter the more humble world of the

Battersea artisan. The elegant squares north of the river, with their classically inspired mansions, their private gardens, their liveried servants, and mews stabling for horses and carriages, had given way to the modest terraces of rented three bedroom houses with attic spaces for a living-in maid-of-all-work.

It was such a servant in a black dress and spotless white apron who answered Parsons' rap on the gleaming brass knocker of the Plumb's residence. The young girl, whom Parsons estimated to be in her early twenties, politely asked him his business and after being told the reason for his call led him a short way along a narrow corridor lit by a single gas lamp to a room she described as the parlor.

"Inspector Parsons to see Major Plumb," she announced to the three people in the room, with what appeared to Parsons to be an unaccustomed formality. Then she dropped a hurried curtsey and left, leaving the door, Parsons noted, slightly ajar. No doubt she would hope to hear something of what was said inside the room from the kitchen at the far end of the corridor.

A broad-shouldered man of average height dressed in a dark tweed suit rose from his chair by the fire, removed his pipe, placed it in a shallow bowl on the edge of the hearth, and advanced purposefully towards Parsons.

"My pleasure, inspector," he said, his firm grip squeezing Parsons' small hand. "Won't you take a seat?"

Plumb gestured towards an empty chair beside an oval table in the center of the room. The table was covered with a red tablecloth with an over-elaborate floral design, and a gas lamp with a gleaming brass base had been positioned exactly at its midpoint.

"Allow me to present my wife, Gertrude," Plumb continued, "and her father."

Parsons made a short bow in the direction of a short, stout woman with a ruddy complexion sitting in the chair opposite her husband's. She was wearing a faded woolen shawl over a simple black dress, and before Parsons' arrival had been playing cards on a small fireside table with an older man dressed in a pair of worn corduroy trousers, an ancient dressing gown and a nightcap.

"I assume you will have heard the news from the barracks," Parsons said, as he removed his overcoat and laid it across the arm of the sofa, across the back of which the view of the street was all but obscured by closely woven net curtains.

"If by that you're referring to the suicides of Colonel Cordell and Audley Simpson," Plumb replied. "Then the answer is 'yes'. Charles Arbuthnot was kind enough to write me a note and inform me on each occasion."

"Were you surprised to learn that they had both taken their own lives?" Parsons asked.

Plumb picked up his pipe and puffed on it thoughtfully.

"That's a difficult question to answer, inspector," he said. "No one ever expects a man to do that. Especially if that man's a soldier. But I've known instances where there was little alternative."

"What exactly do you mean by that, Major Plumb?"

"If you'd been on active service in those parts of the world that I have, inspector, you wouldn't have to ask that question," Plumb said solemnly. "Let's just say that if you're lying wounded on the battlefield and you know there's little hope of surviving, you might choose to blow your brains out rather than die a long and lingering death. Or if you think there's a chance of falling into the hands of the sort of savages we're sent to fight against. I've seen what those heathens can do. In either of those circumstances I'd choose to end it by putting a bullet through my brain."

"But what happened in the case of Colonel Cordell and Captain Simpson seems to have nothing to do with matters such as those you describe," said Parsons.

"Oh, but I think they 'ad," Mrs. Plumb interrupted. "Leastwise they 'ad in the case of poor Audley Simpson."

It was clear to Parsons from what he had heard of their accents that both Plumbs hailed from similar roots. But whereas that of Mrs. Plumb had been unaffected by any contacts much beyond her own part of London, it was obvious that her husband's had been influenced in more recent years by his promotion into the commissioned ranks.

"Can you explain what you mean by that, ma'am?" Parsons asked.

"Audley 'ad to live with the memory of what 'appened to the men on 'is patrol who were left behind," she said. "They found the bodies, and just as Albert 'as said, they natives 'ad done the most terrible things to 'em."

"How do you know that Captain Simpson was concerned about such things?" asked Parsons. "Did he ever tell you?"

"Indeed 'e did, inspector," she said. "Although 'e would never admit as much in front of Albert. But when 'e come here for his Sunday lunch 'e would often confide in me. E'd bring 'is beer into the kitchen while I was preparing the meal and 'e would tell me about 'is terrible dreams. 'E said he would never get over 'is guilt as long as 'e lived. I felt so sorry for the poor boy."

"All soldiers have to live with that sort of thing, Gertie," her husband said kindly. "We just have to get on with life as best we can. That's what's make us soldiers different from other men."

"Well, if you ask me, every man ain't born to be a soldier, Albert," Mrs. Plumb said. "You might've been, and father 'ere might've been, and I might've been born to be a soldier's wife. But from what I know of Audley Simpson 'e was probably better off being a churchman like his father. And maybe much the same's true about Colonel Cordell, although I can't say I ever knew much about 'im other than what you've told me. I was never considered grand enough to be invited to his house or into the Mess."

"Are you saying that you think it's possible that Captain Simpson took his own life, ma'am?" Parsons asked.

"All I'll say was that I wasn't surprised to 'ear the news, inspector. Saddened, yes. But not surprised."

"What about you, sir?" Parsons asked. "Simpson was in your company. What did you think of him as a man?"

"The man I've known in England was much changed from the soldier I knew in South Africa. Simpson and I weren't in the same company then, but from what I heard he was the most promising young officer in the regiment. I wasn't surprised he was the one chosen to lead that patrol."

"And since his return you've noticed a change?"

"I've never seen such a change in a man. It was like chalk and cheese. He lost interest in his men, and his drinking got quite out of hand. I spoke to him several times about it, but he wouldn't listen."

"What about his relationship with Colonel Cordell, both here and in South Africa?"

"They were the best of friends in Africa. As you probably know Simpson was in Cordell's company then, and from what I heard they were inseparable."

"Would you say there was anything unnatural about their relationship?"

Plumb was clearly annoyed by the question.

"I suppose it's your duty to ask me questions like that, inspector," he said. "And, yes, I've heard some of the gossip. To be frank it disgusts me. As far as I'm concerned the two men were good friends. I'll say no more than that."

"But would you agree that the relationship changed after the regiment came home?"

"Of course it did. It had to. Audley couldn't continue calling the colonel by his first name."

"What about the colonel's marriage? How did Simpson react to that?"

"I think he was very surprised, inspector," said Mrs. Plumb. "But I doubt there was an officer in the regiment who wasn't. I know I was, and I hardly knew the man."

"So you don't think the marriage had anything to do with Captain Simpson taking his life?"

"No, inspector," Plumb said emphatically. "I don't."

"What was your opinion of Colonel Cordell as commanding officer?"

"I don't like speaking ill of the dead," Plumb answered. "But the general feeling amongst the rest of the officers was that he should never have been given command of the regiment. He struggled as a company commander in Africa, and were it not for Paddy Whitehead he would've been shown up as being even more inadequate than he was."

"Do you mean RSM Whitehead?"

"I do. At the time he was Cordell's company sergeant-major. Like Cordell, he was promoted when the regiment returned to England. But in Whitehead's case the promotion was thoroughly deserved. He didn't need someone like General Latham pulling the strings for him."

"I'd like to discuss the RSM with you later, but before then I have a few more questions I'd like to ask about Cordell and Simpson. In both their suicide notes they referred to a lie. Cordell's note said *'I can no longer live with that lie, Audley'*. Would you have any idea what that could mean? Colonel Cordell may have been implying that his marriage had been a lie. But what do you think Captain Simpson meant?"

"I couldn't possibly say, inspector," said Plumb. "What were his actual words?"

"He wrote: *'That lie destroyed us both'*," said Parsons. "It was as though Captain Simpson was answering the message Colonel Cordell had left him. Does it mean anything to you?"

Plumb looked towards his wife.

"It means nothing to me," he said. "What about you, Gertie?"

Mrs. Plumb shook her head.

"Audley never said anything about lies to me," she said. "There was only one thing 'e ever mentioned that troubled him, outside of his memories of 'is patrol, and that was somethin' about some money being stolen. 'E told me once that one of the soldiers was punished for somethin' 'e didn't do, and that if Audley 'ad spoken up at the time 'e might've changed things. But I don't think that sounds like 'e were lying."

The idea of someone being punished for an injustice might still be relevant, Parsons thought, making a mental note to pursue the issue later.

"Let's return to the RSM," he said to Plumb. "From what you said earlier you think highly of Mr. Whitehead?"

"He's one of the best soldiers I've ever met. The regiment's lucky to have him as RSM. He was a rock in South Africa. A strict disciplinarian. You might think that that would have made him unpopular with the men. Quite the contrary. Soldiers appreciate discipline if they think it could one day save their lives. Whitehead got a reputation for checking the sentries, especially at night. And woe betide any man he found derelict in his duty. He'd make them sweat, I can tell you. He said the Boers and the Zulus could teach us a lot about night warfare. And I have to say I agree with him."

Plumb began refilling his pipe.

"I was RSM myself once, so I know what Whitehead's up against. It helps if there's a strong commanding officer. But with Cordell in charge, Whitehead found himself running the regiment more or less single-handed. You might think that Cordell would rely more on his company commanders. But he didn't for obvious reasons. Arbuthnot's more interested in things that have nothing to do with the regiment; Holland has no experience to speak of; and, frankly, no one has ever considered my opinion worth listening to. You see, I don't have the right sort of background."

He put a match to his pipe and was silent while he began drawing on it.

"I've only one criticism of the RSM," he said at last, "and that's about the company he keeps."

"Who do you mean in particular?" Parsons asked.

"I mean Sergeant Oakes. He was on Simpson's patrol and for reasons that I still don't understand Whitehead had him promoted. I've always considered Oakes a bad lot. And if making him a sergeant wasn't bad enough, Whitehead has to make matters worse by drinking with him. An RSM is like a commanding officer. He should choose his friends carefully. Better still, it's best not to have any at all."

"What about General Latham?" Parsons asked. "Was he respected when he was commanding the regiment?"

"He was a brave man and a fine soldier. No one would deny that. But there were times when he took unnecessary risks with the men's lives if he thought there was glory in it for himself."

"And was Captain Simpson's patrol one of those times?"

"Yes. In my opinion the whole venture was doomed from the start. But, of course, no one asked my opinion. The opinion of a man like me who's risen from the ranks is never sought by colonels. I didn't go through Sandhurst, so what could I possibly know about higher strategy?"

"Did you attend General Latham's funeral?"

"We did. Gertie and I were both there. But we didn't go to the Mess afterwards. Gertie wouldn't feel comfortable. The other officers think, that like me, she's too common. Especially after they learned that her father was a mere sergeant."

Parsons was grateful that Harris was elsewhere. His reaction would have been predictable and might well have led to a fruitless discussion on what Harris regarded as the unfortunate social strictures that prevailed in both the army and police.

"When did you last see Captain Simpson?" he asked.

"Yesterday," Mrs. Plumb interjected. " 'E come 'ere because 'e was upset about what 'ad been said between 'im and Colonel Cordell. 'E said it was all 'is fault, and that 'e should've known better than to behave as 'e did. 'E told us 'e was beginnin' to 'ate the man 'e'd become, and that 'e was thinkin' of leavin' the army."

"And what did you say?"

"I told him to pull himself together," said Plumb. "I said he had a fine career ahead. I told him not to worry about what the colonel said or what he thought. I said that the colonel was a weak man who'd been put in a position he couldn't handle, and that on top of that he had chosen to marry the wrong woman. I told Audley that he was a far finer man than Cordell and that one day he would be a colonel, perhaps even a general."

"That must've been very reassuring to hear you say that, Major Plumb. Captain Simpson had a very high opinion of you. He told me once that you were the best officer in the regiment. How did he react to what you said?"

"He said that the last thing in the world he ever wanted was to be given high command. He said he never again wanted to have the power of life or death over other men."

"And what was your answer?"

"I told 'im to talk with 'is parents before makin a final decision," said Mrs. Plumb. "I said 'e should listen to their advice. And as far as I know that's what 'e did. 'E said 'e intended seein' 'is parents after leavin' 'ere to talk it through with them. An' because I was anxious to 'ear what they'd decided I invited 'im back 'ere for dinner tomorrow night."

"Do you know where his parents live?"

" 'Is father is the vicar of St. Bride's Church in Cookham Dene," she said. "I've never been there nor met 'is parents, but Audley once told me the church is not far from the station."

Parsons rose from his chair and began taking his leave.

"Thank you for your time," he said. "I'm most grateful for the valuable information you've both given me. I've just one more question before I leave, and I apologize to Mrs. Plumb for discussing it in front of her. Earlier today I learned that soldiers from the Middlesex were flogged while they were in Africa. I was surprised to hear that, as I had thought that that form of punishment was no longer allowed in the army."

"It's still permissible on active service, inspector," said Plumb. "But that, of course, is only at the discretion of the commanding officer. And I regret to say that Colonel Latham, as he then was, was a great believer in that form of punishment. He was one of the old school. He'd seen service in the Crimea and in India during the mutiny, and in those days the punishments were far more severe. There were fortunately few enough cases meriting a flogging while he was in command in Africa, and I'm glad to say that in my company we never saw the need for it. But Cordell had similar ideas to the colonel. It was typical of the man. He was always trying to emulate his half-brother. I remember one instance in particular. Cordell accused his servant of stealing some money. If I remember correctly he was a handsome young lad. But stealing from a comrade is considered one of the more serious offenses in the army. And to be caught stealing from an officer is really asking for trouble."

Mrs. Plumb interrupted her husband.

"Do you think that's the money Audley was talkin' about?" she asked.

"How do I know, old girl?" Plumb said. "He never said anything to me."

"How can I find out the names of any soldiers flogged in Africa?" Parsons asked.

"Speak to the Chief Clerk," Plumb replied. "There should be a record in the Discipline Book."

———

PARSONS WAS ON the point of putting on his overcoat when Mrs. Plumb's father spoke for the first time. Until then Parsons had thought that the old man had been asleep.

"They flogged us like animals in the Crimea," he said. "I remember one sergeant who was flogged for striking 'is company commander as though it were yesterday. The sergeant 'ad got 'old of some vodka after we took a Russian position and 'e got 'imself well an' truly drunk. That's when 'e punched the major. An' the bastard deserved it. But they took away the sergeant's stripes and they give 'im a good flogging in front of us all."

"Why are you telling me this, sir?" Parsons asked.

"Because a'ter 'e bin flogged the sergeant, or private as 'e then was, shot the bloody major. An' then 'e blew 'is own brains out."

39

SERGEANT GEORGE OAKES had drunk a pint of stout at the bar of the Sergeants' Mess before his meal and had taken a second to the table with him. It was far less than he normally drank in the evening, but he needed to pace himself. The session later that night was likely to be heavy.

A few of the junior sergeants had again attempted to draw Oakes out about Captain Simpson and the ill-fated patrol. But he would have none of it. He was in no mood to talk about bloody Simpson and his patrol with men who, at the time, had been miles away from the action. In any case he had an appointment to keep, and it wouldn't do to keep the others waiting.

It was a rule of the Sergeants' Mess that, unless it was a Sunday, formal dress uniform was to be worn for the evening meal. It was not a rule that Oakes agreed with, but as it had been implemented by Whitehead when he became RSM, it was not one that he was going to challenge. Dressing formally for dinner was more time consuming than throwing on an old jacket and trousers, and it left a careless dresser like Oakes open to criticism. On more than one occasion he had been reprimanded by the more senior sergeants and reported to the RSM for having a tunic button undone and for wearing a dirty shirt collar.

He had rushed upstairs after the meal, unbuttoning his tunic as he went, and breathing heavily at the unaccustomed exertion. His small room was the most untidy in the Mess and smelt of stale tobacco, strong body odour and dirty socks. Oakes' uniform shirt and helmet lay on his unmade bed where they had been thrown before dinner beside his crumpled nightshirt, a set of dirty underclothing rested on the floor underneath the boots and socks he had been wearing, and an ashtray on his locker was overflowing with discarded cigarette ends. If the day ever came when the RSM decided to inspect the rooms in the Sergeants' Mess in the same rigorous manner as he did the soldiers' dormitories then Oakes would find himself in trouble. And, in the opinion of his fellow sergeants, that would not be before time.

The only members of the Mess entitled to servants were the RSM and the Chief Clerk, a fact that mattered little to most sergeants, for whom tidiness, after years of military discipline, was a matter of course. But Oakes was an exception. He was incapable of organizing himself. It was another reason why his appointment as Provost Sergeant had seemed unwarranted.

Oakes cast his uniform jacket and trousers onto a chair, and rummaged through a pile of clothing at the bottom of a cupboard until he found an old tweed jacket and black corduroy trousers. Then he grabbed a coat from the hook behind the door, wrapped a scarf around his neck and hurried out of the Mess.

———

CONSTABLE MORGAN WILLIAMS reported to Lambeth Division police station at the conclusion of his day's duty. His feet were sore. When he had joined the police after leaving the army he had fondly imagined that the time spent on the parade ground would be adequate preparation for the hours he would spend pounding the pavements. That had not proved to be the case. He always found himself more tired after a day on the beat than he had ever done after drill. To a great extent the fault was his own. He carried more weight now than when he had been a soldier. The food in the army had never been enough for a big man like Williams, and now that he could choose how much he wanted to eat and at what frequency, his once spartan frame had become bloated.

It had been a relatively quiet day on the streets of Lambeth. There had been no cause for Williams to make an arrest, and other than boxing the ears of a group of ragged boys who were disturbing the traders in Kennington market he had not had to exert himself. That was not to say that Lambeth did not have its share of petty criminals. It was simply a matter of them making themselves scarce. Unless someone intent upon breaking the law were extremely foolish or very drunk it was not difficult to avoid the attention of the police. Williams had also learned from his early days in the police that unless a policeman made a point of looking for trouble he was unlikely to find it. It was a lesson that admirably suited Williams' philosophy.

Like Oakes, Williams was in a hurry. Normally after finishing a day's duty he would stroll slowly from the police station in Kennington Lane to his lodgings in Sancroft Road. Once there he would kick off his boots and lie on his bed for an hour or two before going out for a drink. But tonight was different. The meeting had been arranged for eight, which meant there was barely time to change out of his uniform before meeting the others.

OLIVER BATES HAD left his cab at the cabmen's shelter near Kennington Church in the care of an unlicensed cabbie. It was a common practice amongst cab drivers to do this whenever they felt the need of a few hours break. The agreement Bates had made was that the man could keep any money he made, and he would pay Bates sixpence for every hour he had the use of cab. In addition he would ensure that the cab was spruced up by the time Bates returned at midnight. By that time Bates anticipated being well and truly drunk, and in that condition had no wish to have to clean the cab himself when he returned it to the stables.

Walking was not an activity to which Bates was accustomed. In fact he avoided it as much as possible. But there was little choice tonight. He could, of course, have asked to be dropped off at the pub where he was meeting Oakes and Williams. But he had no wish for anyone to see where he was going or with whom he was meeting. Not that the unlicensed cabbie would have remembered. Like most of his kind he was rarely sober.

———————

WILLIAMS HAD CHOSEN a pub in a quiet lane near Bethlem Lunatic Hospital for their meeting. *The Bethlem Arms* was popular only with hospital porters and those visitors to the hospital who felt in need of a stiff drink after seeing the conditions in which the inmates lived. Its clientele could therefore best be described as transient, and the presence of three strangers unlikely to attract undue attention.

Williams had been the first to arrive and was well into his second pint of stout before the arrival of Bates. Oakes arrived fifteen minutes later, having instructed his cab to drop him in Lambeth Road, several hundred yards away from the pub. At first he thought that he had come to the wrong place or that the others had yet to arrive, but then he saw the two shadowy figures sitting in a dark and secluded corner. Almost at the same time they saw him, and raising their glasses indicated that they required further refreshment.

Oakes ordered three pints of ale and three double whiskies, and joined the others. Few of the customers paid heed to the three men, and those that did would not have imagined that only a short time before they had been redcoated soldiers of the Queen.

"Good 'ealth, mates," said Williams.

The three men raised their tumblers of whisky and clinked them together.

Bates said: "And 'ere's to the others. The ones that never come home."

They both looked towards Oakes, awaiting his toast. The burly sergeant downed his whisky in a single gulp, hammered the empty glass on the table and said bitterly: "And 'ere's to the death of the two men responsible. That bastard Cordell and 'is boyfriend, Audley bloody Simpson."

40

Friday, 31 October

A S MRS. PLUMB had said, St. Bride's
Church was only a short distance from the
railway station, and on a crisp autumn
afternoon Parsons reveled in what was for him the
unfamiliar and agreeable experience of strolling
along a narrow village high street of shops and
red-bricked houses without ever being jostled, as
he was in London, by impatient pedestrians, or
sprayed with mud from the constant stream of
horse traffic. Those few people he passed had
even the time and propriety to wish him a 'good
day'. Only at one point was he forced to break his
stride, and that was to allow a brewer's dray to
unload a few barrels of ale at the picturesque
village pub. It was a stop he was more than
content to make, as it allowed him time not only to
admire the whitewashed wattle and daub building
with its sloping thatched roof, but also to marvel at
the size and strength of the two large chestnut dray

horses who stood contentedly chewing grain from their canvas nosebags. If time permitted he would be sure to visit the pretty pub and sample the local ale before catching his train back to London.

Parsons followed the high street until it petered out at the village green: a wide expanse of grass with a willow-shrouded pond in which one group of mallard ducks scavenged for food amongst the reeds while a larger group of their compatriots watched with apparent disinterest from the bank or slept with their heads tucked under their wings.

The green was bordered on three sides by handsome Georgian houses, each with its own extensive front lawn and flower beds. A church of ancient gray stones surrounded by gnarled yew trees and a graveyard of weathered slabs occupied the fourth side, the square tower and Romanesque entrance bearing testimony that a place of worship had stood on the spot since at least Norman times. Parsons broke his stride and paused in admiration. Each time he saw a religious building of such antiquity and reflected upon the countless thousands that had worshipped there over the centuries he felt his oft-flagging beliefs revitalized. There was time, he decided, to enter for a few minutes before seeing the Simpsons.

A profound silence settled over the gloomy interior of the church as the thick oak door closed behind him, broken only by the sound of Parsons' footsteps on the irregular flagstones. He passed the large stone baptismal font and the bell ropes hanging loosely at the base of the tower, before moving slowly along the single aisle through the muted colors cast by the stained glass windows. As he approached the altar with its solitary brass crucifix, he tried to imagine how much grander the church must have looked before Oliver Cromwell's men destroyed the elaborately painted wooden screen that would once have stood at the entrance to the chancel. In spite of the reforms that had followed his victory in the Civil War and which had proved to be of such importance for England's parliamentary democracy, Cromwell had never been a hero of Parsons. As far as he was concerned, no man, no matter what his merits, had the right to destroy a religious artifact that any person in their right mind would regard as a work of art.

Many of the stone slabs along the aisle bore testimony to those buried in the church or in the cemetery outside. A lack of space on the floor had meant that in more recent years these memorials had taken the form of brass plaques on the walls. Parsons paused to read a few. Some recorded the brief lives of those men who had fallen in battle thousands of miles distant from this quiet English village: a naval lieutenant who had perished at Trafalgar, a captain of infantry who had died of the wounds he received during the Indian Mutiny, and an ensign who had fallen at Waterloo.

There would be no such memorial for Captain Audley Simpson. Had he lived to receive his Victoria Cross his brass plaque would have ultimately taken pride of place in his father's church. As it was, as a suicide his body would not even be allowed the propriety of being buried in consecrated ground. What greater sadness could befall his parents than that?

Parsons was resolved of one thing as he left the church. Whatever it took, he would see that Audley Simpson was laid to rest in a dignified manner in keeping with hs parents wishes.

———————

THE VICARAGE WAS the house nearest the church. From what Parsons could see it had doubtless been built by an ancestor of the present lord of the manor, on a scale in keeping with that of the other houses around the green, all of which exceeded the size of the humble church itself. As he approached along the long gravel drive Parsons could see that the curtains had been drawn and that a large wreath was hanging on the front door; and not for the first time in his career he regretted having to intrude upon a family's grief at such a time.

The elderly maid who answered his discrete knock politely informed him in appropriately hushed tones that Canon Simpson and his wife were at home. She escorted Parsons to a parlor at the rear of the house, where, away from the prying eyes of the village, the Simpsons were sitting in silence on either side of an empty fireplace, the mantel of which bore a solitary photograph of their late son in a frame draped in black silk. With its fine view of a wide expanse of neatly trimmed lawn and well-tended flower beds the room must, on normal occasions, have been a delightful place in which to sit. But now it felt as welcoming as a crypt.

Canon Simpson was a tall man, with a sensitive countenance upon which the effects of his grief could clearly be seen. He had narrow shoulders, a head of unruly hair and the beard of an Old Testament prophet. Both father and son, Parsons noted, as he shook hands, had the same long and slender fingers; although, unlike those of his son, the senior Simpson' nails were perfectly manicured. Both he and his diminutive wife were dressed in mourning: he in a black frock cloak, she in a plain dress of black silk without the customary white linen at the collar and cuffs. Other than her plain wedding band she wore no jewelry.

"You can imagine how shocked we were when we received Colonel Arbuthnot's letter," Canon Simpson said sadly. "Especially as we had only learned the day before that Hector Cordell had taken his life."

After offering the Simpsons his sincere condolences Parsons explained the purpose of his visit. He said that during his investigation of General Latham's murder he had met both their son and Colonel Cordell, and had been called to the barracks shortly after the sudden and unfortunate deaths of the two men. Parsons said that he believed that their son had only recently been home to discuss a personal matter, and he wondered whether, during that visit Audley might have said anything that could have explained why he should have taken his life.

"Who told you he was here, inspector?" Canon Simpson asked, his deep voice trembling at the mention of his son's name.

"The Plumbs. I was at their house yesterday. They told me that Audley was there the day before he died, and that he had told them he was thinking of leaving the army. They suggested he seek your advice before making a decision he might later regret. Major Plumb, in particular, advised him against taking a hasty decision, as he thought your son had a promising army career. And it was their understanding that Audley intended to visit you that very afternoon to discuss his future."

"What you say is true, inspector," said Canon Simpson. "Audley did come here on Wednesday for that very reason."

"And what advice did you give him?" Parsons asked.

"We wanted only the best for Audley," said the canon. "We were both very proud of his conduct in Africa and, like any parents, were absolutely delighted when we heard that he was to be awarded the Victoria Cross. And like Major Plumb, we felt sure that Audley could look forward to a long and distinguished career in the army. But it was also obvious to us that his experiences in Africa had been so terrible that his health had begun to suffer. He had told his mother about his terrible nightmares."

"It was difficult for us to comprehend what poor Audley must have gone through," said Mrs.

Simpson. "We live a very sheltered life here in Cookham Dene. What can we possibly know about the violence of war? How can two old people like my husband and I possibly imagine how it feels to be surrounded by bloodthirsty savages? But we could see what the experience had done to Audley. He was drinking and smoking far too much, and he had become very emotional. In fact, we thought he was on the verge of a nervous breakdown. So I, for one, was more than happy to think that he might be considering another career. My husband naturally hoped that Audley might enter the church. But I'm afraid to say that Audley would have none of that. He said that after what he's seen in Africa he doubted whether there was a God at all."

"I'm sure he didn't really mean that," said the canon sadly. "Audley always believed in the existence of God. I'm convinced that he did right until the end. It was just that after hearing the news of Hector's death everything must have become too much for him. I can even imagine him blaming himself for that."

Canon Simpson's voice broke and he sank into his chair. Seeing his obvious distress, his wife rose and placed her arms around his shoulders.

"Why do you say that, sir?" Parsons asked quietly, when he thought the canon had sufficient time to regain his composure.

It was Mrs. Simpson that answered.

"Because shortly before Hector Cordell took his life the two men quarreled. Audley told us that they had exchanged angry and bitter words. We were surprised to hear that. We had always thought that they had been such good friends. Whenever he wrote to us from Africa Audley's letters were always full of what he and Hector had been doing together."

"Did you ever think there was anything unusual about your son's relationship with Colonel Cordell?" Parsons asked, unsure whether the question might offend Simpson's parents or whether they would even understand what he was implying.

"Not in the least, inspector," said Mrs. Simpson. "We were only pleased to think that Audley had made a friend in the regiment. You see his younger brother and sister both died of typhoid when he was only ten, and after that he became very withdrawn. He never seemed to have any special friends at school or at Sandhurst. So we were delighted when he told us about Hector."

"Did your son ever say anything about Colonel Cordell's marriage?"

Canon Simpson and his wife looked at each other in surprise.

"We had no idea Hector had married," Mrs. Simpson said. "Audley never mentioned it."

"Do you think that was because Audley was in any way upset by the marriage?" Parsons asked.

"I really have no idea, inspector," Mrs. Simpson said. "I would have hoped that Audley was happy for Hector."

She patted her husband's shoulder affectionately.

"Marriage is such a wonderful institution," she said. "After all, it is one of God's sacraments."

Parsons refrained from commenting. From what he had seen of Hector Cordell's marriage it appeared to have been made in Hell. Instead he asked:

"Did Audley discuss anything else while he was here?"

Simpson's parents exchanged an uneasy glance.

"In view of Audley's obviously confused state of mind I'm not sure whether we should tell you this, inspector," said Canon Simpson.

"Please allow me to be the best judge of that, sir. I have to consider every scrap of information, no matter how trivial or unimportant it might appear to others."

"What Audley suggested seemed so unlikely," Mrs. Simpson said. "We talked about it after he'd gone, and decided that the poor boy was beginning to lose his mind."

"But if you think it's important, we'll tell you," said her husband. "Although I pray that this will not lead to an innocent person getting into trouble."

"I hope you will accept my assurance that that will not happen," said Parsons. "But please, just tell me what it was your son said."

"He said that he thought he knew who had murdered General Latham," said Mrs. Simpson. "At first we didn't believe him, but when he persisted we told him it was his duty to inform the police. But he said he didn't dare. He had no actual proof, he said, just a strong suspicion. He said he'd seen the wife of one of the officers going into a hotel with a man he recognized as having once been a soldier in the regiment. The man was a thoroughly bad lot. He'd been flogged while the regiment was in Africa, and Colonel Latham, as he then was, had ordered the punishment."

"Did he tell you the lady's name?"

"No," said the canon. "We asked him but he wouldn't say. In fact he used an unfortunate word to describe her that I wouldn't wish to repeat. All he would say was that this lady had never forgiven General Latham for failing to make her husband a colonel."

"I'm afraid it was all Greek to us, inspector," Mrs. Simpson said. "We had absolutely no idea at all who Audley was talking about. You see we never really knew anyone in Audley's regiment. The only person he ever mentioned was Hector Cordell."

"Do you know if your son ever mentioned his suspicions to anyone else?" Parsons asked.

"I don't think he believed that anyone else would take him seriously. Perhaps he wanted to tell Hector. But it seems he never got the opportunity. And now that you've told us that Hector was married I can well understand why. Poor Audley. What with Hector's marriage and his promotion he probably had little time for Audley."

"So you have no idea what he was going to do about his suspicions?" Parsons asked.

411

"None at all, inspector," said Mrs. Simpson. "But I'm a mother, inspector, and I could see that my son was afraid."

"What about the letter, my dear," said Canon Simpson. "Now that we've told the inspector everything else you might as well mention the letter."

Mrs. Simpson crossed the room to a writing desk on which there were two other photographs of her son, both of them draped with black silk. She looked at them wistfully for a few seconds. Then she opened one of the drawers, removed an envelope, and handed it to Parsons.

"We received this letter from Audley on Wednesday morning," she said. "I assume that was before he knew of Hector's death, because there was no mention of it. Audley merely told us of his intention to come here. You may read the letter if you wish. There's nothing of a personal nature in it."

The envelope had been postmarked in Kensington, and, as Mrs. Simpson had said, the letter inside was brief. Audley Simpson had merely said that he would be arriving in Cookham Dene on Wednesday to discuss a matter of importance.

"Your son had a fine hand," Parsons said, referring to the free-flowing handwriting. "Did he normally choose to use this color ink?"

"Ever since I can remember, inspector," said Mrs. Simpson. "He always preferred blue ink. Audley took great pride in his penmanship. That's why we brought him the expensive fountain pen when we were in America. We never knew that such pens existed, and as soon as we saw it in the shop in Boston we knew that Audley would love it."

"I was in Boston giving a talk to the Episcopalian Church about the journeys of St. Paul," the canon explained.

Mrs. Simpson bent forward and gently kissed her husband on the top of his head.

"My husband is a great authority on the subject," she said. "He's often called upon to deliver lectures on St. Paul to other congregations, although this was the first time he'd ever been invited to visit another country.

Parsons took the note he had found on Simpson's desk from his pocket and showed it to his parents.

"Do you think that your son wrote this?" he asked.

Canon Simpson took the note first and then passed it to his wife. They both shook their heads.

"This is not Audley's hand," his mother said. "He would have been ashamed of such clumsy work."

Her comment only served to strengthen Parsons' suspicions.

"And what of the message?" he asked. "Have you any idea what lie Audley was referring to?"

"I've absolutely no idea," said the canon. "But I can tell you one thing for certain. Audley would never lie. That would break one of God's Commandments."

413

It was likely that Audley Simpson had broken more than one of those, thought Parsons, although he was not going to offend his parents by saying that. Instead he asked:

"Was your son right or left handed?"

"Right handed, inspector," said Canon Simpson. "Why do you ask?"

"Because at the time of his death there was heavy bruising on his right thumb which may have prevented him using that hand. Do you know if Audley recently injured his thumb?"

"Indeed I do, inspector," said Mrs. Simpson. "I could see there was something wrong with it as soon as he arrived. He didn't make a fuss. Audley wasn't like that. But I could see he was in pain. I noticed he used his left hand rather than his right to stir his tea and hold his cup. And when I asked him what he'd done he laughed and said he'd been clumsy and jammed his thumb in the train door. I thought it might be broken, and I suggested that he see a doctor. But I don't suppose he did."

Parsons did not answer. The only doctor who had seen Audley Simpson's broken thumb had been the police surgeon.

"Would his injury not explain the badly written note?" he asked "If he had trouble holding his pen with his right hand might he not have used his left?"

"I can't deny that, inspector," Canon Simpson said. "But even allowing for his injury I can't imagine Audley being content with such a badly written note."

"You still haven't explained why you wanted me to see this letter," said Parsons.

"It wasn't the letter as much as the envelope, inspector," said Mrs. Simpson. "You see, when I first saw it I was convinced it had already been opened and then resealed. And if Audley had done that, there would have had to be a good reason. I imagined he would have only done it if he'd decided to add a postscript. But as you can see, there is no postscript. If you care to look you will see where I used a paper knife to open the letter, but if you look at the back of the envelope it looks as though someone has used glue to reseal it."

"Did you ask Audley whether he had any explanation for this?"

"I'm afraid I didn't, inspector. You see we were so concerned about what he'd told us that it quite slipped my mind."

Parsons could see that what Mrs. Simpson had said about the envelope was true. Someone had obviously wanted to see what Simpson had said to his parents, and after learning that he intended visiting them to discuss a matter of importance had probably concluded that he had some knowledge about General Latham's murder. Perhaps this person was even aware of his suspicions and had decided that it was too dangerous to allow him to live.

"You may keep the letter, ma'am," Parsons said. "But with your permission I will take the envelope with me and endeavor to solve this little mystery."

41

PARSONS HAD ALWAYS found a stroll along Fleet Street to be exhilarating. The narrow street between the east end of the Strand and the bottom of Aldgate Hill was no more than a quarter mile long, but it was home to the nation's most illustrious newspapers. Newspapers, which each day, through the wonders of the electric telegraph, brought news of national disasters, political unrest, famine, and war from the furthest corners of the globe to millions of avid readers such as himself.

The *Daily Telegraph*, like the *Times*, had been one of the first British newspapers to send journalists onto the battlefield, and their reports had often made disturbing reading. No longer was war the sole province of poets and romantics. Instead it had become a serious matter for factual analysis and debate, much of which reflected sadly upon the woeful inadequacies of the commanders, rather than their glorious deeds. The heroes, if any were to be found, were frequently from the ranks of the common soldiers, men who were, more often than not, following foolish orders and fighting and dying for causes they barely understood.

William Howard Russell's epic reports of the Crimean War for the *Times* had set the standard. And for a nation accustomed to believing in the invincibility of the British Army and the brilliance of its leaders, these reports made salutary reading. For the first time readers could not only follow the progress of the war at their breakfast tables, they could also read of the terrible conditions experienced by the troops, their inadequate food, the lack of proper medical care for the wounded, and most damning of all, the incompetence of senior officers. Such open criticism of the organization and command of a military campaign was unprecedented. After reading Russell's reports, Alfred Lord Tennyson, the Poet Laureate, had been inspired to write his widely acclaimed poem about the ill-fated charge of the Light Brigade at the Battle of Balaclava, in which he expressed the appalling futility of the action. *'Not tho' the soldier knew,'* he wrote, *'someone had blundered.'* And Tennyson left little doubt on whose shoulders that blunder rested.

Cedric Hardcastle was the *Daily Telegraph's* most celebrated war correspondent. It was Hardcastle to whom Sir Archibald Prosper had directed Parsons for more information on the Middlesex Light Infantry's action against the Boers. At the time Parsons' interest had been only in General Latham's murder. But since then

Cordell and Simpson had died. Both men had served under Latham's command in Africa, had fought in the Boer campaign, and had been closely involved in the execution of the ill-fated patrol.

AFTER MAKING ENQUIRIES at the *Daily Telegraph* offices Parsons had been directed across the road to the *Cock and Bottle*. Cedric Hardcastle, he was told, had finished work for the day, and was likely to be found drinking with his fellow journalists. From the description he was given, Hardcastle would not be difficult to find. He was a large, loud man, with a mop of unruly red hair and a matching beard.

It was as well that Hardcastle had a distinctive appearance, thought Parsons, as he peered through the dense haze of tobacco smoke. For it seemed that every man in the *Cock and Bottle* - and as far as he could tell there were no women present - was shouting at the top of his voice.

Parsons ordered himself a glass of ale and, after asking where he might find Mr. Hardcastle, was directed to one of the private booths opposite the long public bar. There he found four men seated around a dark oak table on which there were four pewter mugs, an empty pewter jug, and a large plate with only a few crumbs to indicate that it had once been piled high with sandwiches. They ignored his presence and continued their heated conversation.

"Mr. Hardcastle?" Parsons shouted, looking directly across the table at a man smoking a cigar, whose top hat was perched precariously on a head of unruly red hair.

"Who wants him?" Hardcastle demanded. "Can't you see that we're busy."

"So I see," said Parsons. "But what I have to discuss is probably more important. My name is Parsons. Inspector Parsons. And I'm investigating the recent deaths of General Latham, Colonel Cordell and Captain Simpson. I believe they were all serving in the Middlesex Light Regiment at the time you were in South Africa. I was hoping you might remember something of the Middlesex, and especially the incident that led to Simpson being recommended for the Victoria Cross. I believe that it was an event that, at the time, you were unable to report in full."

Hardcastle took the cigar from his mouth, drained his mug and examined Parsons slowly from head to foot.

"You don't look much like a policeman to me," he said, with a twinkle in his blue eyes. "Nor do I know where you've got this story about what I did or did not report about Africa, or what any of that's got to do with the deaths of the three officers you just mentioned. But if you will be kind enough to replenish my mug and do likewise for these three gentlemen I'm sure they'll be kind enough to move elsewhere and allow us a few minutes private conversation."

Parsons picked up the pewter jug from the table and handed it to a passing waiter.

"Will you kindly refill these gentlemen's mugs," he said as Hardcastle's companions began leaving the table, "and then bring whatever is left in the jug back here."

"And while you're about it," Hardcastle shouted after the waiter, "I'll have another cigar and a large glass of single malt as well. The Balmenach. It's by far the best whisky in the house," he informed Parsons with a wink. "And the most expensive."

Hardcastle flicked the ash from his cigar onto the empty plate.

"Now young man," he said. "Exactly what is it you want from me?"

———————

PARSONS WAS AWARE of the danger of saying too much to a newspaper reporter. He described the background of his investigation to Hardcastle but made no mention of his suspicions about Cordell and Simpson's deaths, nor that he considered them to be linked to that of General Latham. But he could see from the glint in Hardcastle's eyes that the reporter had already began to form his own opinion.

"There's nothing you've told me about these deaths that I don't already know, Parsons," he said. "I'm a journalist, young man, and we journalists are an incestuous lot. We like nothing better than gossiping and speculating. You may think that we do nothing but sit around and drink.

But when necessary we can add the numbers up and reach the right conclusions."

Hardcastle blew a long stream of cigar smoke into the air.

"I know what brings you here," he said. "You may not have said it in as many words, but I've little doubt that you believe that the three military deaths are connected. And if I understand the purpose of your visit today it's because you think I may know something that will confirm your suspicions."

"That indeed is what I'm hoping, sir," said Parsons. "And I'd like to start with Simpson's patrol."

He paused to take a sip of ale.

"Apart from the unfortunate fact that men died under Simpson's command, I think something else happened during that patrol, that is germane to my investigation. It's my belief that you know what that was; and regardless of the instructions you may subsequently have received from the military authorities, you have a duty to inform me. It's no longer just a matter of military incompetence. We are now dealing with murder."

Hardcastle tossed off the last dregs of whisky.

"Don't try appealing to my conscience, Parsons," said Hardcastle. "Journalists can't afford to have them. But I'll make a bargain with you. If what I tell you helps you in your investigation I want an exclusive."

Parsons knew he could never promise that, and he suspected that Hardcastle would not expect him to give such a guarantee.

"I'll do what I can, sir," he said. "But these things are never easy. You must know that or you would've printed what you know about Simpson's patrol long before now."

Parsons realized Hardcastle's predicament. As matters stood he was bound by government or military red tape from reporting the events surrounding Simpson's patrol. His only chance of revealing the truth relied upon that incident being linked to other events, like General Latham's murder and the deaths of two other army officers.

"All right, Parsons" he said, after he had smoked his cigar for several minutes in silence. "I'll tell you what I know. But you never heard it from me. And before I say anything I'll have another glass of Balmenach. And make it a large one."

"THE ARMY HEADQUARTERS for the advance into the Transvaal," Hardcastle began, "was at Pietermaritzburg. That's on the Indian Ocean in the state of Natal, and just south of Zululand. It was a fairly desolate spot and little to the liking of many of my newspaper colleagues. Especially after the Zulus defeated us at Nyezane and Isandlwana and it became general knowledge that they treated their prisoners rather badly. Not many journalists chose to accompany the army. They preferred to stay on the coast in the flesh pots of Durban, the capital city of Natal, and compose their war stories from the information they gleaned from the telegraph. I was one of the few reporters who chose to venture inland."

Hardcastle paused to sniff appreciatively at the fresh glass of whisky.

"How those heathen Scots manage to produce a nectar of this quality has always amazed me," he said, before raising the glass to his lips and drinking slowly. "They must have more intelligence than I grant them."

Hardcastle's expression suddenly changed. His eyes hardened, and it seemed to Parsons that his mind had drifted back to the events that had taken place in Africa earlier in the year.

"It was far from comfortable trekking through that country, I can tell you, young man," he said. "For a start the senior officers made it quite clear that they didn't want reporters in the front line. Who could blame them. They were probably tired of reading how the great British Army was being made to look foolish by a handful of Boers and a bunch of black heathens armed with nothing but spears. So, as you can imagine, I wasn't exactly made to feel welcome. And apart from that the living conditions were dire. The flies were a nightmare. They were everywhere. There were so many of the bastards that the simple act of eating and drinking became a major operation. You had to cover your cup with your hand when drinking and sip through your fingers, and even then the little devils got into your mouth. And apart from relatively small inconveniences like that there were more serious ones like dysentery, typhoid, and God knows what other fevers to contend with.

It was no wonder my colleagues chose to stay on the coast."

Parsons was becoming impatient with Hardcastle's reminiscences. His readers might enjoy them, but he had not the time. And he had not spent his own hard-earned money plying Hardcastle and his friends with drink just to hear how hard life was as a war reporter.

"How did you become attached to the Middlesex?" he asked.

"Latham, their commanding officer had a reputation for being a man of action. I'd heard he wasn't afraid to take a few risks to get the job done. So I reckoned if I kept close to him I'd be sure to see some action. Our readers like that. They like to think of war correspondents as being in the thick of the things dodging bullets and native spears. Well, it didn't take long for me to see that Latham deserved his reputation. He drove his men hard, and it was clear he wasn't going to let a few Boers get the better of him."

"Was Simpson's patrol one of the risks that Latham took?"

"It was. And to be honest I was surprised when I learned that Latham had decided to send soldiers through Zululand. It seemed to me that the regiment was making good progress as it was, and stirring up the Zulus was an unwarranted risk. And I wasn't the only one who thought that. As far as I could see none of Latham's officers agreed with him, especially Major Cordell. And I could see why Cordell was unhappy. His company was in the vanguard at the time, and Cordell knew that

Latham would choose one of his officers to lead the patrol."

"Are you sure that it was Latham and not Cordell who made the decision to send Simpson."

"Quite sure. I was skulking around regimental headquarters at the time and I heard the two of them arguing. Cordell wasn't at all happy I can tell you. But eventually Latham convinced him that everything would be fine. He said that he was certain that the patrol was going to be a great success, and he'd see to it that the officers concerned - and by that there was no doubt he meant Cordell and Simpson - would receive appropriate recognition."

"And so they did," said Parsons. "Cordell was made colonel and Simpson got a medal."

"And don't forget Latham himself," Hardcastle said. "He became Sir Maxwell Latham and was made a general. But I suspect he was hoping for even more than that from the patrol."

"Whatever do you mean?" asked Parsons, hoping that Hardcastle was about to say something that would prove to be especially pertinent to his investigation.

"Well, I won't bore you with the details, but our advance into Transvaal wasn't just about teaching the Boers a lesson. There was far more at stake. There had been rumors that gold had been discovered in the Transvaal, and that naturally attracted the attention of people with influence who knew how to exploit such things. Men like Cecil Rhodes. Men who had already made a fortune from Africa, and whose ambitions knew no boundaries. If there was gold in the Transvaal, Rhodes wanted to be the first to make a claim. And he was relying upon the army to do that for him. All he needed was a senior officer prepared to take the necessary risks."

"But what could Simpson and a few ignorant soldiers possibly know about whether or not there was gold in the Transvaal? Or where they might be expected to find it?"

"That's just it, Parsons," said Hardcastle impatiently. "Bless their cotton socks they had absolutely no idea what it was they were looking for, or where they might be expected to find it. But there was one man on the patrol who did. He could smell gold from a hundred miles. His name was Jeremy Brett. As far as Simpson knew he was just a scout with expert knowledge of the country. I was never sure how much Cordell knew, but I suspect it was the truth and he hid it from Simpson. Well, unfortunately for Rhodes and the others involved things didn't quite work out as planned. I don't have to tell you what happened. The Zulus didn't just sit back and allow a bunch of redcoats to go wandering through their lands. They ambushed the patrol and killed most of the soldiers. Only Simpson and a few others managed to save their lives."

"What happened to Brett?" Parsons asked.

"Oh, he managed to escape, but then he disappeared. That's when I began to suspect that not everything about the patrol was above board. So I decided to track Brett down. It took me some time, but eventually I found him drinking himself stupid in a bar in Durban and trying his best to forget what he'd been through. That's when I learned that he was a surveyor working for Rhodes. It wasn't difficult after that to put two and two together. Rhodes could not have sanctioned the patrol himself or have arranged for Brett to go on the patrol without the appropriate authority. That instruction would have had to come from someone high up in the British Government, from someone prepared to by-pass the normal military channels and go straight to the commander in the field. And that man was, of course, Latham."

"And you think that the Government minister was Lord Frederick Sayers," said Parsons.

"I've no doubt. And I was about to go to press and expose the whole damn thing. But somehow Rhodes or Sayers or even Latham must have got wind of what I was about to do, because the next thing I knew was that my editor was invited to dine with a senior government minister. He's never told me who that was. But it was the end of my story. And it was a damn good one. It must've been, because not long afterwards Lord Frederick Sayers handed in his resignation."

"Were you ever able to establish a link between Latham and Sayers?"

"That wasn't too difficult. The members of those so-called gentlemen's clubs in Mayfair may think that what goes on there remains a secret only for a privileged few. They seem to forget that servants have eyes and ears, and for the sake of a few pounds are prepared to reveal what they see and hear. It only took me a few discrete enquiries amongst the club servants at Sayers' and Latham's clubs, the Reform and the Army and Navy, to discover that the two men had been in contact whenever Latham was on leave from Africa."

"And what happened to Brett?"

Hardcastle emptied his glass and smiled ironically.

"Would you believe he died in a mining accident," he said. "Rhodes probably didn't want too many witnesses to his botched scheme. He probably felt he couldn't do much about the soldiers who survived the patrol, and maybe Latham or Sayers were able to convince him that they were too stupid to have ever known what was actually going on. The only person who might have the brains to work it out was Simpson, and they thought they could be assured of his silence if they gave him the Victoria Cross.

42

Saturday, 1st November

PARSONS HAD SENT a telegram to Harris' home the previous evening arranging a meeting at Dobies coffee house in Poultry. It was a convenient location for them both. Parsons could take the underground railway from Sloane Square to Mansion House and Harris would have only a short omnibus ride. Apart from the convenience, the last thing Parsons wanted at this sensitive time of the investigation was to run into Superintendent Jeffries. The superintendent would doubtless want a progress report, and if Parsons was to be completely honest he would have to admit that, in spite of his well-founded suspicions, he was far from clear exactly where he was going. And recent events had only served to make matters more confusing.

After meeting the Simpsons, Parsons was more than ever convinced that there was substance in his suspicions about Lady Cordelia Arbuthnot.

Audley Simpson had told his parents that he believed that the woman who had murdered General Latham was the wife of one of the officers in the regiment; and she had been aided by an soldier who had served in the regiment in Africa, but had since left with a grudge against the general. Simpson had not told his parents the woman's name, but as far as Parsons was concerned it could only be one person: Lady Cordelia Arbuthnot. And if, as it seemed, she had found a willing accomplice with a motive of his own for killing Latham, there was every reason to think that the same accomplice could have helped her murder Cordell and Simpson.

The reason for Cordelia wanting to murder Latham and Cordell seemed obvious. In one way or another they had both stood in the way of her husband becoming colonel. It was less clear why she would want to kill Simpson, unless for some reason she had become aware of his suspicions about her involvement in Latham's murder. Perhaps she knew he had seen her with her accomplice. If that was the case, it would account for Simpson's mail being opened.

Parsons knew that this was all extremely tentative. Even Simpson's parents had their doubts about some of the things he had told them. They had thought that the state of his mind was such that he had become confused.

But Hardcastle's story put matters into an entirely new context. After hearing what the journalist had to say Parsons could imagine the link between the murders extending as far as

Sayers, and that what had happened on Simpson's patrol was at the heart of the matter. The presence of Cecil Rhodes' surveyor on the patrol and the fact that Sayers and Latham had been in frequent contact suggested a high level conspiracy to use a military operation to disguise an attempt to discover gold in the Transvaal. And if it was Sayers and Latham who had put Rhodes' plan into operation, then it was Cordell and Simpson who had executed it. There was an obvious link between the four men, but, as yet, no motive to connect the four murders. And where did that leave his theory about Lady Cordelia Arbuthnot's involvement?

———————

HARRIS WAS NURSING a cup of tea when Parsons arrived at Dobies. The crowd in the coffee house was beginning to thin, the City clerks who had come for an early breakfast had already left for their offices, leaving only a sprinkling of the older men in more senior positions who were not expected to be at their desks until later.

"You're sure that's all you want, Harris," said Parsons. "I'm going to have the full works myself."

"I'm fine, sir. I've already had one of Mrs. Harris' fry-ups."

"Ah, the blessings of marriage, Harris. Will I ever be fortunate enough to savour them?"

It occurred to Parsons that this might be an appropriate time to mention Louise. But he decided against it. There was a certain incompatibility about mentioning Louise within the context of a fried breakfast, and, in any case, there were more important things to talk about. Somehow he doubted that Louise would ever provide him with the same substantial breakfasts that the thoroughly domesticated Mrs. Harris provided for her husband. As far as he knew Louise was unable to cook.

Fortunately, that dispiriting thought was banished by the arrival of a pot of coffee, a large plate containing two fried eggs, three rashers of bacon, and a large pork sausage; together with a smaller plate with two rounds of hot, buttered toast. Parsons sighed contentedly and began to attack his breakfast with his customary enthusiasm.

"Now, my dear Harris," he said after his first mouthful of bacon. "Tell me what you've been doing."

Harris opened his black notebook and placed it on the table in front of the salt and pepper.

"I visited the police station in Brompton first thing on Thursday, sir," he said. "I wanted to see if they knew anything about the Arbuthnot's coachman. And as luck would have it they did. The man's name is Albert Cooper, and by all accounts he's a rough diamond. Not the sort of coachman I'd imagine working for the Arbuthnots, especially for a woman like Lady Cordelia. Cooper, as it turns out, was once in the army. He was Major Arbuthnot's servant, but apparently Lady Cordelia took a shine to him and wanted him as her coachman. At least that's what he's told the local police on the frequent occasions they've apprehended him for being drunk and disorderly."

"So Cooper's got a police record," said Parsons, as he sliced his sausage into five equal parts and began dipping them into his egg.

"Not exactly, sir. He's not even spent a night in the cells. Normally the Arbuthnot's butler, Grayson, arrives to smooth things out. But on a couple of occasions recently it has been no less than Lady Arbuthnot herself. Each time she makes a significant donation to the police Christmas fund."

"That sounds like a nice little racket the police have going for them in Brompton," said Parsons with a smile. "They must hope that more of the wealthy inhabitants in the area decide to employ drunken coachmen. But how about Major Arbuthnot? Has he ever bailed Cooper out?"

"No, sir. It was always the butler or Lady Cordelia."

"There must be something very special about Cooper," said Parsons. "Either that or Lady Arbuthnot wants to keep him out of police custody for reasons of her own."

"Exactly my feelings, sir. So I decided to investigate him further. At first I thought of talking to him directly. But then I decided against it. If he told me anything it would probably be a pack of lies. So I decided to talk to another member of Arbuthnot's staff. Grayson, the butler, seemed an obvious choice. As the senior member of the household he ought to know what's going on."

"Good thinking, Harris. But how did you manage that? After the way Grayson greeted us on our visit to Eaton Square I don't imagine him being too forthcoming."

"Nor did I, sir," said Harris with a mischievous smile. "So with the help of the local police I decided to set a little trap for our Mr. Grayson."

"I hope I'll approve of what you're going to tell me, Harris," said Parsons, as he used the last of his toast to mop the egg from his plate.

"I'm sure you won't sir," said Harris, his smile broadening. "But I'm afraid there's little you can do about it now."

"Then proceed, Harris. After such a splendid breakfast nothing you say will shock me."

"Well, sir. According to the desk sergeant at Brompton, most gentlemen like Major Arbuthnot have their cigars supplied by a tobacconist in Buckingham Palace Road. I made a few discrete enquiries of my own and found it to be true. Major Arbuthnot does indeed have an account there. I was also informed that the proprietor has been known to sell tobacco and cigars to his special customers on a Sunday when the shop is not officially open. For instance, someone like Major Arbuthnot. Well, as you know, sir, Sunday trading is illegal, and if the police were to press a point the tobacconist could lose his license."

"This is all very interesting, Harris. But where is it all leading?"

Harris ignored the interruption.

"It's leading to me setting a trap for Grayson, sir. That's where it's leading. It's leading to me telling the proprietor that I was not just a local policeman but a detective from Scotland Yard. I said I knew all about his illegal trading and I was finally going to do something about it. And when he heard that he was more than willing to do as I asked. He sent one of his staff to Eaton Square with a message for Grayson about a discrepancy in Major Arbuthnot's account that required Grayson's immediate attention. As it happens, the shop is only fifteen minutes walk from the Arbuthnot's house and I imagined that it would be a simple matter for him to slip away and attend to the problem."

"Harris," said Parsons irritably. "Will you get to the point!"

"Patience, sir. I'm nearly there. Mr. Grayson has almost fallen into my trap."

Parsons cooled his impatience by calling for a fresh pot of coffee.

"As soon as I saw Grayson enter the shop I followed him," said Harris. "And while he and the tobacconist were discussing the account I asked one of the staff to show me a selection of their most expensive cigars. These were laid out on the counter for me to examine. This was signal for a policeman in plain clothes who'd been standing outside the shop to make a noisy entrance, and I'm afraid that while Grayson was temporarily distracted I slipped some of these cigars into his pocket. I expect you can guess what happened next."

"I think I can, Harris. You and your plain clothes colleague had a perfect excuse to arrest the hapless Grayson, take him to the station and threaten him with the possibility of being dismissed from his job unless he told you all you wanted to know about his employers."

Harris stroked his mustache and beamed.

"I knew you'd approve, sir," he said. "Especially when you hear what Grayson had to say about the Arbuthnots."

Seeing that he had Parsons' full interest, Harris paused and made a point of examining his empty cup.

"I think I'll have that other cup of tea now, sir," he said. "If you would be so kind."

Harris returned to his notes.

"As we thought, the house in Eaton Square belongs to Lady Cordelia, and it is her money that allows them to live in the style they do. But according to Grayson all is not sweetness and light between the two. Apart from Lady Cordelia being disappointed by her husband's lack of ambition she has also become increasingly annoyed at having to pay his gambling debts. Since his return from Africa these debts have become considerable, and have lead to furious rows between him and his wife. Grayson says they effectively live separate lives: the major spends most of his evenings at a gambling club and she has increasingly taken to being driven around by Cooper."

"Very interesting," said Parsons. "And did you discover where they were on the night General Latham was murdered?"

"Grayson says that there was a terrible scene after the Arbuthnots returned from the Cordell's dinner party. Arbuthnot accused his wife of making a tedious dinner worse by behaving like a sour-faced cow, and in return she told him that he was a pompous ass and that she had no wish to spend another evening in the company of a stupid drunken boy like Simpson, a boring sycophant like Holland, and a French strumpet like Venetta. As a result Arbuthnot stormed off to his club, but not before Lady Cordelia had reminded him that she had been serious when she told him she would no longer pay his debts."

"And what did Lady Cordelia do after Arbuthnot had gone?"

"As soon as her husband had left the house she summoned Cooper and went out again."

"Does Grayson know what time she and Cooper returned?"

"He didn't actually see Lady Cordelia, but he heard Cooper returning the coach to the mews around about one o'clock."

"What about the other nights? The nights that Cordell and Simpson died?"

"Grayson is certain that Lady Cordelia went for a ride with Cooper on the night Captain Simpson died, but she was at home on the night of the colonel's death. Both she and her husband returned from the Officers' Mess after Latham's funeral and dined together. By all accounts it was another stormy affair. She took great delight in discussing the scene that had taken place between the colonel and Captain Simpson. In the process she proceeded to pour scorn on Cordell for his weakness and accused her husband of being no better. She said that Cordell had no idea how to handle a wife, and neither did he. As soon as dinner was over Arbuthnot went out and Lady Cordelia went to her room."

"And where was Cooper?"

"Grayson didn't know, sir. All he could say was that he didn't attend dinner with the other servants. But that's not unusual. Cooper rarely does."

"So on the nights Latham and Simpson died Lady Arbuthnot and Cooper were out together, and Cooper was also out on the night Cordell died. Very interesting. Opportunity and motive, wouldn't you say, Harris. But what about the gallant major? Does he really spend every evening gambling?"

"I'd say that was true, sir. Although Grayson was reluctant at first, he eventually gave me the name of Arbuthnot's club. *Lasiters* in Mayfair. Very exclusive, sir. They didn't want to admit me into the premises at first, but when I explained I was investigating General Latham's murder and that one of their members might be involved they were more than happy to show me the Attendance Book. They keep a record of the comings and goings of all their members. The duty manager told me it was a convenient way of knowing who was at the club on a particular night in case there was ever a need for witnesses. When I asked why there was ever a need for 'witnesses' I was told that there had been times when certain members had attempted to avoid paying their debts by swearing they were not in the club when the debts were incurred."

"Good work, Harris. But what did you learn about Arbuthnot on the three nights in question?"

"He was definitely in the club until the early hours of the morning on the nights Latham and Cordell died, and on the night of Simpson's death he left the club just after midnight and went with some friends to the Cafe Royal in Piccadilly to celebrate his good fortune. Apparently Arbuthnot had won a lot of money that night. Enough to pay his debts for the month."

Harris took a mouthful of tea before continuing.

"I'd say from what we know of Arbuthnot's relationship with his wife that they make unlikely fellow conspirators, sir."

"Well, you never know, Harris. Stranger things have happened. For all we know these domestic scenes between the two of them may have been a clever attempt to throw everyone off the scent. They might well be a couple of love birds all the time."

Harris laughed.

"I find that difficult to believe, sir," he said. "Especially after what I learned next from Grayson. By this time the poor man had become so concerned about his own reputation that he was willing to tell me anything if he thought it would mean him being released from police custody before anyone in Eaton Square missed him. That's when he told me that Arbuthnot frequents a brothel in Bayswater."

"However did Grayson discover that?"

"He found the address when he going through the pockets of Arbuthnot's evening dress before having it cleaned. It was not an address with which he was familiar, and being naturally curious he decided to make enquiries."

"And were you equally curious, Harris?"

"I was, sir. I went to the house in Bayswater yesterday afternoon. I decided there was little use going there in the mornings. That's when most people in establishments like that are asleep."

"I'll take your word for that, Harris," said Parsons with a smile. "But did you discover anything interesting?"

"I did, sir. I had a long talk with Kate Hamilton, the lady who owns the house in Newton Terrace. Quite a respectable neighborhood, sir. But there again Kate has a very respectable clientele. Rather like Lady Cordelia she contributes to the local police Christmas fund and they leave her alone. After all, the police don't want the embarrassment of arresting the distinguished military gentlemen they're likely to find there."

"Did you discover any interesting names amongst Kate's clientele?"

Harris produced a sheet of paper from inside his jacket.

"Here's the list, sir. Kate was extremely reluctant to give me the information, but I told her that it was not just a simple matter of sparing her customers an embarrassment. I said I was investigating a series of murders and it was quite possible that one of her clients might be involved. Even then she seemed a little reluctant to give me the names. So, I simply told her that if she didn't cooperate I'd have her business closed."

"Excellent work, Harris. Remind me to tell the superintendent what a fine fellow you are."

"Much good will that do me, sir. A sergeant I am and a sergeant I'll stay."

Unfortunately that was likely to be true, thought Parsons. No matter how hard he worked or how successful he was Harris was unlikely ever to be promoted. When it came to judging a person by his background there were striking similarities between the army and the police force.

"How many girls does this Kate have?" Parsons asked "And are any of them French?"

"I thought you might ask me that, sir. There are four girls working for Kate at present, and one of them is French. But if you're thinking she murdered Latham I'm afraid you'll be disappointed. She spent the night Latham was murdered with another senior army officer. I've put an asterisk against his name."

For the first time Parsons examined the list of names.

"Kate seems meticulous in her record keeping," he said. "She's very wise. Apart from protecting her customers she also has a useful weapon to use against them should the situation ever arise."

There was a grim smile of satisfaction on Parsons' face when he had finished reading the list.

"I'm most impressed, Harris," he said. "If you have no objections I'll keep this list for a few days. For a start it proves that Major Holland is a liar. And there's one other name here that is of particular interest to me."

43

WARRANT OFFICER JONAS Smallwood unbuttoned his red serge jacket, loosened the top three buttons of his navy trousers, and broke wind loudly. Then he turned to the sports page of his morning newspaper to examine the list of football fixtures.

Excellent, he thought, Fulham are playing at home. With the RSM away I'll be able to slip away this afternoon and watch the match.

In his younger days Smallwood had represented the regimental football team. He frequently boasted that since then there had never been his equal at center forward. With his commanding height and strength he had been a match for most defenders. But that had been many years ago, and since then Smallwood's burly chest had made way for an even larger stomach.

Smallwood had never married, and had few interests other than supporting Fulham Association Football Club and propping up the bar in the Sergeants' Mess. As a result of the latter and his sedentary life as Chief Clerk he now moved with some difficulty, and anyone seeing him in civilian clothes would have been surprised to learn that he was still a soldier.

As Chief Clerk he had reached the summit of his ambition. After the RSM he was the most senior noncommissioned officer in the regiment, and had intelligence enough to have long since mastered the mundane nature of his job, a job that rarely demanded that he leave the comforts of his warm office. Seldom did the colonel or any other of the commissioned officers involve themselves in the detailed paperwork for which he was responsible. Only Whitehead ever saw fit to scrutinize his work and ask to be informed about matters that were really none of his business.

The morning promised to be peaceful. The monthly returns had already been completed and signed off by Colonel Arbuthnot, the RSM was absent, and Smallwood had nothing to do other than read his newspaper until it was time to go and watch Fulham.

In consequence it was with some dismay that he learned that there were two policemen wishing to speak with him.

"I suppose you'd better show them in, Preston," he said with a sigh to the pale-faced clerk who had delivered the message. "And take my empty cup away."

Smallwood thrust the newspaper into one of the desk drawers, opened one of the files on his desk, buttoned his jacket and trousers, and adopted an appropriate expression of studious concentration as the two men were shown into his office. He recognized them. He had seen them with the RSM on their previous visits to the barracks.

"What can I do for you, gentlemen," he said. "If you're looking for Mr. Whitehead I'm afraid he's at the rifle range with B Company. With Major Plumb on leave and Captain Simpson no longer available the RSM has taken it upon himself to keep an eye on things."

The touch of irony in Smallwood's voice at the mention of the non-availability of Captain Simpson was not lost on Parsons. A large, overweight man with heavy jowls, prominent veins in his florid cheeks, and a stained uniform jacket with straining buttons, the Chief Clerk provided a remarkable contrast to the meticulously dressed RSM. That was not to deny Smallwood's competence. Handling the paperwork for a regiment approaching one thousand men required a special talent.

"No, Mr. Smallwood, it is you we have come to see," said Parsons, "as I believe that an oversight of the regimental mail is part of your responsibilities."

"It is indeed, sir," said Smallwood apprehensively, wondering what possible interest the regimental mail could be to the police. "Allow me to explain how the system works. We have an arrangement with the local postal sorting office that mail for the regiment is delivered here twice a day. It comes to regimental headquarters and my clerks sort it into bundles for the Officers' and

Sergeants' Messes, each of the three companies, and another bundle for anyone else, like the band or the mess servants. One of my clerks then takes the mail to the various parts of the barracks and brings back any outgoing mail for the postman to collect when he returns."

"So if someone in the Officers' Mess had written a letter one of your clerks would have collected it and brought it here to be collected by the postman."

"That's correct, inspector," said Smallwood. "Is there any particular officer or letter that you have in mind? The officers write so few letters that I'm sure my clerks would remember."

"It's this letter from Captain Simpson," said Parsons taking the envelope from his pocket. "He wrote it only the day before he died. Would you happen to know which of your clerks would have collected it from the Officers' Mess?"

"Let me see," said Smallwood. "That would be Wednesday, wouldn't it?"

He rose from his chair, went to the door of his office and opened it.

"Preston!" he shouted. "Come here!"

The thin-faced clerk grew even paler when he saw the letter in Parsons' hand.

"I would imagine you recognize this writing, Preston," said Parsons, holding the envelope in front of the clerk's face. "The blue ink is quite distinctive, wouldn't you agree?"

"Yes, sir," said the clerk, looking nervously from the envelope to the Chief Clerk, and back to the envelope again. "It looks like Captain Simpson's writing."

"Correct, Preston. Captain Simpson wrote this letter shortly before he died. And would you happen to know what he said?"

Smallwood rose to his feet, walked around his desk and confronted Parsons.

"Are you accusing one of my clerks of opening an officer's mail?" he said indignantly. "If so I hope you have good evidence."

Parsons handed the envelope to the Chief Clerk.

"I think you will agree that at some time this envelope has been opened and then resealed with glue," he said. "I've seen the letter that Captain Simpson wrote and I assure you that there's no evidence to suggest that the captain reopened the letter himself. So I must assume that it was done by someone handling the letter. Either the postman who collected the mail from the barracks, the one delivering it to Captain Simpson's parents, one of the sorters at the Post Office, or one of your clerks. It is my guess that it was one of your clerks."

"Well, Preston," shouted Smallwood. "What have you got to say to that?"

At first Parsons thought that the clerk would attempt to brazen it out. But in the presence of two policemen and his brawny superior his courage failed him.

"I only did it because my brother asked me," he said with a whimper. "He said one his mates wanted to know about Captain Simpson's mail.

My brother said I was to steam open any letters the captain wrote and make a copy of what he said."

"Preston has an older brother in the regiment," explained Smallwood. "A bit of a trouble maker."

He glared at the trembling clerk.

"I never thought you were like him, Preston," he said. "And more fool you for following in his footsteps. You're for the Guard Room as soon as these gentlemen have gone, where you can spend the rest of the weekend at the tender mercy of Sergeant Oakes. We'll decide your punishment when I see the RSM on Monday. But before that, I want to know why your brother asked you to do this. And who's the friend of your brother that's so interested in Captain Simpson's mail?"

"A man called Cooper, sir. Albert Cooper. He was in the regiment in Africa, but now I think he works as Colonel Arbuthnot's coachman."

"THERE ARE STILL one or two other matters I'd like to discuss," said Parsons, after Preston had been dismissed.

Smallwood looked at his watch in dismay. If these detectives kept him much longer he could see himself missing the start of the match.

"I trust you will be brief, sir," he said. "I've a very important appointment this afternoon."

Parsons ignored the remark.

"I believe that some of the soldiers were flogged whilst the regiment was in Africa," he said. "Is it possible that there is still a record of those who were punished?"

Not for the first time Smallwood congratulated himself on the efficiency of his filing system. It was one of the few things for which the RSM had ever complimented him. Mindful that the time for Fulham's kick off was fast approaching, he hurried from his office and in less then two minutes returned with two ledgers.

"The Discipline Books," he said proudly. "These will cover the period that the regiment was in Africa. Is there any particular year you are interested in?"

"Only the years that Colonel Latham was in command. And I am only interested in those cases where corporal punishment is involved."

"That shouldn't be difficult. It was rare for a soldier to be flogged. As far as I remember there were only two occasions in Africa that Colonel Latham sanctioned a flogging."

Smallwood flicked through the pages.

"Here you are," he said. "I was right. Only two men were flogged."

Parsons looked at the two names. Private Albert Cooper and Private Daniel Hobson. They had both received twenty lashes, Cooper for being drunk and striking an officer named Matheson, and Hobson for stealing from Major Cordell. The floggings had been administered by the sergeant majors of the companies each soldier was serving in at the time. Cooper had been whipped by CSM Brown, and Hobson by CSM Whitehead.

"What happened to CSM Brown?" Parsons asked, thinking that Cooper might well bear him a grudge.

"He died in action shortly afterwards. As did Lieutenant Matheson"

"And what about Hobson?" It had crossed Parsons' mind that RSM Whitehead himself might be in some danger.

"He was selected for the patrol," said Smallwood. "It was Whitehead's idea. Hobson had been Major Cordell's servant at the time of the theft, and Whitehead persuaded the major to send the lad on the patrol and give him a chance to redeem himself. No one in the army likes to be labeled a thief. But he never came back. The Zulus must've taken him alive. When we found his body later you could see he'd been tortured."

"That brings me to my last question," said Parsons. "Who other than Captain Simpson survived the patrol?"

"I don't need my books to tell you that, inspector," said Smallwood. "There were only a handful. Oakes, Williams, and Bates. Oakes is the only one still in the regiment. The others left as soon as we returned to England. As did Simpson's platoon sergeant, Sergeant Fox. Fox wasn't on the patrol. He was wounded at the time. But he knew all the lads who went. He trained them all and said he felt like a father to them."

BEFORE LEAVING THE Chief Clerk's office, Parsons had obtained sufficient information about Williams, Bates and Fox to enable Harris to begin tracing them. Williams had become a policeman, Bates a cab driver and Fox now ran a public house.

"I'm afraid that will mean you'll be working tomorrow, Harris," he said as they walked through the barrack gate. "I'm beginning to feel we're making real progress at last, but I don't think we can afford to wait until Monday. If and when you find these men I don't want any of them to feel that they're suspects for any of these murders. Just tell them that you're trying to get some background on Simpson for the coroner's court, and as they were in his platoon in Africa they might know something about him that would be useful. But what I really want is your opinion as to whether any of them are capable of murder. In the meantime I'm going back to Eaton Square to speak with Lady Cordelia and Albert Cooper, her coachman."

44

THE SHADOWS OF the trees in the central gardens of Eaton Square were already encroaching upon the lower floors of the houses and creeping into the portico of St. Peter's church when Parsons' cab arrived. Only the upmost windows captured the last glorious red rays of the setting sun. Few people were abroad: a primly uniformed nanny pushing a perambulator, an elegantly dressed elderly couple taking a late afternoon promenade, and a baker's boy with a large wicker basket delivering a late order of bread.

Parsons had instructed the cab to drop him and the police constable from Chelsea Division in Grosvenor Place. He stationed the constable behind a tree at the entrance to the square, from where he had a clear view of the Arbuthnot's house, and then continued alone.

He was already climbing the steps to the front door when Charles Arbuthnot emerged wearing a black frock coat and a black silk top hat, and carrying a silver-topped ebony cane.

"Good afternoon, inspector. I'm just off for a stroll," he said jovially. "But I can put that off for a while if you wish to have a few words."

"It's actually Lady Cordelia I'm here to see," Parsons said. "Is she at home?"

"As a matter of fact she is. But what's this all about? If you want to speak with my wife I really think I should be present."

"I'd rather you weren't, sir. I suspect that your presence may inhibit what Lady Cordelia has to say."

"Now look here, Parsons," Arbuthnot said angrily. "If you intend to speak with my wife I've a right to be there."

"You have a perfect right, sir, and I cannot stop you if you insist," said Parsons. "But I should warn you that were you to do that I would be obliged to disclose the fact that you were at Kate Hamilton's on Wednesday night. And you will probably know better than I how your wife will react when she hears you were visiting a brothel."

Parsons had half expected Arbuthnot to bluster and deny the allegation, but from the rather bemused expression on his face it seemed unclear how he thought his wife would receive this news. For a moment Parsons feared that the colonel might be prepared to take whatever risk there might be in his wife learning about his whereabouts for the sake of discovering whatever it was that the police wanted to discuss with her.

But then it appeared that Arbuthnot changed his mind.

"Perhaps it's better you didn't mention my visit to Kate to Cordelia," he said genially. "No point in upsetting the old girl unnecessarily."

He raised the silver tip of his cane to the brim of his hat.

"Then, I'll wish you a good-day," he said with a wry smile. "And good luck with my lady wife."

HAVING JUST SEEN his master off the premises, Grayson was surprised and mildly irritated to find Parsons on the doorstep. In view of the butler's recent brush with the police Parsons could well understand Grayson's concern, and was amused to see the obvious relief on the butler's face when he learned the real purpose of the young inspector's visit.

"Lady Cordelia has been taking tea in the morning room," Grayson said solemnly. "You are fortunate that the last of her visitors has just gone. Please be so good as to follow me."

Instead of taking the stairs Grayson led Parsons to one of the doors off the circular hall.

"Inspector Parsons," he announced.

From behind the butler Parsons could see the sour expression on Lady Cordelia's face. She dabbed gently at her mouth with a white linen napkin.

"I'm busy, Grayson" she said. "Tell him to go away."

"I'm afraid that that will not be at all convenient," said Parsons, stepping from behind the butler and advancing into the room. "What I have to discuss with you cannot wait. Thank you, Grayson."

Parsons closed the door behind him. In a household of this stature it was normal for the morning room to be used exclusively by the lady of the house. In that sense it was rather like her boudoir, although unlike a boudoir, the morning room would generally be used for more public matters. It would be here that Lady Cordelia would meet with servants to discuss their duties, deal with her correspondence, and organize the household accounts. It was also the room in which she would entertain her lady friends.

Parsons immediate impression was that it was a room dominated by the use of imported Indian floral chintz for both curtains and upholstery. And it was one in which Lady Cordelia had attempted to make herself the centrepiece by choosing to adorn herself in a dazzling dress of fawn silk.

As he crossed the room to where she sat he could see the evidence of her earlier visitors. On the occasional table beside her rested a silver teapot, four delicate monogrammed china cups and plates, and a silver dish with the remnants of what had once been a tasteful arrangement of thinly-sliced sandwiches.

"How dare you enter this room without my permission," she said icily as Parsons approached.

"If you insist upon staying I'll have my coachman throw you out."

"I had also intended speaking with him, Lady Cordelia" said Parsons calmly. "But not until after I'd spoken with you. However, if you summon him now I'm sure I can accommodate you both. And if you are thinking of having me evicted I should point out that I have taken the precaution of bringing a police constable with me. If you care to look from your window in the direction of Grosvenor Place you will doubtless see a police constable's helmet protruding from behind one of the trees."

Lady Cordelia rose from her chair in one furious movement and strode towards the window. She drew back the curtain a few inches and looked out.

"As you can see he is not on public display outside your house," Parsons said, "as I am sure you would not want your neighbours to be aware that you are being interviewed by the police. But I can assure you that from where he is standing the constable has an excellent view of your front door and will be here in a trice if I summon him."

Lady Cordelia returned to her chair with an angry rustle of silk.

"Well, what is it you want?" she demanded.

"I want to know where you and Cooper went on the nights of Wednesday, the twenty-second of this month, and on Wednesday, the twenty-ninth. And lest you have forgotten, those were the nights on which General Latham was murdered and Captain Simpson died."

At first a look of surprise crept over Lady Cordelia's face, but then her azure eyes blazed with anger.

"How dare you, young man," she said furiously. "How dare you come into my house and make assertions like that."

"I am making no assertions," Parsons said calmly. "I merely want you to answer my question."

"I have no intention of answering that question without having my lawyer present," she said. "In the meantime I will summon my coachman and have you removed from my house."

She walked to the fireplace and pulled a bell cord.

"Grayson," she said when the butler arrived. "Fetch Cooper."

———

PARSONS SETTLED INTO one of the easy chairs opposite Lady Cordelia. He had no wish to become involved in a scuffle with anyone, especially a man as strong as he imagined Cooper to be. During his years in the police he had managed to avoid any physical confrontation, and he had no intention of starting now.

Cooper's arrival brought Lady Cordelia to her feet.

"I want you to evict this man," she said imperiously.

Cooper's dark eyes scrutinized the small man with long hair. He was clearly overweight and, judging by the size of his hands, unlikely to present any sort of threat. He might, of course, be armed, and that would considerably change the odds. And Cooper was no fool. He was not going to get himself shot or take any preemptive action without finding the reason the man was in the house, and why his presence had so obviously upset Lady Cordelia. His first guess was that the man was a blackmailer, and if that was the case there was no harm in listening to what he had to say. Perhaps he would learn something of benefit to himself.

"Well, Cooper. Why are you standing there like that?" Lady Cordelia demanded. "I've just given you an order."

"An' I'm not lifting a finger against this man until I 'ear what 'e 'as to say," said Cooper with a scowl.

The coachman's impertinent response to his mistress came as a welcome surprise to Parsons. Cooper had not followed her orders blindly, and he must feel very sure of his ground for him to dare speak to her in such a fashion. For most servants that would risk instant dismissal.

"Before laying a finger on me, Cooper," he said calmly. "You should know that I'm a detective inspector in the Metropolitan Police investigating the murder of General Latham."

It was the last thing that Cooper had been expecting. He looked uneasily towards Lady Cordelia and then back again at Parsons.

"But I thought you arrested someone for that," he said. "Some French woman."

"That is correct, Cooper," said Parsons. "Colonel Cordell's wife was charged with the general's murder, and she is still in police custody."

Parsons looked directly at Lady Cordelia.

"However," he said, "recent information has led me to believe that Mrs. Cordell is not guilty of that crime, and as it happens I was discussing the general's murder with Lady Cordelia at the time she sent for you. I had actually just got to the point of asking her where you both were on the night the general was so brutally murdered."

Cooper's swarthy features creased into a frown.

"Are you saying that you think that Lady Cordelia murdered this bloody general, and I 'ad a part in it?" he demanded.

Lady Cordelia had grown increasingly concerned at the way in which the conversation was progressing. She had wanted Parsons thrown out of the house, and she had imagined that Cooper would do that without complicating matters by asking questions.

"Cooper," she said, a trace of nervous hysteria creeping into her voice. "I've already told you once what I want you to do. Now get on with it."

"Not so bleedin' fast, your ladyship," said Cooper. "I want to know more about this. If you've been sticking spears into bloody generals that's one thing. I wouldn't put that past you. But don't get me involved. The next thing I know some fancy bloody lawyer of yours will be convincing a jury that it was really me that done it. I can just hear what he'd say."

Cooper adopted a tone that he assumed would sound like that of an upper class barrister.

"Gentleman of the jury," he said. "I would like to draw your attention to the fact that while 'e was in the army this man Cooper was flogged for striking a superior officer. 'E 'as also been in trouble with the police on several occasions for common assault. Can you seriously believe that such an eminent lady as my client could commit such a crime, when as she 'as already told you it was done by 'er coachman."

Cooper glared at Lady Cordelia.

"Yea. And I know what the bloody jury will think. They'll take one look at my ugly mug, then they'll look at you in your bloody silk dress and your title and your fine upstanding husband who is now a bloody colonel, and they'll say that man Cooper must be guilty. I know your sort, my lady. You need me whenever you want a good screwing, but sure as 'ell you'll say nothing in my defense if it's murder we're talking about."

"You fool, Cooper," shouted Lady Cordelia. "Don't you see that there is no way that either you and I could be involved in General Latham's murder. Don't you remember where we were that night?"

Cooper opened his mouth and closed it again. As Parsons had suspected the coachman was a man who had a tendency to speak before thinking.

"Oh, yea," he said, suddenly aware of his injudicious comments. "We was at *The Marchioness*."

From the expression on Lady Cordelia's face Parsons had little doubt that if she had been given a whip at that moment she would not have spared her coachman.

"Perhaps you will be kind enough to enlighten me as to what you are talking about," he asked. Where and what is this Marchioness?"

"It's a hotel in Paddington," Lady Cordelia explained, her face a composite of suppressed fury and exasperation. "Cooper and I have been known to visit it from time to time."

"And the reason for those visits was the matter that Cooper has previously referred to?" Parsons asked, still stunned by what he had just heard.

Cooper laughed heartily.

"What d'you bloody think?" he said with a raucous laugh. "That we went there to discuss the bleedin' weather. I jus' told you, didn' I. Her ladyship 'ere wanted my body."

Parsons watched Lady Cordelia carefully. There was no doubt of her anger at such a public humiliation, but he was also sure that she had the sense to realize that the exposure of her sordid relationship with Cooper was actually in her best interests. Whatever suspicions the police might have had about her involvement in General Latham's murder had been shown to be groundless. Even as he watched he could see her displeasure giving way to her more usual arrogance. For his own part Cooper was enjoying the situation exceedingly, aware that what he had said unwittingly had completely wrong-footed the police.

The news of the relationship between Lady Cordelia and her coachman had been the last thing Parsons had been expecting. He had come to Eaton Square in order to confirm his suspicions and then to arrest them both. And all he had learned was that they were involved in a tawdry liaison. He would, of course, need to check their alibi, but he had little doubt that it was true. Why else would Cooper have dared speak to Lady Cordelia in the way he did.

But if they were innocent of Latham's murder, Cooper still had to answer for his movements on the night Simpson died.

"And what exactly was your reason for wanting to see what was in Captain Simpson's mail?" Parsons asked, with considerably less authority than before.

Cooper did not attempt to deny his guilt.

"It was just a precaution," he said. "Lady Cordelia thought he might know about us."

"It was something that foolish young man said to me when we were dining at the Cordells," Lady Cordelia explained. "He told me he'd seen me going into a hotel in Paddington with Cooper. I wouldn't like that to become common knowledge. Charles and I have to think of our position."

Cooper snorted with laughter.

"Whereas the only position you 'ave to consider with me is being flat on your bloody back with your legs open," he said.

Parsons gave her no time to respond to this latest coarse remark. He could feel his investigation falling apart, and the last thing he wanted was for Lady Cordelia to lose her temper with Cooper again when there were still questions he needed her to answer.

"And on the nights Colonel Cordell and Captain Simpson committed suicide?" he asked "Where were you both then?"

"I came back to Eaton Square with Charles after that disgusting exhibition in the Mess between Cordell and Simpson," said Lady Cordelia. "And I stayed home. You are welcome to check that with Grayson or any other member of my staff. As for the other night you refer to, Cooper and I were at the hotel in Paddington. I'm sure you'll have no problem in verifying that."

Parsons was by now beginning to feel completely deflated. His two chief suspects both had alibis for the nights Latham and Simpson died, and Lady Cordelia was at home on the night Cordell met his death. There remained only a brief glimmer of hope that Cooper would fail to prove his whereabouts at the time Cordell was murdered.

"And I suppose, Cooper, you can account for your movements after you brought Lady Cordelia and her husband back from the Mess last Wednesday?"

The triumphant smirk on Cooper's face made Parsons' last hope fade.

"That I can, mate," he said. "I was watching some terriers slaughter a few rats. I'll give you the address of the house in Clapham if you want it. There were dozens of witnesses who saw me. If I'm not surprised some of them were titled ladies and gentlemen like yourself, Lady Cordelia."

It was clear from the brazen expression on Cooper's face that he was relishing the chance of making a fool of the police yet again.

"And after that I found myself a woman," he said. "One who was prepared to do a bit of work 'erself. Not like some I could mention. You can check 'er out as well if you want."

The expression of incandescent fury on Lady Cordelia's face was Parsons sole consolation as he left the room.

45

Sunday, 2nd November

PARSONS WOULD NOT have slept well even had the rain not been lashing on the roof slates just above his head for most of the night. He had rarely felt more despondent. His foolish presumption of the guilt of Lady Cordelia and her coachman had managed to lead him down a blind alley, and now he felt further than ever from discovering the truth.

They had both seemed to him to be well capable of murder, and their motives had been compelling. It was Latham who had ordered Cooper's flogging, and Lady Cordelia who held the general responsible for having Cordell promoted rather than her husband. And the opportunity to redress that situation had presented itself after Latham's funeral. Cordelia would have seen how emotionally distraught Cordell had become and how much he was drinking, and with Cooper as an accomplice she would have been little difficulty in staging a convincing suicide. Even Simpson's death fitted this scenario. The young man had seemingly known too much for his own good about the sordid relationship Cordelia was having with Cooper.

That was the most ironic part of all, Parsons thought morosely. For had he known previously about that affair, he would have thought it even more likely than he did that Cordelia and Cooper were guilty of all three murders.

But as it happened, their relationship had instead provided them both with a perfect alibi. They had been together in a cheap hotel in Paddington on the nights Latham and Cordell were murdered, a fact that had been confirmed when Parsons called at *The Marchioness* after leaving Eaton Square. He had neither the time nor inclination to follow up Cooper's story about attending a dog fight in Clapham and visiting a prostitute. But he had little doubt that it would prove to be true.

———

WHEN HIS ALARM clock woke him Parsons had only just fallen into a deep sleep. He rose with great reluctance and gazed sullenly through his bedroom window at the rain falling on the nearby rooftops. It was not a day to venture out, and were it not for his promise to escort his mother to King's Cross Station he would probably have returned to the warmth of his bed.

He put on his dressing gown and made himself a cup of tea before starting to dress and begin his ablutions, and it was fully fifteen minutes before he stood in front of his shaving mirror wearing a clean vest, and with his braces hanging down loosely over his trousers. The reflection in the mirror was far from pleasing. He saw a young man whose tousled head of hair was badly in need of a trim, and with the sort of dark bags under his eyes that made it appear that he had been up all night drinking. He could imagine what his mother would say when she saw him.

Parsons lathered his face and began sharpening his razor on the leather strop hanging at the side of his wash basin. And then his mind froze, and all he could see was Cordell's body in the bath, and the deep lacerations on his wrists. He remembered the cut on the inside of the left wrist being deeper than that on the right. At the time he had thought it only logical that a right handed person like Cordell would choose to cut his left wrist first. But Doctor Grainger had disputed that. He had said that in view of how much Cordell had drunk that day it was irrelevant which hand he used to inflict the first wound. But they had never discussed the angle of the incisions!

Parsons held his razor in his right hand and looked down at his left wrist. Surely, he thought, if I was going to cut my left wrist I would place my razor in a line parallel to my left thumb. And similarly when using my left hand to cut my right wrist. But that was not how he remembered seeing the cuts on Cordell's wrists. They had sloped in the opposite direction. It was not impossible to imagine Cordell choosing to cut himself in that fashion, but what was far more likely was that someone else had made the cuts. Someone had taken hold of Cordell's hands one at a time and slashed his wrists in a direction roughly perpendicular to his thumbs. It was a clear indication that Cordell had been murdered. What other logical explanation could there be? And what did it matter that Lady Cordelia and Cooper were innocent? If it was not them, then it was somebody else. And Parsons knew it was his duty to find that person, and feeling sorry for himself was no way to go about.

He completed his shave in haste, neglecting to wipe the specks of blood from his face where he had cut himself, and ran a brush quickly through his hair. Then he dressed in a dark three-piece suit that was both suitable for Sundays and for an occasion like meeting his mother and the Chapmans, put on his gray worsted overcoat and, after confirming that his black leather gloves were still in the overcoat pockets, seized his umbrella and set off down the stairs.

IT WAS LESS then two miles to the Chapman's house in Holland Park, and had the weather been less inclement Parsons would have chosen to walk. But knowing how critical Louise's parents and brother had been in the past about his appearance, he had no wish to arrive on their doorstep looking like a drowned rat. So he decided to take a cab. But before that there was time for tea and toast at his favorite coffee house on the King's Road and the opportunity to catch up on the week's news in the *Sunday Times*.

In Dublin and other cities in Ireland, he read, there continued to be demonstrations against the arrest of Charles Stewart Parnell, the Irish Home Rule activist; although in the last few days it had been an English parliamentarian who had been attracting the nation's attention. Charles Bradlaugh, the newly elected Member of Parliament for Northampton, had only a few days ago been physically assaulted and forcibly ejected from the Houses of Parliament. As well as being an advocate of trade unionism, republicanism, women's suffrage, and birth control, Bradlaugh also supported Irish Home Rule. He was also an avowed atheist. And it was this atheism, rather than his support for the Irish cause, that had propelled him into national prominence.

Bradlaugh had refused to swear the religious Oath of Allegiance to the Crown that was required of members of parliament. Instead he had claimed the right to affirm, a choice that had proved unacceptable not only to a majority of members of both the House of Lords and the House of Commons, but also to leading figures in both the Church of England and the Roman Catholic Church. Bradlaugh had unsuccessfully attempted to take his seat in the House of Commons on several previous occasions. Once he had been imprisoned in the Clock Tower in the Palace of

Westminster, and more recently assaulted by parliamentary officials and dragged from Parliament by the police.

Parsons considered the whole affair to be a disgrace. After all the voters of Northampton had elected Bradlaugh to Parliament in full knowledge of his policies and his beliefs. As far as they were concerned a belief in God was not a prerequisite for being a Member of Parliament. Parsons agreed with them. He was a staunch monarchist himself, and one who attended church as regularly as most, although of late his faith had become less firm than it had once been. In this respect he was no different from the majority of people in the country. They remained as loyal as ever to the Queen, but were turning away in increasing numbers from organized religion. So it was nonsense for the Establishment to insist that only elected representatives expressing a belief in God should be allowed a say in how the country was governed. Such an attitude could lead to civil disorder and give political extremists yet another reason to call for the abolishment of the monarchy. But he knew that his views would find little favor in the Chapman household, or indeed with his own dear mother.

A CAB DROPPED Parsons at the appointed hour outside the porticoed entrance of the Chapman's residence. He ordered it to wait, confident that his mother and her luggage had been ready for some time.

The butler greeted him with a disdainful expression that had much in common with that normally reserved for him by Louise's brother. He relieved Parsons of his overcoat and umbrella, and escorted him in a condescending manner to the large drawing room on the ground floor where Louise, her brother, and his mother awaited him.

With paneled and gilded walls, and a high ceiling with garlands and elaborate friezes, it was a room clearly intended to reflect the Chapman's wealth, and one in which comfort was less important than style. The spindly legged chairs and the impossibly elegant settees were of such proportions that, although they might accommodate ladies of a more diminutive stature like Louise and Amelia Parsons, portly crinolined ladies and well-upholstered gentlemen such as Mildred and Jasper Chapman, would, out of necessity, have had to lower their weight onto them with the utmost of care. Reginald, their son, with one long leg draped languidly over the arm of one of these delicate chairs, looking as equally out of place in the room as Parsons felt. But it was clear from the superior sneer on his face as Parsons entered, that he did not wish to forego the pleasure of making a final derogatory remark.

"How nice to see you again, Everett," Louise said stiffly, as Parsons crossed the room and bowed awkwardly to her. He had intended making a more favorable impression by kissing her hand, but aware that his every move was being watched with amusement by her brother, he settled for a nervous handshake.

"My parents have gone to church," she said. "They wanted me to accompany them. But I said I preferred to stay and see you."

"Thank you, Louise," said Parsons. "That was most thoughtful." He bent to kiss his mother on both cheeks. "And how are you, mother? How was the journey yesterday?"

"It was very tiring, my dear," Amelia Parsons replied. "I will be glad when I am in my own dear home again. Of course, the holiday was wonderful, and I can never thank Louise's parents enough for inviting me, but at my age I find such long journeys to be very wearisome."

Parsons was dismayed to find how awkward he felt in Louise's presence. In the Lake District they had taken enormous pleasure in being together, and now, after less than two weeks apart it was as though they were strangers. It was, perhaps, too much to have expected a small show of affection from Louise. He knew that, like himself, she felt uncomfortable about expressing her emotions in the presence of her brother, but her reception had been unusually cold.

If Parsons was to be honest he would have to admit that he had never felt at ease in the Chapman's house. Louise's parents, her brother, and even the servants, had made little attempt ever to make him feel welcome. But the atmosphere today seemed even more strained than usual. No doubt the fault was his. He had become engrossed in the complex case he was investigating that whatever social graces he might previously have displayed had abandoned him. And Louise had more than likely sensed that remoteness when he had entered the room.

As far as Parsons could see, the awkward situation was beyond redemption. His mother was clearly anxious to leave, and Louise did not seem to want him to stay. Only Reginald Chapman appeared to be deriving any pleasure from his presence, although so far he had done no more than watch the proceedings with a supercilious grin on his face. But as Parsons and his mother were preparing to leave he followed them out into the hall with the intention of making a final barbed comment.

"I see that you fellows in Scotland Yard are incapable of catching Lord Fwedewick Sayers' assassin," he drawled. "but we've come to accept that sort of incompetence fwom the police."

In the past Parsons would have chosen to ignore the remark, especially if he was engaged, as he was at that moment, in assisting his mother with her luggage. But his feelings had been bruised by Louise's attitude, and it was as much as he could bear to see the foolish grin on her brother's face.

Making his excuses to his mother, Parsons took Reginald's arm and led him into a quiet corner of the hall.

"Are you planning to visit Kate Hamilton's again now that you're back in London, Captain Chapman?" he asked.

The smile evaporated from Reginald's face.

"I've no idea what you're talking about, Parsons," he blustered.

"Oh, but I think you have, sir," Parsons said coldly. "You see I have in my possession a list of the army officers who habitually use a brothel in Newton Terrace, and you will no doubt be dismayed to find that your name is on that list. And if I ever hear one more facetious comment from you, I will ensure that this information is conveyed to your parents. Perhaps even to your doting sister."

It had been a cheap trick, but it was one that had put a gloss on what, for Parsons, had hitherto been a depressing morning; and it was with a lighter step that he returned to the front door to supervise the loading of his mother's trunk onto the waiting cab.

——— ———

AMELIA PARSONS WAS quieter than usual during the journey. Parsons had imagined that she would have had much to tell him about what had happened in the Lake District after he had left. Her silence discomfited him and he found his mood darkening once more. It was fortunate that the sun had suddenly decided to shine and, as their cab sped along Bayswater Road, he could avail himself of the fine views of Kensington Gardens and Hyde Park. But when his mother had still not spoken by the time the cab had reached Marble Arch he felt compelled to speak.

"Is anything the matter, mother?" he asked, in as light a tone as he could manage. "I couldn't help noticing that you are unusually quiet this morning."

Parsons regretted asking the question as soon as his mother began speaking.

"You're a fine one to talk, Everett," she said. "Do you realize how you've upset Louise by your inattention. Only one letter in two weeks! What is that poor young girl expected to think. One moment she is expecting you to propose to her and the next she feels completely abandoned. And what do you suppose her parents think? No wonder they went to church this morning. Louise's mother informed me that it was much better that they did. She had no wish to hurt Louise's feelings any more by telling you just what she thought of you."

In spite of his shock at what his mother had just said it was all that Parsons could do to restrain himself from saying what he thought of Mildred Chapman. But he knew that comments of that nature would only make matters worse.

"For one thing, mother," he said, as calmly as he could, "it has not yet been two weeks. And for another, did it not occur to any of you that I have been involved in a demanding murder investigation."

"Fiddlesticks, Everett. What has that got to do with writing more frequently to a girl who was on the point of becoming engaged to you. Have you no sense of decorum? And just look at you! Your shirt collar is dirty, you are sorely in need of a haircut, and there is still blood on your chin where you cut yourself shaving. And you seem to be the only young man of my acquaintance who doesn't wear a top hat. What a sorry sight you are. No wonder that Louise could scarcely bear to look at you. That brother of hers may be tiresome at times, but at least he takes care of his appearance."

"But, mother," Parsons pleaded. "I have had no time to visit a barber. I've been working all hours of the day and night on an especially tricky investigation."

"Exactly my point, Everett. If this is what your job entails you should consider getting another. You should think about finding a respectable profession. How do you think Louise feels when her parents, her brother, and even the servants think that you are unsuitable for her. You should become a solicitor or a barrister. You're clever enough. Perhaps Louise's father might even find you a position in his bank."

There could not be many worse fates than working for Jasper Chapman, thought Parsons. And he was damned if he really cared what the Chapman's servants might think about him.

"But mother, it is quite unrealistic to think of me becoming a lawyer. I couldn't possibly afford to support myself while I was a pupil or serving my articles, and I have no intention of borrowing money from you. And, in any case, I enjoy my work. Isn't that the most important thing?"

"No, Everett, it is not." Parsons could see that his mother was warming to the task of chastising him. "At least, not if you wish to marry Louise.

How can you possibly support her on a policeman's salary? You need a more respectable profession with better prospects. Don't you know by now that having a liking for your work is less important than what other people think of it?"

PARSONS WAS GLAD to see the handsome Gothic facade of St. Pancras Station. Kings Cross, its less attractive neighbor, but the station from which his mother would catch her train, was but a few hundred yards further along Euston Road. It was rumored that the station had been built on the site of Queen Boudica's final battle with the Romans. That heroic woman had lost that particular battle, but Parsons was under no illusion that the Romans would have been defeated had his mother rather than Boudica been in the Queen's chariot that day.

Parsons paid the cabbie and hailed a porter. Fortunately he did not have to wait long for his mother's train to leave. For once he was not sorry to see her go, although what she had said had given him much to think about.

46

THE EARLY TRAFFIC in Whitehall was lighter than usual, and there were few pedestrians around other than a small crowd outside Horse Guards admiring the mounted sentries with their gleaming helmets, breast plates and sabres, their long black shining riding boots, and their splendid chargers. Only on Sundays was the veritable army of civil servants absent from the nearby government offices. In all probability, thought Parsons, as he stepped down from his cab, they were only now returning from morning worship with their wives and children and anticipating a traditional Sunday lunch of roast beef.

When he had risen that morning Parsons had fondly imagined that he would spend the afternoon with Louise after escorting his mother to the station. But the cool reception he had received and his mother's stern lecture had banished that idea. In the space of two weeks four men had met violent deaths, and all that the Chapmans and his mother could think about was how many letters he had written to Louise. It was really too bad.

He decided instead to go to his office. If Harris was working on a Sunday, and Parsons sincerely hoped that the sergeant was at this very moment engaged in the tasks he had been set, it was only right that he should make a similar sacrifice.

THE CID DUTY Clerk was seated with his feet on his desk reading *The News of the World*, a Sunday newspaper that enjoyed considerable popularity amongst people seeking saucy revelations and scandals, especially if they involved members of the upper classes. The newspaper employed reporters who were especially adept at unveiling indiscretions committed by public figures, and it was one such reporter who had fortuitously been on hand when a Cabinet Minister was caught *in flagrante delicto* only a few days previously.

It was clear that the clerk had not been expecting company. He sprang to his feet when he saw Parsons, gave him a guilty smile, and attempted to conceal the newspaper by pushing it under the desk.

"Cup of tea, inspector?" he asked, opening a cupboard and taking Parsons' distinctive floral-patterned china mug from amongst its more dowdy companions. "You needn't wait. I'll bring it to your office."

Sensing that the clerk was more intent upon returning to his newspaper than engaging him in conversation, Parsons walked along the corridor to his office. The room was desperately cold. It was several days since he had been in his office and during that time it was unlikely that the fire had been lit. The office cleaners had, nevertheless, dutifully laid the fire in anticipation of his eventual return, and it needed only a match to ignite the kindling of old newspapers and wood.

There were only two pieces of information on his desk that were of interest: the police surgeon's report on Simpson's death and a telegram from Paris. Parsons turned first to the telegram.

According to the French police the military authorities had no record of an officer named Major Claude de Verney dying within the past two years. An officer by that name had once served in the army, but he had died in 1870 at the Battle of Sedan and had never risen to the rank of major. But the police in Rochefort were well aware of Venetta de Verney. She was well known as a woman who lived by her wits and frequented the company of the wealthy men who patronized the town's spas and casinos. On more than one occasion a man she was escorting had reported losing his wallet, but although the police had taken her into custody and questioned her, there were never any conclusive evidence that it was she who had stolen it.

So Lady Cordelia was not far off the mark, Parsons mused. The beautiful Venetta was not only a courtesan, but in all probability a light fingered confidence trickster. She had certainly managed to deceive Colonel Cordell about her pedigree, as Parsons had little doubt that it had been she who had instigated their relationship. Yet from the French police's description of her it seemed an act that was out of character. From what they had said, regardless of the fact that she claimed to be a widow, Venetta had shown little interest in marriage. On the other hand she was possibly tiring of the life she had chosen, or might even have felt that it was only a matter of time before her luck ran out and she found herself serving time in a French prison. In either case she could no doubt see the advantage of a new life in England as the wife of a senior army officer.

There had been no record of a Venetta de Verney ever being involved in political activities. Indeed the authorities in Rochefort had found the idea altogether amusing. From what they had seen of her they thought it highly unlikely that a woman such as Venetta would ever abandon her wealthy clientele for the sake of a bunch of Irish fanatics.

The envelope containing Doctor Grainger's report also enclosed the single bullet that the surgeon had found embedded in Captain Simpson's brain. Parsons placed the bullet on the blotting pad on his desk and searched through his desk drawer for his ruler. The bullet measured point four five inches across its base, confirming that it had been fired from a Webley service revolver like the one found in Simpson's hand. So far, so good, he thought.

The police surgeon also confirmed that the time of death was somewhere between two and three in the morning. Much to Parsons' delight the doctor expressed his doubt about Simpson choosing to hold the revolver in his right hand, and to have pulled the trigger with his right thumb. The severe bruising Parsons had noticed had been the result of a compound fracture in Simpson's *proximal phalange*, the longest of the two bones in his thumb. In the doctor's opinion Simpson would have been in such pain that he would have chosen to avoid using the thumb if at all possible. It confirmed what Simpson's mother had said about his severe discomfort after trapping his thumb in a train door. She had advised him to see a doctor, and he had chosen to ignore her. Had he done so his thumb would doubtless have been bandaged, a fact that could not have escaped his murderer.

Parsons leant back in his chair and steepled his fingers. If Simpson had been murdered then it confirmed his suspicions about Cordell's suicide. And if Cordell had been murdered it was possible to draw a simple line of command from Simpson, the leader of the ill-advised patrol, through Cordell and Latham to the ultimate instigator of that patrol, Lord Frederick Sayers. It was exactly that line of command that had been at the heart of his conversation with Hardcastle.

Parsons cursed himself for being sidetracked by his suspicions of Lord Cordelia and her coachman when the truth had been staring him in the face all along. The motives for the murders had to be far more substantial than the petty jealousies of Lady Cordelia or Cooper's desire to avenge himself for a flogging. Whoever had murdered a senior politician and three army officers must have been aware of the conspiracy that linked them. But what was the motive for killing them? Could it have been punishment for their greed? To some extent that made sense. But if Sayers and Latham, and even Cordell, had been murdered for their greed, how would that involve Simpson. If anyone was a pawn in the game it was he.

The more Parsons thought about it the less he was convinced that gold had anything to do with the murders. It was the patrol itself. Something so terrible had happened on that patrol that the murderer had seen fit to revenge himself on everyone responsible for its planning and execution. Everyone from a Cabinet Minister to the officer leading the patrol.

Parsons went back into the general office.

"I want to see all the papers on Lord Frederick Sayers' murder," he told the clerk.

"Very good, sir," the clerk replied, trying not to show his displeasure at having his Sunday reading once again interrupted. "I'll bring you the files at once."

———

PARSONS WAS PARTICULARLY interested in the time of Lord Sayers' death and the description of the policeman who had come to Constable Dewhurst's aid. Sayers, he read, had left the

Houses of Parliament around about half past ten, and his body had been discovered at ten minutes to eleven. So, allowing for the time for him to walk from Parliament to where his body was found on Lambeth Bridge, a distance of about six hundred yards, it was likely that he was shot at approximately ten forty-five. General Latham had been murdered shortly after eleven forty-five. And his murderer had arrived by cab.

Parsons examined the large map of London on his notice board and with the aid of his ruler made a few calculations. As the crow flies the distance from Lambeth Bridge to Chester Place was just over three miles. London hansom cabs, he had once read, had been designed with a low center of gravity, with the purpose of combining speed and safety. Benjamin Disraeli, the Conservative Prime Minister before Gladstone, had referred to them as the gondolas of London. Parsons had heard that a hansom was capable of traveling at fifteen miles an hour, and although he had no wish ever to be driven by a London cabbie at such a speed, he could well imagine that at the late hour that Sayers and Latham were both murdered it would be quite possible to sail through the streets of West London comfortably at half that speed.

Parson's finger and ruler traced a likely route on the map. The policeman Dewhurst had seen at the scene of Sayer's death had departed in the direction of Lambeth. If, as had been speculated, this man was involved in Latham's death he could have boarded a cab at the Lambeth end of the bridge and then traveled south along the Albert Embankment to Vauxhall Bridge. A cab crossing the river at that point would travel northwest along Vauxhall Bridge Road past Victoria Station - Parsons speculated that heavier traffic in the vicinity of the station would cause a delay - before turning north up Grosvenor Place to Hyde Park Corner and thence into Chester Place by way of Park Lane and Bayswater Road. The total distance was just under five miles, a distance that a cab could have traveled comfortably in the hour that elapsed between the two murders.

Dewhurst's description of the policeman who had come to his aid on Lambeth Bridge was unfortunately vague. In fact it was completely lacking in detail. All that Dewhurst had said was that the man was of average height, and that because he was wearing a cape over his uniform Dewhurst had been unable to identify him by the letter and numbers on the collar of his uniform.

There were also the bombs earlier that evening in Kensington to consider. They were obviously part of a plot to associate Sayers' murder with the Fenians, and thereby sever any connection the police might have been inclined to make between his and Latham's death later that evening. And, in spite of the limited damage the bombs had caused, as far as Parsons could see the diversionary plan had worked extremely well.

Parsons left his office in a high state of excitement, all thoughts of his unfortunate reunion with Louise forgotten. He now felt confident of convincing Superintendent Jeffries of the common thread between the four murders. He could also prove that with the aid of a policeman's uniform and with a cab driver as an accomplice one person could have murdered both Sayers and Latham and also have detonated the bombs. And it so happened that Williams and Bates, two of the three soldiers to survive Simpson's patrol, were now respectively a policeman and a cab driver. The third survivor was Sergeant Oakes.

47

Monday, 3rd November

"COME IN, PARSONS," Superintendent Jeffries boomed from behind a thick cloud of tobacco smoke. "I was wondering when you would be gracious enough to honor me with your presence."

Parsons could tell that the omens were not favorable. Whenever Jeffries resorted to irony it was a sign that his patience was beginning to wear thin. And Parsons was well aware that he had been dilatory in keeping his superior in touch with his progress.

He took the only available seat, the one directly in front of Jeffries' desk. It was placed there purposefully. With his back to the window Jeffries had a clear view of Parsons, whereas the superintendent's face was in shadow.

"And what have you been doing with yourself since Thursday, Parsons," said Jeffries grimly. "As I remember you had arrested Mrs. Cordell for the murder of General Latham, but were having second thoughts about her guilt. It seems you thought that another officer's wife might have stabbed the general. If I remember correctly she was a titled lady."

"That's correct, sir," said Parsons nervously. "Lady Cordelia Arbuthnot. She is now the wife of the new commanding officer of the Middlesex Light Regiment."

"Well, that's very convenient for her, Parsons," Jeffries said caustically. "And didn't you think that this Lady Cordelia had murdered the general because she was seeking to further her husband's career?"

Parsons cleared his throat with a nervous cough.

"Your memory serves you well, sir. That was indeed what I thought at the time. But since then I have had good reasons to change my mind."

"Is that so, young man," said Jeffries coldly. Parsons sensed rather than saw the muscles of the superintendent's jaw tighten as his teeth clenched the stem of his pipe. "Then you had better explain them."

Parsons' mouth suddenly became dry, his tongue excessively large and immobile. In a few hurried sentences he described his investigation of Lady Cordelia and her coachman in as positive a light as possible, praising Harris for his initiative in the way he had obtained information on the Arbuthnots and their staff. At the time, he explained, all the signs had indicated that Lady Cordelia and Cooper had murdered Latham and

Cordell, both of them having what he regarded as a strong motive. But his suspicions had been unfounded. The association between the two suspects had proved to be more to do with carnal desire than revenge.

"So you're telling me that you're still no closer to discovering Latham's murderer, Parsons, unless you've changed your mind again about Mrs. Cordell's guilt."

"I'm more convinced than ever of her innocence, sir. I'm certain the general was already dead when she arrived at his house. The only reason I haven't released her before was because I had thought there was a slight chance that she was involved in a political conspiracy to murder prominent figures like Lord Sayers and General Latham. It was just possible that, as as Frenchwoman, she was working with the Fenians. But since I last spoke to you I've heard from the French police, and there is no reason to think that she ever had any connection with any political group."

"I could've saved you that trouble, Parsons," said Jeffries gruffly. "I knew that was all stuff and nonsense, and merely that vivid imagination of yours getting the better of you. As I've told you before there is absolutely no connection between the murders of Lord Frederick Sayers and General Sir Maxwell Latham."

Parsons took a deep breath. The next few minutes were going to be crucial if he was ever to convince Jeffries of the validity of his latest theory.

"Oh, but I think that there is, sir. And what is more I also believe that whoever murdered Sayers and Latham was also responsible for the deaths of Colonel Cordell and Captain Simpson."

In spite of being hidden in a cloud of smoke, Jeffries' disbelief was palpable.

"What in God's name are you talking about, Parsons!" he shouted. "As I understand it Cordell and Simpson took their own lives because, according to you, they were involved in a homosexual relationship. And now you sit there and tell me they were murdered. Have you completely lost your senses, young man?"

Parsons had expected Jeffries to react in this manner, but what he feared more than his anger was his complete disbelief, and of being dismissed before ever having the opportunity to plead his case. And to his relief Jeffries had not dismissed his theory out of hand. He might well be incensed by what Parsons had said, but it was clear that he was prepared to hear more.

Parsons began talking rapidly before Jeffries had the opportunity to say anything else. He began by reminding the superintendent that Sayers and Latham had been related by marriage, although he neglected to mention his visit to Sayers' wife in Manchester, as it had been made in defiance of the superintendent's warning to keep out of the Sayers' investigation.

"I first began to realize that the two men were linked by something other than marriage when I realized what was written on the page of *Hansard* found in Sayers' mouth," Parsons explained. "It was that that made me see the connection between Sayers, Latham and Africa."

Parsons sensed that Jeffries was on the point of interrupting him. His shoulders hunched aggressively, he removed his pipe and he leaned forward over his desk. But then he clearly had second thoughts. It was Jeffries, after all, who had assumed that the page of *Hansard* found in Sayers' mouth was no more than the Fenians making it clear that they viewed the murder as a political assassination.

"In fact, sir," said Parsons, "the speech of Lord Frederick's referred to in *Hansard* dealt specifically with Africa and the great opportunities the continent had to offer."

Jeffries grunted and made a play of re-lighting his pipe. It was clear that the superintendent was embarrassed by his oversight. Parsons would have preferred to avoid doing that, had it been possible. But in the circumstances he felt he had little option. There was no other way of convincing Jeffries of the logic of his argument other than to put all his cards on the table. And if, in the process, Jeffries was made to feel that he had been negligent, that was just unfortunate.

"When I realized that Sayers was interested in Africa, sir," he said. "I began to wonder if it was possible that he had exploited his relationship with General Latham in any way. If you remember, Latham was commanding the Middlesex during their march into the Transvaal, and by all accounts was conducting his campaign with considerable vigor. It was for that reason that he was subsequently given a knighthood and promoted. As a result of that promotion his half brother, Hector Cordell, became commanding officer of the Middlesex, and for his part in leading a dangerous patrol Audley Simpson was recommended for the Victoria Cross. However, I have recently been told quite a different story by a journalist who was accompanying the regiment at the time. According to him the main purpose of Simpson's patrol was not to outflank the Boers but to claim mineral rights for a South African politician called Cecil Rhodes. Rhodes has already made a fortune from African diamonds, and although he could have no direct say about the military strategy in the Transvaal, he was able to get what he wanted with the help of men like Sayers and Latham. No doubt Rhodes promised Sayers a share in the fortune he imagined he would make, and Sayers possibly made a similar promise to Latham. I think it worth noting, sir, that Sayers was dependent on his estranged wife for his income, and Latham had little private money to speak of. So it is easy to see why Rhodes' plan would be attractive to both men."

"Go on, Parsons," said Jeffries. "Spare me the lecture. I just want to know what it was you thought a bunch of British soldiers were expected to achieve. From what I read of our gallant men in red they have trouble in knowing where they are on any day of the week let alone being able to decide whether one piece of ground they're tramping over is more valuable than another."

"That may be true, sir. But someone on that patrol knew exactly what to look for. He was a man called Brett, and as far as the soldiers were concerned he was a scout with an expert knowledge of the country. But he was actually one of Rhodes' surveyors. As it happened he was one of the few to survive the patrol, but unfortunately died later in a mining accident."

"Cecil Rhodes covering his tracks?" mused Jeffries.

"Who's to say, sir. That's for the South African police to determine. That's, of course, if they're interested. All I know is that the journalist later found Brett and discovered the real reason for his being on the patrol."

"But what about the soldiers? Didn't they know what was going on?"

"I doubt it, sir. I'm sure they just accepted Brett as a scout. Latham obviously knew what was going on, and perhaps Cordell. But they're both dead. Even Simpson may have worked it out. After all he was the patrol leader. And now he's dead as well."

"What about the other men on the patrol? How many of them survived?"

"Three, sir. One is still a sergeant in the Middlesex. The other two left the army when the regiment returned to England. One's a policeman and the other drives hansom cabs. It's my belief that one or all of them were involved in these murders. It's possible another man was as well. He was Simpson's platoon sergeant, but he was wounded at the time and never went on the patrol.

Sergeant Harris has spent the weekend trying to trace these three men, and after I hear what he's discovered I'm going back to the barracks to see what the sergeant has to say for himself."

"So what exactly are you trying to tell me, Parsons? As far as I can see there's still a great deal of speculation in what you've said."

"I agree, sir, but don't you think that it's too much of a coincidence that four men with obvious links to a single incident in South Africa should all die within a few days of one another?"

"When you say four men, Parsons, I assume that you're including Cordell and Simpson."

"That's correct, sir. I've no doubt that both their suicides were staged."

Parsons explained the inconsistencies in the suicides that had led him to believe that the two men had been murdered.

"And the motive, Parsons. What have you got to say about that?"

"I believe that all four men were murdered because they were part of the chain of command that resulted in a foolish decision to send a patrol into hostile enemy country for no good military reason. A patrol on which many of the men died cruelly at the hands of the Zulus. I believe that the motive was nothing more than revenge."

There was a lengthy silence before Jeffries spoke.

"You've half convinced me, Parsons," he said. "But I have some difficulty in believing that the survivors of this patrol have waited all this time before deciding to murder these four men. If I were to stretch my imagination far enough I might give some credence to a group of disgruntled soldiers deciding to murder one of their officers if they thought he had let them down. But for the life of me I can't see ignorant soldiers deciding to assassinate a politician. Most soldiers can barely read or write, let alone understand what the likes of Rhodes and Sayers are trying to do."

"From what I know of the army I'm inclined to agree with you, sir. But perhaps we're underestimating the intelligence and cunning of some soldiers. All I ask is that you give me free rein to treat these four murders as a single investigation."

"You've got forty-eight hours, Parsons. After that I'll decide the next step. In the meantime what do you intend to do about Mrs. Cordell?"

"I think I'll leave her where she is for the time being, sir. Were I to release her it might put the real murderers on their guard."

48

SERGEANT HARRIS WAS slumped in the leather armchair in Parsons' office, with his hands clasped over his chest, his legs stretched out in front of him, and his eyes closed. A mug of cold tea lay on the floor beside the chair.

"Good morning, Harris," said Parsons cheerfully as he took his customary seat behind his desk. "Has working on a Sunday made you that tired?"

Harris reluctantly opened his eyes, drew his legs back and sat straighter in the chair.

"It's my girl, sir," he said. "I'm sure she's sickening for something. Her stomach's upset, and the wife decided that she should spend the night in our bed. So with one thing or another I didn't get much sleep."

"I'm sorry to hear that, Harris," said Parsons. "But I'm sure that a man with a philosophical nature like your good self will have accepted all that as being part of a loving family. But more to the point. What did you discover about Bates and

Williams? It had better be something substantial as I've just spent a rather uncomfortable half hour with Jeffries trying to prove to him that there's a link between the four murders. I did better than I thought, but he's still far from convinced. He's given me forty-eight hours to come up with something more substantial."

Harris reached down for his mug and sipped his tea, frowning when he found it had grown cold.

"I managed to find Bates and Williams, sir," he said. "It was easier than I imagined. After I left you on Saturday I came back here to check the Metropolitan Police records, and I was pleasantly surprised with what I found. Not only do they have details about every policeman and the Division in which he's employed, they also keep a register of all the licensed cab drivers in London. So it didn't take me long to find the whereabouts of Morgan Williams, late of the Middlesex Light Regiment. And out of over four thousand licensed cab drivers there was only one Oliver Bates."

"Excellent, Harris," said Parsons enthusiastically. "Let's start with Constable Morgan Williams. Where is he stationed?"

"In Lambeth Division, sir. He works out of the station in Lower Kennington Lane, less than a mile from Lambeth Bridge."

Parsons face was radiant.

"And very convenient for Lord Sayers' murder," he said. "Now that is a welcome coincidence. You know, Harris I'm at last beginning to have a good feeling about this."

"That's what I thought at the time, sir. But I must warn you that the news isn't all good. Just let me tell you what I discovered."

Harris took another sip of cold tea.

"I went to Lambeth Station first thing on Sunday hoping to catch Williams before he went on duty, only to discover that it was his day off."

"While you were there did you find out if he was on duty on the night Sayers was murdered?"

"I did, sir. And he wasn't. And I'm afraid to say that it doesn't look as though it was Williams who murdered Sayers. Whilst I was at Lambeth I learned that Constable Dewhurst, the policeman who found Sayers' body, had been to the station several times to try and identify the policeman he saw on Lambeth Bridge. According to the station sergeant, Dewhurst has seen every policeman in the Lambeth Division, including Williams, and failed to make a positive identification. The handful of men answering Dewhurst's description were also interviewed by one of our detectives. And it proved to be impossible that any of them could have been on the bridge at the time Sayers died. Before going home last night I came back here and checked all their statements. Each one of them has a witness who can vouch for him being miles away from Lambeth Bridge at the time Lord Sayers was murdered."

"Where was Williams?" Parsons asked.

"As I said, he wasn't on duty that night, sir. And not only that, the man Dewhurst saw looks nothing like Williams. Williams is far taller than the policeman seen on Lambeth Bridge, and he has a thick mustache. The man Dewhurst saw was clean shaven."

Parsons felt his enthusiasm ebbing. He had been expecting better news than this.

"Did you find Williams?" he asked disconsolately.

"I did, sir. I got his address from the station sergeant and went to his lodgings in Sancroft Street."

Parsons got to his feet and examined the map of London pinned to his notice board.

"And where exactly is that?"

Harris joined Parsons in front of the map. He placed his finger on a narrow street leading off Kennington Road.

"You can see it's not far from the station, sir. It took me less than fifteen minutes to walk there. Williams wasn't in when I called, but I spoke with his landlady. She said that Williams has been living there for three months. He's one of four people renting rooms in the house. The landlady lives on the ground floor with her cat, there are three lodgers on the first floor and another in the attic."

"And the other lodgers? Who are they?"

"She said they're all respectable working men. One's a bank clerk, one's a shop assistant, and the other is a gardener in Kennington Park."

"And what did the dear lady have to say about Williams?" Parsons asked.

"Not a great deal, sir. She said he wasn't always prompt with his rent, and on more than one occasion she'd seen him the worse for drink. But you expect that from a policeman, don't you, she said."

In spite of the discouraging news that Harris had brought about Williams' appearance Parsons could not help but smile.

"I hope you informed her of your own exemplary character, Harris. We can't have every law abiding citizen thinking that all policemen are drunks."

"She had only to look at me to see that, sir," said Harris, stroking his mustache fondly. "But as it happens she had some kind words to say about the police. She said it was comforting to have a policeman in the house. It made her feel that much safer now that her husband had passed away."

"And where was Williams while you were talking with his landlady?"

"In a public house in Prince's Road. *The Marquis of Granby*. His landlady directed me there."

Harris pointed to the map again.

"Not a pub quite up to the standard of your Chelsea haunts, sir," he said. "Sawdust on the floor, a pretty rough bunch of customers, and very little in the way of food. But Williams seemed to fit in there pretty well. He's a large, loud Welshman with a pretty foul tongue."

"Was he surprised to see you?"

"He was, sir. In fact he was downright suspicious at first. But when I told him I was just closing the books on the suicides in Kensington Barracks he seemed to relax. I told him that it seemed pretty clear to me that Captain Simpson was suffering from a delayed melancholia brought about by his experiences in Africa, especially the patrol he'd led. I said I'd learned that Williams was one of the few survivors of that patrol and I hoped he could tell me something of what actually happened. I said it would be useful information for the coroner's court."

Harris returned to the arm chair.

"He was far from complimentary about Captain Simpson, sir," he said. "In fact he as good as accused him of being a coward. He said that the Zulus attacked them at night while they were bivouacking, and that Simpson made no attempt to organize a defense. He just ran. Williams said that when he saw what was happening he took to his heels as well, along with Corporal Oakes, Private Bates and the civilian."

"What did he know about this civilian?"

"Not much, sir. Williams said they'd been told he was a scout. But if that was what he was supposed to be he wasn't very good at his job, because he knew very little about the country they were going through and less about the Zulus than anyone else on the patrol."

"Did you ask Williams how many men died?"

"I didn't have to ask him, sir. He told me. He said that Simpson abandoned fifteen of his men. Those that died in the attack were the lucky ones. A few were taken prisoner. Williams said the advance guard of the regiment found their mutilated bodies a few days later. He said that for Simpson to get a medal for what he'd done was a disgrace."

"I don't imagine that Williams was sorry to hear that Simpson had taken his own life."

"I didn't ask him that, sir. But I think it highly unlikely."

"You were probably right not to mention it, Harris. The last thing we want is to put Williams on his guard by asking him about his feelings towards any of the four men who've been murdered. Now what about the cabbie, Bates? Where did you find him, and what did he have to say about Simpson?"

"In Alfred Road, in a run-down house behind the workhouse in Paddington. He was snoring away in the filthy room he rents there."

Harris returned to the map and pointed to a narrow street near the railway line.

"Not a particularly attractive part of London, sir. In fact it reminded me of where I grew up. And if Bates is anything to go by, then what they say about cabbies is true. If ever there was a drunkard, it's him. His room looked worse than a pig sty and smelt like a sewer, and he was most offensive when I woke him. He quietened down as soon as he realized who I was, especially when I explained the purpose of my visit. At first he denied all knowledge of Simpson's death. He said he never had time to read newspapers. But I sensed he was lying. I'm sure he already knew that Simpson was dead."

"What did he say when you asked him about the patrol?"

"Much the same as Williams, although if anything his language was even more foul when he described Simpson's leadership, and what he thought about him being given a medal."

"It seems to me that both Bates and Williams are hypocrites," said Parsons. "Simpson wasn't the only coward that day. He wasn't the only one to run. And who are we to judge how it feels to be attacked in the middle of the night by a crowd of angry Zulus?"

The prospect must have been truly terrible, thought Parsons. In similar circumstances he had no idea how he would act. Only one thing was certain. If he ever decided to run he doubted whether his short legs would carry him far.

"Is that all you learned from Bates, Harris?"

"No, sir. My visit was really quite informative. Much to my surprise Bates became quite talkative once I'd moved off the subject of Simpson. I picked up some useful knowledge about the cab business. Very few cabbies, it appears, actually own their cabs. Bates certainly doesn't. They rent them from a dozen or so large cab-owners in London for between nine and twelve shillings a day depending upon the length of time they have the cab. The cab-owners are not concerned about how much the cabbies make as long as they pay their rent and return their horses and cabs in good condition. The cabs are rented for set periods. The 'morning men', as they're called, rent them from seven in the morning until six in the evening; the 'long-night men' from six in the evening until ten the next morning; and the 'short-night men' from six until six. Most cabbies are 'long-day men'. That means they rent their cabs from nine or ten in the morning until between midnight and one. Sometimes they're out until four or five. No wonder that so many of them take to the bottle. If I had to work those hours to make a decent living I might think about it myself."

"Did you find out where Bates rented his cab, and what hours he normally worked?"

"Yes, sir. He rents his cab from Havers in Paddington, and generally chooses to work the long-day shift. Most cabbies choose that shift, he said, because they can make the most money. But, in his case, he said he chose it because he didn't like getting up early. After being in the army he said he had wanted a job that allowed him to lie in in the mornings."

"Was he working on the night Sayers and Latham died?"

"I thought you'd ask me that, sir," said Harris. "I didn't want to arouse Bates' suspicions by asking him directly, so I went round to the stables and enquired there. He did work that night. But unusually for him he worked a short-night. In fact he booked out at about five fifteen, rather than at six.

"That's interesting isn't it, Harris," said Parsons excitedly. "And it fits, doesn't it? If Bates was involved in the plot to kill Sayers and Latham he would want to be sure that his horse was reasonably fresh and that he hadn't inadvertently got himself a fare that took him a long way from where he wanted to be, which was in the area between Lambeth and Bayswater. And the best way of doing that was to start work in the evening, and not in the morning as he usually did."

Parsons leaned back in his chair and toyed with his paperknife.

"What does Bates look like?" he asked.

"He's quite the opposite to Williams. Small, wiry, with mean-looking eyes. And I'd say he had a temper."

"Does he have a mustache?"

"I wouldn't say he was exactly clean shaven, sir. But he definitely did not have a mustache when I saw him."

"As I remember, Constable Dewhurst thought the policeman he saw on Lambeth Bridge was clean shaven. Like Bates. Do you think Williams' uniform would've fitted Bates?"

"At a pinch I think it would, sir. He might've need to turn up the trousers, but in the dark that would hardly matter. And don't forget that the policeman Dewhurst saw was wearing a cape. That could hide a lot."

"Good work, Harris. You've done well," said Parsons. "But now that you've met them, can you imagine either of these men committing murder?"

"I've thought about that, sir, and in my opinion they're both capable of violence. They must've seen plenty of death while they were in the army, and more than likely they actually killed other human beings at close quarters. So, yes, I do think they could have been involved in these murders, but I don't think they acted alone. Someone with more brains than Bates and Williams must've done the planning."

"You're probably right about that, Harris. Whoever's behind all this is no fool. You only have to look at the suicide notes to see that. They may have been written in a childish scrawl, but the actual words suggest that whoever wrote them has a fondness for words. That doesn't sound like either Bates or Williams. And there's another important consideration."

"What's that, sir?"

"Neither of them is a woman. And we know it was a woman who murdered General Latham."

49

PARSONS HAD DECIDED that he and Harris should pursue their own lines of enquiry and return to Scotland Yard later in the day to compare notes. Parsons intended interviewing Sergeant Oakes, and in spite of his protests insisted that Harris visit Nathaniel Fox, Simpson's former platoon sergeant, and now the landlord of *The Tanners Arms* in Bermondsey.

"But Fox wasn't even on the patrol, sir. Don't you remember he was wounded."

"I'm well aware of that, Harris, but we can't afford to leave a single stone unturned. I know it's unlikely, but it's just possible that Fox had a part to play in all this. The young men who died on Simpson's patrol had all been trained by him, and from what the Chief Clerk told me Fox considered himself almost like a father to them. But more important than that he could be an important character witness. If he was the platoon sergeant you can be sure that to all intents and purposes he ran the platoon rather than Simpson, and that would mean that he'd have a pretty good idea of the qualities of each of the men. So apart from hearing what he has to say about Simpson, I'm also anxious that you get his opinion on Bates, Oakes and Williams."

Harris was about to leave when Parsons remembered the other task he had in mind for him.

"And on your way back from Bermondsey I want you to go to Clapham and follow up on Cooper's alibi for the night Cordell died. He said he was at a dog fight, and after that he visited a brothel. I have both addresses here. After the success of your visit to Kate Hamilton's it sounds just up your street."

———

PARSONS KNEW THAT it was never going to be easy to speak with Sergeant Oakes without the RSM being present. So when he arrived at the barracks he informed the sentry that he had come to interview Preston, the clerk who had opened Captain Simpson's mail, and who was probably still confined in the Guard Room. As he had anticipated, the sentry first relayed his message to Sergeant Oakes in his capacity as Provost Sergeant, and shortly afterwards Oakes appeared on the scene. At first he was reluctant to admit Parsons without the RSM's permission, and conceded to Parsons' request only when it was pointed out that the RSM's presence might intimidate the clerk and prevent him from answering any questions honestly.

As they made their way to the Guard Room, Oakes explained that Preston's misdemeanor had yet to be dealt with, the RSM having already determined that the offense was serious enough to warrant Preston being brought before the commanding officer.

"An' Colonel Arbuthnot ain't in yet," said Oakes. "It's Monday 'in'it. I doubt we'll see 'im much before lunch. Then 'e'll read the bloody papers an' 'ave a few drinks before 'e eats. Preston won' be dealt with 'til sometime this afternoon. But I've got plenty in mind fer 'im to do before then. Some of the pan closets in the men's accommodation is blocked, an' we need a skinny clerk with a long arm like Preston to clear 'em."

What a charming prospect, thought Parsons. If Preston did not feel sick after that, the clerk had a stronger stomach than he.

PRESTON WAS ON his hands and knees scrubbing the already spotless floor of the Guard Room when they arrived, but at the sight of Oakes he sprang to his feet and stood to attention.

"At ease, Preston," Oakes said, his face pressed so close to the clerk's that Parsons could see the clerk instinctively recoil from the sergeant's offensive breath. "The police inspector 'ere would like to 'ave a few words with you."

"Thank you, Sergeant Oakes," Parsons said. "Perhaps you would care to withdraw slightly so that I may speak more directly to Private Preston."

Oakes stepped to one side. He ran his right hand across his mouth, stroking his thick mustache as he did, enabling Parsons to see the mass of dark hair on the back of his hand and on his fingers. There were heavy tobacco stains on his index and middle fingers and his nails were badly bitten. His breathing was heavy and uneven, and his small, bloodshot eyes peered angrily from beneath his helmet. If one were to include the sagging flesh on his cheeks and the prominent stomach straining against the buttons of his red jacket, Oakes presented a most unflattering image of a British soldier.

God help us all, if this is an example of the men we send to fight our wars, Parsons mused. Is it any wonder that a handful of Boers and uneducated heathens armed with nothing more than spears have proved more than a match for us?

He approached the clerk.

"You can relax, Preston," he said. "I'm not going to bite you."

"Yes sir," the clerk said. His lips barely moved and he watched Oakes apprehensively from the corner of his eyes.

"I want you to tell me again why you opened Captain Simpson's mail."

"I told you, sir. My brother asked me to."

"And your brother had done that on behalf of Albert Cooper, a man who once served in this regiment, and who is now Colonel Arbuthnot's coachman."

Preston barely moved his head in acknowledgment.

"And would you care to hazard a guess as to why Cooper would want to know what was in Captain Simpson's mail?"

"No, sir," said Preston. "What I mean is, I don't know, sir."

"But you surely must have some idea," said Parsons. "Most people in the regiment seem to have a opinion one way or another about Captain Simpson. He was, after all, a brave man, and one who was about to be rewarded for that bravery."

Parsons walked behind Preston to a position from which he could see Oakes.

"And what about the relationship between Captain Simpson and Colonel Cordell. Do you not think that Cooper might have wanted to know about that?"

Preston shook his head.

"I don't know anything about that, sir," he said.

"What do you think about that, Sergeant Oakes? Do you think Cooper was thinking of blackmailing Captain Simpson?"

"I don't see 'ow 'e could do that, sir," Oakes said. "The colonel bein' already dead. What sense would it make Cooper blackmailin' the captain 'bout anythin' that went on between 'em."

"Then you think that it might have been something else. Something to do with Captain Simpson getting the Victoria Cross. A few of the people I've spoken to don't seem to think he deserved it. You were with him, weren't you, Sergeant Oakes? Perhaps you've got something to say on the matter."

Oakes small eyes blazed.

"'E were a coward if that's what you mean," he said bitterly. "We all knew that even before we started. God knows why 'e were picked for the patrol. There was talk that the colonel, that's Colonel Latham, only chosin' 'im 'cause 'e wanted to spite Major Cordell. But whatever anyone thought we all knew we was in for trouble. As soon as we knew we was going without Foxie we knew."

"Who is Foxie?" Parsons asked.

"Sergeant Fox. 'E were the platoon sergeant. 'E knew what 'e was doin'. If 'e 'ad been with us we'd been all right. But Foxie was wounded. 'E didn't go on that bloody patrol. 'E wouldn't 'ave 'ad us bivouac where we did an' 'ave those bloody Zulus surprise us like that. 'E'd 'ave done things better."

"You mean he would have organized a better defensive position from which to fight the Zulus."

"Yeah. That's what I mean. Proper soldiers like Foxie know what they're about. Foxie was one of our best sergeants. 'E'd been trained by Mr. Whitehead when 'e were our company sergeant major."

"As I understand it you are a close friend of the RSM's."

"I wouldn't say that, sir. It's jus' that Mr. Whitehead and I 'ave a drink together now and again."

Oakes voice had grown noticeably louder. Preston, Parsons noticed, had also become aware of this and had turned his head apprehensively in the sergeant's direction.

"So you think Captain Simpson was incompetent?" Parsons asked. "And not only incompetent, but from what you've just said he was also a coward. Didn't he run away and abandon his men?"

"Yeah. 'E did that. The bastard run away."

Oakes had taken a pace or two towards Parsons.

"We found the bloody bodies, inspector," he said. There were flecks of saliva gathering at the corners of his dry lips. "An' we seen what they bloody savages done. None of us will ever forget that. There are men in the regiment who would kill Captain bloody Simpson for that."

There was a few seconds of silence before Parsons spoke.

"And would you be one of those men, Sergeant Oakes?" he asked quietly.

The pause before Oakes replied was almost imperceptible. But it was a pause nevertheless.

"No, I bloody wasn't," he shouted. "Ev'ryone knows that Captain Simpson done 'imself in."

Parsons had heard many confident denials in his time, but this was not one of them. He knew that Simpson had not died by his own hand, and he sensed that Oakes knew full well who was responsible.

"Thank you, Preston," he said. "I'm obliged to you for your information. "And thank you, Sergeant Oakes. No doubt we will speak again. But in the meantime I trust you will not be too hard on Private Preston."

But Parsons could tell from the fierce anger burning in Oakes' eyes that it was a request that had fallen on deaf ears.

50

SAM TANNER WAS a mudlark. He had known no other life. He was seven years old and lived with his mother in a back alley off Pratt Street, a few hundreds yards from Lambeth Bridge. Each day as the Thames retreated he and his mother joined the other mudlarks on the steps leading down to the river, waiting for the water to fall to a level that would allow them to begin their scavenging. Dressed in a pitiful array of garments that had grown stiff from long hours immersed in the river, there were no more wretched creatures to be found anywhere in London.

The mudlarks gathered along the length of the Thames between Vauxhall Bridge and Woolwich. In the few hours between tides this ragged army of men, women and children spread across the shore like crabs, before moving out into the retreating waters to forage for any flotsam or jetsam the river might yield.

Like other mudlarks, Sam and his mother wore crude baskets around their necks made from strips of old coal sacking. These baskets allowed them the free use of their hands while they searched for anything that might be of value: pieces of coal, odd bits of iron, lengths of rope, bones of any variety, copper nails, and any item that might have fallen from a passing vessel. Indeed anything that might be worth a few pence or exchanged for a bite to eat. The coal they sold to the poor people in the neighborhood; the iron, bones, rope and copper nails went to the rag shops. Occasionally they would find tools, such as saws or hammers. These they would sell to sailors or exchange for biscuits and meat.

Although Sam knew how old he was, his mother had no idea of the year she was born. In all likelihood she was less than thirty years of age. But the dried dirt in her wild hair, the deep lines on her face, and her crooked body were those of a woman twice her age; although the chances of her reaching such a ripe old age were slim. Sam's father had been a sailor. He had gone to sea shortly after Sam was born and never returned, leaving his wife uncertain of whether it was the sea that had claimed him, or that he had simply abandoned her and her child. Since then his mother had lived off whatever the river could provide, and as soon as his little legs were strong enough to wade through the thick mud, Sam had joined her. He had once had an older brother, Cal. But Cal had cut his foot on a broken bottle whilst wading in the river, and the mud had poisoned his blood.

More often than not now Sam searched in deeper waters than his mother. Countless hours spent bending over the cold river had deformed her body and crippled her hands and feet, so that she strayed less frequently into the deep mud, preferring instead to stay near the shore with other women of a similar age and infirmity. As a result her pickings were generally poor, and increasingly she relied upon whatever young Sam could find. He would often wade out until the level of the river reached his waist, at which point he would be forced to forage as much with his feet as with his hands.

It had become his practice within the past few months to work the river nearer Lambeth Bridge. Although the mud was deeper and there were greater dangers, there was a better chance of finding not just the items that had fallen from boats but also the occasional article that had fallen from the bridge itself. Only a few weeks before another boy had found a pocket knife, which had been worth more than all the coal and nails any one person could collect in a week.

Sam's decision to head for the deeper water meant that he was neglecting the chance of more assured but slimmer pickings closer to the shore. But he was a determined child, and having struggled through the thick mud for almost an hour to reach his position under the bridge he had no intention of retreating until forced to do so by the incoming tide. The tide was always something to be wary of. He had never witnessed it himself, but there were stories of boys being trapped in the mud and drowning.

There were other dangers lurking in the mud. To step on the jagged edge of a broken bottle or a discarded tin can was to risk death. Sam's brother had born testament to that.

Sam's basket was not even half full when the tide began to turn. Even at his tender age he had learned to heed the state of the river lest it trap him whilst he was still floundering in the mud. His whole body had become numbed by the cold water, and to add to his misery it had begun to rain. In the distance he could see his mother looking anxiously in his direction. She waved towards him, indicating that he should return. As old and crippled as she was she could not risk losing another son to the Thames.

It was just then that Sam's left foot brushed against a solid object. At first he thought it was the piece of machinery he had seen sailors using to raise and lower the sails. He had never found anything like that before, but he reckoned that it might be worth as much as a pocket knife, and considerably more than anything else he had found in the past few hours.

Keeping his foot firmly on the object Sam bent over slowly and groped towards it carefully with his right hand. The mud was deeper than he had imagined, and he was forced to close his eyes and hold his nose as he lowered his face into the mire, while at the same time gripping his basket tightly with his forearm to prevent the contents spilling back into the river. Sam's outstretched fingers grasped what he took to be the arm of the winding gear and brought it slowly to the surface. Were it to slip from his cold fingers he would be unlikely ever to find it again.

But what he had found was more valuable than any piece of ship's machinery, and such was his excitement, that in spite of his fierce concentration he nearly dropped his find back into the mud.

"Ma," he cried when he was eventually close enough for her to hear him. "I've found a gun!"

Had Sam been less exhilarated by his find, his mother and he would have dined well for many days on the proceeds of the sale of the Webley revolver. But his cries had attracted the attention of the police constable at that moment patrolling Lambeth Embankment.

"Let's have a look at what you've found, my lad," he said as Sam dragged his weary legs from the mud.

51

HARRIS HAD STILL not returned when Parsons arrived back at Scotland Yard. But regardless of what Harris might unearth he had already decided upon a course of action. From what Harris had told him about Bates and Williams, and from what he had seen of Oakes, he thought there was a very good chance that all three men were implicated in some way with the murders. But which of them was the ringleader? Before meeting Oakes, Parsons had been anticipating that because of his rank Oakes might prove to be that person. But he now felt that he had been mistaken. There was nothing about the uncouth sergeant to make him believe that he had either the imagination or intellect to mastermind four murders. And from what Harris had told him about Bates and Williams it did not sound as if it could be either of them.

Parsons had decided that there was only one way to proceed. He intended to arrest all three men and offer each the opportunity of implicating the others. Were any of them to turn Queen's Evidence there was every chance of him being excused a trial or given a reduced sentence. It was a ploy that was frequently employed by the police and prosecution lawyers in the case of a serious crime like murder.

———

IT WAS WELL after six before Harris poked his head around Parsons' door, and from the despondent look on his face Parsons could see that the news was not good.

"Cooper's alibis stack up, sir," he said, "As he said he was in Clapham on the night Cordell was murdered. And I don't think what I learned in Bermondsey will prove to be of any great use to us."

"Let me be the judge of that, Harris," Parsons said. "Just tell me what Nathaniel Fox had to say for himself."

Harris sank gratefully into Parsons' armchair, cradling a mug of tea.

"Fox is a cut above the likes of Bates and Williams," he said. "He seems quite intelligent, unlike most of the soldiers I've met in the course of this investigation. He reminds me a little of RSM Whitehead. Perhaps if Fox had stayed in the army he would have been just as successful. In fact he told me that when Whitehead learned of his own promotion he said that Fox was in line to be his replacement as company sergeant major. But Fox wasn't interested. After losing so many of the young soldiers he'd trained on Simpson's patrol he'd had enough of the army. He didn't choose to say much about the patrol other than that he knew it would be a disaster with Simpson in charge. But at the time he could do nothing about it. As a mere sergeant no one was going to listen to him, and as he was still recovering from the effects of having a Boer bullet removed from his shoulder he was in no position to go with Simpson."

"He sounds like someone else who doesn't think that Simpson deserved his medal."

Harris took a sip from his mug.

"You're right about that, sir," he said. "According to what Fox later learned from the men who survived, the patrol was a shambles from beginning to end."

"What about the surveyor, Brett. Did he mention him?"

"It was news to him that Brett was a surveyor. Like most of the other soldiers, Fox thought that Brett was just an army scout."

Parsons could barely conceal his disappointment.

"Then it doesn't sound that Fox is involved in any way," he said.

"No, sir, I don't think so. For a start I don't see how he could spare the time. He's got a nice little business in Bermondsey, and from what I learned from a few of the customers who were in the pub while I was there, Fox and his wife have little free time. That can't be unusual? You must know from your own extensive knowledge of public houses that it's more than a full-time job for any landlord and his wife wanting to make a success of their business."

"You're quite right, Harris. A first-class landlord has to work every hour God sends him. So must his wife if he has one. Apart from being a natural philosopher and everyone's good friend, a landlord needs a good woman running his kitchen and helping out behind the bar."

An impish grin unexpectedly appeared on Harris' tired face.

"As far as I could see Fox has certainly got himself a good woman," he said, stroking his mustache appreciatively. "Apart from being pleasing on the eye, she brought me a cheese and pickle sandwich that was as good as any I've ever tasted. If there were more like her I might have a change of heart and visit the occasional public house without having to be prompted by you. But I don't suppose Mrs. Harris would encourage that. I think you know what my wife and her mother think of pubs."

"I do, Harris. And I can only commiserate. Although your good lady has many admirable qualities, I regret to say that we will always differ on the subject of pubs. But apart from discovering the virtues of this excellent Mrs. Fox, did you learn anything that is at all relevant to our investigation?"

Harris thought for a few moments.

"I shouldn't think it's relevant, sir, but Fox did mention that not all the men on the patrol were from his platoon. At the last minute Whitehead persuaded Cordell, who was then his company commander, to include a young soldier called Hobson."

"Hobson?" said Parsons. "Now where have I heard that name before?"

"He was one of the two soldiers who were flogged, sir. Their names were in the Chief Clerk's Discipline Book. The other one was our old friend Cooper. Cooper was in Arbuthnot's company, Hobson in Cordell's. If you remember it was Whitehead's idea that Cordell give Hobson the chance to redeem himself."

"How unfortunate for the young man. Instead of redeeming himself he met a sad fate at the hands of the Zulus. But, as you said, Harris, I hardly think that's relevant now."

Harris had been right, thought Parsons ruefully. His visit to Bermondsey had achieved very little. It would have been far more productive had he spent more time investigating Bates and Williams.

A clerk stuck his head around the door.

"Telegram for you, Sergeant Harris," he said, handing Harris an envelope.

"Harris I do believe that you're blushing," said Parsons, as he watched a look of embarrassment slowly spread across the sergeant's face. "Come now, tell me what's in the telegram. Don't keep it to yourself."

Harris passed the telegram to Parsons.

"Read it for yourself, sir," he said.

"I have something of importance to tell you," Parsons read in amusement. *"Come to the pub before ten tomorrow morning. Ada Fox."*

"Well, Harris, you do seem to have made quite an impression on Mrs. Fox. I assume that if I can spare you, you will want to go alone."

"Not on your life, sir. I'll need some moral support. Nathaniel Fox is far bigger than me. And, besides that, I'm sure you'll enjoy the comforts of *The Tanners Arms* as much as I."

52

Tuesday, 4th November

"WHERE IN HEAVEN'S name have you brought me, Harris?" Parsons asked. "This place is like a scene from Dante's *Inferno*."

"You've got me at a loss again, sir. I've never heard of Dante or his Inferno."

"Inferno, my dear Harris, is Italian for Hell, and the *Inferno* I'm referring to is the first part of Dante Alighieri's epic fourteenth-century poem *'Divine Comedy'*. The other parts of the poem are *'Purgatorio'* and *'Paradiso'*, words that I'm sure you will recognize even though they are in Italian. The *Divine Comedy* describes the soul's journey to God through the nine circles of suffering that represent Hell. And as I look around me, I'd say we've almost reached the half way point, probably somewhere between Gluttony and Greed."

Parsons and Harris had met at London Bridge Station at eight-thirty that morning and had then walked south, away from the river, along Bermondsey Street to the leather market. It was there that Parsons had had his vision of the *Inferno*.

In every direction carts were piled high with bloody hides, each with matted scraps of hair or fragments of wool attached. The men attending these carts were of like appearance: their hands, leggings and shoes, and even the whips they carried, streaked with blood. There were even marks of the carnage on the horses lashed to these terrible carts, each of them snorting and shaking their heads in distress at the scent of the flayed skins of their fellow creatures. Buyers, sellers and blue-smocked porters swarmed amongst the carts; poking, prodding and hauling the grotesque hides, some of which still had fierce horns attached to what remained of their skulls. Beside them the innocent-looking calves, sheep and lambs seemed almost serene, as though resigned to the fate that had befallen them. But everywhere there was the foul stench of death.

"Are you expecting me to believe there is a decent public house amongst all this, Harris?" Parsons asked in exasperation. "I should've known better when I saw the name of the Fox's hostelry. Anything associated with tanning is bound to be bloody and smell like a slaughter house."

Harris pointed to a narrow street leading off the square.

"It's not far now, sir, and I'm sure once you're inside you'll soon forget what's going on out here."

Parsons had to admit that Harris was right. *The Tanners Arms* was as neat a pub as any in Chelsea. The outside walls were chocolate colored, with the doors and window frames painted in a darker shade; and judging by the black beams forming the skeleton of the building it had been standing for many centuries, perhaps even from Tudor times.

A few customers clustered around a welcoming fire nursing glasses of dark porter. In keeping with their trade they wore aprons and gaiters of rawhide; and to hide the stench of their clothes smoked dark shag in clay pipes stained red from constant contact with unwashed hands.

"Well, Harris," said Parsons, more pleased than he had expected by the interior of the pub, "we may not have reached *Paradiso*, but at least we've made it as far as *Purgatorio*."

A small woman with a mass of red curls and rosy cheeks was busying herself behind the bar stacking glasses and bottles. She turned from her task as the two policemen approached and gave Harris a warm smile, which noticeably cooled when she saw he was not alone.

"Thank you for coming, Sergeant Harris," she said. "But who, pray, is this gentleman?"

"This is Inspector Parsons," Harris explained. "He's my boss. Whatever you want to tell me you can say in front of him."

Ada Fox did not reply. Instead she inspected Parsons from head to toe, and seemingly satisfied by what she saw led the two men through a door into an adjoining bar.

"Don't think I don't have eyes in the back of my head," she said to the men around the fire. "And if you imagine you can help yourselves while I'm talking business with these two gentlemen, you can think again. This door stays open so's I can keep my eyes on the bar."

She pointed to a table and four straight-backed chairs.

"Sit yourselves down, gentlemen," she said. "This is my snug bar. I reserve it for the more senior men from the market. I never let the dirty tanners in. We won't be disturbed here."

"Where's your husband, Mrs. Fox?" asked Harris apprehensively.

"He's gone to the brewery," she replied. "He won't be back until around eleven when we start getting busy."

She took a box of matches from the mantle and put a light to the kindling under the coals.

"That should catch in a minute or two," she said. "But while we're waiting, perhaps I can get you two gentlemen something to drink."

Parsons and Harris both settled for tea, and Parsons watched approvingly as Ada disappeared behind the bar and returned almost immediately with a wooden tray bearing a large china pot, two cups and a plate of biscuits.

"The tea needs to stand for a few minutes," she said, "and while we're waiting I'll explain why I sent that telegram to Sergeant Harris."

Ada Fox took two folded sheets of cheap lined note paper from a pocket in the front of her apron and laid them on the table beside the tray.

"You can read this letter after I've told you about the woman who wrote it," she said, folding her small, strong hands over her apron.

"Twenty years ago I was working in a pub in Leicester Square," she explained. "Though I say it myself I was a pretty young thing then. I turned more than a few young men's heads, I can tell you. And I wasn't the only one. That dirty old landlord knew what he was doing. All his barmaids were young girls like me. It's what made the pub so popular with the men."

Parsons reckoned that Ada Fox was probably in her late thirties. If she had been working as a barmaid twenty years ago she would have been possibly sixteen or seventeen at the time. Any younger and the landlord might have found himself in trouble with the law.

"At the time I had a very dear friend by the name of Norah Hobson," she said. "She had come from the Isle of Sheppey in Kent. She said that there was no life there. The people were mainly fisherfolk. Most of them knew nothing else, and for all they cared about the world outside it might never exist. She told me she couldn't abide it. She wanted to see the bright lights of London. Well, anyone like me who'd been born and brought up here could've told her that those lights are not always as bright as people imagine. But when I met her, Norah was still excited by the idea working in the center of a big city."

Ada stirred the tea in the pot.

"I expect it's ready now," she said.

She poured a small amount of milk into two cups and filled them with tea.

"I'll let you help yourselves to sugar," she said. "And to the biscuits."

She waited for the two men to sweeten their tea and take a few biscuits before continuing.

"Norah and I were working in the pub one evening when two young men came in. I gave Norah a nudge, because in spite of being a little drunk they were really quite handsome, and they were clearly excited about something, as they kept slapping each other on the back and laughing. You couldn't help but notice them even though the pub was full. So when one of them came up to buy more drinks I asked them what they were so pleased about. And he told me they'd just taken the 'Queen's shilling' from a recruiting sergeant in Westminster. They had just become soldiers in the Middlesex Light Regiment. To be honest I couldn't see what was so wonderful about that. What young man in his right mind would want to be a soldier. But as it happens it was a fortunate night for me, because one of those soldiers became my husband, Nat. The other man was Patrick Whitehead."

It was all she could do to restrain a smile when she saw the look of surprise on the faces of both men.

"At the time Patrick was a much shyer young man than Nat. He'd just come down from somewhere up north and Norah and I had some trouble at first in understanding what he was saying. But he was good-looking enough and I could see that Norah was quite taken by him. Well, to cut a long story short, the four of us went out together a few times. Then Norah received a letter telling her that her father had drowned at sea. I remember how upset she was. Not just because of her father, but because she knew that meant she would have to go home to look after her family. So she went back to Kent and I never heard of her again. Until a few weeks ago. Then I received this letter."

She picked up the two sheets of paper and handed them to Harris.

"Perhaps it'll be best if you read it out loud, sergeant," she said.

Harris unfolded the paper.

"It's dated the second of October," he said.

"I didn't receive it until a few days after that," Ada explained. "It was delivered by hand by a friend of Norah's family, and he took some time to find me."

"Go on, Harris," Parsons said. "Let's hear what this is all about."

"Dear Ada," Harris read. *"By the time you receive this letter I will've gone. I've got the coughing sickness, Ada, and the doctor says there's no hope.*

During these past months I've thought a lot about our time together in London when we were young girls. Believe it or not, Ada, those were some of my happiest days. After I left London my life became one long drudge. But I won't bore you with that.

My reason for writing to you now is to tell you about my son, Daniel. I named him after my dad, but I'm sure you can guess the boy's father. Why else would I be writing to you after all these years?

Well, Ada, things were really bad when I come back here, what with dad dead and ma not well. Not to mention my six younger brothers and sisters, and no money to speak of. And then I found I was with child.

I knew I couldn't keep it. What chance had I of a decent man marrying me with a bastard for a son? And we had troubles enough of our own without another mouth to feed. So when the child was born I took him to an orphanage in Sittingbourne and I left him there. That's the last I saw of Daniel.

As you can imagine I thought about him many times over the years, but it was not until I become ill that I went back to the orphanage to see what had become of him. Of course, by then he had long gone. But I thought they might know where. And they did. And when they told me I decided to write to you.

You see, when I left Daniel at the orphanage I told them his father was a soldier. I never told them his name. What good would that have done. But they must've told him what I'd said, 'cause when Daniel left the orphanage he said he was going to enlist. And if that's what he done I want you to find his father and tell him that he's got a son in the army.

Do this last thing for me, Ada. Please.
Your old friend,
Norah"

————

"ARE YOU TELLING me that RSM Whitehead is the boy's father?" Parsons asked.

Ada nodded.

"What did you do when you received the letter?" Harris asked.

"I went to the barracks and I did as my friend asked. I told Paddy Whitehead about his son."

"But you didn't give him the letter."

"No. Norah was my friend. She had chosen to write to me. It was my letter, and I decided to keep it."

"Does you husband know anything about this?" Parsons asked.

"No, inspector. I decided not to tell him. I didn't want Nat to get involved. I felt it was better if Mr. Whitehead heard it from me."

"What did he say when you told him?"

"He merely asked me the boy's name. He said he would make enquiries. That's all he said."

"Why did you decide to tell me, Mrs. Fox?" Harris asked.

"Because I heard my husband mention the name Hobson when he was talking to you the other day. And I wondered if it might be the same boy."

"I'm afraid you may be right, Mrs. Fox," said Parsons. "There was a Daniel Hobson in the Middlesex, but I regret to say that he died in South Africa before his father ever discovered he existed."

53

AFTER LEAVING *THE Tanners Arms* Parsons and Harris retraced their steps towards London Bridge. Parsons remembered seeing a coffee shop inside the railway station which he thought might be quiet now that the majority of the morning commuters had dispersed to their places of employment.

"Charming though Mrs. Fox may have been, Harris," he said. "I wasn't sorry to turn my back on Bermondsey and all that gore. And we need somewhere quiet to discuss the implications of what we've just heard."

But as they approached the station Parsons began to think that he was going from one gruesome scene to another. Either that or he was dreaming.

Outside the station a large woman of what appeared to be African descent was beating a monotonous rhythm on a drum, much to the obvious disapproval of a small donkey standing disconsolately between the shafts of a two-wheeled cart. The woman was wearing a dress of cheap gray material that looked as though it had been stitched together by a person altogether unfamiliar with the use of paper patterns. Of equally unappealing appearance was the shapeless, white, wide-brimmed hat with a sad-looking feather that was perched on top of the woman's head, and the scrawny blue woolen stole that was draped around her neck.

It was not until he was closer that Parsons realized his mistake. The 'woman' was in actual fact an unattractive looking man with a crudely blackened face. Yet even more bizarre was the huge shapeless effigy of indeterminate gender that was perched precariously on the cart.

"Who's that supposed to be?" Harris asked good-humoredly as he dropped a few coins into a cap that was lying on the ground beside the cart.

"Charles Stewart Parnell, mate," the man replied. "That Irish bastard deserves to be burnt if ever anyone did."

———

"WHAT WAS ALL that about, Harris?" Parsons asked after they had ordered their coffee. "Other than what I saw earlier today in Bermondsey I don't believe I've ever seen anything quite as hideous."

"You probably wouldn't living where you do, sir. They may not have effigies in Chelsea, but we see plenty of them in Shoreditch. And they're all over the East End at this time of year."

Parsons looked puzzled.

"November the fifth, sir," said Harris with a smile. "I thought an educated man like yourself would know all about Guy Fawkes."

"Of course I do, Harris," Parsons said irritably. "Guy Fawkes was one of a group of Catholic sympathizers who, in 1605, tried to blow up the Houses of Parliament along with King James I. But what has that ridiculous exhibition outside to do with Guy Fawkes? I thought I heard that creature with the black face mention Charles Stewart Parnell. "

"Guy Fawkes or Parnell, sir. It's all the same to some people. It's just another way of raising a bit of money. In all probability that man's a costermonger or someone down on his luck. As you can see he's dressed himself up to attract attention, made a rather poor attempt at making an effigy, and in all probability will spend the next few days standing outside railway stations or places that are equally busy in the hope of getting a few coins."

"But that dreadful figure on the cart has no artistic qualities whatsoever, Harris," said Parsons in exasperation. "Even someone like you who obviously knows about such things had no idea who or what it was supposed to represent. Why should anyone bother to give that man money for something quite so pathetic?"

"You're a harsher judge than I, sir. I wasn't considering the artistic merits of the effigy. I just saw a poor man trying to raise a bit of money for his family."

Parsons was momentarily nonplussed by Harris' comment. But he was not going to allow himself to be diverted from the point he was trying to make.

"Well that's extremely commendable of you, my dear Harris," he said. "And I wouldn't like you to think for one moment that I was criticizing your generosity. I merely wish to point out that if you, and similarly magnanimous people like you, continue to reward a man like that for doing as little as he clearly has, then he will never consider it worth his while producing anything better. I regret to say that I have never witnessed the great carnivals held each year in Venice and Rome, but from what I have read of them they are truly artistic, colorful and picturesque events. In addition the people themselves derive enormous pleasure from them. What we see in this country is something quite different. That hideous monstrosity outside the station represents a complete lack of any artistic sensibility, which I regret to say is a hallmark of many of we English."

Much to Harris' relief the arrival of the coffee interrupted Parsons' rhetoric. Much as he envied and admired the inspector's education and his use of language, there were times when he found him overly pompous.

"I think we have more serious matters to discuss than effigies, sir," he said quietly.

"You're absolutely right, Harris," said Parsons as he spooned sugar into his coffee. "And I've been talking too much. Now it's your turn.

Why don't you give me your opinion about what we've just heard about RSM Whitehead and this unfortunate young man, Daniel Hobson."

Harris took a sip of coffee before replying.

"I confess that I'm a little confused by what I've just learned, sir. While we were walking here I tried to imagine how I would feel if I was in Whitehead's shoes and discovered after all these years that I had a son. And frankly I've still no idea."

Parsons watched the emotions playing out on Harris' face. At times like these he was always surprised to see how sensitive Harris was. Not everyone with a background like his would be the same.

"It must've been a terrible shock for Whitehead to realize that his son was dead," Harris said after a lengthy silence. "I'm a father myself. And I know how I would feel if one of my children died."

"Even if you had abandoned that child? After all, that's what Whitehead did."

"But he didn't know anything about a child, sir. As far as he was concerned, and from what Mrs. Fox told us, the relationship between Norah Hobson and Whitehead was a short one. What would he know about any child?"

"So you think Whitehead would have acted differently if Norah had told him she was pregnant?" said Parsons. "Don't forget he had just become a soldier and probably had little money. Do you think he would've been prepared to accept the responsibility of being a father?"

"How are we to know what he would've done, sir? And even if he'd done the decent thing and recognized the child as his, it's still likely that Norah would have chosen to give the child to an orphanage. As she said in her letter, at the time she had more than her share of family responsibilities."

"Well, all that's history now, Harris. What we have to consider is how we think Whitehead reacted when Ada Fox told him what was in that letter. Let's just examine the facts. Whitehead discovers that he has a son. A son who, unbeknown to him, had followed him into the army, and actually joined the same regiment. And not just the same regiment, but the very company in which Whitehead was the sergeant major. How do you think he'd feel after learning that his son was the handsome young man he'd been ordered to flog for stealing money from his company commander; a flogging that had been sanctioned by the commanding officer, Colonel Latham. And what happens after that? Whitehead actually volunteers the young lad for a hazardous patrol in order to give him an opportunity to redeem himself. A patrol that Latham and Cordell had planned and which Simpson was going to lead. And we both know what happened. As a result of Simpson's apparent incompetence Daniel Hobson was amongst those soldiers who were left behind to die at the hands of the Zulus. Whereas Simpson himself escaped."

Parsons paused to drink his coffee.

"I think we can understand what Whitehead would have felt. He would've decided that the blame for his son's death really lay with Latham, Cordell and Simpson; perhaps even Sayers, if Whitehead had any inkling of the real purpose of the patrol?"

"Well, if you put it like that, sir, it certainly fits."

"It fits like a glove, Harris," said Parsons excitedly. "We have a single motive for all the murders at last, and we also have a man with the means to carry them out. There's little doubt that whoever planned them was clever. And I think we can both agree that Whitehead is smart. To murder Sayers and Latham in the space of an hour and a half required excellent planning. And then there are the suicide notes. I've always thought that whoever wrote them was no fool. They may have been written in a rough hand to hide the writer's identity, but there was also a subtle meaning to the words that I'm still uncertain of. We know that Whitehead always had his ear to the ground, and not much happened in the barracks without him knowing. So I'm sure he would've heard about Cordell and Simpson's argument. He would also have known that Cordell had had far too much to drink, and would've guessed Simpson's state of mind after learning of Cordell's death and what was written in his suicide note. There could never have been a better time to murder them both and make it appear like suicide"

Parsons was warming to his task, and barely noticed that Harris had refilled his coffee cup.

"But let's start with General Latham's death," he said. "If we can prove that Whitehead had a hand in Latham's death then everything else falls into place. We know from what Bradley told us that Whitehead was in the general's house earlier in the evening. According to Bradley, Whitehead took him a bottle of brandy to celebrate some battle they'd been in together. Whitehead knew Bradley's weakness for brandy and would've been confident that he would drink enough of it by midnight to be unaware of anyone entering the house provided they had a key. And I think we can assume that Whitehead had taken the key during his first visit to Chester Place."

Harris had become increasingly sceptical as he had listened to Parsons' elucidation.

"But I thought that it was a woman who murdered Latham, sir," he said

"So did I, Harris. But your good lady and her mother knew better than that, and I was foolish enough not to listen to them. If you remember they said that a woman would not have stabbed General Latham with an *iklwa* in the way that the murderer did. And they were right. And if you want to know how we were misled by the woman's clothes you have only to look outside the station. If that overweight, ugly man with the crudely blackened face could fool me into thinking he was a woman, how much easier would it be for a slim, clean-shaven man of average height like Whitehead; especially if it was dark and he was wearing a heavy veil."

"So what next, sir. Do we arrest Whitehead?"

"Not yet, Harris. We're not going to leave here until we have worked out how Whitehead managed to murder both Sayers and Latham in the same evening. He would've needed help for that. I suspect he could've managed to kill Cordell and Simpson by himself, but it's likely that Bates, Oakes and Williams were involved in the first two murders. But we need proof. Speculation in itself is not enough to convict anyone."

"So why don't we arrest the others?" Harris asked.

"I think that's what we have to do, Harris. But not Oakes. That would only put Whitehead on his guard. Let's concentrate on Bates and Williams. There's a good chance that faced with the possibility of the gallows one or the other of them will turn Queen's Evidence."

54

B Y THE TIME Parsons and Harris left London Bridge Station they had established what they considered to be a likely scenario for the night of the twenty second of October. It only remained to make the necessary arrangements to have Oliver Bates and Constable Morgan Williams arrested.

That in itself presented its own problem, as it transpired that Williams was on duty until six in the evening and Bates was not expected back at the stables until the early hours of the following morning. As Parsons had no wish to do anything to forewarn either Oakes or Whitehead of what might be in store for them he decided that there was no alternative but to allow both men to continue their day's work as though nothing was amiss.

Parsons had decided to hold both Bates and Williams at Paddington police station. In that way neither he nor Harris would have to waste valuable time traveling from one station to another. And time was of the essence. For all he knew Oakes and Whitehead were in frequent contact with the other two men, and their sudden disappearance would sound alarm bells.

The police station at Paddington was also conveniently near the barracks, the newsagent's shop in Silver Street, and the general's house in Chester Place. And Parsons had questions he needed answering in each place.

Harris had previously learned during his visit to the stables that Bates had been using the same horse for the whole time he had worked as a cabbie. For all his ill temper and fondness for drink, it appeared that Bates had always been especially attentive to the animal. According to the foreman, Bates would often come to the stables on his infrequent days off to give the animal a special grooming. The horse was a chestnut mare with a distinctive white blaze on the bridge of its nose and white socks on its hind legs. One hansom cab might look much the same as another, the foreman had informed Harris, but no two horses were ever alike.

The two men had gone their separate ways after leaving the railway station. Harris went first to Paddington to make arrangements for adequate policemen and carriages to be made available for the two arrests. After that he returned to Kennington to further question William's landlady about the night Sayers and Latham were murdered. He had not felt able to ask too many searching questions before lest she should inform Williams and rouse his suspicions. But it was unlikely now that Williams would to be returning to his room for sometime. Perhaps not at all.

Parsons took a cab to Chester Place. At first he feared that Bradley might be out or even have left the house, as the brass knocker had not been cleaned for several days. But he eventually answered the door to Parsons' persistent knocking.

Bradley's appearance had not improved. He was unshaven and had neglected to brush or comb his hair, but much to Parsons' relief appeared sober enough to answer his questions.

The decanter of whisky had been removed from the table in the general's study, but other than that little else had changed. Ash remained in the fireplace, and Parsons could still see the marks left by his fingers in the dust on the general's desk. It was evident that Bradley continued to neglect his household responsibilities.

"I've a few more questions to ask, Bradley," Parsons said. "And I want you to concentrate, as you may be required to repeat your answers under oath in a court of law. Do I make myself clear?"

Bradley nodded.

"Yes, sir," he said.

"On those occasions you delivered the general's notes to the newsagent in Silver Street, did you at any time see RSM Whitehead in the shop or anywhere near the shop?"

"No, sir. I tol' you before that there were generally plenty o' soldiers around. But I never seen the RSM. I'm certain about that."

"Did you ever see a woman dressed in black with a thick black veil? Rather like the woman you saw here the night the general was murdered."

"No, sir."

"What about a cab? Was there a cab ever parked near the shop?"

Bradley's brow creased in concentration.

"Now that you mention it there were, sir. I thought at the time that it were strange. The cabbie didn' seem to be waitin' for a fare and the nearest cabbies' shelter is either in Holland Park or Kensington Park Road."

"That's very good, Bradley. Now I don't suppose there's any chance you could describe the cabbie."

Bradley looked at Parsons in amazement.

"Are you serious, sir," he said. "How can you tell one of those cabbies fr'm another. They all look the same, what with their 'eavy coats and the scarves round their faces."

"So you wouldn't be able to identify this cab from any other?"

"Not the cab nor the driver, sir. But I certainly remember the 'orse. I'm a country boy. M' father worked in the stables. So I can certainly tell one 'orse from another. And I know a good one when I see it. An' there's few 'orses in London pulling cabs as pretty as that chestnut mare with the white blaze and the white socks."

"You're sure of that, Bradley?"

"As sure as I'm standin' 'ere, sir. I saw that 'orse twice, and the second time I went over and stroked it and give it one of the carrots I'd just bought from the vegetable shop."

"Thank you, Bradley. I'm most impressed by the clarity of your memory. But don't forget. You may have to testify about that horse in court."

"Don't you worry about that, sir. That 'orse were a beauty. I'm not likely to forget 'er in a 'urry."

AS IT WAS only just over a mile from Chester Place to Silver Street, Parsons decided to walk. With the major exodus from central London just beginning there was little chance of finding a cab on Bayswater Road. Had he the time he would have chosen to walk across Kensington Gardens, but instead he took the most direct route, following Bayswater Road to Notting Hill and then turning south into Silver Street.

An elderly man with a long black beard flecked with gray was serving cigarettes to a customer when Parsons arrived at the newsagent. Like many small shopkeepers, the newsagent was a Jew. He wore a long black coat that had seen many years of service, and a *yarmulka* on his head out of respect for the God he was sure was continually watching him from above.

Parsons waited for the handful of customers to leave before introducing himself.

"My sergeant was here last week asking about the post box that General Latham rented," he said.

"As I told the sergeant I couldn't svear that it vas General Latham who rented the box, inspector," said the newsagent, "because I never saw him. It vas always a servant who paid me the rent for the box. At least I assumed the man vas a servant by the way he dressed."

Parsons described Bradley.

"Yes. That vas the man."

"You told my sergeant that the notes that this man delivered were normally collected by a young French woman."

"She certainly sounded French to me," the newsagent said, bending his arms and waggling his hands to emphasize the point. "But on the other hand she may have been Italian. I speak only Yiddish and English myself, and the French and Italian languages sound very much the same to me. So please don't expect me to svear that this young lady vas one nationality or another. But she vas definitely young and very pretty, inspector, and she had beautiful brown eyes. If any of the soldiers vere here when she came they always tried to start a conversation with her. But she vanted nothing to do with any of them. Who can blame her. Vhat future is there for any girl who goes with a soldier?"

"So you would recognize this young woman again?"

"Oh, without doubt, inspector. You don't see many pretty young vomen with such charming accents around here."

"But if I remember correctly you told my sergeant that the last note the young French woman collected had been delivered, not by the man you took to be General Latham's servant, but by a second woman. A woman who was probably much older. I believe that she was wearing a black dress and had a heavy veil over her face. Is there any chance at all that you would recognize that woman again?"

The elderly Jew raised his hands and shrugged his shoulders.

"I vould like to be able to help you, inspector," he said. "But as you said, I couldn't see her face. All I can remember is that she was taller than the average voman."

"What about her voice?"

"As I told your sergeant she had some sort of accent. It might have been French, but if it vas it vas not as pleasing to my old ears as that of the young voman."

"Can you remember what she said?"

The newsagent seemed taken aback by the question.

"Inspector," he protested mildly. "I see hundreds of different people in this shop in the course of a week. How can I be expected to remember vhat they all say?"

"But this woman was very different than most," said Parsons, trying to prevent himself from sounding equally piqued. "She was dressed in black, she was wearing a veil, she was tall, and she spoke with an accent. Surely that helps."

The newsagent stroked his beard and mumbled to himself.

"She said she had a note she vished to put in General Latham's post box," he said, after considerable thought. "That's all she said. So I asked her vhere the other young voman vas."

"And what did she say?"

"She said that she was sick."

"So you took the note?"

The shopkeeper was becoming increasingly irritated. Two other customers had entered the shop and were waiting to be served.

"Of course I did, inspector," he said. "Unless a customer specifically says that only certain people are to use his post box I allow anyone to use it who asks."

"I'm not questioning your judgment, sir," said Parsons. "I merely want to confirm exactly what happened. Do you remember how each of the women came to your shop. Did they walk or did they come by cab?"

"The older one came in a cab."

"And the other woman walked?"

"That's true. The young voman always walked, but the other one came in a cab."

"I don't suppose you can describe the horse pulling the cab."

"The horse?" the newsagent said in surprise. "Now you vant me to describe a horse?"

"Yes. The horse. What color was it?"

The old man mumbled to himself again before answering.

"It vas a chestnut," he said excitedly. "Yes. A chestnut. And now that I think about it, I seem to remember seeing it before."

The shopkeeper became increasingly excited.

"Yes," he said. "I did. It vas on the other side of the road on a couple of occasions. I couldn't understand vhy it was there for so long. I thought to myself at the time, that's no vay for a cabbie to be earning a living."

"Just one final question, sir," said Parsons, who was equally delighted at what the newsagent had recollected, "and then I'll allow you to serve these customers. You said the second woman spoke with a French accent, or at least an accent that sounded French. But how would you describe her voice?"

"Vhat do you mean by her voice? I already told you she sounded French."

"Well, did she speak in a high voice or a low one."

"She had a low voice."

"I see. Like a man's voice."

"No. I vouldn't say that." The newsagent stroked his beard again. "But I vould say that if a man vas trying to make himself sound like a voman he might sound like she did."

———————

KENSINGTON BARRACKS WAS only a short distance from the newsagent's shop, and within ten minutes Parsons had reached the main gate of the barracks where the familiar routine was performed of the sentry summoning Sergeant Oakes, who in turn sought permission from the RSM for him to enter. This time, however,

Whitehead did not choose to make an appearance. It was, perhaps, because the RSM had more important matters to attend to; or it may have been that Parsons' request to question the staff in the Officers' Mess about matters relating to Captain Simpson's death seemed of relative unimportance. Whatever the reason might have been, Parsons was grateful to be allowed to proceed without the customary escort.

Mindful of the RSM's earlier admonition he skirted the parade ground, where even now, in the failing evening light, squads of soldiers continued to be put through their paces by the bevy of junior noncommissioned officers whose faces had grown puce through the constant use of their vocal chords throughout the day. Parsons had by now become inured to what he regarded as one of the more foolish military practices, and was not surprised to see that not a single commissioned officer was present to watch the drill. Doubtless they had more pressing demands upon their time like riding in Hyde Park, exercising their right to take excessive leave, or simply idling about in the Mess.

Two of the younger idlers looked disdainfully down their noses at Parsons as he entered the Mess and asked them where he might find the Mess Sergeant.

"How can you possibly expect us to know," said the taller of the two, with a sneer of the sort that Parsons had become accustomed to hearing from Louise's brother. "We've just come from the billiard room."

"You might try the kitchen or the bar," said the second, indicating a corridor leading in the opposite direction to that which Parsons had taken when he had interviewed Holland and Simpson.

As he made his way along this corridor Parsons could see the dining room through two doors on his left, and mess servants in starched white jackets and white gloves arranging the glasses, silverware, and candelabra on a long mahogany table with as much precision as the soldiers drilling on the square. It would be interesting to know, he reflected, whether meals served in the Officers' Mess were *a la francaise*, which would involve the officers serving themselves from a side table; or *a la russe*, where a servant would appear discreetly at each diner's elbow with a serving dish. With such an abundance of servants, Parsons suspected the latter. As far as he could see the residents of the Mess were not in the habit of doing much for themselves.

Two doors on the opposite side of the corridor opened onto the bar, and Parsons could see several officers, including Holland, sprawled in armchairs around a roaring fire enjoying pre-prandial drinks. None of them noticed him; but Sergeant Barnard, who had been assisting at the bar with another servant, hastened across the room to forestall his entry.

"Whom do you wish to see, sir?" he asked, shepherding Parsons back into the corridor. "The gentlemen will be dining shortly. If you need to speak with any of them I'm afraid that you will have to wait."

"That won't be a problem, Sergeant Barnard," said Parsons with a smile. "I've no wish to speak to any of the officers. It's you that I've come to see."

The startled expression on the mess sergeant's face gave way to one of confusion.

"I don't know whether that's possible, sir," he said. "I have my duties to perform."

"I'm sure you can be spared for a few minutes," Parsons said. "But if you think your absence presents a problem I can ask Major Holland's permission."

Barnard looked anxiously over his shoulder towards the group around the fireplace.

"Perhaps that won't be necessary, sir," he said, wishing to avoid any chance of a reprimand for allowing Parsons to enter the bar uninvited. "We can go to my office."

BARNARD'S OFFICE OPPOSITE the kitchen was no larger than a broom cupboard. His small desk was piled with papers, and there were box files stacked neatly on shelves on one of the walls.

"I'm surprised you have time for all this paperwork," said Parsons.

"I spend a few hours here every day, sir," Barnard said, "Apart from keeping track of the bar deliveries and the collection of the empty bottles I'm also responsible for the officers' mess bills."

Seeing the puzzled expression on Parsons' face, Barnard said: "Whenever an officer orders a drink he signs a bar chit; and at the end of each month I have to provide a mess bill for each officer that, apart from his drinks, also includes the cost of any meals he may have had during the month, any charges for laundry, and any damages to mess property."

"What do you mean by damages to mess property?" asked Parsons in amazement.

"Oh, you'd be surprised what some of these young officers get up to, sir. Especially those who have more money than sense. Only last month three of them had to pay for the windows they broke in the billiard room. It seems they got tired of playing billiards and decided to throw the balls through the windows."

Barnard continued, as though what he had just said had been no more than a routine event in the Mess.

"You'd be surprised how many hours each month I spend trying to sort out the drinks," he said. "Apart from the drinks each officer orders, I also have to account for any drinks that are served at receptions or formal dinner nights. Take for example the drinks at General Latham's wake. The cost of those drinks will be shared amongst every officer in the regiment whether he lives in the Mess or not. Even those, like Major Plumb, who weren't at the wake will have to pay their share. You see that's because the Mess as a whole was entertaining. It would be different if it were the wine and spirits served at a formal dinner night. In that case only those officers present would pay."

"And does each officer pay the same amount regardless of his rank?"

"No, sir. The more senior officers pay more. I have to work all that out. But it's not as difficult as it sounds. There is a fairly simple formula to follow. The colonel pays the largest share, the majors a little less, and so on through the captains and lieutenants."

Much to Parsons surprise Barnard gave him a wink.

"Of course, some of the junior officers have far more money than Colonel Cordell. It was well known that the colonel had little of his own. Why else would he choose to live in the barracks?"

The matter of where Cordell had chosen to live had never before occurred to Parsons. He had thought that living in the barracks had merely been a matter of convenience. But he was clearly wrong. Most commanding officers, so Barnard informed him, normally lived outside the barracks in houses of their own. It was many years since a commanding officer had chosen to live in the barracks. That would be another reason, why many of the officers, and wealthy wives like Lady Cordelia, would have chosen to look down on Cordell.

"How do you know which officers are in the mess at any one time?" Parsons asked "As far as I can see many of them are frequently absent."

"That's true, sir. But when an officer knows he's going to be away he signs himself out.

There's a 'Dining Out' book on the table just inside the entrance to the Mess for that very purpose."

"I hadn't noticed," admitted Parsons. "Perhaps you will be kind enough to fetch it. There's something I wish to check."

Barnard was not entirely comfortable with the request, but he could see that he had little option but to comply. Doubtless if he refused the inspector would only seek permission from Major Holland, and Barnard had no wish to interrupt the senior officer in the Mess just before his dinner without good reason.

"Here's the book, sir," he said, a few minutes later. "Is there anything in particular that you're looking for?"

"I was interested in seeing whether Captain Simpson followed the rules," Parsons said. "For instance did he sign out on the day before he died?"

Barnard flicked through the pages and handed the book to Parsons.

"There you are, sir. As you can see he signed out for lunch and dinner on the twenty-ninth."

That would have been the day he visited the Plumbs and his parents, thought Parsons. He turned the page.

"But I also see that he had signed himself out again for the thirty-first."

Parsons examined the entry more closely.

"And he appears to have done that when he returned to the Mess on the evening before he died. Don't you think that was unusual for someone who'd decided to shoot himself?"

Barnard was discomfited by the question.

"How am I to know what the captain was thinking, sir?" he said. "It's not my place to say, but Captain Simpson was drinking so much I don't think he knew what he was doing most of the time."

"You may be right about that, sergeant," Parsons said. "There's no doubt that Captain Simpson was a very confused young man."

Parsons closed the book and handed it back to Barnard without further comment. But there was no doubt in his mind that when Simpson had signed himself out for the thirty-first of October, presumably to visit the Plumbs for dinner, he had no intention of committing suicide. Although he agreed with Barnard about Simpson being a confused young man, as far as Parsons was concerned the fact that he had signed himself out as he had was just one more indication that he had been murdered. But now it was time to turn to the matter that had really prompted his visit to the barracks.

"It's as well the regiment has a man like RSM Whitehead in these difficult times," he said. "Even an ignorant civilian like myself can see that he's a most remarkable man. I don't believe I've ever met anyone quite like him. He seems to know every single thing that goes on in the barracks."

"Well, that's his job, sir," said Barnard. "There's some that say a commanding officer should be like that. But I've never met one that was. Half the time they're not even in the barracks, whereas most of the RSMs I've known never seem to leave. Mr. Whitehead lives and breathes the regiment. I've heard him say many times that the regiment is the only family he's ever known."

"What remarkable devotion," said Parsons in a suitably approving tone. "But tell me, Sergeant Barnard, how do you think the RSM manages to obtain all his information?"

Barnard laughed knowingly.

"Mr. Whitehead's always asking questions, sir. He has spies everywhere."

"Would you say that you were one of Mr. Whitehead's spies, Sergeant Barnard?"

"Not really, sir," Barnard taken aback by the directness of the question. "I see the RSM often enough in the Sergeants' Mess. And if he asks me a question I'll answer it as truthfully as I can. Of course, if it's anything personal about one of the officers then he knows that's something I can't discuss."

Parsons was far from convinced. He was certain that Barnard told Whitehead everything he wanted to know. If he ever refused, no doubt the RSM could make life difficult for him.

"But for instance, the argument between Colonel Cordell and Captain Simpson after General Latham's funeral. Would you have told Mr. Whitehead about that? Especially that part of the quarrel that took place in the corridor. I believe only you were privy to that."

From the expression on Barnard's face it was clear that he was surprised that Parsons had been aware of what had occurred.

"I didn't mean to tell Mr. Whitehead about that, sir. But he asked me who was at the wake and how everything had gone. It was his way, sir. Those are just the sort of things he wants to know. And before I realized what I was saying I'd told him about the quarrel. It just slipped out, sir."

"And what exactly were the colonel and captain arguing about in the corridor?"

"It was something about some money that was stolen from Colonel Cordell in Africa and how the colonel's servant was accused of taking it, but really it was Captain Simpson all along. The captain said that he had only meant to borrow the money, and when he learned that the servant had been blamed he was too embarrassed to admit what he'd done. "

"And you told Mr. Whitehead that?"

"Yes, sir. It didn't seem that important to me."

"What happened to the servant?"

"I don't know about that, sir. I wasn't there at the time."

"Did the RSM also know that the colonel had drunk far more than he was accustomed to before he left the Mess?"

Barnard nodded his head.

"I suppose he did, sir," he said glumly. "Well, that's to say, I told him."

"What about Captain Simpson's drinking? Did he know about that?"

Barnard laughed.

"Everyone in the regiment knew that, sir. That wasn't news. It was common knowledge that Captain Simpson had been drinking like that for months."

"But was it common knowledge that Captain Simpson's favorite drink was Irish whiskey, that he frequently drank alone in his room, and that he kept a loaded revolver in his desk?"

"That's not that unusual, sir. Many of the officers keep a bottle in their rooms, and some even have revolvers. They often take the revolvers with them when they go out. I'm sure I don't have to tell you what a dangerous place London is."

"That may be so, Barnard. But was the RSM as interested in the other officers as he was in Captain Simpson?"

"No, sir," Barnard replied. "I don't suppose he was."

———

PARSONS LEFT THE barracks soon after. He had one more visit to make. And that was to the *Queen Adelaide.*

55

Wednesday, 5th November

WHEN THE CHESTNUT mare turned its head into the stables on Harrow Road just before one Oliver Bates had no idea that in a nearby, dark, side street a police carriage and four large policeman from Paddington station awaited his return, nor that the lone man leaning against the chestnut tree outside the stables was the detective sergeant with the waxed mustache who had interviewed him two days before. He was far too cold and weary after another long day to think of anything other than his bed. Another reason for Bates' oversight was the fact that he was not entirely sober, having sipped liberally during the course of the long, damp evening from the bottle of cheap gin that invariably accompanied him.

The hansom cab shelters in both Bayswater and Kensington had closed at the customary hour of eleven. Since then, apart from a few short distance fares, Bates had done little other than doze fitfully in Park Lane before finally deciding to gently flick his reins and set the mare on the familiar homeward path. As he slipped stiff-leggedly from his seat, he had no sooner begun his nightly task of removing the mare's tackle, feeding her, wiping her down, and cleaning his cab than he was apprehended by the police and bundled into their carriage.

———————

PARSONS HAD BEEN waiting at Lambeth police station for Constable Morgan Williams with a similar reception committee some seven hours previously.

"You'll appreciate that what I've told you is in the strictest confidence," Parsons had said to the desk sergeant after he had explained why he and four policemen from Paddington had unexpectedly descended on his station. "At present the evidence we have against Williams is entirely circumstantial. There are others involved, and it is the ringleader that I'm most interested in getting my hands on."

"I've never liked Williams," the desk sergeant had confided. "He was always too big for his boots, like many of the ex-soldiers we get in the police force. They see a bit of action and they think because of that we should all be impressed. Well, perhaps we are at first, but we soon tire of hearing the same old war stories. Either it's the Zulus or the Afghans or some other godless bunch of natives that none of us have much interest in. And in Williams case the more we heard of his stories the more convinced we became that he wasn't quite the hero he made himself out to be."

"I agree with you," Parsons had said. "From what I know Williams was a coward who deserted his comrades. But if my suspicions are correct Constable Williams will be going to a place where his exploits will mean very little. There are probably more than enough men in prison who, in normal circumstances, would listen to Williams' stories. But not when they learn that as well as being a soldier he was also a policeman."

WILLIAMS HAD BEEN stripped of his uniform as soon as he had entered the station, before being bundled into the waiting carriage in his underclothing, transported to Paddington and left in a cell below street level to contemplate the reason for this unexpected event. During this process Parsons had kept in the background. He had no wish to be seen or heard by Williams.

"Manacle his arms and legs, don't feed him, don't give him a blanket, and don't allow him to sleep," Parsons had instructed the desk sergeant at Paddington. "Another man by the name of Bates is being brought in by your men later tonight. I want him treated in the same way. Put Bates in a separate cell from Williams, and under no circumstances allow them to speak to one another. But I do want each of them to be aware that the other man is in custody. It will give them both the opportunity to consider exactly what that could mean. And I repeat. Neither man is to be allowed to sleep for one minute. This is going to be a long night, and I want it to be as unpleasant as possible for Bates and Williams."

Once he was sure that his instructions were understood Parsons made his final preparations.

"I want you to send this telegram to my superior in Scotland Yard," he told the desk sergeant, handing him the note he had drafted. "It tells him where I am and what I'm doing, and I want to be sure that it is on his desk when he arrives in the morning. I'd also like you to recommend a local pub where I can still get something to eat."

BATES WAS THE first to be brought up from the cells shortly after two thirty. Parsons and Harris could hear the rattle of his chains as he was brought to the interview room. They had waited in an adjoining room until one of the policemen accompanying Bates had confirmed that he was securely manacled to a tall stool in a way that prevented his feet from reaching the floor, and that a gas lamp had been placed on the floor on either side of him. Only then did they enter the interview room and take their places behind the desk facing the prisoner.

Bates was aware that there were at least four people in the room. Two policemen had brought him up from the cells, and two other men had entered the room soon afterwards. But because of the way the lamps had been positioned and their flames trimmed he was unable to see anything of the two men behind the desk except for their legs.

Parsons did not say anything for fully five minutes, during which time Bates became increasingly apprehensive and uneasy. And in spite of the coldness of the room and the fact that he wore only his underclothes he began to sweat.

Finally Parsons spoke.

"Are you Oliver Bates?" he asked.

"What's that to you, mate?" Bates replied, the sound of Parson's voice rekindling his truculence.

"Answer the question, Bates," Parsons said, "or I will ask one of the constables to teach you some manners."

Bates, Parsons was sure, had little doubt what that would mean. If he had not been in police custody himself, a man like him would have known others that had.

"Yeah," he said. "I'm Oliver Bates."

"And did you previously serve in Africa with the Middlesex Light Regiment?"

"Yeah. Am I 'ere to git a medal? Is this what's this is all about?"

Parsons crossed his ankles, a signal that one of the policemen should kick the stool from under Bates. He landed with a dull thud and winced as he grazed the side of his head and one of his elbows on the stone floor. After a minute Parsons ordered him to be picked up and placed back on the stool.

"The two constables have heavy boots, Bates," said Harris. "Next time they will use them before they pick you up."

It was clear from the expression on Bates' face as he cocked his head to one side that he had recognized the new voice.

"'Ere," he said. "Don' I know you? Ain't you the sergeant that come to see me on Sunday? What the 'ell are you doin' 'ere then?"

"I will ask the questions, Bates," said Parsons. "But I'm glad to see that you recall meeting Detective Sergeant Harris. Allow me to introduce myself. My name is Parsons. Detective Inspector Parsons. Like Sergeant Harris, I also work for the Criminal Investigation Department."

Parsons allowed time for Bates to digest the significance of the information.

"Do you know why you are here, Bates?" he asked.

"P'raps 'coz I splashed mud on that bobby in Kensington 'igh Street a few days ago," said Bates defiantly.

Almost immediately the stool was kicked away again and this time Bates was kicked in the lower part of his back while he lay on the floor.

"You were warned, Bates," said Harris as the prisoner was dragged back onto the stool. "The decision is yours. Either you answer a few simple questions or you can continue to allow the two constables to use you as a football."

Parsons was hoping that Bates would take the threat seriously. He had no liking for these methods. Physical intimidation, he knew, was part and parcel of the methods employed in many police stations. They were not methods he approved of, but when he had discussed with Harris the problem of extracting information from Bates and Williams during the course of a single night, it had been Harris who had come up with a strategy.

"It won't take more then a few well-aimed kicks in the kidneys to get people like Bates and Williams to talk," he had said dispassionately. "They may bluster a little at the start, but they'll talk, especially if they think that by doing so they can incriminate others and save their own skins."

Once Parsons knew that he had Bates' renewed attention he repeated the question. Bates shook his head.

"I ain't got nuffin to say," he mumbled.

"Then I will tell you," said Parsons. "You are here because your cab was seen several times outside a newsagent's shop in Silver Street. Altogether it was there for several hours, and on one occasion it delivered a passenger. A lady dressed in black who was wearing a heavy black veil. She went into the shop to deliver an envelope. I want to know who that woman was, where you picked her up and where you dropped her."

The first sign of distress showed on Bates' face. But it appeared to Parsons that he was still going to attempt to brazen his way out of his precarious position.

"Prove it, mate," he said. "'ow can anyone be sure it was my cab? They all look alike, don' they?"

"Indeed they do, Bates," said Parsons. "But not the horses. And it so happens that you have a very handsome and distinctive mare with a white blaze and white socks."

Bates laughed.

"So you're goin' to bring my 'orse into court as a witness, are you?"

"Who said anything about you going to court, Bates?" said Parsons. "Unless, of course, you have done something for which you feel guilty."

Bates said nothing. He lowered his head and looked at the feet under the table opposite him.

"So you have nothing further to say, Bates?"

Bates shook his head.

"Then take him back to his cell, gentlemen. And bring the other prisoner. We'll see what Constable Williams has to say for himself. And after that, Bates, we'll talk again."

———

IT WAS WHILE Parsons and Harris were waiting for Williams that they received a welcome piece of news from Scotland Yard. The telegram Parsons had sent to Jeffries earlier had been read by the Duty Clerk, who in turn had received earlier instructions from the superintendent that if either Parsons or Harris was to make contact during the night they were to be informed that a Webley revolver had been found in the river near

Lambeth Bridge. There was no evidence to say that it was the revolver that had been used to kill Lord Frederick Sayers, Jeffries had said, but in view of where it had been found it was a strong possibility.

"It's a strong enough possibility for me, Harris," Parsons said. "And neither Bates or Williams will know any better when I tell them."

WILLIAMS HAD SEEN Bates when he was first brought down to the cells and later had apprehensively watched him being led upstairs in manacles. But it was the sight of Bates being dragged back to his cell some time after that had been of the greatest concern to Williams, especially as Parsons had instructed that the evidence of Bates' recent injuries be reinforced by sprinkling some red ink onto his face and vest. As a policeman, Williams knew only too well the sort of treatment frequently administered to prisoners during questioning, and after seeing the blood knew what he might expect when it was his turn to be interviewed. Like many bullies, Williams was not a brave man, and he had already made up his mind that he was not going to allow himself to be unmercifully beaten and kicked in order to protect anyone else. As far as he was concerned it was just a matter of deciding how much he should say to save himself.

It was almost three thirty when Williams was eventually brought up from the cells, and by then his imagination had conjured up the most vivid and unpleasant images of what lay in store for him. He licked his lips nervously as he was being manacled to the stool, aware that the two policemen who had dragged him up from the cells were now standing behind him and that there were also two shadowy figures sitting behind the table opposite him.

"You are Constable Morgan Williams, formerly a private soldier in the Middlesex Light Regiment?"

The voice was more cultured and less threatening than he had expected.

"Yes, sir," replied Williams, only too anxious to say anything that might sound helpful to his interrogators even though it might be no more than his name.

"You have lodgings in Kennington at 9 Sancroft Road."

"Yes, sir."

"Were you there between ten and eleven on the night of the twenty-second of October?"

There was a lengthy pause. Williams' mind seemed suddenly to have become blank.

"I can't remember, sir," he said in a weak voice.

"Then let me help you, Williams. It was the night that Lord Frederick Sayers and General Sir Maxwell Latham were both murdered. Does that help you remember?"

Williams could not fail to note that the cultured voice had developed an edge, and gentlemen policemen, he knew, could be bastards as much as anyone else.

"I was off duty that night, sir."

"I'm well aware of that, Williams. Constable Clough, one of your colleagues from Lambeth Division, confirmed that when he made his statement about his own whereabouts that night. Earlier this evening I spoke with Clough, and what he told me was most interesting. He said that in the half hour or so before Lord Sayers was murdered you engaged him in a lengthy conversation while he was patrolling Lambeth Embankment. He told me he was surprised to see you there, and even more surprised that you had chosen that moment to speak to him, as during the whole time you have been at Lambeth Division the two of you had barely exchanged more than a few words. Don't you think that it was a strange coincidence that your meeting with Clough took place shortly before Sayers' murder, Williams?"

"I just happened to be walking along the Embankment at the time, sir" said Williams sullenly. "Is that a crime?"

"Not in the least, Williams," Parsons replied. "But from what I know about you, walking along the Lambeth Embankment late at night is not one of your regular habits, especially after spending the day pounding the beat. From what I hear you're more inclined to spend your off-duty hours in the public houses in Kennington."

Williams did not speak.

"Would you care to tell me the real reason for your being on Lambeth Embankment that night?"

"I was seeing a friend."

"I see. Perhaps you can tell me the name of that friend."

There was a long silence and then Parsons said:

"It seems that there was no friend, Williams. That seems hardly surprising. As far as I can see you have few friends. No one at Lambeth Division has much time for you, and if you call the likes of Oliver Bates a friend I should warn you that he has already told us what he was doing that night."

Before continuing Parsons allowed Williams time to consider what it was that Bates might have already told the police.

"I think the reason you chose to speak to Constable Clough that night was to delay him," Parsons said eventually. "You see, if Clough had been allowed to continue his patrol as normal he might well have intercepted Lord Sayers' murderer."

Another silence, during which Williams squirmed uncomfortably on the stool and licked his dry lips.

"But let us put that to one side for the moment," said Parsons. "Perhaps you would rather tell me why it was that Oliver Bates' cab was outside your lodgings at ten o'clock on that same night?"

Williams' opened and closed his mouth several times without speaking, his sweat now so profuse that his sodden vest clung to his body. He racked his brain for an answer that might satisfy his interrogator, but none came.

In the long silence that followed Williams waited for the inevitable, trying to anticipate what form the punishment would take. It was not long in coming. Without warning the stool was kicked from under him, his heavy body landed unceremoniously in a heap, and the policemen on either side of him began kicking him. Williams began to cry and call for his mother as the pain in his kidneys grew unbearable.

"Pick him up."

This time the voice was different, and it was one Williams thought he recognized. It was a voice he had heard only recently, a more common London voice, but he was too confused to remember when that might have been.

"When I spoke to your landlady again this evening, Williams," the common voice continued, "she told me that someone other than yourself was in your room during the time you were walking on Lambeth Embankment. Would you care to tell me who that was?"

It was then that Williams remembered the police sergeant who had questioned him in the pub. The bastard had been sent there by his landlady.

"How can I, sir?" he said without great conviction. "I wasn't there."

Williams found himself on the floor again, and cried out in pain as the first kick landed in his groin. The interrogation continued as he wriggled and squirmed to protect himself as best he could from the heavy boots.

"Williams, I do not believe that you are a man who would allow anyone to use his room without his knowledge."

It was the cultured voice that spoke.

"Why don't you make it easier for yourself by telling the truth. We know that your part in these murders is a minor one. As far as I can tell it seems you are only guilty of wasting a policeman's time and allowing your room to be used by someone wishing to change their clothes. Admittedly you may have committed an additional offense by allowing that person to wear your uniform. But I do not think that you can be held culpable for what that person did whilst wearing that uniform, nor for what they did after leaving your room dressed as a woman."

Parsons leaned forward and draped a black veil over the front edge of the desk.

"My colleague found this in your room when he searched it yesterday," he said. "Does it happen to be yours?"

Williams attempted to sit up. He shook his head.

"Do you know who it belongs to?"

Williams shook his head again.

"Pick him up."

Williams was dragged to his feet and the stool placed under him.

"I will repeat the question, Williams, and this time I want you to answer 'yes' or 'no'. Do you know who this black veil belongs to?"

"No, sir."

"Williams," the cultured voice continued. "I'm very disappointed in you. I had thought you would see sense and tell me the truth. But I can see that you have decided otherwise. That is unfortunate, as I don't imagine that things will go as well for you as they might have had you been cooperative."

Parsons could see from the troubled expression on Williams' face that he was having difficulty in deciding how much he should say. It was time to put him in a position where he had little option.

"Then let me tell you what I think happened that night while you were on Lambeth Embankment with Constable Clough. I think that during that time a man came to your room and put on your uniform. Then he got into Oliver Bates' cab and was conveyed to Lambeth Bridge where he shot Lord Sayers to death. Bates then picked this man up at a prearranged location and took him back to your room where the man put on a black dress, a black cloak, and a thick veil before leaving with Bates again, this time for Chester Place. It was there that the man murdered General Latham before once again returning to your room to change his clothes. I think it was likely that you were given the task of disposing of the dress, the cloak and the veil. And, I regret to say, that you failed to do that job well, as Sergeant Harris found the veil. That carelessness could prove disastrous for you, Williams, as most juries would consider that you were not merely an innocent bystander, but a person deeply implicated in a plot to murder both Lord Sayers and General Latham."

"But I wasn't," shouted Williams. "I swear to God that I never knew what was going to happen."

"I may believe you, Williams. But I'm not sure that you will convince a jury. They may prefer to think that you knew the details of the plan all along. They may prefer to think that by allowing a murderer to use your room to change his clothes and by distracting a policeman whilst on duty you were in fact part of a conspiracy. If they believe that you will hang. That is, of course, unless you are prepared to tell me the name of the person who murdered those two men. In which case I may well be able to convince my superiors that you were no more than a foolish man who did as he was asked to help out an old comrade. But before I can do that you must tell me the murderer's name."

At first Parsons thought that Williams would call his bluff. The evidence against him, Parsons knew, was thin and based on a chain of suppositions. But if Williams did not talk there was no alternative but to continue with the questioning until he did.

"Of course, we can spend the rest of the night here, Williams," he said allowing the hint of a threat to creep into his voice, "and the two gentlemen behind you can continue to refine their footballing skills. Think about that for a few minutes, Williams, and while you're doing that let me give you something else to consider. A Webley revolver of the sort used by the army was recently found in the Thames near Lambeth Bridge. It is now at Scotland Yard, and doubtless the serial number will allow us to identify from which regiment this revolver, and indeed, the murderer, came. If it actually allows us to identify the murderer then we have no further use of your confession. By then it will be too late. You will simply be regarded as a conspirator in a dastardly plot to murder important people, and you will be considered to be as guilty as the man who shot Lord Sayers to death and stabbed General Latham with an *iklwa*. And for that Williams, you will hang."

Williams eyes opened wide in terror.

"But he told us the revolver could not be traced," he said.

"Who, Williams? Who told you a lie like that?"

"Regimental Sergeant Major Whitehead, sir," said Williams, his voice becoming increasingly distraught. "He said no one would ever be able to trace the revolver even if they found it. How could he lie to us like that?"

Williams, Parsons could see, was on the point of crying.

"I knew nothing of what he was planning or what he did until afterwards, sir," he said, as tears began to mingle with the sweat and blood on his face. "Then what could I do?"

Williams paused, as though expecting sympathy for the dilemma in which he claimed to have been in; and when no one spoke he continued to plead his innocence.

"Bates knew all about it, sir. It was Bates that gave Mr. Whitehead a ride to Lambeth Bridge and it was Bates who took him to the general's house."

Parsons could barely conceal his delight. This was the confirmation he had been seeking. There was just one other issue, and then he had got all the information he needed.

"And the bombs, Williams? Who was responsible for the bombs at Kensington Barracks and Sir William Fawkus' house? From the description I have of the man seen running away from the barracks it could well have been you."

"Oh, no, sir. That was Sergeant Oakes, sir. I was still on duty."

"Of course you were, Williams," Parsons said quietly. "How could I forget that?"

Parsons addressed the policemen standing in the shadows.

"I think we can release Williams from his manacles now. And will one of you find him a more comfortable chair?"

Then he turned to Williams once more.

"Now I'm going to write down all that you told me, and then you're going sign it."

"Yes, sir," said Williams disconsolately.

———————

THE SECOND INTERVIEW with Bates was shorter and, for Bates, less painful. When informed that Williams had signed a confession that included a statement about Bates' involvement in the murders of Sayers and Latham, the cabman knew he had little option but to sign a statement of his own admitting his role. And like Williams he pleaded ignorance of what Whitehead had been planning.

"A GOOD NIGHT'S work, wouldn't you agree, Harris?" Parsons said, as they both sat drinking mugs of strong tea. "I was sorry we had to revert to violence, but sometimes it can't be avoided. And as you said at the start, in this case we didn't have an option. We were up against a deadline. If Whitehead had discovered that either Bates or Williams had been arrested he would know that the game was up. From what he knew of the two men he would know that sooner or later one of them would talk."

"I expect both Bates and Williams have experienced worse things than happened here tonight, sir," said Harris. "They were soldiers after all, and apart from what they had to do while on active service I'd be surprised if they hadn't been involved in a fight or two after having a few drinks. But it takes one sort of courage to fight when the odds are even. It's quite another when one can't fight back. As a policeman Williams knew that. He knew what to expect. And we were both certain he would talk faster than Bates."

"They were both aware of what would happen if they didn't turn Queen's Evidence," Parsons replied. "They would both hang. As the French say: *sauve qui peut*. Save yourself if you're able. That's what they both decided to do."

"Why do you think they helped Whitehead in the first place, sir?"

"I'm still not sure about that, Harris. Maybe we'll find out after we arrest him. But before doing that I'll have to speak with the Duty Inspector. We're going to need reinforcements. I don't think you and I want to run the risk of arresting Whitehead by ourselves."

56

IT WAS UNLIKELY that the inhabitants of Eaton Square had ever seen two police carriages outside one of the houses in their exclusive corner of London; and it was well for the reputation of the Arbuthnots that at six in the morning it was barely light and the steady rain had reduced the visibility even further.

An expression of perturbed incredulity crossed the normally composed face of the Arbuthnot's butler at the sight of the familiar figure of Inspector Parsons on the front steps and the two police carriages in the street behind him. Grayson had not been long dressed himself. He glanced anxiously around the square to confirm that none of the inhabitants had ventured abroad at this early hour. But, regardless of that small blessing, he knew that there were still enough witnesses amongst the servants in other households who were already about their morning tasks, to ensure that the reputation of the Arbuthnot household was forever sullied.

"I want to see Colonel Arbuthnot at once," said Parsons as he walked past Grayson into the annular hall. "If he is dressed, well and good, but if he is not I will see him in his night clothes. One way or another I wish to speak to him without delay."

It was only then that Grayson noticed with some distaste that Parsons himself was scarcely presentable. His long unruly hair was unbrushed, his face was unshaven, and there was a general dishevelment about him that suggested that he had either not gone to bed or had slept in his clothes. At first Grayson feared that the small inspector might have been drinking, but then he remembered the police carriages.

"I will inform the colonel of your wishes, sir," he said with extreme reluctance. "But I cannot guarantee that he will see you at this early hour."

"Grayson," Parsons said as calmly as he could. "I realize that your unfortunate role in this household is that of an intermediary. But if Colonel Arbuthnot is not here within ten minutes I will go and find him myself. I will also see that you are arrested for obstructing the police. And I'm sure you have no wish to be taken into custody again."

Parsons would never know what Grayson said to his master, but Arbuthnot appeared in a silk dressing gown well within the allotted time. He was, if anything, even more incensed than his butler at the police presence.

"What's all this about, Parsons?" he said indignantly. "Whatever brings you here at this ungodly hour?"

"I think it might be wise for me to explain that to you in private, colonel," Parsons said.

"If you insist, inspector," said Arbuthnot. "But it had better be good. Thank you, Grayson," he said dismissively. "That will be all."

Grayson reluctantly returned to his morning duties, casting a last anxious glance in the direction of Parsons and Colonel Arbuthnot as he opened the door behind the staircase that separated the servants' quarters from the remainder of the household.

"I'm on my way to the barracks to arrest RSM Whitehead for murder," Parsons explained to an astonished Arbuthnot. "I've no time, nor do I wish, to explain the details to you now. You will learn them soon enough. For the moment you will just have to accept that the evidence I have against him is conclusive, and as you are his commanding officer I would like you to be present when I arrest him."

In spite of the seriousness of the situation Parsons allowed himself a smile.

"I can offer you a ride in one of the police carriages, colonel," he said. But doubtless you will prefer to make your own way to the barracks."

"Thank you for the kind offer, Parsons," Arbuthnot replied. "But I prefer the latter. I'll have my horse saddled right away, and allowing for the time it will take me to dress I should be at the barracks within half an hour."

"Then you will probably be there as soon as us, colonel. Do you happen to know the RSM's routine? Where can we expect to find him at this time of the morning?"

"Whitehead's an early riser. He'll almost certainly be in one of the barrack blocks inspecting the men's breakfast. Whitehead has an irksome habit of insisting that the soldiers eat well. For some reason he seems to think it's good for their morale. But he's a good man nonetheless, and I wouldn't want to see him humiliated in front of the men. If you'll await my arrival before taking any action I'll send word for him to come to my office. It will no doubt come as a great surprise for him to hear that I'm in the barracks, as with the exception of the mornings that Cordell and Simpson were found dead I don't think I've ever been there before nine."

"Very good, colonel," said Parsons. "When I arrive I'll position a police carriage at each entrance to the barracks, and I'll have a couple of men with me near the main entrance. But until I hear from you I won't enter."

57

THE SOLDIER ON guard duty at the main gate of the barracks might have been forgiven if he thought he was dreaming when he saw his commanding officer riding towards him on his handsome black stallion. It was unheard of for Colonel Arbuthnot to arrive at the barracks at this hour. A more observant soldier would also have noticed that Arbuthnot's attire was less than sartorial, an equally unlikely event in one who invariably paid such meticulous attention to his appearance.

"Fetch the Guard Commander," Arbuthnot instructed the incredulous sentry, and waited impatiently for the unfortunate sergeant in charge of the night guard to emerge from the Guard Room buttoning his tunic.

"There are a group of policemen on the opposite side of the road," Arbuthnot said. "When I send for them I want you to escort them to my office. In the meantime have one of your men open up regimental headquarters and send another to find the RSM. I'm sure you'll find him inspecting the men's breakfast in one of the barrack blocks. Give Mr. Whitehead my compliments and ask him to come to my office immediately."

———————

"MAY I ASK what this is all about, colonel," said Whitehead, when he saw Parsons, Harris and two policemen. The fact that his commanding officer was unshaven and appeared to have dressed in a hurry was also not lost on him, nor that Parsons and Harris looked as though they had been up all night. Something quite out of the usual had clearly occurred. And that greatly concerned the RSM. In Whitehead's carefully orchestrated life there was little room for surprises.

"I'm sure Inspector Parsons will explain in his own good time, RSM," Arbuthnot said calmly. "In the meantime, perhaps you would be so kind as to take a seat."

Parsons first impression of Arbuthnot's office was that it was at least three times the size of Superintendent Jeffries' office in Scotland Yard. But unlike that of Jeffries, it appeared little used. The large desk with its leather inlay was as spotless as the scrubbed and well polished wooden floor and the white-painted walls. A painting of the Queen in her younger days hung on the wall behind the desk, flanked on one side by a red, yellow and blue regimental flag and on the other by the red, white and blue of the United Kingdom.

Two windows faced west towards Church Street, and two on the opposite side of the room overlooked the parade ground.

"I'd prefer to stand, sir," said Whitehead, visibly surprised by his commanding officer's unaccustomed civility. During previous visits to the office he had never once been offered a seat.

"And I would prefer that you sit, Mr. Whitehead," said Parsons politely. "What I have to say is extremely serious and may take some time."

Whitehead bridled at the request, and was on the point of challenging it, when Arbuthnot spoke.

"Do as the inspector says, and sit down, RSM. I want to hear what this is all about as much as you."

Whitehead sat on one of the brown leather arm chairs in front of the colonel's desk, half facing towards Arbuthnot, and half facing Parsons in the arm chair opposite. He removed his hat and placed it on the floor beside his cane, which he had previously placed exactly parallel to the side of the chair.

"Before we start proceedings, colonel," Parsons said, "may I ask that you send one of the guard to fetch Sergeant Oakes? No doubt at this time of the morning he is breakfasting in the Sergeants' Mess. Tell him that the RSM wishes to see him in his office. One of my men will be waiting for him and will ensure that he stays there until we need him."

Arbuthnot waved his hand dismissively at the young soldier who had opened his office.

"Do as the inspector says." he ordered.

The soldier left, accompanied by one of the policemen. The other policeman took up a position by the closed door. Harris leaned his tired body gratefully against the wall opposite Whitehead, his eyes fixed intently upon the RSM, and noting with some satisfaction the anxious expression on the RSM's face at the mention of Oakes.

"With your permission, colonel," Parsons said. "I will now describe the events that have brought us all here this morning."

He took a sheaf of papers from his coat pocket.

"Let me start with the evening of the twenty-second of October. That was the night that Lord Frederick Sayers and General Sir Maxwell Latham were both murdered. Earlier that evening, around half past six, Mr. Whitehead had visited the general's house in Chester Place with a bottle of brandy for Bradley, the general's servant. The reason for this generous act, so Bradley informed me, was for the RSM and he to toast a famous action in which they had fought together. I believe the action concerned was at Nyumaga. Is that not so, Mr. Whitehead?"

"That is correct, sir. It was a famous victory, and one worthy of celebration, and it's a custom of mine on such occasions to have a glass or two with old comrades."

"A commendable custom," Parsons said, "and one I'm sure that an old soldier like Bradley much appreciated, especially as he is very partial to brandy. But when Bradley informed me of this later he said he had no recollection of this particular battle being in October. He attributed that to his poor memory. At the time I thought nothing of it. But, in fact, Bradley's memory had served him well. When I checked the date for myself I discovered that the action at Nyumaga was not fought in the month of October, but in January 1878. So I began to wonder why it was that the RSM had chosen to celebrate it when he did."

Parsons leaned back in his chair and steepled his fingers. In spite of his tiredness he was beginning to enjoy himself. It was at times like this that he knew his mother was right. He should have chosen the law as a career. He could well imagine himself as a prosecuting counsel making a closing address to the jury.

"Now you may think that such a small mistake over dates is of little consequence," he said. "And in isolation I would agree with you. But when a series of similar events of seemingly little importance follow one another they become something altogether more serious."

Whitehead opened his mouth as though to speak. But then he thought better of it. At this stage of the proceedings he decided it more prudent to remain silent and see where all this was leading.

If Parsons noticed the movement from Whitehead he chose to ignore it, instead he said: "Now I think that this visit served three purposes. First of all it enabled Mr. Whitehead to exchange a few words with the general. It would have been a perfectly normal thing for him to do. After all the two men had served together in Africa when the general was Mr. Whitehead's commanding officer. By all accounts they had a great deal of respect for one another. But, more importantly for Mr. Whitehead, his visit established beyond doubt that the general was alive at the time of his visit. The second reason the RSM went to Chester Place was to ensure that when he returned later he could be sure of finding Bradley drunk. He was well enough acquainted with Bradley's drinking habits to know that he would not be content until the brandy bottle was empty. And the RSM was correct in making that assumption, because when Bradley went in search of help after discovering the general's body, the policeman who came to his assistance noted that he appeared to be inebriated. And finally, the third reason for the RSM's visit was to enable him to take the key to the front door from the drawer in the hat stand when Bradley was otherwise occupied. Mr. Whitehead would have need of that key when he returned later that night."

"This is outrageous, sir," Whitehead said angrily to Arbuthnot. "I don't deny that I took a bottle of brandy to Bradley. And if I was mistaken about the date of Nyumaga that is just an unfortunate mistake. We all get our dates confused at one time or another. But the other insinuations are downright lies. There are several witnesses who can confirm I was drinking that evening with Sergeant Oakes."

Arbuthnot looked questioningly towards Parsons.

"Well, inspector," he said. "You are making some very serious allegations against Mr. Whitehead. I hope you can substantiate them."

"Rest assured that I can, colonel," Parsons said.

He held up some of the papers.

"I have here two signed statements from Mr. Whitehead's accomplices, Oliver Bates and Morgan Williams, that are very precise in their description of Mr. Whitehead's movements that night. You may not remember these two gentlemen, colonel, but they were once soldiers in this very regiment. In fact they are survivors of Captain Simpson's ill-fated patrol into Zululand. However, they have since left the army. Bates is a now a cab driver and Williams a policeman. But with your indulgence, colonel, I would like you to hear the full story. You may not be willing merely to accept the word of men like Bates and Williams against that of your RSM. And I would not expect you to release Mr. Whitehead into my custody until you are convinced of his guilt."

Arbuthnot nodded his agreement.

"Please continue, inspector," he said.

"Mr. Whitehead is quite correct when he said that he was drinking with Sergeant Oakes in the *Queen Adelaide* in Victoria Road that evening," Parsons said. "The landlord remembers them both being there. But if this was an attempt by Mr. Whitehead to establish an alibi for himself I'm afraid to say that it was not altogether successful.

Although the landlord and his staff are prepared to say that both Mr. Whitehead and Sergeant Oakes were present on the night in question, none of them will swear that both men were there for the whole evening. From what I learned at the *Queen Adelaide* it appears that Oakes left the pub at one stage, and shortly after his return Mr. Whitehead also departed. Of course, the landlord cannot be expected to be precise about the times of these comings and goings, as there were several other people in the lounge bar at the time; but, as I said previously, I have a statement from Bates that makes everything quite clear. You see Bates acted as the RSM's personal driver for the most part of that evening, and he knows exactly where Mr. Whitehead went from the time he collected him near the barracks prior to taking him to Chester Place to deliver Bradley's brandy, to when he returned the RSM to the barracks in the early hours of the next morning. There is, of course, no record of the RSM entering the barracks at that time. And that is hardly surprising. As one of a select group with keys to the back gate, he would doubtless have chosen to use that entrance."

Parsons allowed the full significance of his statement to register with Arbuthnot before continuing.

"Bates has also confirmed that he collected Sergeant Oakes from the *Queen Adelaide* at eight forty-five, and that he had in his cab two explosive devices that Mr. Whitehead had previously given him. Bates first took Oakes to Kensington High Street and then to Pembroke Road, and although he claims that he did not see what Oakes actually did when he left the cab, I have little doubt that it was Oakes who planted the bombs at the barracks and at Sir William Fawkus' residence. Oakes certainly answers the description given to me by a witness who lives near the barracks of a man seen fleeing from the scene shortly after the first device was detonated. No one, fortunately, was injured in either attack. But it was never intended that anyone would. The two bombs were no more than a side show: part of an elaborate attempt to blame the Fenians for Lord Frederick Sayers' death."

Parsons paused to confirm that he still had Arbuthnot's full attention.

"But I will come to that later," he said. "For the moment let us stay with Bates returning Oakes to the *Queen Adelaide* and then taking Mr. Whitehead to Constable Morgan Williams' lodgings in Kennington."

Parsons turned and spoke to Harris.

"I think this is an opportune time for you to fetch the two newspapers we spoke of, Sergeant Harris," he said, noticing with some satisfaction the look of confusion on Arbuthnot's face and the growing concern on Whitehead's. "We will need them before much longer."

"I'm on my way, sir," said Harris with a grin.

"As I was saying," Parsons said after Harris had left the room, "Bates took Mr. Whitehead to William's lodgings. Constable Williams was there at the time, although he now claims that he knew nothing of what the RSM had planned. However, in his statement he does admit to allowing the

RSM to wear his uniform; an action that I'm sure you're aware, colonel, is an offense in itself, although admittedly a relatively minor one. What is far more serious as far as Williams is concerned is that he later prevented Constable Clough of Lambeth Division from performing his duty by needlessly distracting him. At the time, and we are now speaking of somewhere between ten fifteen and ten forty-five, Clough was patrolling Lambeth Embankment, and were it not for Williams might well have been close enough to Lambeth Bridge when Lord Sayers was shot for him to have seen what had happened and even to have made an arrest."

Parsons directed his next words to Arbuthnot.

"As you may remember from the newspaper reports of the time, colonel," he said. "The general consensus was that Lord Sayers' assailant was a policeman. My colleagues in Scotland Yard were certainly of that opinion, but were unable to find anyone answering the description of that policeman, either in Lambeth division or elsewhere. The reason for that is simple. Lord Sayers' murderer was none other than Mr. Whitehead dressed in Constable Williams' uniform and cape. It would have been difficult for me to prove that were it not for Bates' confession. It was Bates, of course, who drove Mr. Whitehead, dressed in Williams' uniform, over Lambeth Bridge towards the Houses of Parliament, and waited with him for Lord Sayers to appear and begin walking towards the bridge. The two men then followed Lord Sayers to Lambeth Bridge, where they overtook him on their way to a quiet back street on the Lambeth side of the river. It was from there that Mr. Whitehead returned to the bridge to commit the first of his murders."

Whitehead again attempted to interrupt Parsons.

"Sir, I must protest at this nonsense," he said to Arbuthnot.

"You will do nothing of the kind, Mr. Whitehead," Arbuthnot replied irritably. "The inspector is entitled to make his case. If you have a quarrel with anything he says you will have the opportunity of defending yourself later in a court of law."

He turned to Parsons.

"Please continue, inspector," he said.

"Putting the page of parliamentary proceedings inside Lord Sayer's mouth was a masterstroke, in my opinion," said Parsons. "Most people, and I'm afraid to say that includes many of my colleagues at Scotland Yard, assumed that the page had been torn at random from *Hansard* and merely indicated that his lordship had been assassinated for his strong political views. In other words, it was assumed that the Fenians had murdered him for his outspoken attacks on Home Rule for Ireland. It was only after doing some research of my own that I discovered that the actual page of *Hansard* found in Lord Sayers' mouth referred to a speech he had made about Africa. Why that particular page was chosen will become clear later. But unless Mr. Whitehead cares to enlighten us now I fear we will never know for certain why it was he took the risk of drawing the attention of someone like me to events in Africa. Unless, of course, it was simply his way of making his victim literally eat his words."

Parsons allowed the RSM the opportunity to respond. But he said nothing, and when Parsons engaged Whitehead's eyes, unlike on the occasion of their first meeting, it was the RSM who lowered his gaze.

"But for whatever his reason, Mr. Whitehead's decision was a mistake," Parsons said. "A small one admittedly, but as I have already implied, it was not the only one that Mr. Whitehead was to make. It was also a mistake for him to return to the scene of his crime to admire his handiwork. Had he not done so no one would ever have assumed that Lord Sayers' murderer was wearing a policeman's uniform. And I would never have thought of making a connection between Mr. Whitehead and Constable Williams."

"What about General Latham, inspector?" Arbuthnot asked. "I thought you said that the RSM was involved in that murder as well."

"Oh, indeed he was, colonel," replied Parsons. "And that particular murder required careful planning, accurate timing, and great ingenuity. Not unlike a military manoevre, I'm sure you will agree. It also required knowledge of General Latham's affaire with Venetta Cordell. And that needed one of Mr. Whitehead's most remarkable skills: his ability to acquire a vast array of information from a variety of sources. He once boasted to me of that special ability of his. I seem to recall him saying that as RSM it was important that he had eyes and ears everywhere. And the more I learned about these murders, the more true I found that to be."

Parsons addressed himself to Whitehead again.

"For that quality you have my utmost respect, sir," he said. "I admire a man with your curiosity. However, when one gains a reputation for that you must accept that one day it may rebound upon you. You see, it is one thing to press information from servants like Bradley, or Colonel Cordell's servant, Pound, or even from Sergeant Barnard, the Officers' Mess steward. But it is quite another matter when those same people confide in someone like me who is every bit as inquisitive as yourself."

"You see, colonel," Parsons said, turning to Arbuthnot. "It was Mr. Whitehead's curiosity that enabled him not only to find out about the relationship between General Latham and Mrs. Cordell, but also to discover their means of communication. And by introducing a message of his own into that arrangement he persuaded Mrs. Cordell to go to Chester Place on the same night as him, and even managed to make it appear that she had murdered the general."

Harris returned at that moment carrying two newspapers. He passed them to Parsons, and whispered a few words to him at the same time.

"Excellent, Harris," Parsons said. "As ever your timing is perfect. I was just about to explain to Colonel Arbuthnot the role played by the newsagent in Silver Street, and the use that was made of these two newspapers in compiling the messages that passed between the general and Mrs. Cordell."

Parsons described how it was a common practice for small newsagents such as the one in Silver Street to rent private post boxes for messages of a personal nature; and how it was one such post box that General Latham and Venetta Cordell had used to communicate. He explained that they were circumspect enough not to go to the newsagent themselves, but instead had used Bradley and Mrs. Cordell's maid, Edith, as their messengers. But even that attempt at discretion had failed, as both Bradley and Edith had attracted the attention of the many soldiers from the barracks who used the newsagent; Bradley because he had once been a member of the regiment, and Edith because she was so pretty."

"So the information eventually reached Mr. Whitehead," Parsons said, "and it raised his curiosity to such an extent that he decided to send Bates and his cab to Silver Street to investigate. Bates went there on several occasions, and although he might have thought that no one noticed him, both Bradley and the newsagent remembered him being there because of Bates' handsome chestnut mare and its distinctive white blaze and white socks. And once I knew that, I was able to persuade Bates to admit his role in keeping watch on the newsagent's and of reporting the comings and goings of Bradley and

Mrs. Cordell's maid to the RSM. Bates also told me that he actually dropped Mr. Whitehead at the shop on the Sunday evening prior to General Latham's death. This was also confirmed by the newsagent. And that is when the RSM delivered the message that persuaded Venetta Cordell to go to Chester Place on the night of the twenty-second of October."

"However would the RSM have done that without running the risk of being recognized?" asked Arbuthnot.

"The same way that he made it appear that Mrs. Cordell had murdered General Latham, colonel," said Parsons. "He disguised himself as a woman."

Arbuthnot's expression changed rapidly from one of surprise to one of disgust, and he appeared to be on the point of making a comment when Parsons distracted his attention by handing him some of the messages Venetta Cordell had received from General Latham.

"Look at the last message to Mrs. Cordell, colonel," he said. "Do you notice anything that is different from the others?"

"Only that the time has been written in manuscript. In all the others each of the words appears to have been cut from a newspaper."

"Very good, colonel. And what about the typesets?"

Arbuthnot studied the messages again.

"I'd say the words used in this last message had been cut from a different newspaper than the rest."

Parsons passed him the two newspapers he'd received from Harris.

"Excellent, colonel," he said. "You're absolutely right. Now take a look at those newspapers. General Latham, as you might expect of a man in his position, read the *Times*; and I think you'll agree that the words used in most of the messages match the typeface of today's *Times* that Sergeant Harris has kindly collected from the Officers' Mess. Mr. Whitehead, on the other hand, as his servant has just informed Harris, favors the *Daily Chronicle*; and if you care to compare the words on the last message Mrs. Cordell received with the newspaper that has just been collected from the RSM's room you will see that the two typefaces are identical."

Whitehead interrupted angrily.

"And what the hell does that prove? Am I the only person in London who reads the *Chronicle*?"

"Not at all, Mr. Whitehead," said Parsons calmly. "Taken in isolation your choice of a daily newspaper is a matter of little importance. Rather like the page from *Hansard* found in the Lord Frederick Sayers' mouth, and the bottle of brandy you gave Bradley. But, as I've said before, when all these relatively trivial matters are considered together they become something far more significant. My reason for bringing these facts to Colonel Arbuthnot's attention is simply to illustrate your cunning. Had I merely wanted to inform him that you murdered General Latham as well as Lord Sayers, I would simply have told him that Bates has already admitted taking you from

Williams' lodgings to the general's house dressed as a woman. And in the black cloak and heavy veil you were wearing you bore a passing resemblance to Venetta Cordell. It was a likeness that would probably have been good enough to convince Bradley had you encountered him. But as it happened, as you had planned, by the time you arrived Bradley had already consumed most, if not all, of the brandy you had given him. So Bradley was unaware that you had entered the house using the key you had previously taken. Your few words in French for the benefit of a passing policeman could not, of course, have been planned. But they were, nevertheless, most opportune. They substantiated Bradley's story of Venetta Cordell visiting the house, and they confirmed her guilt. But we now know that by the time she arrived General Latham was already dead: stabbed to death with the *iklwa* you had previously taken from Colonel Cordell's study."

Parsons clasped his hands over his chest and inclined his head towards Whitehead.

"As I said earlier, Mr. Whitehead, we have Bates' confession to tie all these loose ends together. But even without Bates' evidence I regret to say that your choice of weapon to murder General Latham was somewhat at odds with your attempt to impersonate a woman. And I am obliged to Sergeant Harris' wife for bringing this to my attention. Not only did Mrs. Harris consider an *iklwa* a most unlikely weapon for a woman, in her opinion no woman would have used it in the manner it was employed. Armed with such a weapon, a woman would invariably have chosen to stab her victim with a downward blow; whereas you, no doubt had seen how an African native thrusts his short stabbing spear beneath his victim's ribcage and upwards towards his heart. There was also the matter of your strength. Had a member of the weaker sex like Mrs. Cordell stabbed the general, I would have expected him to have grasped the shaft of the *iklwa* and fallen forward. But such was the strength behind the thrust that you exerted he was driven backwards. It was the thrust of a trained soldier like yourself. And there is one final point about the *iklwa* you used. Like a good soldier burnishing his bayonet before going into battle, you had taken the precaution of sharpening its blade. I don't imagine any woman would have thought of that."

Before continuing, Parsons allowed himself a brief smile of satisfaction at the forlorn expression on Whitehead's face.

"You also made an error in relying upon Constable Williams to dispose of the dress, the cloak and the veil. Although he remembered to burn the dress and the cloak he unfortunately overlooked the veil. Sergeant Harris found it under the bed when he searched his room yesterday."

Parsons addressed himself once more to Arbuthnot.

"And now we come to the murders of Colonel Cordell and Captain Simpson. And I have to admit that the evidence against Mr. Whitehead for these two deaths is far more circumstantial. But, nevertheless, I think it compelling enough to convince a jury."

"But I thought Cordell and Simpson had committed suicide," Arbuthnot said. "They both left notes, and as far as I could see each of them had good reason for taking his own life."

"I'm sure a lot of people would agree with you, colonel," said Parsons. "But from the first I suspected otherwise. For a start there are the suicide notes. Both were extremely informative, firstly for what they actually said, and secondly for the fact that they were printed in childish capitals to disguise the author's hand. In my experience it is very unusual for anyone to print a suicide note unless they are barely literate. And that did not apply to either Cordell or Simpson."

Parsons searched through his papers for the two notes.

"I have little doubt that neither Colonel Cordell or Captain Simpson wrote these notes," he said. "Suicide notes are, after all, deeply personal communications from people in the deepest despair and on the point of taking their own lives, and they are intended to be read by those nearest and dearest. Apart from that they often give an indication of what has driven the authors of these notes to take such a terrible and final step. But in the case of Cordell and Simpson that doesn't seem to have happened. Cordell's note says: *'I can no longer live with that lie, Audley'*. Simpson's follows a similar theme. It says: *'That lie destroyed us both'*. If these notes were indeed the final thoughts of these two gentlemen, then they are extremely unusual; and I confess that I had great difficulty when I first read them in seeing any connection between the contents of each note and the likely reason each man might have had for taking his life. As far as I could see both men had far more to contend with than an ill defined lie, and I became convinced that they only made sense if it is assumed that the murderer had written them."

Parsons leaned back in his chair, steepled his fingers, and directed his next words towards Whitehead.

"Perhaps," he said, "rather in a similar fashion to the page of *Hansard* found in Lord Frederick Sayers' mouth, and the Zulu *iklwa* used to kill General Latham, Mr. Whitehead was using the suicide notes to explain his reason for killing the two men. Of course, he did not intend anyone to actually understand what he was saying. It was merely a game of his own that he was playing, and he was arrogant enough to think that no one else would understand it. Especially Sergeant Harris and me. That was why he felt confident enough to summon us to the barracks after Cordell and Simpson's bodies were discovered rather than merely inform the local police. He chose to tell us because he knew we were already investigating General Latham's murder; and he had seen how he had successfully duped us into arresting the wrong person."

"You're beginning to lose me, Parsons," said Arbuthnot. "Spell it out in words a simple soldier can understand."

"With pleasure, colonel. Allow me to remind you again of what was in the notes. The first, allegedly that of Colonel Cordell, said: *'I can no longer go on living with that lie, Audley'*. What lie you might ask yourself? And why was the note addressed to Captain Simpson?"

"In normal circumstances I'd expect a man to write a note to his wife," Arbuthnot said. "But in Cordell's case the marriage was a sham. We all knew that. It was common knowledge that Cordell had been overly foolish in his haste to marry, no doubt because he felt that as commanding officer he needed a wife. Well, so he did. Every commanding officer should have a wife with some social standing to run his household for him and help entertain. But Venetta was the wrong woman. For a start she was a foreigner, she had no influential friends, and, as far as I know, little money to speak of. And to cap it all she had an affair with Cordell's half-brother. On the other hand Simpson and Cordell had been close friends. There had even been allegations of a homosexual relationship, although I must say that I never saw any evidence of that. Nevertheless, it's not unreasonable to think of Cordell dwelling upon that friendship rather than his disastrous marriage at the time he was contemplating suicide. Especially after the very public and bitter argument he'd just had with Simpson."

"That is an excellent summary of the facts, colonel," said Parsons. "But it only makes sense if Cordell wrote the note. And as I've already said, I don't believe he did. The note was written by Mr.

Whitehead, a fact that becomes even more apparent when you understand why he chose to write *that* lie rather than *this* one."

"Parsons, for Heaven's sake," said Arbuthnot in exasperation. "What are you getting at? *This* lie or *that*. Whatever is the difference?"

"There is a great deal of difference, colonel. You see, if the murderer had written *this* lie he would have been suggesting an event that was current. Like Cordell's unfortunate marriage or his tortured relationship with Simpson. On the other hand, *that* lie suggests an event that had happened in his past. I found it particularly instructive that the same word was used again in Simpson's note. If you remember it said: *'That lie destroyed us both'*.

Parsons smiled triumphantly.

"It was only yesterday that I learned what *that lie* actually meant. Only then did the motive for Cordell and Simpson's murders become finally clear. It was the same motive that had driven Mr. Whitehead to murder Sayers and Latham"

"Do we have to listen to this nonsense any longer, sir?" Whitehead interjected. "It's quite clear that Inspector Parsons has taken leave of his senses."

"Let me be the judge of that RSM," Arbuthnot said coldly. "If I get any more interruptions from you I'll have you taken to the Guard Room. And as things stand I have no wish to inflict that indignity upon you. Inspector Parsons, of course, may ultimately have other ideas."

Arbuthnot turned to Parsons.

"I hope you will be getting to the point soon, inspector," he said in mild exasperation. "This is beginning to sound more like an English lesson than a police investigation."

"Please bear with me a little longer, colonel," Parsons said. "As I said it was only yesterday that I discovered what the lie in the suicide notes actually referred to. You see Cordell Simpson quarreled about it shortly before Cordell's death."

"I heard no talk of any lie, Parsons," said Arbuthnot. "And I was in the Mess on the afternoon they quarreled."

"As were many others, colonel. But I am not referring to the angry words that Cordell and Simpson exchanged in public. I am talking about what was said shortly afterwards in the corridor outside the anteroom. And there was only one witness to that. Sergeant Barnard, the Officers' Mess steward. He heard the two men arguing about a lie and the theft of some money that had led to a soldier being unjustly punished. Barnard, of course, would not have known what they were talking about, as he was not in Africa at the time."

Parsons gathered up his papers, rose from his chair, and began slowly pacing around the room. In spite of the exhilaration he felt at finally being able to expound his conclusions he could feel the onset of fatigue, and knew that there was a danger he might lose his train of thought were he to remain sitting.

"You see, colonel," he said "Simpson had taken money from Cordell without his permission.

And that had led to Cordell's servant being accused of theft. Simpson could have admitted his guilt. But he chose not to. Perhaps he was too embarrassed. We shall never know. But because of his moral cowardice an innocent soldier was punished. In fact he was flogged; a very severe punishment, in my opinion, for what seems to have been a relatively trivial offense. But theft from a colleague, I am led to understand, is considered to be a serious offense in the army. And in this case the theft was construed as being an especially serious matter, as it was a breach of trust by a company commander's servant."

"I remember the incident now that you come to mention it, Parsons," Arbuthnot said. "I was never one for punishments of that sort. In my opinion there are better ways of dealing with such matters, even where theft is involved. But Latham believed in the lash. He'd served in the Crimea and in India during the mutiny, and they flogged unmercifully in those days."

"And that is the very point, colonel," said Parsons, interrupting his pacing at a point directly opposite Arbuthnot. "It was Colonel Latham, as he then was, who sanctioned the punishment; and it was Cordell's company sergeant major who administered it. And at that time that was Mr. Whitehead."

"You're absolutely right, Parsons," said Arbuthnot. "Now that I recall, it was the RSM. But I still fail to see any connection between these suicide notes and the flogging."

Parsons resumed his pacing.

"When I spoke with Sergeant Barnard yesterday," he said, "he confirmed that the RSM had questioned him about anything significant that had occurred in the Officers' Mess after General Latham's funeral. Mr. Whitehead frequently asked for information of that sort. And in that way he learned about the quarrels between Cordell and Simpson; both the one in the anteroom, and more importantly, the one that only Barnard had been privy to. Sergeant Barnard, I regret to say, has been a constant source of such information for the RSM. I don't think you can blame Barnard for that. No doubt in his privileged position Mr. Whitehead could make life uncomfortable for the likes of Barnard if they failed to do his bidding."

Parsons paused and directed his next remarks directly at Whitehead.

"But Sergeant Barnard's latest information was more important than most," he said. "Because Mr. Whitehead had recently become aware of a tragedy in his personal life that had been very much influenced by the lie that Cordell and Simpson were arguing about."

"What in Heaven's name are you talking about, Parsons?" Arbuthnot demanded. "And what has the RSM's personal life got to do with all this?"

"I'll explain that later, colonel. For the moment just accept that Mr. Whitehead heard about Cordell and Simpson's quarrels. Of course, he knew something of the state of mind of each of the men. And it was because of that, and what he had just learned, that he decided to murder them and make it appear like suicide. He knew that there would probably never be a better time."

"My God, Parsons," said Arbuthnot. "This is beginning to sound as though you think Mr. Whitehead is some sort of monster."

"That will be for a jury to decide in due course," said Parsons. "But for the moment let me deal with the events leading up to each man's death. First Colonel Cordell. You were in the Mess the afternoon before he died and you must have seen that he was drinking far more than usual."

"Without doubt, inspector. I can't say I've ever seen him drink as much. Cordell was by nature an abstemious fellow; and I assumed, like most people, that it was just a reaction to his half-brother's death, Venetta's arrest, the ill-mannered behavior of some of his guests, and his argument with Simpson."

"I'm sure that each of them may have contributed, colonel. In the circumstances I'm sure many men would have behaved in a similar fashion. But it seems that Cordell took matters further than most. Not only did he drink to excess in the Mess, from what his servant, Pound, told me he continued drinking when he returned home. Pound said he had never seen the colonel in such a state. So I think we can assume that when Cordell finally went to bed he would have consumed enough to make him sleep soundly, and it's unlikely that he would have woken if an intruder had entered his room. Now, as it happens, Pound had neglected to lock the front door that night. He told me that he was so concerned about the colonel that he had overlooked it. But even were it locked it would have been of little consequence, as Mr. Whitehead had probably taken the spare key from the Orderly Room. From what I learned about the RSM from Major Plumb he was especially skillful in moving at night without being seen. It was a skill I can imagine him employing to enter the Cordell's house, firstly to steal an *iklwa*, and then to murder the colonel. I don't doubt he already knew the layout of the house from speaking with one or other of the servants. So, after watching the house and waiting for the servants to go to bed, it would have been a relatively simple matter for him to enter the colonel's bedroom and smother him with a pillow. After that it was just a case of running a bath and staging the suicide."

Parsons paused in front of the chair in which Whitehead was sitting, and noted for the first time a remote, almost detached expression in the RSM's eyes. If he had been listening to what he was being accused of he showed little sign.

"For a reason that I still don't really understand," Parsons said as he continued his perambulation, "The RSM chose to leave a bottle of Jameson Irish whiskey by the side of Cordell's bath, in an attempt to make it appear that his unfortunate victim was drinking from it whilst he was bleeding to death. That was another of Mr. Whitehead's unfortunate mistakes. According to Pound the colonel never drank whiskey, of the Irish or Scotch variety. Pound told me that there was a bottle of Jameson in the house. It had been bought especially for Captain Simpson when he attended the dinner party at the Cordell's. And when Pound checked, it was still in the drinks cabinet. That could mean only one thing: the bottle of Jameson found in Cordell's bathroom had been placed there by his murderer."

Parsons stopped in front of Arbuthnot' desk.

"The whiskey was a serious enough mistake," he said. "But Mr. Whitehead made one that was even greater when he cut the colonel's wrists."

Parsons showed Arbuthnot how Cordell's wounds had actually appeared and how they would have looked had they been self-inflicted.

"And you have no doubt that it was the RSM who murdered him."

"Not in the least, colonel."

"And you think that he did that just because of some stolen money. Surely there was more to it than that."

"There was indeed, colonel. And I will come to that later. First let me deal with Captain Simpson's death."

Outside on the barrack square there were the first signs of life. Soldiers were coming out of the accommodation blocks and lining up in squads in preparation for the first drill of the day. As the first words of command echoed across the parade ground the RSM instinctively turned his head in their direction.

"My boys," he muttered to himself, and shook his head sadly. "What will they do without me."

"They will survive, Mr. Whitehead," said Arbuthnot dismissively. "Just as they did before you became RSM."

Arbuthnot turned towards Parsons.

"Now, inspector," he said. "What have you got to say about Simpson's death."

Parsons returned to his chair, clasped his hands together and leaned forward.

"Captain Simpson must have been one of the last in the regiment to hear about Cordell's death," he said. "He had left the barracks before the body was discovered and did not return until much later that day, after first visiting the Plumbs, and then his parents."

Parsons could see that Arbuthnot was surprised to learn that Simpson had visited the Plumb's house.

"Simpson often visited Major and Mrs. Plumb," he explained. "He told me once how much he respected the major, and how greatly he enjoyed Mrs. Plumb's Sunday roast lunches. In fact, the Plumbs were expecting him to return for dinner on the day he died. He was going to tell them what had been decided during his visit to his parents. You see, Simpson was thinking of leaving the army. He discussed that decision both with the Plumbs and with his parents; and as he was seriously considering options for his future life I think it most unlikely that, at the same time, he was contemplating suicide. In fact that was so far from his mind that, after returning from his parents, he had actually signed himself out of Mess to attend dinner at the Plumbs. But admittedly, when he did that it was still possible that he was unaware that Cordell was dead, and had not heard what had been written in his suicide note."

"Then you admit that it was possible that Simpson did take his own life," said Arbuthnot in exasperation. "Surely he would think himself in some way responsible for Cordell's death."

"I'm sure you're right about how the unfortunate young man felt, colonel. And it's true that Simpson's state of mind, like that of Cordell, was such that he could be considered a likely candidate for suicide. And that is exactly what the RSM was assuming everyone would think. But I'm certain that Simpson did not take his own life. When I saw his body he was still holding the revolver that had killed him in his right hand with his thumb on the trigger. Admittedly, Simpson was right handed, but at the time he died he would not have chosen to use that hand. He would have been obliged to use his left. You see, colonel, on the way to visit his parents he had trapped his right thumb in the door of the railway carriage. The police surgeon has confirmed that it was badly broken and that he would have been in considerable pain. Simpson's mother had previously noticed his discomfort and advised him to visit a doctor. Had he taken her advice his thumb would no doubt have been bandaged. But it was not, and as Mr. Whitehead was unaware of the injury, after shooting Simpson he placed the revolver in the wrong hand."

Parsons noted a demented smile playing at the corners of Whitehead's mouth. It was possible that Arbuthnot was right. The RSM could well have become deranged.

"Not only was Mr. Whitehead unaware of Simpson's broken thumb, he also made the mistake of writing the suicide note before he went to his room. There was a new moon that night, and visibility was poor, much as it was on the previous night when Colonel Cordell was murdered; so that it was relatively easy for the RSM to move around the barracks without being seen. But even the RSM would have little excuse for being in the Officers' Mess in the middle of the night; and by choosing to write Simpson's suicide note before going to his room he was, doubtless, trying to save himself as much time as possible. But by using black ink and writing in childish capitals he overlooked an important aspect of Simpson's character. Simpson took great pride in his handwriting. Not only that, but he used blue ink and a special fountain pen that his parents had bought him in America. According to them, their son would never have written a note as badly as the one found on his desk. Not even with a broken thumb."

Parsons took an envelope from amongst his papers. It was the last letter that Simpson had written to his parents.

"You can see for yourself how well he wrote," he said, passing the envelope to Arbuthnot. "Can you imagine a man with such an elegant hand being satisfied with the way his so-

618

called suicide note was written. Even with a broken thumb he would have done better. And he would most assuredly have used his own pen and his own ink."

"I'm inclined to agree with you, inspector," said Arbuthnot. "But nothing you have said so far has entirely convinced me that it was the RSM who murdered either Colonel Cordell or Captain Simpson."

"I can well understand your quandary, colonel," Parsons said. "What possible motive could he have had? Until a few days ago I was at a loss to answer that question myself. But then I learned of an incident that occurred shortly after the RSM joined the army. Until recently he had been unaware of it himself."

Parsons rose from his chair again and began pacing slowly backwards and forwards in front of Arbuthnot's desk.

"I don't know how much you know about Mr. Whitehead," he said, "and I hope you will forgive me if I repeat things with which you are already familiar."

Parsons paused and gestured towards Whitehead.

"By any standard the RSM is a most remarkable man," he said. "He grew up in the squalor of the Manchester slums, and received little schooling. The army has been his salvation. It enabled him to educate himself, but more than that it allowed his natural talents of organization and command to flourish to such an extent that he has become one of the most important figures in this regiment."

Parsons addressed himself to Arbuthnot.

"I do not know whether you are aware, colonel," he said. "But Mr. Whitehead had serious ambitions of becoming the commanding officer of this regiment. And I believe that given time he might well have done so. He had the necessary qualities of leadership, he had experience, and more than anything he loved this regiment more than anything else in his life."

Parsons began pacing once more.

"Now imagine yourself for one moment back in Africa, colonel," he said. "Mr. Whitehead here is the company sergeant major of A Company, Major Cordell's company at the time. Lieutenant Simpson, as he then was, was one of the company officers. Everyone can see that Cordell and Simpson are close friends. I will say no more than that, as any speculations about the nature of their relationship is irrelevant. What was relevant, however, was that at the time Simpson was short of money and took some from Cordell without his permission. And when Cordell noticed the money missing he accused his servant, Private Daniel Hobson, of stealing the money. For reasons that we will now never understand, Simpson chose to remain silent about his own guilt; which ultimately led to Hobson being punished. And as we already know, he was flogged."

Parsons addressed his next words directly at Arbuthnot. The present commanding officer, he knew, was in no way responsible for Hobson's flogging. In fact, he had already expressed his dislike for such punishments. He was nevertheless the most senior military figure in the room, and Parsons felt a need to express his disgust at what had happened.

"I was relieved to hear that such barbaric punishments are rare," he said bitterly, "and as I understand it, are only awarded on active service with a commanding officer's approval. And I'm confident that there are many commanding officers who would not have sanctioned such a punishment. Especially for a relatively minor offense. But Colonel Latham, as he then was, was clearly not one of them. As you said earlier he was a disciplinarian of the old school, and probably did not think twice about ordering Private Hobson to be flogged. And whatever Mr. Whitehead's feelings might have been at the time about the punishment, as Cordell's company sergeant major, he had little choice but to administer the lashes."

Whitehead stirred uneasily in his chair. He refrained from speaking but Parsons could see that the distant look in his eyes had given way to one of anger.

"Shortly after this," Parsons said, as he continued his pacing, "Colonel Latham ordered Major Cordell to send a patrol into Zulu territory to outflank the Boers and attack them from their rear. I have no doubt that there were many in the regiment who doubted the wisdom of such a patrol. Mr. Whitehead may even have been one of them. Apart from Zululand being neutral territory there must have been reservations about the military advantage to be gained from such a patrol. However, let us not pursue that for the moment."

"Many of us thought it was a damned waste of valuable manpower," said Arbuthnot. "But Latham would have none of it. He was going to have his patrol no matter what anyone else said."

"And I believe that I'm correct in saying that Latham insisted that Lieutenant Simpson be given the task of leading the patrol. Perhaps that wasn't altogether surprising, as from what Major Plumb has told me, Simpson was considered one of the best young officers in the regiment at the time."

"You're right about it being Latham's decision, Parsons," said Arbuthnot. "And as I remember Cordell wasn't too thrilled about it. He knew it would be a dangerous mission."

"If my information is correct there was also a civilian scout on the patrol," said Parsons. "Someone by the name of Jeremy Brett. I believe he was included because of his specialist knowledge of the territory."

Unexpectedly it was Whitehead who spoke.

"He was no bloody scout," he said bitterly. "He was a surveyor working for Cecil Rhodes!"

"I'm obliged to you for that information Mr. Whitehead," said Parsons. "It was a point I was about to make myself. It is true, colonel, Brett was employed by Cecil Rhodes. The same Cecil Rhodes who had already made a fortune from diamonds, and who had prevailed upon the British Colonial Secretary, at the time none other than Lord Frederick Sayers, to authorize this illegal military excursion through Zululand into the Transvaal with a view to staking a claim on the rich mineral deposits there. And to facilitate that Sayers by-passed the normal chain of command and ordered the commanding officer of the Middlesex Light Regiment to send a patrol through Zulu territory."

"How in God's name could he expect to get away with that, Parsons?" Arbuthnot exclaimed.

"Because the commanding officer of the Middlesex was Lord Frederick's brother-in-law."

"My God," said Arbuthnot. "I had no idea."

"The family relationship was probably not close enough for it to have been an important factor, colonel," said Parsons. "I think we can assume that the motivation for both Sayers and Latham was the chance of sharing in the wealth that would arise from Rhodes' surveyor staking a claim to mineral rights in the Transvaal."

Parsons began pacing again.

"So I hope you're beginning to see the direct link between Lord Sayers, Colonel Latham, Major Cordell and Lieutenant Simpson. It was a direct chain of command that ultimately led to the unnecessary deaths of many young soldiers. Young men that, doubtless, Mr. Whitehead had trained. The young soldiers died, and their officers were rewarded. Latham was knighted and became a general, Cordell was promoted above his ability to colonel, and Simpson was recommended for the Victoria Cross for what appears to have been little more than an act of cowardice in abandoning his men to a terrible fate."

"Yes, I take your point, Parsons," said Arbuthnot. "But that is the nature of war I'm afraid. Young soldiers die and officers get promoted. It's regrettable, but it's a fact."

"No doubt Mr. Whitehead mourned the loss of all these young men; but I suspect that until a few weeks ago, Private Daniel Hobson meant little more to him than any of the others who died at the hands of the Zulus. You see, colonel, after Mr. Whitehead had flogged the unfortunate Hobson for the sake of a few pounds stolen from Major Cordell he prevailed upon that same gentleman to include Hobson on Simpson's patrol. He thought that if the young man acquitted himself well in action it would go some way towards him redeeming himself. How Hobson performed is irrelevant now, as he was killed by the Zulus. But I think all of us in this room can imagine how Mr. Whitehead would have felt when he discovered recently that Private Daniel Hobson was his own son. It's possible he blamed himself for the young man's death, although I think most people would agree that the fault was not his. At the time he had no idea that he had a son. He was only obeying orders when he flogged Hobson, and he was only acting in what he considered to be that young man's best interests when he requested that he be included on the ill-fated patrol. There might even be those who, like the RSM, believed that if anyone was to held responsible it was Sayers, Latham, Cordell and Simpson."

Parsons resumed his seat.

"I hope I have finally convinced you, colonel," he said.

Arbuthnot remained silent for sometime. Then he turned to his RSM.

"But the regiment was your family, sergeant-major," he said. "I've heard you say that more times than I can remember."

"I do not blame the regiment for what happened," Whitehead said bitterly. "There is no dishonor in this regiment. But there was every dishonor in the four men responsible for my son's death."

58

THE SIGHT OF the Regimental Sergeant Major and the Provost Sergeant being escorted from Regimental Headquarters with their hands manacled behind their backs was cause enough to disrupt the age-old disciplines of the parade ground. Heads turned in the ranks and words of command died on the lips of drill sergeants as Patrick Whitehead and George Oakes were led past the openmouthed sentry at the main gate to the waiting police carriages. Bareheaded and stripped of their red serge frock coats there was little to identify them as serving soldiers other than their navy trousers. Whitehead managed to maintain a straight back and continued to hold his head erect, but the lumbering figure of Oakes presented an altogether more sorry picture.

Following Parsons' disclosure of Whitehead's major role in the four murders the interview with Oakes had been short. When confronted with Bates' confession, Oakes had been swift to admit his responsibility for placing the bombs at the barracks and at Pembroke Road, and when it was pointed out that his sentence would likely be shorter should he further implicate Whitehead he was swift to acknowledge that in providing an alibi for Whitehead on the night Sayers and Latham were murdered he had lied.

Oakes had denied any knowledge of Whitehead's intention to commit murder, but whether a jury would be convinced of that was another matter. In Parsons' opinion no jury would accept that Oakes was entirely ignorant of what Whitehead had done. It was far more likely that they would assume that he, along with Bates and Williams, had jointly conspired to commit murder. Much would depend upon how a judge regarded their willingness to turn Queen's Evidence, and on his final instructions to the jury.

———

ONCE THE FORMALITIES of Oakes and Whitehead's arrests had been completed and they had been charged and incarcerated along with their fellow conspirators, Parsons returned to Scotland Yard with Harris to report his success to Jeffries. By this time his exhaustion was so apparent that even the normally hardhearted Jeffries was concerned.

"Get yourself home and into a hot bath, Parsons," he said. "And tell Harris to take the rest of the day off as well. I hate to admit being wrong, but like many others I was way off beam in my thinking; and without that dogged perseverance of yours we might well have never got to the bottom of this. I'm sure I don't need to tell you how pleased the Commissioner will be when I give him the news."

"I'm glad to hear that, sir," said Parsons, who was more delighted by the praise from Jeffries than he cared to admit. "But I would be prepared to bet that whatever pleasure Colonel Wilson may derive from the arrests may be dampened by some of their ramifications. Not only will Lord Frederick Sayers' reputation be tarnished, but the army's competence will again be brought into question. How do you think the public will react when they read that a regimental commander sought to further his own ends and those of his brother-in-law by needlessly sending young soldiers to their deaths; and that his reward for this scandalous conduct was to be knighted and promoted to general. And in an attempt to cover this same commander's tracks, one incompetent officer was made a colonel and another recommended for the Victoria Cross. And to top it all the regimental sergeant major turns out to be a mass murderer."

"But who's to say any of them will ever learn the full truth from the newspapers, Parsons?"

"Oh, I think they will, sir. I know of at least one reporter who's been waiting a long time to tell this story."

———————

BEFORE GOING HOME Parsons took a cab to Brompton. Venetta Cordell had languished in her cell long enough. But he felt he had little choice but to leave her there long after it had become apparent that she was innocent, in order to avoid putting the real murderer on his guard.

It was clear from her black silk dress and well-groomed hair that her maid had been visiting her. According to the desk sergeant, Edith had been to the police station several times to wash and set her mistresses hair and provide her with food and fresh clothing. The ruddy-faced sergeant confessed that he would miss these visits. In much the same way as the newsagent in Silver Street, he had become enamored by the obvious attractive qualities of the young French woman.

"Life 'ere won't quite be the same again, without young Edith brightening an old man's day," he said wistfully. "But I'm pleased to hear Mrs. Cordell's goin' to be released. In spite of her feisty nature I never quite reconciled myself to her sticking a spear in someone's guts. She's far too much a lady for that."

Parsons was not sure that he agreed. He considered Venetta Cordell to be well capable of murder. But it surprised him to see her wearing black. He had not imagined she would mourn her husband. But, quite obviously, the customs and conventions of the day were important to her, even in a prison cell.

"What are your plans now, madame?" Parsons asked.

Venetta's shoulders raised in a Gallic shrug.

"I will not stay in England longer than is necessary," she said. "I will see my 'usband buried. And then I will return to France.

She gave Parsons a charming smile, the like of which must have first enamored Hector Cordell.

"Per'aps as the widow of an English colonel I will 'ave more chance of finding myself a suitable French husband," she said. "Especially when I tell people that my brave 'usband died leading 'is troops into battle. 'Oo knows, perhaps some good will come from all this after all."

———————

IT WAS ONLY when Parsons was drying himself after his bath and contemplating the celebratory meal to which he was going to treat himself that he noticed the date on the calendar. It was a Wednesday, and he had yet again failed to keep his Tuesday evening whist appointment with Thomas Mann. He knew that Thomas would be especially annoyed this time, as the first Tuesday of each month was competition night; and he always eagerly anticipated the opportunity of them both pitting their wits against the best players in the club. Doubtless he would understand once Parsons had told him what he had actually been doing at the time, but it would be better if that explanation was given sooner rather than later.

Parsons looked at his bedside clock. It was just after four. There was still time to send Mann a telegram inviting him to join Parsons for dinner. Thomas might still be vexed, but Parsons had never known him to turn down a dinner invitation.

59

Southampton Docks, three months later

A LIGHT DRIZZLE was falling as the soldiers of the Middlesex Light Regiment dressed in full marching order and each carrying a canvas bag holding spare clothing and personal items, moved slowly up the gangplank into the troopship. They were followed by the few dozen fortunate wives allowed to accompany the regiment, whose names had been drawn by lot from the hundreds of eligible regimental dependents. Many of the women carried babies or held the hands of small children. For them it was the start of the greatest adventure of their lives. They were embarking on a sea journey that would take them halfway round the world to the mysterious country of India, and thence by railway and horse drawn vehicle to the remote North-West Frontier.

After its lengthy service in Africa most officers and men in the regiment had been anticipating an extended period of home duty. But the powers that be in the War Office had decided otherwise, and at indecently short notice had posted the regiment to one of the most desolate and dangerous places in the British Empire. In the opinion of the majority of Government officials and senior military figures it was a sensible decision. After the shameful events that had occurred in Kensington it was only sensible to remove the regiment from further public scrutiny. It was also an opportunity for the officers and men of the regiment to redeem themselves under new leadership after the disgraceful business in Africa.

A large crowd had gathered at the dockside to see the regiment off. Many held small Union flags in one hand and umbrellas in the other. Mothers and fathers, and those wives and children unfortunate enough to be left behind, had tears in their eyes, fearful that this might be the last sight of their loved ones. They knew the uncertain fate that awaited them in the vast subcontinent that had already taken thousands of British men, women and children to its bosom.

After attempting to warm the spirits of the crowd with a selection of rousing military marches, the regimental band played 'God Save the Queen', bringing the soldiers on the troopship and the spectators on the dock to a position of attention as they all bellowed out the familiar words. As the last strains died away the bandmaster marched his men onto the troopship, their red jackets, white Foreign Service helmets, and brass instruments making a final brave show as they boarded.

———————

PARSONS STOOD SELF-CONSCIOUSLY in the new top hat he had recently bought. It was not an item of clothing that he felt suited him, but he was prepared to suffer it if it pleased his mother and Louise. He had found himself surprisingly moved by the spectacle of the regiment's departure. No loved one of his was leaving, but Louise was much saddened by the departure of her brother. Major Reginald Chapman, recently and unexpectedly promoted, was on his way to India to join the staff of the newly formed headquarters at Peshawar on the North-West Frontier. It was a posting that had left both him and his family with mixed feelings. Reginald had never been a man with ambition, far preferring his indolent military life in London to the prospect of real soldiering in a desolate trouble-spot, and when he had received the news of his posting he had considered resigning his commission. But that would likely have meant working in his father's bank, and even he could not bear that thought. For their part, his family had mixed feelings. They had been thrilled by his promotion, but his doting mother and loving sister had been much saddened by the thought that it could be years before they saw him again.

Parsons had been far more sanguine. Since informing Reginald that he was acquainted with his visits to Kate Hamilton's brothel he had been far less troubled by his boorish behavior. He was, nevertheless, still uncomfortable in Reginald's presence, and could never regard him as anything other than pompous and overbearing, and lacking in any sense of decorum. Nor could he imagine his relationship with Louise ever developing further as long as her brother remained on the scene. And after his recent dealings with the Middlesex Light Infantry, if he were never to see an army officer again for some time he would not be unduly dismayed.

One such officer, Mark Holland, stood at the railings of the troopship at this very moment with his new wife, the only daughter of an India Army general whom Holland had met whilst the family was on leave in London. At much the same time that Parsons had read of the regiment's deployment he had seen a photograph of the wedding and learned of Holland's unexpected promotion and appointment as the Middlesex's new commanding officer. Arbuthnot's decision to retire from the army and forego the chance of leading the regiment into the wilds of the North-West Frontier had not been unexpected, and the idea of fresh blood at the helm had been welcomed in the corridors of power at the War Office. Lady Cordelia, it appeared, had been more than content for her husband to resign his commission. The alternative of accompanying the regiment to India had been far less agreeable than accepting her position in London society as a retired colonel's lady. She had even deigned to join her husband at the docks to wish the regiment *bon voyage*. And for his part the gallant colonel was delighted to have even more opportunity to follow his real interests on the faro table at *Lasiters*.

PARSONS HAD MANAGED a few words with Major Plumb before he embarked. It was their first meeting since Parsons had visited his home shortly after Captain Simpson's death.

"Is Mrs. Plumb not accompanying you?" Parsons had asked.

"Not for the moment," Plumb had replied. "Her father is fading and needs constant nursing. If he passes on she may well join me. But that, of course, depends upon where we are at the time. The North-West Frontier is no place for a woman at the best of times, and we may be heading for somewhere far worse. The latest rumor is that we're bound for Afghanistan. It seems the tribal leaders there are threatening the Kabul government again, and we're one of three regiments being sent to Peshawar to strengthen the garrison in case the powers that be decide to invade."

"Then you have my sympathy," said Parsons. "Afghanistan has been a problem for as many years as I can remember."

"If our masters in the War Office consider this regiment capable of fighting a war in that sort of country," said Plumb, "then they need to have their heads examined. We're still under-strength, and although there's a core of good men who saw action in Africa, most of our young noncommissioned officers are not battle hardened. It's one thing to fight natives on the open plains of Africa, it's quite another to deal with armed tribesmen in the mountains of Afghanistan. To add to that we've got a new RSM and a commanding officer who doesn't know his arse from his elbow. If we thought Cordell was a disaster, let me assure you that this one will be worse. Holland's only been promoted because he married a general's daughter who came to England to find herself a suitable husband. As though India isn't already full of young men worth twice as much as him. All I can say is God help us if we ever see action."

Plumb looked Parsons squarely in the eye.

"I know you were only doing your duty, young man, but the Middlesex could well do with Paddy Whitehead at a time like this. There was no one quite like him for maintaining the sort discipline that keeps men steady under fire."

———

THE REVOLVER FOUND in the mud below Lambeth Bridge had proved to be of little use in the case against Whitehead and his accomplices. The serial number had enabled the weapon to be traced to a batch the manufacturer had sold to the army in 1875, but after that there was no trace. There were no records in the Quarter Master General's department to indicate to which regiments the weapons had been sent, the opportune excuse being that paperwork had been misplaced during the many departmental reorganizations following the Cardwell reforms.

But there was evidence enough, especially that given by Mrs. Fox. Together with the confessions of Bates, Oakes and Williams it had been more than enough to convict Whitehead. And it had been Mrs. Fox's story and Parsons' evidence that had enabled the jury to assemble the pieces of the complex jigsaw into a picture they could understand and set the four murders in context.

The irony, of course, was that it had been Mrs. Fox who had first made Whitehead aware of his son, and had set him on his vengeful path.

The jury had not accepted the plea by Whitehead's counsel that he had become insane after learning that Daniel Hobson was his son. In their opinion any man who could cold-bloodedly murder four men, three of whom were his brothers in arms, could not be considered to be anything other than in full control of his senses.

Whitehead had been hanged and Bates with him. Turning Queen's Evidence had not persuaded the judge to mitigate the punishment he had awarded the cab driver. In the judge's opinion a man in Bates' position must have been well aware of Whitehead's intentions. There was also the more serious matter of ensuring that anyone closely involved in the murder of senior public figures member had to be seen to receive an appropriate punishment.

Oakes and Williams had both received long prison sentences for their more minor roles. As a policeman Williams' offense had been considered the more serious. He had been sentenced to serve ten years of hard labor, Oakes to seven.

———————

"DO YOU THINK that sense of discipline was the reason men like Bates, Oakes and Williams remained so loyal to Whitehead that they were prepared to help him commit murder?" Parsons had asked Plumb.

"That's a question I've been asking myself these past few months," replied Plumb. "And I must admit that I haven't arrived at a satisfactory conclusion. Discipline and loyalty are both admirable qualities, and in my opinion are seen at their best in an infantry regiment like ours. But discipline and loyalty don't always produce heroes. You can drill a man until you're red in the face, but that doesn't mean that when he's faced with a mob of howling Zulus he'll stand shoulder to shoulder with his mates like he did on the parade ground. Some men will choose to abandon their comrades. That's what Bates, Oakes and Williams did, and Whitehead knew it. For all their brave talk after the patrol he would know how they really felt about themselves. So when he asked them to help him exact revenge on those responsible for sending them on a suicide mission, it's possible he rekindled in them the courage they thought they'd left in Africa with their dead comrades. Perhaps what he was proposing offered them the chance to be men again."

PARSONS WAS REMINDED of Plumb's last words as the troopship pulled away from the dock and the faces of the red coated soldiers lining the decks became gradually more blurred and indistinguishable.

"Who knows what Whitehead told those three men, inspector," Plumb had said. "All I can say is that you're never the same man once you've faced death on the battlefield. Once you've put on the that redcoat you may be sure that Death is standing beside you wearing his."